CW00547523

KEEP IN TOUCH WITH THE AUTHOR HERE

Visit my website online:
https://www.evabielby.co.uk
or
Join me on Facebook:
www.facebook.com/eva.bielby/
or
Join me on Twitter:

https://twitter.com/AuthorEva69

ACKNOWLEDGMENTS

ACKNOWLEDGMENTS

I would like to take this opportunity to thank my son
and daughter for their never ending support over
the last few years. I love you both to the moon and back.
Also, I would like to thank many of my friends
and author friends from around the world,
who have given me constant support, encouragement,
and advice, whether acted on, or not!
And a special mention goes to authors Ian Grant and Mel
Comley!
Thanks again for making this journey
an absolute pleasure.
Eva xx

CHAPTER 1

We finally managed to get up the stairs, but it was a struggle. I wanted him so badly and my body ached with growing need. His denims were around his ankles; my panties discarded somewhere half-way up the stairs. His cock entered me three times already only to lose contact again, such was our desperation to keep moving and reach the bedroom. His breathing was heavy and laboured and he gasped with excitement and frustration.

As we stumbled through the bedroom doorway, our mouths desperately searching each other. He tripped, taking me down onto the floor with him. Once down, there was no way we were going anywhere in a rush. We scrabbled frantically at each other's remaining clothes. I pushed down on his denims and boxers with my foot until they were off. In my desperation to see his well-toned body, I tugged hard to try to get his T-shirt over his head. For a few seconds he reluctantly stopped his fight with the hooks of my bra to raise his arms for me.

I didn't want to wait a second longer; I needed his cock

inside me. I was sick with wanting, positively ached for him, and he was a like a man possessed, wanting to be inside me. Our antics on the stairs aggravated my need, but I prayed that this time there would be no loss of contact. I would do my best to make sure of that.

"Ram it inside me... now. I need..." I urged, and with rash exuberance he shoved it hard into me. The breath was knocked out of me and I gasped before I could get my next word out,

"...fucking."

I squeezed my hands under my back to undo the bra for him but he couldn't wait and quickly pushed the cups upwards to reveal my breasts.

"Oh, Helen! What ...beautiful tits, just...beautiful."

After a struggle with the last of the hooks, I was finally free of the bra and he was onto me, squeezing, kneading and caressing my nipples with his thumb. He thrust deep into me, slow but deliberate movements, as I eyed his amazing physique - his perfectly toned abs and chest. He was stunning in every way possible: lean, muscular, manly and tanned. He could have any woman he wanted....and yet...he was here with me....fucking me. I couldn't believe my luck that he was mine.

`He flipped over onto his back, and after a little shuffling about I sat astride him but facing his feet, his cock buried deep inside me. I'd never been in a position like it before. What a difference from the usual feeling when I faced him... a totally new sensation. I could feel every inch of him but from a different aspect. I loved how it made me feel; it was mind-blowing. What I didn't like, however, was not being able to watch the pleasure on his face as we fucked. I thrust my hips towards him this time, slow, steady, and it felt that with the slower moves the intensity was perfect. Every little muscle within his cock throbbed. His arms came around my body and he tweaked my nipples and stroked my breasts tenderly once more, before cupping them in his hands and kneading them with his thumbs.

"Step up the pace, Helen, fuck me faster, nip my cock with those pussy muscles. Take me to the point. I'll tell you when to stop."

I whispered back to him in what I hoped would come out as my most seductive voice,

"I'll take you there. I'll take you there and beyond and then I'll back off. I'll leave you wanting."

"Perfect, bring it on, baby!"

Just as he asked of me, I stepped up the pace, riding him faster and faster still. I ached for it. I needed to climax. Although I couldn't see that handsome face, I closed my eyes and pictured him, imagined I could watch the pleasure in his eyes. Onward I rode, getting more frantic by the minute. The tip of his cock hit my G-spot and I was close to coming. I could feel the dampness inside of me and spreading outwards to my folds. His throbbing started to drive me to distraction so I clenched my muscles and gripped his cock tightly. I felt like I was on fire, and I didn't want those flames extinguished. I wanted those flames lapping at my body forever.

"Lap at every inch of me and never die." I was amazed to find myself whispering the words.

They were beautiful. If this was Heaven, I was well and truly in the spot; a place where I wanted to stay for all eternity.

"Ooh...I...I'm...coming! I'm coming...right now! Wow!" I purred. My whole body jerked, as if I was experiencing convulsions that would never cease. He quickly dropped his hands from my breasts and they reached around my waist at the height of orgasm and his fingers rubbed slowly on my clit, driving me to dizzying heights.

"Go, baby...let go...let your cum drench my cock. Close your eyes and keep feeling it, hard inside your pussy."

He kept still while I rode him, but now that my orgasm subsided he pounded hard at my body in return. Perhaps he thought he could keep my orgasm going.

"Keep squeezing yourself around my cock, keep riding, honey. Now, take me to the point and back off again."

Of course, my pace slowed as I'd cum, so I did it again, rode him as if I was galloping over the dunes on a white horse, faster, faster...I was almost at the point again. His cock moved inside me so perfectly, so...

"Stop, Helen! Stop! I'm not...ready to...cum...just yet."

He muttered urgently as he struggled to breathe. But I didn't want to stop yet. I was being greedy and wanted to cum again.

"Whoa...whoa!"

His gentle hands grabbed my waist and dragged my body up his stomach and away from his cock. I groaned as he manoeuvred me around until I was laid next to him.

"So you want to cum again? I'll make you cum as much as you want, baby." He whispered his promise.

He eased himself back on top of me and, taking his time, slid down my body, his tongue tickling at my skin as it slowly worked down my front, inch by phenomenal inch. He licked between my boobs, down to my navel and towards my pubic region, taunting, tantalising a million nerves. He placed some fingers inside my wetness and pushed hard into me, heightening my excitement. Within seconds, his tongue tasted me, licked at my clit, tormented and teased yet again, until my deluge was there ready to free flow. I suddenly felt his other hand move up the inside of my right thigh. My lower body, receiving the attention of both his hands and his tongue, hurt all over; burning with lust and I wanted it bad. I was eager to have my every need filled with any part of him I could get. I could feel the glow from within and the soft sheen of perspiration forming all over me. He also glistened; his hair looked extremely damp from his exertions and his expression bore a look which verged on wild and reckless. His finger stroked over the area around my anus and ever so gently he inserted a fingertip. I was tipped over the edge, my body bucked in the throes of orgasm again, more intense than the last. I fought to catch my breath; such was the feeling of being blown away.

"Was that beautiful, honey? I can feel your cum all over my fingers. I can taste it on my tongue. You taste gorgeous, Helen. Taste!"

He played his tongue over my lips and I swept my tongue over it and tasted my own secretion. He moved to the side of me and onto his back.

"Now, you on top!"

"Not yet. It's time for your treat now. Lay still." I smiled up at the gorgeous face that stared down at me. He made me smile; he made me happy. I could see the pleasure on his face, the anticipation of what was yet to come for him making him pant and sometimes hold his breath. First of all, I leant over him and slowly planted little kisses up every inch of his cock to its head, and I circled the tip of my tongue around the little orifice at the end of its head. He moaned out loud and it gave me a real kick to know that he felt wonderful as I pleasured him. I couldn't resist dragging it out, tormenting him for what seemed like an age. His groans were longer, but barely audible, and I was aware that he could hardly utter his words.

"Beaut…iful!" he stammered.

"But… it's not as beautiful…as it's going to get," I answered between my kisses and licks.

His cock was the perfect specimen. I was torn, unsure whether I wanted to look at his handsome face or his amazing length. It was anguish but I decided to focus my attention on his thighs and scrotum and lick the creases that form the sexy v-shape at the top of the thighs; the V-shape where the lines start mid-hip, almost coming to a point near the base of his cock, that extremely desirable feature on many a sexy man. He though, was not many, not any; he is the sexiest man. Lucky for me, I was here with him and enjoying every inch with my eyes and my body.

I fondled around his scrotum; his testicles felt as if they too were on fire. I caressed his stiffness with one hand and his scrotum with the other. It thrilled me to hear him moan and groan and heightened the pleasure for me. Feeling desperate for more physical pleasure to my body and with a minimal loss of contact, I swivelled my lower body around the bed to position my legs straight up the bed towards his head and face. He quickly cottoned on and between his groans he teased me.

"Who's being a greedy girl then?" I giggled as I asked him,

"Can I then? Let me sit on your face. Drive me insane with your tongue and your fingers."

I taunted him, running my tongue around my own lips in an overtly sexy manner, and he took a deep breath and growled at me.

"Do it! I'm waiting to taste your juices again, babe!"

I raised my right leg up and swung it over his head. As I lowered my bottom to his face, his tongue came into contact with my wet folds and I briefly lost contact with his cock. I arched my back with yet another explosive gush of cum. My body was taut yet I shuddered in ecstasy; my nerves alight. I was flushed and my face felt like an inferno; everything burned. He paused for a few seconds and, after what seemed like forever, just as my orgasm silenced, his fingers entered me and his thumb slithered over the area around my anus.

"Do you want my cock now, Helen? It's ready and waiting to explode inside you. Only if you're ready, though! Or do you want me to keep making you cum? I really don't mind. I love watching your face when you climax."

I was breathless; barely able to get my words out.

"Yes!" I whispered. "Yes, I need it in me, darling, do it from behind."

I climbed off him and was about to lay face down on my stomach, but before I finally got into position, he eased his cock into my warmth and we were laid there like spoons. His lower arm squeezed beneath me and I felt his left hand move around my hip. His fingers encircled his cock as it was thrusting into me, but then he began rubbing at my clit. Little circular moves at first, it was delicious. Once again I was on the verge of coming but suddenly both his hands moved and he gripped tight at my hips as he pushed harder and harder. I could feel the tell-tale twitches and we both came together. He yelled out loud and I stilled, moaning inwardly, concentrating, as if my silence would make the pleasure more intense and infinite.

He rested his chin on my shoulder as his breathing gradu-ally calmed over the next few minutes. I closed my eyes, savouring every beautiful second. I was wet; pleasantly, wonderfully wet. Suddenly, he pulled at my left side and rolled me until I was on my back. He moved on top of me and I wondered if he wanted to carry on fucking.

"Helen, open your eyes, babe. Look at me."

I opened my eyes, cautiously. Something wasn't quite right. I gazed around the room with my eyes half open. He'd gone. I was alone and my only wetness was that from my eyes, dampening my cheeks. It had all seemed so real. His touch, his smell, and I could still hear his words and moans of sexual delight ringing in my ears. I cried some more. David paid me a visit in my dreams yet again, as he had done most nights for the last six months. The visions were always different scenarios, not always about sex, but we were always together. I was devastated once more to wake up to the reality.

CHAPTER 2

*T*he taxi dropped me at Charles De Gaulle airport with five minutes to spare. Their flight would have landed fifteen minutes earlier; nine twenty. Before the cab picked me up, I logged onto my laptop to check if there were any delays. Fortunately, after a trying five minutes of browsing, I found that none had been reported. Allowing the girls time to get through passport control, customs and then baggage reclaim, I reckoned on twenty to twenty five minutes before they would emerge into the arrivals hall. Taking a slow saunter to start with, I picked up my pace a bit when, from about fifty yards away, I could see crowds around the barriers. Half a dozen or so arrivals started to filter through from the corridor. I wasn't sure whether they would be from Catherine and Ruby's British Airways flight from Heathrow or some other flight that recently landed, but I hurried along regardless.

My stomach churned nervously as I waited. A thousand worries flitted through my head and carried on doing circuits. Would their bedrooms be okay for them? What if they didn't like the food I cooked? What if they didn't really want to go to the places that I planned for the week's itinerary? What if Ruby didn't like me? I met Catherine on one occasion already and we got along fine for the day. Maybe a week would be too long. What about Ruby? Would I take to her? I never met her. She might take an instant dislike to me. How would they like to be entertained each evening? Bugger! They were young girls for heaven's sake. Catherine might like to visit a nightclub, she was nineteen after all, but there was no way I wanted to go out clubbing. But then I remembered that Ruby was only sixteen and wouldn't manage to get into a nightclub anyway. We couldn't go out and leave her alone in my apartment.

Oh shit! They're here!

I was standing near the barriers facing down the long corridor from where they would exit and I could see Catherine waving frantically, her beautiful face breaking into a smile the instant she caught sight of me. My heart melted at the sight of her, so like her father. She was dragging her suitcase along and was surrounded by older folks. I searched eagerly amongst the faces of all the strangers around her and I couldn't see anyone closely resembling the only image I ever saw of Ruby; a holiday snap. For a fleeting moment it crossed my mind that she decided not to come after all. Catherine ran the last few yards and with the barrier between us, flung her arms around me and kissed my cheek. "Oh, Helen, I've been so exc…"

She didn't get to finish as I butted in rudely with my concern.

"Catherine, where on earth is Ruby? Hasn't she come with you?"

Looking back for a second or two down the corridor, she stood on her tiptoes, trying to see above what must have now become two or three flights' worth of arrivals.

"Oh, don't worry about her, she'll be along shortly. She's busy throwing her undies haphazardly back into the suitcase. It happens all the time with Ruby. I left her muttering obscenities under her breath, directed at the customs guy who stopped her."

Relieved to hear that Ruby would be joining us shortly, I turned back to Catherine and folded my arms tight around her. I wondered whether David would be watching over us. I hope so. Catherine was beautiful and charming and a true credit to him.

It was another couple of minutes before Ruby ambled towards the arrival hall. I was flabbergasted when I saw her. She was a couple of inches taller than Catherine, natural blonde hair, full make-up and just sixteen years old. To anyone who didn't know the pair, they would readily have thought Ruby to be the older sister of the two. Catherine waved and shouted to attract her attention. Ruby gazed straight ahead and, it seemed, didn't put much effort into looking for us. Catherine shouted at her three times before she turned her head sulkily towards us and grumbled something I didn't quite catch. She suddenly stopped dead in her tracks and crouched down setting about emptying the contents of her handbag onto the floor, as though she was looking for something. After carefully and slowly sifting through it all, oblivious to all the people having to weave around her, she began to throw all the items one by one back into the bag. I was transfixed as I watched every move she made. I scrutinised her face and the determined expression as she rifled through loose items of make-up, pens, paperwork and goodness knows what else. The whole charade I was witnessing appeared to have no purpose. There was no jubilant expression to note about her face at finding a specific item; nothing. I'd been told by David some time ago how troublesome Ruby could be, and Catherine verified the fact when we first met. But then…maybe I was being ridiculous and reading too much into it.

Rather than walk around the barrier towards us, she crouched underneath and strode off towards the main entrance without a word to me or Catherine. By the time we caught up with her outside in the sunshine, she was lighting up a cigarette. Offering my hand I greeted her.

"Hi, Ruby, pleased to meet you. I'm Helen."

The minute I started to speak, she turned her head away, her eyes following the butt of a tanned and extremely fit guy who was, at a guess, in his early thirties. I could feel utter panic creep into my bones.

"RUBY!" Catherine snapped.

She thumped the upper part of Ruby's left arm. "You haven't even acknowledged Helen yet and she's been kind enough to have us as guests for the week. Show some bloody manners."

Bugger!

The last thing I needed was my guests at each other's throats all week. Maybe this wasn't such a good idea after all. The sharpness of Catherine's voice, however, did elicit a reaction. She finally faced me, as though she'd only just been made aware of my presence.

"Oh hello, Helen. It's just that the flying stresses me out. Sorry!"

Catherine looked at me helplessly and apologetically. Ruby's words hadn't sounded the least bit sincere and Catherine positively squirmed. I could feel the anger building up inside me. How the hell was I expected to get through a week of *this*? I was torn between wanting to slap her senseless or set about to organise a return ticket for her to London. My face was burning and I couldn't help but notice a sad look of regret on Catherine's face. She was feeling bad, I know she was. I beamed at her and walked away to organise a taxi back to the city.

The tension continued for the first few minutes after the taxi left the airport. Catherine and I were sat next to one another in the cab and Ruby sat facing us; or rather, she sat with her body facing us as she watched the countryside whizz by. Totally out of the blue, after ten minutes or so, she spun her head towards me.

"So…you were Dad's bit on the side then, Helen?" She gave a wicked grin.

I couldn't believe that this sixteen year old was actually challenging me; waiting for a reaction.

"RUBY! What the hell…?" Catherine's face dropped and she looked mortified.

Determined not to rise to the bait and give her what she wanted, though reeling inwardly, I managed to stay calm and met her gaze.

"No, Ruby. Not quite his bit on the side. I was a prostitute; a call girl. I used to visit him in his hotel rooms."

I held her gaze even though Catherine whipped her head round to stare at me. The pair of them had their eyes wide open in astonishment and mouths gaping. My eyes never faltered, then the shock on Ruby's face morphed into a big grin and she howled with laughter. Catherine, assuming a wind-up, burst into laughter too and I couldn't help but join in. My laughter, though, was for a different reason. My mouth had spilled out the spur of the moment comment and both girls took it to be a smart-arse remark, made with the intention to score a point back from the obnoxious Ruby. Little did they realise, my quick-witted comment was the truth. Ruby was the last to stop laughing. "Respect!" she sang in delight. "You're actually quite cool, aren't you?"

In my mind, I chalked up an imaginary score on the board

with my index finger, yet I had a terrible feeling about the seven days that were to follow. Deep in thought for a second, I wondered who would be top of the scoreboard before Ruby returned to England.

CHAPTER 3

*T*he remainder of the journey passed without incident and Ruby contributed a few comments to the conversation that had mainly been between Catherine and I. Catherine updated me on how her course was progressing at university and Ruby, not to be left out, had volunteered information on the subjects she would be studying for her A-level courses. It was her intention to study psychology at Reading University if she achieved the grades required in maths, biology and psychology. I couldn't help but wonder how, as a future graduate psychologist, Ruby would have interpreted her own behaviour of earlier on. As the taxi pulled up outside my apartment block, I pointed upwards to the windows to show them roughly where my apartment was situated.

"Wow!" was Ruby's first word as she walked into the apartment and I blushed with pride – that is until her next words floored me. "Did you buy this with my father's money?"

"RUBY! Catherine scolded. "I think an apology is in order, now!"

Again, I was almost rendered speechless by her outspokenness. I felt deeply sorry for Catherine, who no doubt was going to be apologising far more than she needed to over the coming days. Part of me wanted to indulge in a verbal attack on Ruby for being so thoughtless and a total embarrassment to her sister, but feigning a calmness that was fast deserting me, I answered her.

"Sorry to disappoint you, Ruby, but no, I haven't touched the money that your father left me. This apartment was bought in my name, by my father when I was in my teens. I also own a villa in Marbella, which is rented out as holiday lets forty eight weeks of the year. My parents' home in Richmond was sold a few months ago and I'm an only child. I didn't expect, ask for, or need your dad's money."

I could see that Catherine was cringing. Ruby, however, stared at me totally expressionless. I don't know if she planned on making any further smart-arse comments but if she had, she clearly thought better of it.

"Okay, girls, I'll show you where your bedrooms are."

I gave them a quick tour of the kitchen-cum-diner and they followed me through to the long hallway where in passing, I pointed out the bathroom. Opening the door to the first of the bedrooms, I stood back letting Ruby enter first.

"This is your room, Ruby."

Her eyes flitted quickly around the room, taking in every square inch of the space in a few seconds.

"Cool."

She gave us a quick glance before doing an about turn and going back down the hallway. I assumed she was going to fetch her suitcase, so Catherine and I headed off to the next room along; her bedroom.

"Don't let her get to you, Helen. She never shows enthusiasm at the best of times, unless it's for men, mobile phones, wacky baccy and alcohol. I'm sorry she's behaving like a total shit. We don't know what to do with her at times. Mum despairs."

"You're also despairing of her, Catherine," I stated. "I think perhaps she's going through a tough time. For what reason, I don't know but bear with it. It will pass, I'm sure."

Her eyes glazed over and her chin started to quiver a little.

"I...I wanted...this week to be p..perfect for...Dad." She stammered.

I was surprised by the held-back tears and stifled sobs. Catherine struck me as sensible and level-headed but maybe the mention of David contributed to her little show of weakness. I folded my arms around her and held her tight. David came to the forefront of my mind. Catherine was so like him both in looks and in nature, I felt as if I was holding him once more. The slamming of the apartment door jolted us from our embrace and we broke apart looking at each other rather puzzled. Without speaking, her look must have mirrored mine, a mutual dawning of the knowledge that Ruby had gone out.

On returning to the lounge, we found Ruby's suitcase where she left it, the one we thought she'd gone to collect to take through to her bedroom. I didn't know what to say to Catherine and she must have been able to tell from my face that I wasn't too happy with the first hour of their stay.

"Yes, Ruby's gone out. Sorry, Helen. She tends to do her own thing. This is typical of her, causing people to worry."

My heart ached for her. It was a difficult enough time for her as it was; still grieving for her Dad and having to constantly apologise for her wayward sister. Something told me that it was Catherine who needed some help to cope.

"Sit down, Catherine. We'll have a glass of wine. Do you want to talk?" Hesitating, she eyed the suitcases which still graced a corner of the lounge.

"Yes, we can talk. But can we not mention Ruby, please?"

I looked around the room in confusion as I figured out what I would say next, but before I reached a decision, my mouth just spewed out the words.

"Catherine, she's just…gone. She's sixteen…and…Paris…"

"Believe it or not, she can look after herself. She's done self-defence and has a brown belt in karate. She's very street wise."

Trying not to appear too intense when I looked at her, I wondered who she was trying to convince. I couldn't think of an appropriate remark to make, so I shrugged my shoulders and smiled. It was merely a front. I didn't want her brooding over the deep stress that I could feel coursing through my body and mind. Sick to the stomach didn't quite cut it, and my neck and shoulders were taut.

"I'll just take these cases into our rooms so they are out of the way. If we're having wine, I like something simple like a White Zinfandel if you have some. If not…I'm open to suggestions."

I'd put a selection of wines ready in the fridge. I found a bottle of one I thought she would like and poured two large glasses for us and returned to the lounge. Catherine appeared a few minutes later and sat down next to me.

"It's a beautiful apartment, Helen. I've just had a quick freshen up. I hope you don't mind?"

"Of course I don't mind. Catherine, you are to treat this as your home while you are staying with me, understand?" She nodded.

A long silence followed. We both sipped at our wine and it seemed as though Catherine didn't know what to say next. I wanted to broach the subject of Ruby but as Catherine had mentioned earlier, she had no desire to discuss her sister, so I let it lie.

"Tell me what you've been doing since you came to France. What gossip have you got?"

I wasn't at all sure how to answer that one and I tried hard to pluck at least one thing from memory to tell her, something that was positive. but I failed miserably. Then before I had chance to wonder where the words had come from they spilled forth from my mouth.

"I've done absolutely nothing, Catherine. Nothing. Or would you count grieving as a daily activity? I have left this apartment once every three to four weeks to go for essential shopping. I walk a few blocks to the supermarket, get stocked up and call for a cab to bring me back. Other than that I do nothing."

I felt terrible for bombarding her with the truth and the look of concern on her face was touching. She didn't really know me that well and yet, her eyes glazed over as if she was going to shed a tear or two, such was her compassion.

"Oh, Helen...I..."

I shook my head to stop her interruption.

"I cried constantly for the first few months, drank too much, way too much, and ate very little. I was throwing out more food than I was consuming...and...I never bothered getting dressed unless I was going shopping. There didn't seem to be any point."

I was lost in my own world for a few moments, my mind so busy that, until I snapped myself out of the reverie, I was unaware that I had scraped the nail polish off my left hand fingernails. Little flakes of dislodged fuchsia varnish were scattered in my lap. I glanced up at Catherine. Her face was expressionless as she gazed at me, but her eyes burned into mine, seeking more than I'd already given, but my words had left me drained. I went along to my bedroom and returned with nail polish remover and cotton wool. Her eyes were on me again as I sat. She seemed to be struggling, as if she wanted to say something. She opened her mouth to speak, but the words that came out were not what I expected.

"Let me do that, Helen."

She sat next to me on the sofa and soaked a cotton wool pad ready to remove the damaged nail varnish. There was a long silence between us as she removed the remaining nail polish from my left hand and gently took my right hand in hers to start on the undamaged polish. I watched her as she worked away with the cotton pad. My heart ached for her. She was still dealing admirably with her own grief for her father, yet unselfishly she was trying hard to cope with the difficulties that Ruby was presenting. Then there was me. She knew very little about me, other than that I had loved her father, but she was here with me, being an angel; kind, thoughtful and caring. I knew in that moment that I loved the girl with all my heart. I couldn't stop myself. I eased my right hand away from her and wrapped my arms around her. She jumped a little, surprised by my impulsive action.

"What...what was that for?" she asked when I finally released her.

"I want to say thank you, Catherine. Thank you for coming here and thank you for being you. I am so proud of you; proud for David. You are a true credit to him. I..." My voice tailed away.

I had been on the verge of telling her that I loved her, but reigned myself in just as quickly, as she was already looking embarrassed and tearful again.

Our afternoon passed quite quickly but it was approaching eight o'clock and Ruby had not returned. We had taken a short walk mid-afternoon, knowing we couldn't go far because Ruby didn't have a key. Catherine was doing her best to cover up her stress. She carried on chatting and laughing with me, but I noticed the tension in her neck and shoulders. She seemed slightly detached from the conversation and her smiles were forced. I was at a total loss to know what to say next, especially as I was worrying for Ruby as well. Sixteen years old and roaming the streets of Paris; a wild teenager who looked at least twenty years old.

She arrived back shortly after nine o'clock, calmly walking through the door with a stack of shopping bags... and smelling of cannabis. Catherine stood up the moment she heard the door knob turn. Flying through to the hall, she vented immediately.

"RUBY! WHERE THE HELL HAVE YOU BEEN?"

Ruby stared back at her through glazed eyes. She wobbled where she stood and let the bags drop from her hands on to the floor. She was spaced out; not even capable of shouting back at her sister. She spat out her reply in a very low but nevertheless venomous voice.

"Don't fucking start on me! Perfect fucking Catherine! Perfect fucking sister and daughter who can do no fucking wrong!"

Rather than argue with Ruby, who was in no state to do so, I went through to the hall and grabbed Catherine's hand to lead her away.

"Come on, Catherine. Leave Ruby to go to bed. There's nothing to be gained at the moment from getting involved in a row."

Ruby slowly turned her head to look at me and her eyes followed seconds later. I could see she was unsuccessfully trying to focus on the face from where the unfamiliar voice came. She looked extremely puzzled. She tried to raise a hand for some reason, but leaden, it dropped back to her side. My blood was boiling. Feeling fucking furious I wanted to lash out at her. Catherine was on the verge of tears but I didn't dare utter a word. As much as I was feeling protective of her, it was clear to anyone who cared enough to notice, that Ruby had some serious issues. I was also livid with myself for feeling helpless. I wanted to help both of them... for David, but I felt ashamed that I didn't even know where to begin. Catherine was reluctant to let me lead her away. She gave me a desperate look, but then turned back to Ruby.

"Go to bed, Ruby. The matter's closed for tonight."

She looked vacantly at Catherine for a couple of seconds and then staggered down the passage and into Catherine's bedroom, apparently having clearly understood. We shrugged our shoulders at each other and slowly followed her. Standing in the bedroom doorway, we both watched on as Ruby collapsed into a heap on the bed and fell asleep instantly, fully-clothed.

"It doesn't matter. I'll take the other bedroom. I'm not bothered."

Catherine went to bed shortly after, but not before she had a quick nosy through Ruby's shopping. Among the expensive clothes in one of the carrier bags, she discovered a litre bottle of whisky. As she verbally expressed her disgust with a few expletives, she tipped every last drop down the kitchen sink, leaving the empty bottle on the counter for Ruby to see the next morning.

My plan for their first full day was to start with a visit to the Pantheon in the Latin Quarter; originally built as a church dedicated to St Genevieve. From there, I intended for us to visit Le Sorbonne, followed by the fabulous Notre Dame and The Holy Chapel on Île de la Cité. It was certainly a full day's itinerary and I hoped we could get away by nine thirty at the latest.

I was awake fairly early and got up straight away to make some coffee. Fresh out of the shower, but still in her dressing gown, Catherine joined me at the kitchen table not long after. The sun was streaming through the kitchen window as we sat discussing the plans for the day. She told me she'd visited Notre Dame previously, but assured me she would love to return. After we sat for almost three quarters of an hour she went off to get dressed and wake up Ruby, ready for our early start, when I heard her hysterical screaming.

"HELEN? HEL-LEN! Quick! Come here please!"

My heart was beating like crazy as I dashed down the hallway from the kitchen, expecting some sort of problem in Catherine's room. However, she was stood by Ruby's bed (with Ruby totally oblivious to Catherine's shouting) pointing to the nightstand. Until I was through the doorway it was impossible to see just what it was that she was pointing at. I followed her through the door and was horrified to see one empty and one almost empty wine bottle, both of which had come from my stash of wine in the fridge. There was no sign of a wine-glass. She'd been drinking straight from the bottle. Clearly, she'd woken from her weed-induced sleep in the early hours and checked through her bags to find the whisky gone. The only conclusion I could reach was that she thought it was me who had poured her fire down the sink. My mouth gaped and I didn't know what to feel, until I chanced a look in Catherine's direction. Her shoulders were slumped and she had a look of desperation in her eyes, they were glassy and dulled with pain and worry. We needed to do something and fast; she had consumed far too much alcohol for a girl of her age.

"Let's wake her, Catherine. She's flat out. She needs to vomit or else that stuff is going to poison her system. I'll go and get a jug of water and a glass."

I left Catherine trying to wake her by rolling her body back and forth.

"Ruby! Ruby!"

I could hear her shouts from the kitchen. There can't have been a response as the next thing I heard was Catherine bellowing at the top of her voice.

"RUBY! RUBY! WAKE THE FUCK UP! COME ON!"

Halfway across the kitchen with the water and glass, I turned back and grabbed a bucket from beneath the sink. I couldn't imagine Ruby would be capable of walking to the bathroom. As I walked into the bedroom her eyes were rolling backwards into her head and her lashes flickered. She gave a rasping groan and my stomach clenched tight with dread. I have never been good around vomit and I knew in an instant that it was imminent. Catherine was almost kneeling on the pillows trying to haul Ruby up into a sitting position, but she was a dead weight. I knelt on the opposite side and with an arm each we managed to drag her up the bed. I quickly stuffed a pillow behind her, ready in case her head flopped backwards.

With my hands shaking nervously, I poured a large glass of water and thrust it into Ruby's hand, but I didn't dare let it go until she had a firm grip around it.

"Here, Ruby. Drink this…but small sips, right?"

She raised her head took a small mouthful then greedily took another couple of sips, before shoving the glass back at me.

"Don't…want…any…anymore."

She struggled to get the words out before she started retching. I reached for the bucket and thrust it towards Catherine.

"Here, I'll get behind her to push her into a sitting position."

I felt guilty for giving her the tough part but there's no way I wanted to be on the receiving end, bucket or not. I pushed one arm behind the top of her shoulders and levered her upwards and away from the pillow. I just got my other hand in there and heaved her up in time. Catherine positioned the bucket just under Ruby's chin and up it came. Turning my head to face the wall didn't stop my gag reflex from kicking in, though. I knew from past experience that I wouldn't vomit but I put one hand over my mouth all the same.

She vomited three or four times in all. After twenty minutes with nothing further coming up, I encouraged her to sip some more water. There was no way she was going to be fit enough to go on our day's outing. Once I was fairly happy that she brought up sufficient alcohol, my worry faded away to be replaced by downright fucking anger.

"Ruby, what the hell were you thinking? Coming back in a state like you did and then stealing my wine through the night. You're bloody sixteen for heaven's sake."

She glowered at me, a weak one, but definitely a glower. She looked exhausted.

"My whisky was tipped down the sink. I was pissed off about that."

I looked to Catherine who, judging by the way she stood with hands on hips and tight-lipped, her mood had changed to anger as well as mine.

"It was me who tipped your bloody whisky out, Ruby. You're too damned young to drink spirits and you shouldn't have taken Helen's wine, either."

Ruby turned to face me, a hint of shame passed over her face before she grudgingly uttered a 'sorry'.

At Ruby's insistence, Catherine and I went out for the day and left her recovering, or rather, sleeping it off. As hard as we tried, it was difficult to put our previous night and morning behind us to take some enjoyment from the day. Other than chatting over a lunchtime snack, we toured the fine old buildings without much in the way of conversation. I'm sure Catherine felt the same as I did; that we were merely going through the motions. She seemed in a sad and low mood. I wondered how often she and her mum had gone through similar traumas with Ruby at home. We were walking down Rue du Pont Neuf in the direction of home, before I dared to broach the subject.

"Catherine, I would like to try and help Ruby, if I can. Do you think she would talk to me if we were alone? Something seems to be troubling her."

She linked arms with me and her eyes burned deep into mine as she thought about my suggestion.

"I don't know if it would do any good, Helen. She's always been…well, difficult. We've tried, Mum and I, but she seems to shut everybody out."

"Is this since David…sorry, your dad died?"

"No….yes…I don't really know. Yes…maybe she has got more…self-destructive since then. I'm not sure."

There was no chance of me sitting down for a chat with Ruby when we arrived back at my apartment, however. She'd gone out yet again. She hadn't even bothered using the spare key I'd left for her. The door was closed but she left it unlocked. Catherine slumped onto the sofa and sobbed for ages. I held her close to me and did my best to console her, although I also felt as if I could break down at any moment. They had hardly been in Paris for thirty six hours and Ruby already managed to wreak havoc on my plans for a fun-filled week for the three of us.

"Catherine, do you think this is likely to continue for the rest of the week? At a push, I could maybe cope without losing my temper, but I'm more concerned about the effect this is having on you. She's not being fair to you."

"No offence to you, Helen, but I'm wishing we hadn't come, or at the very least, that I'd left Ruby at home."

Her words brought on a fresh wave of sobs and another stream of moisture to further sully her beautiful, already tear-streaked cheeks.

"Phone your mum, Catherine. She needs to be aware of this." She gave the matter some thought for five minutes or so, until she calmed down. Without another word to me, she picked up her phone, still sniffing but perhaps a little more resolute. I disappeared through to the kitchen to start preparing some food, giving her some privacy, while she spoke to her mum.

A short while later, as she told me about her mum's reactions to the call, we tucked into chicken and pineapple stir-fry and some fresh salad.

"Mum is disgusted with Ruby's behaviour. If there are any more incidents, she has told me to get Ruby's things packed up and take her to the airport. It's best that she returns home instead of you having to put up with all this shit, especially after the kind hospitality you have shown to us both, Helen."

It saddened me to have to listen to what Catherine was saying. I loved her to bits and was dying for a chance to get to know Ruby better, but my sense of foreboding was telling me that it wouldn't be happening during their visit to Paris. She was out there again, somewhere on the streets, doing goodness knows what, and I had a bad feeling about it. I had set aside some stir-fry for her return, I only hoped that if she was drinking again she had the sense to eat something first.

We sat around getting depressed for what seemed like hours before we heard a few sharp raps on the front door. I looked at Catherine and shrugged, unable to understand why Ruby wouldn't just walk in as the door was still unlocked. Both of us hurried to the door and when I opened it I was rather downcast to see that it wasn't Ruby stood there. I was surprised to find myself face to face with an absolutely stunning vision of male good looks, sexiness and testosterone. Nicely toned body, perfect white teeth, steely, grey eyes and light brown slightly mussed hair; he was gorgeous. His urgency, however, prevented me from being able to indulge for longer than a few seconds. He spoke in rapid French and I tried to translate as he spoke. I missed some parts of it but I understood the important bits.

"I am sorry to disturb you. My name is André. I am your neighbour. Your sister is outside. She is very drunk and vomiting. I will need some help to bring her upstairs."

Turning to Catherine, who was stood slightly behind me, I started to explain, not aware that she understood the language better than I did.

"Yes, I got the gist of it. Let's go and get the stupid little bitch."

André glanced back and forth between the two of us with interest.

"Ah, you are English?"

Catherine roughly pushed past him without answering and she was leaping down the stairs, two or three, at a time. I turned to André.

"Thank you so much. Would you be able to help us please?" He smiled and looked me up and down appraisingly.

"I think I will have to carry her for you. Even you two girls will not be able to manage her in that condition."

I checked out his clothing; he was immaculate.

"But…but you'll get covered in vomit…from her." His grin shifted into genuine amusement.

"It won't be the first time. I've had some pretty vomit filled evenings myself in the past!"

He carried her upstairs over his shoulder and took her straight into my bathroom and placed her in the shower cubicle, still wearing her sick streaked clothes.

"Right, ladies, I will say goodnight. Turn the shower on and then it won't be such a daunting task to remove the sicky clothes. It will help get her sobered up with a bit of luck."

I smiled, not knowing what else to say for a few seconds, I was still reeling at Ruby's under-age inebriation and stunned to have this gorgeous man helping us with her.

"Thank you for your help, André. Thank goodness you saw her laid there in the street. I dread to think what could have happened to her."

"It was no problem." About to close my front door after himself, he added, "No doubt I will be seeing you again sometime."

Once Ruby was cleaned up and in bed sleeping it off, Catherine called her mum and told her about the latest incident. I was mortified to hear that not only was Ruby going back to England, but Catherine would be returning with her. She persuaded Heidi that Ruby should not be allowed to travel alone. Catherine booked the flights online and printed off the e-tickets while I organised a taxi. To much protest from her, I said I would go to the airport with them and wait around until their flight departed.

Without Catherine knowing, I stayed awake all night listening for any sound from Ruby. The last thing we all needed was a repeat performance of the previous night; Ruby waking up and looking for alcohol. It was vital to me for her to be on the plane tomorrow morning without fail. I was desperate not to let David down. I wanted to help Ruby, but I couldn't think how best to achieve that while she was staying with me. I needed time to think. She had serious problems and her answer was to turn to drink and cannabis. She wasn't that different to me, after all. I'd had serious issues too which resulted in me suffering from an obsessive compulsive disorder. Ruby was a few years younger than I was when my problems started, and I didn't think much to her chances of good A-level grades if she carried on the way she was.

Fortunately, during my night's vigil, there was no nocturnal activity from Ruby. She was rather shocked on waking, to be told that tickets had been booked for their flight home to England. She ate breakfast and got ready in total silence; speaking only when spoken to. When I gave them both a hug and kiss before they went to the baggage drop, I was surprised to hear her whispered apology.

"I'm sorry, Helen. It's no excuse, but life is tough at times."

"I know. We must talk sometime, Ruby, just the two of us. Perhaps we can exchange details about our tough times and try to help each other."

Her eyes met mine and I registered the shock in hers at what I just said.

"Not just losing my father, then?"

"You don't know the half of it, Ruby. I'm still waiting for the healing process to begin."

She gave me another hug before they were summoned to the check-in desk.

CHAPTER 4

I t was a refreshing change to have a friendly cab driver for once, and one who spoke excellent English. It helped considerably. My French was at best, passable, and most of the locals could understand what I was trying to convey. My main problem was that I struggled to understand *them*, mainly due to the speed that the language came out of their mouths. I would slowly translate their first sentence in my head and miss the rest of what they were saying.

Although it was such a short journey home from the supermarket, we crammed in quite a conversation and a few laughs too. He even helped me to carry all my shopping bags into the main entrance hall, before treating me to a beaming smile, and bidding me goodbye. His kindness was appreciated, as some of the bags were bloody heavy. Too late, it occurred to me that I should have asked him for his number. I never laid eyes on the guy before and I somehow doubted I ever would again. I sighed as I picked up three of the carrier bags and made the first of what would be three journeys up the stairs to my apartment.

Hurrying back down the stairs, I turned sharply on the landing to take the second flight and almost collided with André, my neighbour.

"Whoa! Slow down. You almost sent us both flying down to the bottom."

He placed his hands on my shoulders to steady me then asked

"Where are you rushing off to?" Then it must have dawned on him.

"Oh…I see. Is that your shopping in the hall? Let me help please."

He held me by the elbow as he escorted me back down the stairs.

"It will only take one journey with the two of us," he stated needlessly.

"This is much appreciated. Thank you, André"

I was struck yet again by how handsome he was and wondered how I managed *not* to come into contact with him over the last six months, until the Ruby incident. His intense grey eyes sparkled. He grinned like a superhero as he gathered all the shopping into his arms.

"You can carry that one, Helen."

He nodded towards the last carrier, full of nothing but bread and weighing so little. I laughed and followed him up the stairs. His tight denims, or rather, his nicely rounded arse was a welcome distraction from my usual dread when returning from shopping; putting the bloody stuff away in the cupboards and fridge. When my eyes were suddenly drawn away from his tight butt, it was because I noticed for the first time the back of his white tee-shirt. In large letters and in English it read 'I AM A FUCKING IDIOT!' and below in a much smaller font 'An idiot who likes to fuck'. Smirking to myself at the bold statement, I decided not to pass comment.

Once we arrived at the door to my apartment, he bent down, ready to place the shopping on the floor. Immediately impressed that he wasn't going to make the assumption that he would be invited in, I more than likely played right into his hands when I asked him if he'd like to join me for a glass of wine or a coffee. He smiled, and I could tell he was tempted.

"Well, I was going... Yes, that would be lovely, Helen. Thank you."

Going out, maybe? Or going to say?

I hadn't been expecting the quick turn around and acceptance of my offer, but I was pleased. He straightened up, maintaining his hold on the shopping so I opened the door and gestured for him to go on in ahead of me.

"Wow! You've got this place beautiful already, Helen. Great taste!"

His eyes peered into each room as we headed down the hall with the shopping, in the direction of the kitchen.

"I'm not responsible for any of it. My parents had all the work done a couple of years ago before they...yes, they did have good taste."

After dumping the bags on the worktop I was astounded as he started to take the shopping out and sort it into piles around him; things for the fridge, tins and groceries. He tried to be discreet about it, but I felt sure I saw him raise his eyebrows briefly as he spotted the wine carriers I carried upstairs on my first trip. Busying myself putting coffee on to filter, I was amused to watch him open and close each unit door, trying to locate exactly where to put everything. He must have sensed that my eyes were on him because he turned towards me and smiled before posing the question.

"So...have your two sisters returned to the U.K. now?"

"My sisters?" I laughed out loud and he looked puzzled, wondering what he said that appeared to be funny.

"They're not my sisters. I look on them as...stepdaughters, though they're not even that."

He screwed up his face, his curiosity piqued, trying to figure out what I was getting at. Although I didn't have to, I felt the need to explain, (some of it at least), particularly after his help with Ruby that night.

"Sorry. Let me fill you in. Their father, David, was my... erm...partner. He passed away last November; pancreatic cancer."

"Helen, I'm sorry. Sorry for your loss."

He moved towards me to take me into his arms, but I swiftly turned away, the coffee machine providing a more than convenient distraction. As gorgeous as he was, I didn't want his arms around me at that point. I thought that the sympathy and understanding he was offering would simply start the next round of tears.

"I'm getting there...but it's not been easy."

As he approached again, I felt the need to keep talking, so I offered some more details and he hung back respectfully.

"I didn't know the girls before David died, but it was one of his wishes that I get to know them, and them, me. They're lovely, but as you've already seen, Ruby is going through a bit of a troublesome time."

"Yes. It sure seemed that way. Poor kid, it can't be easy losing your father."

With all the shopping away and the pot of coffee ready, we went through to sit in the lounge. Keen to try and ward off further questions, I decided it was time that I knew more about him.

"How come you speak perfect English, but have a French name? Are you actually French or English?"

He laughed, evidently amused, but was quick to set me straight.

"Ah, that. No. I am a Frenchman. Both my parents are

French, but because of his business my father was based in England throughout my school years. I returned to France when I was eighteen years old and studied at Université Paris Dauphine. My parents moved back here until I got my degree and then moved back to England afterwards. They still live there."

"So you're bilingual. That explains why there's not a hint of an accent. I'm envious. I can speak French well enough to get by, but I struggle to understand when certain individuals speak rather fast."

His easy laughter was there again and he settled back into the sofa, quite relaxed this time, leaning forwards, elbows resting on his knees.

"What did you study at university if you don't mind me asking?"

"Computer Sciences. I run my own company and have eight employees. I'll never be mega rich, but I do alright. My parents co-own this place but the mortgage is colossal, so I'll probably never be able to afford a flashy car. But we can't have it all, I suppose."

He sipped at his coffee, but his eyes were fixed on mine. I wondered what he was thinking and I started to feel a little uncomfortable, as if I was being scrutinised. Eventually I looked away from his intense stare and straightened a few items on the coffee table. For once, I was at a loss to know what to talk about, and I was grateful when he broke the silence.

"Helen, would you allow me to take you out for dinner at the weekend? How would Friday night suit you?"

I was staggered. A dinner invitation was the last thing I expected. A guy like him; totally gorgeous, well-mannered and thoughtful would surely have a girlfriend or plenty of love interests. My stomach did a back flip with excitement, but I needed to know. If he had somebody on the scene, I certainly wasn't going to muscle in and spoil anything.

"You look rather surprised, Helen, if you don't mind me saying."

My heart rate was increasing by the second. My stomach lurched in excitement and I felt flushed as I stammered.

"Y..yes…I am. Don't you have some gorgeous leggy blonde somewhere who'll be pining for your attention? You…you must…have a girlfriend of sorts?"

His face darkened with a frown and in an instant he found something rather interesting to focus on in the middle of his right thigh. He brushed away a speck of lint from his denims while he considered his answer. "Did! It must be around four months since we split up. It wasn't going anywhere. We would have parted company anyway. I didn't love her or anything. What hurt me the most was not that she cheated, it was the fact that the person she chose to shag behind my back happened to be my older brother. He dropped her shortly after we split. He didn't really want her. He's done it all my life. Anything I have, he has to take. I haven't spoken to the bastard since. And yes, she was a blonde bimbo."

I saw the flash of anger in his eyes as he mentioned his brother and I felt sorry for him. Although I was an only child, I could imagine how the betrayal by a jealous sibling must have caused him such heartache.

"André, that sucks. I'm sorry. I haven't any siblings but I do understand the hurt of being betrayed like that. With me, it was my first love and my best friend. That was in my uni days. After that it was my ex-husband with a rent boy."

It was his turn then. His face was agog with a look of utter disbelief.

"Helen, I…"

Not wanting to hear his sympathy or indeed any further

questions, I nipped in, cutting him off rather rudely. Besides, I felt that a compliment was in order. He was in need of some nice words.

"Your brother, surely he could never be as gorgeous and attractive as you? She must have been mental."

It worked. He didn't give me a full smile but the corners of his mouth twitched with the beginnings of one. He was flattered by my comment, the twinkle in his eye revealing all I needed to know.

"I wouldn't go as far as that. But my brother and I are like peas in a pod. I am his mini me. Except for personality, of course; he's a wanker."

There was still the shadow of hurt across his face, the memory slow to leave his mind, too recent to be erased just yet. With the pair of us subjecting ourselves to more misery, I knew it was time to uplift the conversation from the morbid direction it was taking.

"How would you feel if I was to accept your dinner invitation? Friday night would be perfect. Let me know what time?"

His smile almost split his face in two. His eyes shone with delight as he downed the dregs of his coffee, deposited the cup and saucer on the coffee table and pushed himself up off the settee. Once stood, he shuffled nervously. If he was trying not to let too much excitement show, he failed miserably. It was rather cute and attractive, especially coming from a guy as breathtakingly hot. (I doubt he would have wanted to let any friends, employees or any guy, for that matter, bear witness to his loss of street-cred.)

"I…I…well, that's…wonderful, Helen. Can…should I put a note under your door telling you what time? After I've booked somewhere, of course? I don't want to impose any longer on your hospitality. I must go."

With his face raspberry-coloured, he turned and headed

for the door rather abruptly, I suspect to belatedly hide his embarrassment or nervousness. I followed him down the hallway, thanking him once again for the help with my shopping.

When I closed the door behind him, I rested my back against it for a few seconds, my mind was racing. Was it too soon after David to get involved with someone? Then I berated myself. It wasn't an involvement. I only accepted an offer of dinner. That was all. It didn't have to be any more than that, though I guessed it could, if he was keen, be anything I wanted it to be. Would I settle just for the one date? I would just have to wait and see what developed, and whether I was ready to move on.

CHAPTER 5

*H*e obviously pushed his note under my apartment door sometime during the night. It was brief and to the point.

'Helen, Dinner is booked for seven thirty this Friday night. Be ready for seven pm. I will give you a knock. André x'

I finished applying my make-up by six. Opting for a neutral look, I took it easy with both the lipstick and eye shadow. The pale beige on my eyelids gave a 'barely there' look and I used a lip dye that was only a shade different to my natural colour. I was pleased with the result. Maybe I was wrong, but my instinct told me that André was not the kind of man who would appreciate heavily-made-up women. I opened my wardrobe doors and lay sprawled across the bed on my tummy, looking at the contents for some inspiration amongst the garments and hangers. I hadn't appreciated exactly how difficult it was going to be to select an outfit, and after half an hour and no further forward, I felt my nerves kick in. I shuffled along to the kitchen in my slippers and poured myself a glass of chardonnay, mistakenly believing it would have a calming effect.

I knew time was running out, so after I downed most of the wine I made a more serious and determined effort to sort out my attire for the evening.

Simple, keep it simple, Helen.

Within five minutes, my fingers nervously fumbled to fasten up the zip, which was at the back of my charcoal grey silk pants. All fingers and thumbs! Now I know how that expression came about. I was feeling like a teenage girl on a first-ever-date. Only this was not all about the thrill of being asked out by a drop-dead gorgeous specimen of testosterone, there were other things amongst the mix of excitement and apprehension. The first guy I really had contact with since David, how would I feel as the evening progressed? Would I compare every aspect of him to David? What if the matter of sex cropped up? And more importantly, what would David think if he happened to be watching over me? Was I ready to get back out there and socialise, be available? Available for what, and to whom? Perhaps Catherine was right when she said I should move on. But would I ever be able to move on from David if I got back into the limelight and started social-ising, enjoying life?

I glanced at my alarm clock; ten minutes before he'd be knocking on the door. I didn't have time for soul-searching or to take stock of my life right now. I wasn't even capable of making a decision as to what top to wear with the grey pants. Closing my eyes, I reached forward and grabbed a hanger. Luck was on my side. In my 'lucky dip' I selected a suitable colour match, a pale lilac, floaty sleeveless top that wasn't too low cut. Standing back from the wardrobe, I gave a quick appraisal of my image in the full-length mirror. I was satisfied. Nothing further was needed, other than something for my feet. The day had been a scorcher, and although the temperature dropped slightly, it promised to be a sultry evening, at least from a weather point of view.

André had given no hint as to where he was taking me, but I couldn't imagine he would be the type who liked driving, especially if he wanted to drink. I selected a pair of pale grey mules on a small heel, but I never got the opportunity for another glance at the mirror. There was a barely audible tap on the apartment door. I scooped up my evening purse off the bed as the second tap followed.

"Coming!"

I shouted in response and was shocked at the throatiness of my voice and the somersaulting that was occurring deep in my stomach. For the briefest of moments it crossed my mind to shout out to him again, feign some illness, make my apologies and close the door on him, for good. I held my hand to my chest. My heart was racing away and I couldn't catch my breath. A bit of a panic attack descended on me.

"Helen? Are you okay? I must confess to feeling more than a tad nervous too."

His voice came from the other side of the door, showing his concern and understanding. He must have picked up on how I was feeling, my voice having given me away. As fast as the onslaught was, the terror retreated and I got control back. I inhaled deeply and opened the door to him. I was floored by the vision of male sexiness that greeted me. He was beautifully dressed in smart black chinos and a white short-sleeved shirt with a very feint stripe running through the fabric. He wore the shirt unbuttoned at the collar and it was adorned by a plain, loosely fastened, light blue tie. As banal as it would seem to most, his overall image was red hot, and despite his grin, he coloured up quickly.

"I didn't know what…" I blurted out, without so much as 'hello, André.'

"You look perfect, Helen, stunning, in fact. Shall we make a move then?"

Out on the street, there was no cab in sight, so when he made to turn left I fell in beside him. It was a beautiful evening, a slight breeze from over the Seine making the temperature more bearable that it would otherwise have been. The street was a hive of activity, with traffic hooting, tourists and locals alike strolling in all directions, making the best of the mid-summer heatwave. We sauntered along in near silence for a few minutes, having to manoeuvre at times to skirt around the odd group of people taking up the pavement as they stopped to chat to others.

"Where are we eating, André?"

As if suddenly remembering something he had forgotten to do, he held a palm up to his head.

"Shit! I forgot to book somewhere. We'd better carry on walking until we find a cafe, shall we?"

I shot him a warning glare.

"I know you're trying to joke with me, André, but you already told me in your note that you booked somewhere. And let me tell you this, if you did take me to a cheap café, it would be the first and last date we'd ever have."

He howled with laughter before reading into what I just implied.

"Oooh! Does that mean that you're already thinking there could possibly be another date? If I end up not taking you to a café, that is? Seems like I'd better take you some place half decent then? It's just as well I've booked us into La Regalade Saint-Honare, isn't it?"

I joined in with his blatantly playful mood and hit him around his shoulder with my clutch bag. He pretended to cower away in fear and we chuckled. The joviality rapidly broke the ice and we relaxed, his arm draped loosely around my shoulders as we neared our destination.

From what my parents told me two or three years previously, the restaurant had an outstanding reputation. Mum and Dad ate there on a few occasions, though it was not a place where we went when I had stayed with them. Once I started to relax in André's company, I realised how hungry I felt. The food was rather pricey but delicious. I was convinced that I had just eaten the best food I ever tasted in all the times I'd been to Paris, although the portion sizes could have been improved upon. We talked non-stop throughout the meal yet, rather than giving our conversation his full attention, André was closely watching my facial expressions as I ate. I could see the pleasure on his face as I tasted each mouthful of food and showed my enjoyment. I got the impression that his sole aim for the evening was for me to be impressed at his choice of restaurant and the culinary delights that were served up. Well I have to hand it to him, I was impressed, very much so. We sipped our way through two bottles of wine during the meal, but the effects were minimal because of the food. I made a point of watching him carefully, his eyes and his body language, unsure as to whether there were any ulterior motives. His eyes shone with pleasure and his smile appeared readily, yet there was no innuendo, no touching, and no undressing me with his eyes. I was totally at ease with that.

After we left the restaurant we wandered aimlessly for an hour or so. The streets were alive with people, the hot night bringing them out to enjoy the late night temperatures. Most just roamed around with no destination in mind, rather like André and I.

It was just before eleven when we took the final few hundred yards back to our apartments. He kissed me on the cheek.

"Goodnight, Helen. Thank you for your company. I have really enjoyed this evening."

"André, I thoroughly enjoyed the meal. Thank you so much, it has been lovely, really pleasant." Placing my hands on his shoulders for a second, I gave him a peck on his cheek.

"Goodnight!"

He stood and watched me turn the key in my lock before walking towards his own door. He mouthed "goodnight" once more before I closed my door. I heaved a sigh of relief that it was over and sat around for an hour or more, running through every aspect of the evening in my head. First steps taken!

CHAPTER 6

*I*t was clear that André must have enjoyed our dinner date as much as I had. We hadn't yet made any further dates but he had taken to popping in to see me every other night, usually just after he arrived home from work. I was delighted. Much as I enjoyed his company and found him breathtakingly hot, I did not want to be seen as the one giving chase. I wasn't one hundred percent comfortable with the situation, but more than happy that if things did develop any further, it would be at a pace that I felt right with.

On some occasions he would only stay long enough to have a coffee or a glass of wine and tell me amusing stories and gossip about some of the characters who worked for him. The more I watched him and listened to his tales, the more I thought how appropriate the message on his tee-shirt had been. He was indeed 'a fucking idiot', but an intelligent, interesting, caring, handsome and fuckable one at that. His sense of humour was typically British and, in his case, the sarcasm that could spill from his mouth was not the lowest form of wit. It was clever, off the cuff and highly entertaining. I loved his presence, but I spent many hours pondering whether it could ever be more than that, as much as I wanted it to be.

Some of his visits were longer; frequently reaching midnight or after, before he left my apartment. I assumed he'd already eaten on these occasions as it was usually later than eight o'clock when he knocked on my door. Whether he'd eaten or not, I never felt the inclination to offer to cook. It hadn't reached that stage. At best, I brought out snacks and nibbles; crisps, nuts, chocolate and as a one-off - fresh strawberries and ice-cream. André always seemed to have more conversation to offer than I did. He had a life, a business, and plenty of news. With no job, therefore no colleagues, no family, hence no news, the only topic I could offer was that of my past. He hadn't clicked just how skilled I was at discreetly side-stepping painful discussions about ex partners and my parents. My career (the unsavoury one) was something that obviously escaped a mention, too.

We both had similar tastes in music, films and books, and as far as I was concerned it was much safer ground. We watched a few recent box office successes, mostly of his choosing, but nevertheless, enjoyable. What I enjoyed the most was when we decided to have a wander down by the riverside. Maybe this was down to my months of self-inflicted confinement, or that I enjoyed being out and about during Catherine and Ruby's recent visit. My newly born craving to be out in the open air was such that if André and I didn't venture out for a walk at some point during his visit, I would make a big thing of going out the following morning for a lonesome stroll. I found it to be therapeutic and it gave me other things to focus on, something I hadn't allowed myself to do for a long time; the healing process.

Wearily climbing the stairs one night after a walk that

took us further off our regular route, André affectionately squeezed the left side of my waist and asked,

"Helen, would you let me cook for you at the weekend, please? My apartment? I've wanted to ask you for the last few days but never got around to it. I always come to see you, but I feel it's time I had you as my guest."

Although he'd already taken me out for a meal, I was still taken aback by his request. Up to that point, he pecked me on the cheek just once or twice, and I presumed that he was happy to go along with our 'friends' arrangement for the time being and take things slowly, if indeed there was anything there to be taken slowly.

"Oh! I…" I started.

"Don't worry. I won't try to poison you, Helen." He laughed. "I'm a decent enough chef."

"I'm sure you are. I…It's just that your invitation has surprised me. Anyway, I would love to come for a meal. I'd like to see your apartment as well, since you never asked me round before now."

I could tell by his expression that he was pleased with my acceptance. His eyes shone with evident delight though he was trying to cover it by suppressing a wide grin, such was his transparency at times.

We said our goodbyes at the front door to my apartment. He told me he was planning the meal for Saturday night at six thirty and he'd stressed the word 'informal'. I couldn't fathom whether he was jesting or deadly serious when he told me he would need two or three nights off to plan and prepare. He'd also thrown in some comment about needing to spring clean from top to bottom. He was always so immaculate that I somehow doubted his flat would be kept to anything other than a high standard.

I lay in bed that night with my head in total turmoil, unsure as to what dinner at André's place would mean for me and what it meant to him. Did he see the prospects of a romantic meal for two and cosying up afterwards on the sofa? Or perhaps he was thinking if he provided the main course the dessert would somehow involve two naked bodies and oodles of scorching hot sex. He was everything that most women would dream of, and yet I didn't know how I would feel if he tried to give me a full on kiss and if the matter of sex cropped up, heaven forbid. I wanted to move on and live a normal life, possibly even to have a relationship, but until the situation came smacking me on the nose end I wouldn't know if it was too soon.

I didn't sleep too well and woke up with a head that felt like it was ready to split in two. Foregoing my day-to-day morning routine of two cups of coffee and a croissant, I poured a large glass of fresh orange juice and washed down the couple of paracetamol I felt were necessary. I showered and dressed, determined to get out into the fresh air and walk off the damned headache. I paused at the door wondering what I'd forgotten and then dashed back to the kitchen to grab the bottle of water I left on the worktop.

It was uncomfortably muggy outside and large, heavy black clouds threatened a torrential downpour as I took a leisurely saunter along the side of the river. Although I felt refreshed and wide awake after my shower, there was a feeling of weariness gradually taking over which could have been due to the headache that was proving reluctant to disappear. Along the walkway I noticed I was approaching a bench and decided I would make use of it until my fatigued body recovered. I sat back and watched the world go by; hordes of people on their way to work, shopping, walking their family pets or visiting the sights and attractions that Paris had on offer. Later in the morning the couples would appear; loving twosomes on romantic breaks, possibly getting engaged or sometimes there were even honeymooners. Paris had a reputation, after all, for being the most romantic city in Europe.

With the troubles my mind unwillingly encountered, I started searching the faces of the passers-by, for once ignoring the physical things like clothes, shoes, handbags or whether they were walking with a particular gait. I was oblivious to the size of their noses or whether they sported the latest designer specs that the opticians had on a half price offer if you signed up for a monthly plan with contact lenses. The physical didn't matter to me anymore. Minds and lives were more important. Picking out random people as they passed me by, I scanned each face, looking deep past their eyes and into their souls. What were they feeling? Were they happy in their lives? Had they been hurt by anybody? I abandoned that one quickly. Everyone had been hurt by somebody at some heart-breaking period in their lives, hadn't they? I found jealousy lurking in my bones as I looked at those my age and younger who I imagined would still have loving parents to offer their help and guidance with life's traumas.

Of the souls I searched, I wondered if any had lost both parents in such tragic circumstances as I had. I probed the eyes of the men who strode confidently past, some of whom would loiter too long and mentally undress me before going about their business. Would they cheat on their wife or girl-friend, the one they were supposed to love? Would I trust them with a best friend? Then the question changed as I tried to pick out the ones who would stoop so low as to visit a prostitute or use the services of a call-girl. Like somebody had just thrown a switch, I found myself despising the clients who I'd entertained and allowed to use and abuse me and my body. I was no better than they were. I was engulfed in my shame and guilt at being party to their dirty, unforgivable adultery.

My mind game with the pedestrians suddenly cast aside, I scoured the depths of my own soul, damaged as it was. I hated myself for the sordid way in which I'd sought sexual gratification and accepted money for it. It occurred to me though, that had I not sunk to those murky depths, and swam in that sea of secrets and lies, I would never have met David, the love of my life. He was the exception to the rule; there had been no lady in his life, though I initially went ahead with our first few 'business' transactions unaware of the fact that he was single. Not even for one second could I have regrets about David, even though I since wished I'd met him at another time and in a different set of circumstances. I sighed heavily and jerked myself back to the present.

A distant rumble increased in volume and intensity and, glancing up at the sky, I noticed how black the morning had become and the aggression and intimidation the low-lying clouds now held. Heavy spots of rain hit the footpath and a tall, slim bespectacled gentleman shouted an unnecessary warning as he rushed past in the process of opening his black golfing brolly.

"Hurry home, Madame! The Heavens are about to open! You will get drenched!"

"Oui, Monsieur. Merci beaucoup!"

With an effort, I pushed myself up from the bench. A beautiful streak of forked lightning lit up the blackness of the sky for a second, a very resounding boom of thunder dramatically drowning the sound of the ever hooting traffic. I'd lost track of time and my watch was where I left it on the bathroom shelf. The early morning rush hour was long since over and it seemed that with the threat of an imminent heavy downpour, most people were deserting the streets. Those few that remained outdoors held their umbrellas aloft and hurried onwards to their various destinations. Finding the rain invigorating, I felt no such urgency.

More frequent bolts of white hot lightning continued to flash with their electrostatic discharge, lighting the world with a blinding incandescence. It possessed a vivid, jagged, electrical beauty that bore life and also the threat of death to anyone falling victim to its powerful and lethal tendrils. I was afraid and yet I found a thrill and excitement in the spectacle. The spots on the pavement were soon gone as the shroud of dark grey cloud finally spilt its burden and the pavements and road were instantly awash with much heavier rain. In seconds I was drenched. My hair was heavy with the rat tails that stuck to my face, and the shorts and tee-shirt I wore clung icily to my body; my weariness finally left me, as had the headache that greeted me as I woke. People stared as they passed me, aghast at my casual indifference to the noisy display and my piss-wet-through body and clothes. I smiled cheerily at their faces, defiant and feeling refreshed, alive and amazingly positive.

Thursday and Friday passed by quickly. The hot weather was back with a vengeance, but thanks to the electrical storm the humidity had reduced and it was a pleasure to be outdoors. I walked to the park and sat reading for most of Friday afternoon, remembering to re-apply sun-block regularly. It was an attempt, with Saturday fast approaching, to not fill my head with negative thoughts about the dinner date with André. It worked for a time and then deserted me the moment I let myself back into the flat.

From getting out of bed, Saturday passed painfully slow. There was too much time for thinking. I walked. I shopped, for clothes this time, clothes that I didn't need. Such was my poor judgement and lack of concentration, four of the half dozen items I purchased would need to be returned come Monday morning. Two skirts (I don't know how I'd managed it) were the wrong size, and I had no-one to blame except myself. I was the one who picked them off the rail and taken them to the tills. I tried on a green patterned top in one store and fallen in love with it.

On searching my wardrobe for a skirt or trousers to wear with it, I found there was nothing. What the fuck made me buy something green? I hated green. My fourth mistake was a dress of which I liked the style. It was fitted, short-sleeved, the skirt part being pencil like and came with a belt in the same fabric. It hugged my figure perfectly, but not having tried it on in the store (because the changing rooms were chaotic) I hadn't realised how hideous its fabric with large vibrant flowers would look on me; my biggest fashion disaster to date.

The temperature was above forty throughout the afternoon, and when I started to get ready to go to André's apartment it had dropped, but only by two or three degrees. My face having a natural summer glow, I didn't bother with much make-up, using only a tinted moisturiser and lightly applied mascara. I wore a white ankle-length cotton skirt with a plain white vest top and bright purple leather flip-flops. (He stipulated informal, after all.) Having decided in advance not to be prompt, it was gone twenty five to seven when I rapped on his door.

He didn't answer. I just heard his distant voice shouting,

"Helen, come in."

Hesitating a little, I opened the door to frantic cursing and slamming around of pots and pans coming from his kitchen.

"Hi!" I shouted.

"Find yourself a seat. I'll be with you shortly." He growled again, his frustrations in the kitchen glaringly obvious. I shouted 'okay' to him and walked through to his lounge. Trying to keep a new attach of nerves at bay, I looked around. The decoration was up-to-date and his furniture suited the décor of the room. The whole appearance was very nice but it was lacking a woman's touch. It was totally devoid of artwork, ornaments and modern lighting. I sat in a big comfy armchair, the type I adored where there was room to curl one's knees up. He made a quick appearance, thrusting a glass of wine into my hand before running full pelt back to the kitchen, swearing under his breath én route. As an afterthought, he shouted from the kitchen once more.

"Won't be long."

It was apparent that things weren't going to plan. I sat with my thoughts for almost an hour before he came and collected me, grabbing my hand to lead me to his kitchen diner. Being the gentleman he was, he pulled out a chair for me. I gave the table a quick once over and the first thing that caught my eye was the tea-light holder complete with five tea-lights already aglow. Shit! He fully intended that this was to be a romantic evening, not a returned favour by the look of things.

My stomach grumbled loudly but not with hunger. Something was causing it to flutter and I felt an all-consuming unease settle over my body. The easy friendship André and I had settled into these last few weeks was on the verge of change. Uncertainty loomed about how that change would or could affect our friendship. I couldn't even find a safe place from my worry during our meal. Hoping to leave my thoughts behind and lose myself in conversation, I was disappointed. We ate in near silence and from his body language I sensed that André was harbouring some worries of his own. I made appropriate and positive comments about his food as we ate and watched for a difference but he remained tense, my compliments about the meal unable to appease him.

The three course meal he prepared had been tasty enough (though not presented well), yet neither of us emptied our plates. I watched him carefully as I finished my second glass of wine and stacked the dessert plates and cutlery.

"Leave them, Helen. They can wait. We'll move through there," he tilted his head to indicate the direction of the living room, "and put some music on."

He collected two fresh glasses and another bottle of wine from the fridge and we abandoned the kitchen. It felt as though things were getting on top of me. My head was truly up my proverbial and even though I gave it my best shot, I couldn't come up with a safe topic of conversation. I'd pinned my hopes on André to make things easy with his normal wit and carefree banter, but he wasn't on the planet right when I needed him to be. If I couldn't do anything to give the atmosphere a lift within the hour, I would make my excuses and leave. I'm not someone who can endure prolonged silences.

"You choose. I'll pour us both a glass."

He treated me to what must only have been his fourth smile of the evening. I headed towards his impressive C.D. collection which was the only personal touch in the huge lounge; floor to ceiling shelving built into a full recess and every shelf was crammed full with all genres of music.

"Ignore the ones on the top shelves. They're the ones I don't play these days. It's impossible to see what they are anyway."

I looked round to find him watching me as he sloshed the wine into the glasses. His mood had lifted and he seemed more relaxed. I ran my thumb along one shelf of C.D.s pausing every now and then as I noticed one or two of interest. Selecting an old favourite of mine, 'Definitely, Maybe' by Oasis, I swung around straight into his arms. I hadn't heard him sneak up behind me. It felt nice to be held by him. His body was firm and muscular against mine as he pulled me in closer. I could smell him up close; just a hint of a fragrance so deliciously masculine, but one I couldn't remember the name of. His eyes shone with desire and sexiness. He kissed my cheek and I jumped with the movement, wondering how our previous awkwardness dissipated so swiftly. He brushed my cheek with his lips, and moved towards my ear.

"Oh, Helen."

His breath was heavy and tickled my ear in such close proximity.

"You always look so sexy and...hot. I don't know how I kept my hands off you each time I've been with you these last few weeks."

His voice was that of a stranger. I'd never heard him speak in this raw, throaty and intimate way, and my inhibitions melted away as my body temperature soared through the roof. He kissed me on the lips very briefly and leaned back to gauge my reaction.

"So...why...ha...have you?" I demanded, feeling the onset of wanting much more. I could feel his heart pound against my breast, as he gasped for air.

"I...I..don't know. But I don't...want to...keep my hands... off you...any...anymore." He was on me immediately, our lips smacked together as he kissed me urgently, our tongues danced and tangled, our bodies throbbed together demonstrating our hunger. I wanted him to fuck me at that very moment.

CHAPTER 7

A fire I'd forgotten existed, wondrous, burning flames lapped at my body as our tongues twisted and tasted each other's warmth. Then suddenly we lost contact as he pulled away and eased my vest top up and over my arms and head. He unclasped my bra at the front, leaning back to stop and admire my little breasts before kissing and fondling them, gently at first and then greedily, biting into me with his need. It was a beautiful pain, and I winced each time he repeated the move, groaning, communicating that I wanted more of his touch, the whole of his body, and it seemed that he understood the message loud and clear.

Grabbing at his leather belt, I pulled him up close to me but before I started to unfasten him, I let my fingers roam slowly and teasingly over the outline of his cock, which stood proud and hard against his stomach. He gasped in pleasure.

"Fuck! That's good!"

I tried to put the thought of what this could do to our friendship to the back of my mind. I wanted and needed to stay focused. I wanted to want him. I stroked his hard-on once more, reaffirming what I already knew; I wanted him badly. My urgency increased as I unzipped and unbuttoned him as fast as I possibly could. He tongued my nipples and I thrust my hand down his pants, desperate to feel the heat of his cock. Desperate to explore and caress every inch of it before it became buried hard into my depth. His eyes closed in ecstasy and his wet, hot kisses were all over my face as he blindly sought my mouth. I held his cock, massaging it tightly, up and down, deliberately keeping it slow and with the intention to torment. His girth was perfect and I moaned deeply as my wetness increased, nerves tingled excitedly and I could wait no longer, my stomach ached with a wanting that I hadn't experienced in recent months.

In one deft move, I yanked his denims and pants down his legs, pausing mid-crouch to kiss the tip of his length when I caught my first glimpse of it; a perfect seven-inch specimen. Following suit, he soon discovered the waistband of my skirt was elasticated and caught his thumbs up in my panties as well. He tugged both garments down to my ankles. In an almost like-for-like action to mine, he fleetingly ran his tongue over my clit. I moaned out loud as he repeated the action.

"You're so sweet and tasty, Helen. Delicious." As he straightened up, I thought he was moving in for another kiss, but he took my face in his hands and peered deep into my eyes, searching my expression for reassurance.

"Do you want me to fuck you, Helen?"

My heart pounded and I was unable to voice an answer. It was mental torment, the waiting but I was ready. I nodded my head vigorously making it clear to him that I was certain. He kicked his shoes off and removed his denims and under-wear then reached for my hand. Before he could lead me, I stepped out of my skirt and panties and we headed for the hallway. He couldn't tear his eyes away from my nakedness.

Pushing me hard up against the wall, somewhere between his main door and the lounge door, he shoved two fingers deep inside me.

"Oooh! You're nice and wet for me."

The speed of his move left me reeling and made me feel light-headed and giddy (which could also have been alcohol induced).

"Whoa!" I whispered.

"Sorry, Helen. Did I hurt you?"

Before I could answer he slowly slid his fingers out and I groaned even louder.

"No! No! Wine's affecting me."

"Good. I'm going to fuck you right here, Helen. Right here!"

Holding me with one arm around my waist, he grabbed hold of his rigid cock and guided it towards my warmth. As he tried to nudge into my opening, I couldn't understand, I tensed from the inside.

He shoved hard again trying to penetrate and my attempt to relax made me more uptight.

"You...you've dried up on me, Helen. I thought...you were...ready?"

"I was...I am...I don't know...." I cried out in frustration.

I was devastated and I felt awful for him too. I was ready and couldn't for the life of me understand where it had gone wrong. He knelt down on the floor and pulled me down to join him.

"Perhaps if we indulge in a little more foreplay? Maybe I've jumped in too soon. You need to relax for me, you're so tensed up. Lie down, Helen."

"Can...can we...go to your bed?" I asked, apologetically. "Maybe if I'm a bit more comfortable..."

Taking my hand, he led me to his room. I noticed that his

cock had lost some of its stiffness. Guilt started to eat away inside me.

I tensed even more as I lay down on his bed and he spooned up behind me and reached over to fondle my breasts.

"I'm sorry, André. I…don't know what happened."

"Don't apologise. We'll start again. We'll take it slow." His cock was getting hard again, I could feel it between the top of my thighs, close to my warmth. Every inch of my body needed him. "Roll over to face me, darling." He backed away slightly as he rolled me to face him. His mouth was on mine again and I ached with want as our tongues played together once more. He eased his fingers inside me and my pussy was putting up a little resistance. He teased me slowly, working his thumb lovingly over my clit. Thrusting his fingers in and out slowly, he reached deeper with each move and my nerves tingled with excitement as I gradually started to relax and open up to him. My juices started to flow and I moaned.

"You're getting wet again, Helen. I'm going to shove my cock inside you while you're wet." I couldn't wait. I was warm, and my fingers trailed through the perspiration on his back as I pulled him closer to me. Lifting my bottom off the bed to meet up with his cock, I was horrified when the head nudged painfully at my entrance. I groaned loudly in self-disgust. What the fuck was going on? What was my body playing at? In desperation I grunted at him.

"André, just fucking shove it hard into me, please."

He didn't need asking twice. Holding the base of his cock, he positioned its head in my folds and rammed hard into me. Fucking Hell! It bloody hurt! Screaming out with the pain, I nodded at him to carry on, eager to get something out of this. I was desperate to cum, to feel that euphoria once more that I had all but forgotten. I wanted an explosion to rock my world and consume my body, to dampen my flames. He carried on thrusting into me like a maniac and my pain continued. It felt so abrasive and my warm depths were burning and sore.

"Sweetheart, I'm going to need you to cum as soon as you can. Your pussy needs wetness. It is so fucking tight it's not going to take me long. Cum for me, Helen. As fast as you can."

His eyes met mine and I saw frustration in them. He wanted our mutual enjoyment to last and the behaviour of my body was about to tip him over the edge, prematurely. Closing my eyes tight with the pain, and so that he couldn't see his frustration mirrored in mine, I willed myself to feel excitement. I willed my body to feel that dancing, tingling pre-cum build up. Reaching down with my hand, I frantically rubbed at my clit…to no avail. It was lost to me. Although in my mind, I wanted to be fucked, hard and rough, the way I always liked it, my body was an unwilling participant. I carried on rubbing myself, trying to summon a little more enthusiasm. Then without much warning, and because I was so tight around his cock, I could feel the intensity of his twitches as he was ready to shoot his lot deep into me. Bellowing as loud and enthusiastically as I could muster, I forced my whole body to shake and shudder as if in delight… for the first time ever. I faked what André thought was a violent and intense orgasm. He bit into my neck as if to heighten his imminent ejaculation. Almost simultaneously, he threw his head back as he pumped his seed into me.

"Oh fuck…king hell. Wow!" he growled his ecstasy.

Flopping onto his side, head on my breast, he struggled to calm his breathing.

"Thank fuck you managed to cum, Helen. That was so sensitive. You're tiny, too tight around my cock. I could… couldn't hold on any longer" he stammered, his breathing slowly returning to normal.

I didn't know what to say. He cuddled up to me and I tensed, stressed and unhappy with the way I'd just been. I wanted to go home. Within a short space of time, his heavy breaths turned into contented snoring. The tears came as my emotions ran away with me. I could think of nothing but David, and how I just betrayed him. Soon, the sobs jerked my body and I couldn't do anything about them. André, disturbed by my movements, jolted awake.

"Helen? What's the matter?" He coaxed softly. "Fuck. Have I…have I just made you do something you didn't want to do?"

The look on his face was so full of disappointment, my heart leapt in sympathy for his woe. I knew I had to pacify him. It hadn't been my intent to hurt him.

"André, no! I wanted it…just as much…as you. A gorgeous…sexy guy…like you, what girl… wouldn't want you?" I sobbed and reached for the box of tissues on his nightstand. "I…I managed to cum, didn't I?" I lied. "I…I'm sorry, André. It's…it's my first time…for months…since… since David."

He held my cheeks and looked deep into my eyes. I wanted to turn my head away, not wanting him to see my guilt…my lie. I couldn't bear for him to see the truth in my eyes. I don't know what he saw in my eyes to recognise, but he took me into his arms and pulled me hard into his body. Stroking my hair soothingly, his voice was barely a whisper.

"Sorry, Helen! It was too soon for you. Next time…if you want there to be a next time…" he searched my face, looking for confirmation "…it will be at your instigation, when you feel ready."

"I…I was ready…am ready." I corrected. "I was…torn. I know my body was ready for you, and then…then my mind…closed me down. I think it was…just because…it was…my first time. Next time will…should be better. I…I hope so. It's not fair…on you."

Speaking rather sternly, as well as logically, he gave me his view.

"To hell with me and my feelings, Helen. They'll keep. First and foremost, you have got to be fucking fair to yourself. You have got to be ready…mentally first…then the physical will take care of itself."

Watching his face through watery eyes, I was stunned by his empathy and stalwart unselfishness. He was not only a loyal friend but a more than considerate lover, and he deserved better. His kindness just piled more guilt onto my shoulders and I found it hard to meet his gaze. I felt a total shit.

"Maybe you should go, Helen. You need some 'you' time. Go home and get a good night's sleep. I'll go and gather your clothes up."

He slid out from under the duvet and I watched in awe as he padded down the hall in bare feet, a little shred of tissue stuck to the end of his cock. Though I managed to find a little amusement at the sight, I couldn't even summon a smile. He was a truly lovely guy and all I wanted to do was get out of his sight, get him out of my sight, and be alone.

I dressed in silence. As I hurriedly slipped into my crumpled top and skirt, he threw a towelling robe around himself, watching me with concern. He walked with me across the landing to my door and after giving me a quick hug and a peck on the cheek, he whispered in my ear.

"I'll pop to see you in the morning. I know it's not been easy for you, Helen, but do try to get a decent night's sleep. Don't worry!"

I no sooner locked the door behind him and I let it all come flooding out. My body was racked with my sobs until the early hours, after every last gram of energy was drained from me. What had been a daily process in my life for these last months was still with me. Heartache, grief, guilt, feeling lost, and now my sexual frustrations were back. Would I ever be able to shake them off? Would I ever be fortunate enough to live a normal life again?

CHAPTER 8

*A*ndré and I carried on our lives as normal for a week or two after that disastrous night. All our usual routines stayed the same; walking, listening to music, watching films. There was new warmth between us, a closeness that I felt comfortable with, and I settled down, appreciative of the fact that he'd not mentioned the dinner date at his; he never probed or asked how I was feeling. Perhaps so we didn't fall into a rut, he organised a cinema outing and we went out to a couple of different restaurants. Not once did he push his affections onto me. He did nothing more than give me a lingering kiss on the lips and hugged me close to him. I'd never met a man with such patience; it didn't seem to ring true for a Frenchman. I was always under the impression that they were red-hot lovers with fiery temperaments to match.

On the night that we visited the cinema, I didn't even know the title of the film he'd booked online for us to see. My eyes may have been on the screen but my head was elsewhere. I sat there, my hand in his, feeling safe and content in his company. We took a slow walk back to our apartments, his arm tight around my shoulders, protecting me, watching for any crack in the pavement to steer me around so that one of my heels didn't cause me to stumble. I was proud to be seen with him. Another matter we'd not discussed was our relationship. He hadn't laid any claim on me, made any demands, or asked me to be his girlfriend. I was unsure as to whether he classed us as 'an item' or whether we were just 'friends'. I couldn't help but think that 'friends without benefits' would be a more appropriate terminology for the situation, as it was at the time. But whichever way he chose to look at things, he never voiced his thoughts and I was content with the relationship the way it was.

Three and a half weeks after the sex-from-hell, my want was back, and much to his surprise, in the middle of a film, I watched him watching the film for ten minutes. He looked so goddamn fucking hot sat there, his right finger rubbing the tip of his nose, and I'd have bet any money he didn't realise he was doing it (it was a habit of his I fast caught onto). His arms were tanned and the sun had bleached his hair a shade lighter; fuck me, he was so handsome. I was aware of the wet fabric between my legs as I tingled deliciously with craving. Fuck! I was resolute, determined not to miss the opportunity.

So engrossed in his film, I don't think he realised I'd quietly knelt down at the side of his knees. Jumping to it, a lump in my throat in anticipation, my hands swiftly worked hard at his belt and zip before he understood what was happening. Tugging his denims and pants urgently from under his beautiful arse, I descended onto his soft cock with my mouth before his clothes had even reached his ankles. I massaged the base of it and sucked hard on its tip, looking into his eyes which, wide open in shock, sparkled lustily with the realisation that I was ready to fuck and be fucked.

I watched in pleasure as his flaccid cock grew in my

hands and then my stomach lurched to attention as his size-able hard-on steadily filled my mouth, my teeth grazing his skin as he started thrusting towards the back of my throat.

"Well, fuck me, Helen…what a surprise. But are you…"

Nipping in quickly to verify it before he even finished asking, I groaned.

"Yes! I've never been more certain, André."

He moaned at the moment his cock reached its peak of rigidity and I rushed to stand, urgently removing my skirt and thong. He put his hand on the arm of the sofa and leaned forward, ready to move. "Stay there!" I ordered assertively. "I'm going to fuck you first. I'm wet and I want your cock hard inside me."

"Go…go for it!"

He breathed, taking his length and holding it steady as I placed my knees on the sofa and, straddling him, I lowered myself onto its head. My back arched instantly. Before the head of his cock fully penetrated, I stopped lowering myself, the intensity too much as my orgasm exploded around him. My stomach fluttered and my body tingled, each nerve alive with individual pleasure, causing my body to jerk spas-modically.

He watched me and his face was aghast, his eyes showing disbelief at the violence with which my orgasm took hold.

"Fuck me! You were…really ready, Helen. Fuck!" He laughed. "You saucy bitch, going down on me like that, without any warning. Go you, you dirty bitch!"

Relieved to have finally got back at it, I was fuelled and ready to go. I wanted more. Then, after recovering from the sensitive after-shocks of my release, I lowered myself onto the full length of him, slippery with my cum, until he filled me. It was a beautiful feeling. He was big, at full stretch and I taunted him, clenching around him and then unclenching, clenching, unclenching, and each time I clenched tight I could feel his throbbing, his nerves communicating their need to mine.

"Oh God, Helen. You're so hot in there, so fucking hot."

The mention of it…the hotness…I felt it deep inside. I was like an inferno, fierce, a ferocity not yet dampened by the wetness within. Urging myself to fuck, wanting more, wanting to fuck him and cum again, and then fuck him some more, I rode him wildly, rubbing my clit tight to his pubic frame, awaiting a new wave of tingling, throbbing, aching and letting go. And then it was with me again, another explosive, beautiful minute of juddering, and I lost myself in the moment, biting into his shoulder and growling breathlessly as I soared into a new realm of pleasure.

He let my body still for a few moments, not once taking his eyes from mine as he smiled at my exuberance and my joyous 'coming'. I quietened, and he gently pushed me away and rolled me until I was sat adjacent to where he'd been.

"Let me taste you. I want to run my tongue around your pussy and taste your juices before I add to them. Can you cope with more, Helen? Another cum while I lick you and tongue fuck you?" He snarled dirtily.

I hadn't come back down, my head was still somewhere in the fucking clouds and his head was suddenly tight between my thighs, tasting me, fucking me with his tongue, stroking my clit with one finger and another poised over the puckers that formed my rear entrance.

"Phwoar!" He snarled again between his tongue thrusts and licks. "You're a tasty fucking bitch, Helen…as well as a dirty one," he added jokingly.

"Oh, no! It's too much!" I cried out.

Knowing that my next orgasm was not far away, I didn't know which planet I was on but the thoughts in my head thrashed about, desperately trying to be grounded and get back in control. He must have sensed my distraction and imminent gush and pushed hard into my rear with his finger. I fell over the edge again in a rush of emotions, fire and convulsion of epic proportions.

At the height of my display of wantonness, he quickly backed away and pulled me forwards to the edge of the sofa and rammed straight into me. Thrusting in desperation (as if it was to be his last time ever) he rammed hard and deep, matching my wildness of minutes before. He pulled almost out of me and rammed the full length hard into me again. He repeated, faster and faster with an energy that was borne out of his need. Out, in, out, in. Harder, faster, and then he stilled deep inside me. I knew his spurts were imminent, his twitching so intense, and then he groaned loudly and throatily.

"Yes! Oh, yes! Fuck!"

His seed flowed. And it was my turn to watch his face screw up, eyes closed as he enjoyed every second as he spurted within me. He slept in my bed that night. For once, I didn't dream. I had the deepest, most restful sleep I'd had in a long time. I think I'd burned myself out.

The sex between us started to happen on a more regular basis as we plodded along together, but I started to feel disquieted by my thoughts and feelings. I wasn't always able to let go and enjoy myself. It seemed as if I couldn't relax sufficiently. On those occasions, my body struggled to accept him. Hard as he would be every time, he had to force himself into my tight, dry depths. I should have been honest with him, told him I wasn't in the mood, but not wanting him to feel rejected or unwanted, I let him go ahead and it was wrong of me. It didn't feel right; it hurt and I would always end up feeling extremely sore and uncomfortable. I watched a pattern develop over the next few weeks, until, finally, I faced up to the one fact that had been staring me in the face.

I had always been a horny inquisitive bitch since my early

adolescence and I lost my virginity in the sports equipment storeroom at school. With the exception of when I was studying for my finals and the difficult months following David's death, I always had a healthy sexual appetite and couldn't go for long without. It had been troubling me that the only times I could fully indulge in our fucking were when I took the initiative to start things. On each occasion André took the lead, it seemed I couldn't willingly let him in. I found it hard to take part, ended up sore and felt bitterly disappointed later, usually because I faked yet another orgasm. That was my little soul-search done; my investigation over. How stupid had I been? I could only perform when I wanted the sex. Greedy to be fucked, it wouldn't have mattered who it was, I'd get my kicks. Sometimes, André happened to be there when I wanted to fuck. I was actually quite gutted about it when it finally hit me. André was stunningly handsome, kind, caring and everything but yet, that sexual spark, that chemistry was missing. I was sorry about it but I didn't see a way of being able to put something there that evidently was not. I genuinely wished it could have been possible. Ashamed though I was with myself, I used his body on at least a couple more occasions during my hours of need.

I don't know what possessed me, but one night I decided to fish my mobile out of the drawer of my nightstand and left it on charge overnight. It had been in there, unused and forgotten since I arrived in France.

The following morning, I switched it on and first deleted all the useless texts. Making myself comfortable on the sofa, I listened carefully to dozens of voicemails, half a dozen or so which grabbed my attention. After getting rid of the ones I regarded as junk, I listened more carefully to those that I'd saved. I gave them some consideration for a while before coming to a few decisions. I needed to make some return calls, one or two of which were urgent.

Early evening, once I heard André arrive home from work, I tapped on his door. He threw it wide open and grinned a little too knowingly.

"Helen? My God, you are eager tonight. I've just got home. Come in."

He waved his arm towards the living room.

"I won't be staying, André. I've come to tell you that I've got to go back to England tomorrow. My flight's in the morning."

I was dismayed to see the disappointment wipe the smile from his face.

"Oh! How long for?"

"A week, maybe a little longer."

Then by way of explanation, as he looked so crestfallen, I added,

"I've got to see my lawyer. My ex-husband's trial is more or less imminent, so there are lots of things we have to go through beforehand."

"Oh, right. I had forgotten all about that."

He smiled, evidently pacified to think that I was going through necessity and not just swanning off to enjoy myself without him. I felt like a total arse. All he wanted was to have me around, and although I had a bastard of an ex-husband to face over a crowded court, I was inwardly buzzing with excitement, more so to be getting out of Paris and away from him.

"So will I see you tonight, sweetheart? See you properly, I mean?" he asked, looking hopeful, and a little forlorn.

"Sorry André, not tonight. I must pack. I've got some washing to do and I need to be up at five thirty, so an early night for me."

"Oh! That's a shame. I was hoping to say goodbye. I know it's not for long but I'll miss you. I'll miss our nights together."

The great untruth seemed to roll too easily off my tongue.

"Yes me too, my love." And as if it was a consolation prize, I added, "I'll ring you, promise. I'll be back before you know it."

I hated myself in that moment for lying to him; letting the poor guy believe that all was well. I knew deep in my heart that when I returned from the U.K. I would have to do the decent thing.

Refusing his offer of coffee or wine and leaving his big comfortable armchair for what I envisaged would be the last time, I stood, leaving him looking bewildered and maybe hurting a little. He got up to follow and came right up to the door of my apartment before folding his arms around me in a bear hug. His mouth was over mine in an instant, his tongue forcing my lips to part and he kissed me then with a passion that, up until then, I hadn't felt from him. I gently pushed him away after a while, eager to be on the move, but he kissed me once more before gingerly releasing his hold.

"That was my parting gift to you, Helen. Hopefully, it will keep you going while you're away. Hurry back to me, I'll be waiting."

I forced a cheery smile I didn't feel, and the lie came forth readily.

"Of course, André…I will too."

My British Airways flight took off on time at ten past nine. I boarded the plane with mixed feelings about the trip. I wondered how I would feel being back on British soil after my extended, yet self-inflicted imprisonment. I didn't relish the thought of having to face my bastard of an ex-husband in court. But there were things I looked forward to; catching up with the girls as well as some very dear friends, but not until after a couple of important business meetings. Surely, I could forget about the André situation until I boarded my return flight.

CHAPTER 9

J felt as if I was going to vomit. My forehead and cheeks were burning up, my stomach was churning and my head was in such a mess. What the Hell are you doing, Helen? I asked myself for what must have been the hundredth time in the last half hour. Have you finally lost your mind? No! Rephrase that one. Have you lost your mind yet again?

I poured myself a second G & T, slightly amused (though unable to smile) at the way my hand shook as it held the gin bottle, nearly missing the glass mid-pour. Last one, Helen. Sip it. No knocking it back in one this time. Common sense please. I caught a glimpse of my reflection in the mirror as I raised the glass to my mouth, obeying my self-imposed instruction. One sip.

My eyes remained fixed on my reflection as it stared back at me, shock registering, wide-eyed, mouth gaping. What on earth possessed me to dress in those clothes; a tight royal-blue pencil skirt and a slightly see-through, royal-blue blouse…black stockings? Even though the clothes were classy and expensive, the image seemed to spell out sexy; way too sexy. This was a business meeting, after all, wasn't it? Well…sort of…a business meeting. Denims and T-shirt would have sufficed. It was a casual meeting with an old friend…about… a little bit of business. It suddenly dawned on me what must have been at the back of my mind as I dressed. I could feel panic rearing its ugly head, so I quickly chided myself. Don't give him the wrong impression, Helen. Go and get changed now. You've still got fifteen minutes.

Feeling much calmer once I made the decision to change my clothes, I took a couple of casual sips at my gin, still eyeing my reflection and trying to remember which tops I packed that I could wear with my denims. A plain white cotton shirt; that would do. And wipe the lipstick off or tone it down. A gentle rap at the door disturbed my thoughts. Ah, that would be room service with the bottle of wine I ordered. A quick look at my watch revealed it had been twenty minutes ago. It also served as a reminder that my guest would be here in just over ten minutes. It was time to get a move on. Without another thought I hurried across to get the door. Standing well back as I opened it, and giving him room to enter with his tray, I heard a mumbled,

"Room Service, Ma'am".

Then, tray thrust out at arm's length, in he walked and I gasped in surprise.

"I caught him just outside your door, so I decided to relieve him of his duties" he explained. "I also gave him a tip."

"D…did…you?" I stammered, still stunned at his appearance and swiftly regretting the fact that I hadn't changed my clothes five minutes ago. Why the hell was he early?

"Yes, I told him not to hang around outside ladies' hotel rooms."

A few seconds too slow, I managed a chuckle at his wit, as he plonked the tray down on the nearest surface. As he turned and grasped my hands, he pushed me away a short distance and gave his appraisal.

"Helen Pawson! You are looking just as beautiful… and as hot as ever!"

I couldn't help but think he was looking pretty darned hot himself. He was fifty-ish and balding, but there had always been something fairly attractive about him; maybe the brown eyes, I don't know. He was looking tanned and I noticed immediately that his slight paunch was gone. However, I had no intention of revealing my thoughts to him. I leaned forward to receive his hug.

"Simon! It's lovely to see you again."

As he kissed me on each cheek, I could feel the colour start to rise. I quickly added,

"By the way, it's not Pawson any more. It's Helen Rush-forth…Rushforth is my maiden name."

He took hold of my left hand and turned it over in both of his.

"No wedding ring. Okay, Miss Rushforth it is then. I wouldn't want to upset you."

I laughed and scolded him gently.

"I'll maybe allow you to get away with making the mistake a couple of times, Simon, but after that, I won't be upset, I'll just get cross with you." He laughed.

Despite my earlier reservations about how difficult this meeting was going to be after many months and a solitary phone call a week ago, I felt comfortable in his presence. I laughed with him before suddenly remembering my manners.

"Simon, do forgive me. Would you like a glass of red, or perhaps the white that you just stole from room service? Or I've got…"

"Gin! I know you've got gin, Helen, you always have gin." I watched as he made himself comfortable on the sofa, amused that he felt 'at home' enough to do so. He noticed my amusement and grinned up at me.

"Red will be fine for me, thank you, sweetheart."

Smiling to myself, I wandered over to the unit and poured a generous glass of red for him. I noticed I still had most of my G & T left from ten minutes ago, so I just dropped in another ice cube. About to pick up both glasses, I was aware of a movement and, looking in the mirror, I realised that Simon was right behind me. He kissed the back of my neck playfully while his hands were trying to slide my skirt up my thighs. I tensed.

"Simon...I...you're here...so that we can talk...talk about...Anthony."

He caught on quickly with the tight pencil skirt, it wasn't going anywhere. He fumbled with the button and zip at the back and it dropped to the floor. I didn't know whether to feel angry...or... He sighed loudly and whispered in my right ear,

"That arsehole, Helen? Forget him...for now, at least."

We made eye contact in the mirror. I could hear his heavy breathing in my ear as I looked into those brown eyes; those eyes that were watching for my reaction. I could smell his fragrance, so subtle but...manly, wonderful.

"Suspenders, Helen?"

His whisper was barely audible as he gently caressed the skin around my stocking tops. I held my breath as his fingers inched their way up the inside of my thighs. Further tension crept into my body, his breath on my neck, hot and heavy, before he played his tongue on my ear-lobe, then he whispered,

"Put the glasses down. Turn to face me, sweetie."

My eyes met his again in the mirror and I could hardly breathe but somehow I managed to mouth the words,

"Simon...no. We..."

In a most serious voice and staring hard at me, he asked

"Just who are you trying to convince, Helen? Me? Or you?"

My eyes remained on his reflection and I couldn't take them off his gaze. His hands around both my elbows, he slowly let his fingertips slide down my arms to my wrists. Finally reaching my hands, he carefully removed the glasses from my grasp and placed them back on the cabinet. Gently turning me away from the mirror to face him, he kissed my neck again, his lips edging forward to my throat. I flinched at the touch of his fingers near the top of my thighs again, hardly daring to breathe, wondering whether I should stop things there and then, no harm done. Then he was in my panties and his fingers located my wetness, his thumb found my clit. I was powerless to resist. Hell, I didn't want to resist!

"Helen, beautiful girl, do you remember the first time I... did this to you? You tried to resist me then. I knew instantly that you wanted fucking, just as you want me to fuck you, now."

His whispering was laboured but there was sensuality to it. His heavy breathing was punctuating his words and it was exciting me. His tongue was almost in my ear as he uttered his words and my inner flames passed their infancy. His fingers probed every inch inside of me and I was feeling light-headed so I exhaled at last as I answered him,

"How...how could...I...I...ever...forget?"

There was the tickle of a heavy breath in my ear, and then,

"Do you know, how I can tell that you want fucking, Helen?"

I was at a loss for an answer. I closed my eyes and listened to that whisper and I waited for more; more whispering and...I still couldn't answer him. His whispering only just caught my ears this time,

"It's your wetness, babe; your wet, warm, welcoming pussy. That is what lets me know that you want to be fucked. We are going to relive that first time…tonight."

Suddenly his fingers were gone and he pushed himself close up to me, against the cabinet. He was still fully clothed but I could feel every inch of his hard-on as he pushed it against me, all the way from my pubic bone almost to my navel. I knew that I wanted it, wanted every inch of him inside me…in a while. But there was something I wanted more than that, and then it was my breathing that became laboured as I begged of him,

"Don't…don't stop whispering to me…please. Tell me what you are going to do to me. In detail, explicit detail."

With great urgency, and fumbling fingers, I unbuttoned his shirt, exposing his amazing chest and I needed to feel that hairiness against my bare breasts. His hands started work on the buttons of my shirt, but I pushed them down, wanting them inside me again, wanting him to massage my clit. He obliged on both counts.

My blouse and bra were discarded at last, and it felt amazing to feel the softness of his chest hair against my breasts. His whispering in my ear continued and it was almost driving me to distraction as I unbuttoned his denims.

"You want me to talk dirty, baby girl?" It was almost a moan.

"Yes, yes…I do."

"How dirty?" Shaking violently at these mere words, I also considered how wonderful it was to have his fingers carefully, but meaningfully, delving into my depths, finding my G spot, and I wanted very dirty talk.

"Tell me…about how you're going to fuck me. Say the… fuck word and cum …a lot…" I stammered.

With his denims down below his hips at last, I tugged at

the waistband on his boxers. My breathing stopped again. I was hot with anticipation, hot with need.

"Helen," he groaned, "I will be fucking you very soon. Fucking you, making your juices flow."

His amazing cock was finally free and I had pleasurable memories running through my head of how his rigid cock made me feel on a number of occasions. I started to lower myself, wanting to place my lips around its length and take him into my mouth, but he grabbed me under the arm.

"Oh no!" he gasped. "Not yet, Miss Eager Beaver. Not until I've fucked you hard with my fingers. Fucked you fast… cavorted with your clit…your cum on my fingers"

He moved faster, then gradually increased his speed with those manicured fingers of his, stabbing into me, deeper, harder; his thumb rubbing abrasively on my clit; his teeth biting at my nipples every few seconds between his dirty words.

"You love being fucked dirty, Helen. I'll fuck you dirty with my cock just as soon…as you've let that pretty little cunt of yours let go of your cum, baby girl."

Tipped over the edge with his filthy talk, I came, fast, and as I screamed out my pleasure (hopefully not too loud) he slowed down his movements gradually as he watched my eyes, taking in my shudders and whispered his gently spoken dirty words, talking me down.

"Oooh, yes! Was that a hot finger fuck for you, baby? Lots of your sweet cum all over my fingers, you dirty girl. More fucking, more cum to come…dirty as you want …just say the word."

My body still juddered and jerked in the final throes of my orgasm as I knelt down on the carpet and took his full length into my mouth, and…determined to make him beg for more, make him cry out in his ultimate orgasm. I held tight to the cheeks of his bottom as I pulled him towards me to take him further inside, to the back of my throat. He tasted good and he was rigid as I repeatedly sucked at him, slowly working my mouth up and down that tautness, marvelling at what I had missed.

After a few minutes, he held my shoulders still and pushed me away.

"Helen," he gasped. "Not like this, no! Let me…let me… fuck you properly…with my cock…please!" My forehead and my hair were damp; I was breathless. I wanted him inside me now that he mentioned it. Somewhat reluctantly though, my lips parted company with his hardness. He reached out to the back of one of the dining chairs, swivelled it around and quickly parked his butt.

"Sit astride, babes…quickly!"

I clumsily guided his cock inside me, before lowering myself onto him; we both groaned. Our mouths met and he probed with his tongue for a few seconds, holding my bottom still, allowing me no movement and I growled my frustrations. Pushing my hair away from my ear, he whispered softly to me, "Patience, Helen…nearly there. Work that pussy nice and slowly, fuck my cock. You make me cum, I'll make you cum."

His fingers between us, he worked at my clit. I was gasping as I rode him, slowly at first, and then picking up speed. My eyes were closed, I was picturing what it would look like in a porno movie, his cock moving in and out of me, my labia tight around him, and I was almost letting go…

"You're fucking me good, ba.."

I didn't want him talking any more. I wanted him inside me, in as many ways as he could. I opened my mouth for him and getting the message he plunged his tongue in and out… in and out, like his cock down below. I was on fire…I tightened my stomach muscles as I finally gave in…to another wonderful orgasm…and screamed out in pleasure,

"Fuck..fuck..yes…yes!"

He orgasmed seconds after me. Totally exhausted we sat, my head on his shoulder, my naked breasts against his chest, our heartbeats gradually getting back to normal. Fifteen minutes later (and dressed in the complimentary bath robes), as we sipped at the drinks I poured earlier, I was trying to make sense of everything. I asked myself what this turn of events meant to me. I tried to convince myself that this was not what I wanted to happen, but I was not so sure. I also didn't have a clue what the fuck Simon was thinking. He had been very quiet for the last few minutes. I looked across at him, trying to read those eyes, looking for answers. He smiled back, his eyes sparkling.

"I've really missed you, Helen!"

CHAPTER 10

"*S*imon, our meeting this evening; we are supposed to be discussing things...Anthony...the court case..."

A look of guilt passed over his face, just fleetingly – but definitely...guilt. He seemed to be holding his breath as I spoke, waiting for me to say more, spill my deepest thoughts and probably lay some blame on him.

"I'm not sorry about what just happened. Please don't think that, Simon. I don't regret anything, but the fact remains...we still need to talk."

He moved closer and took my hand in his.

"Look me in the eyes, Helen, look at me...please."

Removing his hand from mine, he tilted my face towards him until our eyes met.

"I just need you to understand that when I came to your room tonight, it was not my intention to...you know, use you or anything. But when I saw you..."

I had to cut in. I had no wish to let him feel that he'd used me and that I had not been a willing partner in our sexual antics. Yet again, I was flattered by his seductive attentions.

"Simon…"

He held both hands forward in a bid to stop me interrupting.

"Helen…let me finish, please!"

"Simon…"

He carried on regardless. "But when I saw your body…I am not going to apologise for wanting you. I've always wanted you. We've had some good times together, haven't we, Helen?"

At last he paused for breath, so I took the opportunity to correct him, raising my eyes to the ceiling as I spoke. "AND, Simon, when you'll kindly let me get a word in. did I actually stop you, huh? I didn't exactly put up a fight, did I? Have you asked yourself that? I wanted you just as much as you wanted me, Mister. So I won't hear any more talk about you using me, or feeling apologetic, right? Is that understood?"

He sighed, but his grin clearly showed his relief and I couldn't help but smile at him, but with the realisation that I was incredibly fond of him.

"Perfectly, and I'm glad about…you know. Thank you, Helen."

Once that little issue was out of the way I had hoped we would get around to the reason for his visit; Anthony. Simon had other ideas though.

"Helen, we've just had some amazing sex, as we have from that first day we met. Can't we just leave our business chat until later this evening? My head is still in the clouds and there are other…shall we say… more informal topics of conversation that we could have."

I tensed. Alarm bells started to ring in my head. Oh no! I should have seen it coming. The only thing I could think of was that Simon wanted to discuss with me a possible return to my former role; Helen, the call-girl. Let's face it, what else did we have in common? He knew very little about my life and I knew nothing at all about his private life, other than the fact that he was married with a grown up son and daughter. I groaned inwardly and yet I smiled at him, waiting for him to hit me with the inevitable. I only returned to London for a short visit, mainly to attend Anthony's court case. My biggest fear was that Simon (against his better judgement) may have arranged a rendezvous for me with one of my former clients. He could be rather inconsiderate at times... jumping in with both feet.

He was the start of it all; my secret career move. He wasn't a pimp...well not in that manner of speaking. He provided the client leads and his payment was that he got my body three or four times a year, for free. Surely he would realise that I wouldn't ever do that again anyway? He was also well aware of the fact that I now lived in Paris, so it would be pointless even to bring it up.

As it turned out, nothing could have prepared me for his next words and I was horrified.

"So...tell me about David Barnard then, Helen. I couldn't believe your phone call that day. I was stunned to say the least. What a disaster...I'm sad for you that he died, of course, but...fucking hell!"

I was mortified by his words and almost speechless too. So many different emotions, but more than anything, the shock kicked in. I sat open-mouthed for a few seconds, reeling inside, and then the anger followed, and for at least half a minute I wanted to slap him senseless. That wonderful post-shagging satisfaction deserted me in a split second and I bit back at him with a venom that I found hard to control.

"Disaster? What the fuck are you talking about, Simon? It was a disaster that I fell in love with him? Is that what you meant?"

He shuffled about on the sofa, clearly uncomfortable with the quick turn of the conversation and finding himself on dangerous ground. He tipped the dregs of his wine down his throat and got up to pour himself another, maybe in an attempt to avoid my anger and my vicious stare.

"What did you think, Simon? That I'm some common street-walker who became obsessed with a rich client and hounded him all the time? Did it not even cross your mind that my love for David was not one-sided; that he also fell in love...in love...with me?"

I jabbed at my chest several times with my finger as I spoke, lest he be in any doubt as to who it was that David had loved - me! My voice started to crack. He spun around to face me and, in anticipation, quickly snatched up a handful of tissues from the dispenser and brought them over. Pressing them into my hand, he knelt down next to me, looking up into my watery eyes. Having kept a tissue back for himself, he used it to gently dab at the tiny rivulets of tears as they rolled down my cheeks.

"Helen? Forgive me...I...I didn't think," he said, and then added "As usual! I am so sorry. It must still be very raw."

How could I stay angry at him for long? He was a lawyer when all was said and done; they did that kind of thing for a living, didn't they; make assumptions, in with both feet, and suspicious to boot? I knew that he wasn't aware of the full facts (how could he possibly have been) and it was up to me to put him right on a few matters. As I snivelled and sobbed into the wad of tissues Simon handed me, he got off his knees and sat to the right of me on the sofa. Placing a welcome arm around me, he spoke in the gentlest voice I would never have expected to hear, from him at least.

"The wrong topic of conversation, Helen, I truly am sorry."

This was a side to him that I never saw before and I was touched, almost feeling sorry for him in return, as he was the guilty one at that moment, and he recognized the fact. I softened.

"Simon, it's fine, honestly. You were not to know." I paused for a while, pondered and made a quick resolution, "Seeing as the subject of David is still open, I will tell you everything…and show you."

"That will not be necessary, Helen. Right, I'm going to pour that drink and I'll pour you one too."

I sensed he was embarrassed and needed time to gather his thoughts and prepare for what was yet to come. Once he moved off the sofa and back to the drinks cabinet, I shuffled my bottom along to where he'd been sat and reached over the arm of the sofa to grab my handbag. I extracted the slim-line leather wallet that always accompanied me on my travels. Simon, having poured the drinks, gave me a rather sheepish look as he handed me my glass, but hesitated before sitting down again.

"Am I forgiven? Or will I be the victim of another tongue lashing? Will I be safe if I sit next to you, Helen?" he asked cautiously.

He tried to give the impression that he was joking, but his eyes gave him away. I could see behind them; he was genuinely worried and once more I found myself softening towards him. I had seen a tender, caring side to him that for some reason he didn't usually put on display.

"Of course you will." I thrust my leather wallet at him as he sat. "There you go…read it."

"No! I…Helen, if this is personal…no."

"Just do it. I want you to understand."

Waiting, and keen to see his reaction as he read the letters I carried everywhere with me, I stuffed a cushion under my head and reclined, in a better position to gauge his reactions. He leaned forward, placing his glass on the floor before removing the contents of my wallet.

"Read the solicitor's letter first," I ordered.

He glanced up at me, maybe giving me a last chance to change my mind before he dug into the depths of my, until now, closely guarded secret. I nodded, just once.

"Go ahead!"

Giving me a quick appraisal, he then assumed a serious face and unfolded Bill Douglas's letter to me. His face revealed nothing as I watched his eyes scan, and his mind absorb, each and every word. Without making a comment, he carefully folded the letter and retrieved the one which consisted of several sheets bearing David's last tender words to me; his confession of love. After reading the first few lines, he inhaled sharply and closed his eyes briefly. Recovering from those first revelations, he read on, mouth agape and raised eyebrows as at last he understood the grim reality of my relationship with David, and how devastating the effect his death had been for me. After returning both of the letters to my wallet he lowered his head, sighing heavily, and once more reaching for his glass.

"Helen...I...what can I say? I'm stunned." Then considering the way his words may have come across. "Not that I'm implying that...you know...Oh, shit!"

I laughed as he was getting himself into knots.

"Don't worry, I know what you meant." Then without thinking, I added, "Two million pounds, Simon."

He cocked his head to one side and frowned, evidently puzzled.

"Pardon? I'm not under...standing, I...think."

"Two million pounds! That is my compensation for David being taken from me. That is the figure he left me in his will, Simon. A very expensive hooker, wouldn't you say? I have already had an interim payment of five hundred thousand. I don't want any of it...not a single bean. I loved that man,

Simon. I didn't want his fucking money. I wanted him, my David."

"Christ Almighty, you're wealthier than I am, Helen."

"You know everything now, Simon, so can we please put this matter to bed? That was my only intention, to make you aware. Now, you came here so we could discuss Anthony, and we mustn't put it off any longer."

TWO DAYS PREVIOUSLY ...

...I switched on my Nokia cell phone for the first time in ages. After I arrived in France all those months ago, and settled into my apartment at Rue de Rivoli, I'd text my Paris landline number only to a small number of people who I was interested in hearing from. Browsing through my list of contacts, I considered whether there was anybody else I wanted to add to the privileged few, but decided against it and switched off the mobile. Once abandoned in the drawer of my bedside unit, it remained there, without a second thought from me. The beeping of the text messages and missed calls continued for quite some time when I finally decided to switch the phone on, after it had received an all-night charge up.

Of the missed calls and texts remaining after a mammoth deleting session, most had been from Simon. Simon asking me what or who I was running away from. Simon asking me where the fuck I was. Simon asking questions about my affair with David. Simon telling me that my clients were missing me. But the two most recent voicemails grabbed my attention and made me sit up sharply.

"Helen, please return my call. I need an answer to my question. I need to know if a certain Anthony Pawson is your husband, or ex-husband, or whatever."

I pressed '2' to listen to the message again and noted the

date and time (a week ago) of the recording, before listening to 'next message'.

"Helen. Ring me urgently, please. There are things I need to ask you about Anthony Pawson…if he does happen to be your husband, that is. I cannot stress how urgent this is now becoming."

I had not bought English newspapers on a regular basis, but the few I did purchase were within a month of my arrival in Paris. The British press were usually on the ball where drug hauls were concerned and I had eagerly scanned the columns looking for news of anything that might have involved Anthony's stash, but to no avail. Strangely enough, after all the trauma the bastard caused me, I managed to put it all to the back of my mind after accepting the fact that obviously I missed any newspaper write-ups.

After pouring myself a glass of wine, I sat in the lounge, aware of the clock ticking away loudly, aware of the TV, though its sound was muted. I could feel the tension creep into my neck and shoulders, accompanying the anger that was surfacing from my very core. Why did his fucking name have to crop up again, triggering a re-run of the nightmare; the disaster that had been my marriage?

Damn you, Simon! Why did you have to contact me again? Why did you have to rake up all that fucking…shit?

Tentatively picking up the mobile again, as if it would bite me, I quickly located his number and pressed 'call' before I had a chance to change my mind.

Not bothering with a greeting, polite or otherwise (he'd know it was me calling anyway), I launched into such a volley of abuse at him, before he even managed to utter one single word.

"Simon! What the fuck are you ringing me for, and about that asshole? He's a drug-dealing piece of shit, who the fuck would want to defend him? I...you don't even know anything..."

I couldn't believe the amount of venom with which I spat out my words, but he cut me off rather rudely, and yet, he remained calm.

"Helen...Helen...listen to me, ple...!"

"You haven't a clue what he's..."

"HELEN!" he snapped, "Stop jumping in, please. What the fuck makes you think I'm defending him? I'm prosecuting for the Crown, for your information young lady!"

I was flabbergasted. That was me, well and truly put in my place and I couldn't apologise enough to him for jumping to the wrong conclusion. We chatted for well over an hour. I answered all of his questions and then went into detail about how I anonymously dropped a packet of drugs off at the police station, along with my statement and some printed photos. (I'd taken some snapshots of evidence with my mobile phone; pictures of dealer's cars in our driveway,) Simon was pretty quick to put an end to some of my assumptions, though. Apparently, Anthony hadn't been dealing in drugs. As a user himself, he had, in return for free cocaine to feed his own habit, foolishly agreed to let the dealers store the stuff at our home. The big boys involved feared a raid on their own homes and various other premises they used in the past. Anthony hadn't even needed to give the names of those involved in his statement as the police already tracked the dealers through the car registration numbers involved. His bank accounts were thoroughly checked and no evidence had been found of him having received any large amounts of money. Even the dealers corroborated his story that he received a small supply of cocaine in return for 'storage facilities', and that no money changed hands.

I agreed to return to London for a week to reluctantly

attend the court case. He went on to suggest that we should meet up before the court date, to talk in depth. Simon told me that he would book into his usual hotel (the place where I had once been employed for a short time). He suggested I ring him to make further arrangements once I arrived at Heathrow. We ended our call at that stage, and once I booked my return flights online, I made a hotel booking for the Park Lane Hilton for a week, my intention being to catch up with one or two close friends whilst back in London. The thought crossed my mind, that if Simon expected me to use the same hotel as him, he would be bitterly disappointed.

Thanks to my determination to keep Simon on track, our earlier shagging session and my revelations about the love affair I had with David, were now pushed to the back of my mind. Simon was sat opposite me, his business head well and truly in place, pen and legal notepad at the ready. I sniggered inwardly, wondering what his colleagues at the Bar, and even more so, his clients, would think if they could see him now; tight boxer shorts, courtesy bathrobe wide open, glass of wine in one hand and his pen poised in the other. Suppressing the broad grin that threatened to expose my growing amusement, I pushed to get the matter over and done with as soon as possible.

"So…about Anthony, what questions do you need answering?"

"Just talk, Helen. Talk! Tell me everything I could possibly want to know about him…even things that you think I wouldn't need to know. There may be something that might be relevant, even though it could seem insignificant to you."

I was not really in the mood for dragging all the shit up again; painful memories that needed taking down, dusting off and smashing to smithereens once and for all, never to surface again. I knew that wouldn't be possible until this court case was out of the way. This was going to hurt and I felt the tension beginning to hone in on my neck and shoulders. I curled my feet up underneath me and plumped the cushion behind my neck in the hope of relaxing. Meanwhile, I fixed my gaze onto the pattern of the carpet, desperately searching for the words that wouldn't come.

"Helen, let me get you started. How did you come to meet Anthony?" he encouraged, with one of his winning smiles, those brown eyes searching mine.

On edge all of a sudden, dreading some of the memories that I had buried deep within me re-surfacing, I didn't know if I would be able to cope. Then from nowhere, the answer to his question was spilling from between my lips. My mind didn't feel forthcoming, but nevertheless, the words seemed to form without much help.

"He...he worked for my father, for his advertising company...Rushforth Advertising and Media Limited." I paused and he nodded, acknowledging that he heard of the company before.

"Yes, go on. Keep it coming."

The memories of those early days re-surfaced but I pushed the Anthony memories back and focused on Dad.

"My dad thought the sun shone from his arse, he was his right hand man. He pushed us together, Dad did. I was studying for my finals at the time and didn't really want a...a relationship with anyone, but we dated a little. When I was qualified it...it got more serious. After we were married, we went to Vegas on honeymoon. Anthony played the casinos, he won...big, and sort of...got hooked on gambling."

I snatched up my wine glass and gulped greedily, deep in thought, before I could carry on.

"His mother hated me, you know. I was never good enough. She tried to humiliate me and he never defended me."

The memories of the dinner party and her cutting

remarks were still very vivid. He tapped his pen on the pad impatiently and raised his eyebrows, before sighing heavily.

"Not relevant, sweet thing. Get back to the story."

I wasn't listening, though. I was on a roll and the words continued to spew out, as my mind took me on a backward journey.

"We had a dinner party once with his parents as the only guests. She belittled me all evening. Maybe I was a little rude stomping off to bed like I did, but the things she said... He followed me upstairs later, shouting and cursing at me. Things changed after that. I still loved him. We still had some fun, but...yes, things changed."

I paused at that point and looked across the room. For a few seconds I was puzzled to see Simon sat there, staring across at me. So lost in my horrible memories, I had forgotten about the here and now. Simon gave me an encouraging smile, but there was an underlying hint of sympathy in his eyes.

"You're doing fine, Helen..."

Somehow, I found my momentum again.

"He was gambling and he was drinking heavily. I could frequently smell alcohol on his breath when he'd driven home from work. One day, I arrived home from work much earlier than usual and was surprised to see his car in the drive. I thought he must have come home ill from work or something. I walked into the house to find him receiving a blow job from a rent boy."

I broke my gaze at the carpet to look up and gauge Simon's reaction to that revelation, to see him scribbling away furiously. Giving him some time, I unfurled and went to fetch the bottle of wine. Pouring myself another generous measure, I looked across at him again, tilting the wine bottle at him questioningly. He shook his head...no. He had his business head on...and this was serious business.

Simon watched my every move as I settled myself down on the sofa again. I took up the story where I left off and, once more, searched deep into those brown eyes of his to see what they gave away.

"Digressing slightly before I go on, you need to know that I have suffered from O.C.D. since quitting university, hence the cleaning job I had when…when I met you that day."

With not the slightest hint of emotion in his eyes, he stared back at me intently, waiting patiently.

"I ended it then; told him it was over. Not wanting my parents to know about the rent boy and that Anthony was potentially gay, I agreed to keep it to myself. We carried on living in the same house, but I told him it was over between us…no going back. We maintained a sort of…polite indifference to each other, speaking only when we had to."

I got up again at that point, paced the room, and felt distinctly uncomfortable and traumatised as I built myself up for what was coming next. I closed my eyes as I came to a standstill behind one of the dining chairs, my back to Simon, loathe for him to see the tears that had been inevitable, for the second time that evening.

"One night, a few months later, I had been out clubbing with the girls from the office and went home rather the worse for wear. I staggered upstairs and as soon as I hit the bed, I was asleep. Sometime later…it was the early hours, but the exact time I don't know…I was awakened as my clothes were ripped off me. It was him. He raped me – my own husband raped me, Simon. I…"

Almost instantly, I could feel him behind me and he placed his hands gently on my shoulders.

"Helen…I…"

The tears streamed down my cheeks; their very substance almost burning, but it was nice to feel the comfort he offered.

"No, let me carry on, Simon, please."

Drawing in a deep breath, hoping to gain some inner strength that seemed to be lacking, I determined to reach the end as soon as I possibly could.

"Afterwards, I kicked out at him and he put his fist in my eye. My parents were away on a cruise for three weeks, so after he left the house on the Saturday morning, I threw some things in a bag and went to stay at my parents' empty house. I needed some time to think…and to recover. I had to stay off work that week because of the…black eye. I still had no intention of telling my parents…or the police, or anybody for that matter. I planned to go back home before my parents returned. The following weekend, Saturday it was, I needed some more suitable clothes for my return to work on the Monday, so I drove over to the house. I walked into the house to such a scene. Bodies were laid all over the lounge; semi-comatose bodies. Anthony was in his bed with two girls, and another girl was in the guest bedroom with two men. There were the remains of lines of cocaine on the coffee table and alcohol bottles and tins everywhere."

I rambled on about how I returned home just before my parents cruise ended and my visit to the sexual health clinic to get tested for STDs and HIV. I quickly reassured him that the tests had all returned negative. His face remained impassive. While I talked, I watched as his pen flew across his pad, getting down as much detail as he could, and once he caught up, he tilted his head towards me, pointed the pen at me accusingly and said,

"And you went back! You're something else, Helen!"

I took that bit as he intended it to sound; certainly not a compliment. Carrying on with my story, I went into detail about the drug envelopes in the greenhouse and the tragic accident that took the lives of my parents.

"I think you can hazard a guess at the rest, Simon. So there you have it. I couldn't cope with my accountancy work, so I became a skivvy...met you...met David...fell in love...and..."

"Right!" he cut in, bringing me to a halt.

I glanced around quickly at his tone of decisiveness. He snapped his pad shut and replaced the top on his fountain pen with determination.

"That's enough for today, Helen. It's been an emotional ride for you. We'll carry on tomorrow, there's plenty of time. I'd better get myself back to my hotel and we'll..."

"Wha...what?" The tears were close again and I shivered; icy tentacles seeming to brush every square inch of my skin. That hated feeling of loneliness was looming again. He was going to do a runner and leave me with my mental anguish.

"But...I thought after we'd...you know...got this Anthony case out of the way...I thought you'd stay...you'd want to fuck me again. I..."

I was genuinely shocked at how desperate and needy I sounded.

"Helen, there's nothing I'd love more than to fuck you all night, but how can we? David...Anthony...you've been upset with what we have covered tonight. I've caused it for you. You're not in the right frame of mind...you.."

He looked so apologetic and, as I searched his eyes, he looked away from me guiltily.

"So you put my mind through...fucking torture. Dredging up things I'd rather fucking forget.....has it not crossed your mind that after all that shit...after being hung out to dry...that I need to...I need to be fucked!"

I struggled to control my voice and as he turned his softening brown eyes towards mine again, he raised his eyebrows questioning my words.

"Are you...sure...? He enquired, warily.

"Sure? Of course I'm sure! I need fucking, Simon. Dirty,

anything-goes type of fucking. Stay. Fuck me all night, but just fuck me please…any way you want me."

He was on me in seconds, needing no further encouragement. His mouth and hands were everywhere and I lost myself, lost all sense of time and those most unpleasant of memories, as we indulged in the dirtiest that sex had to offer. I took immense pleasure from his amazing cock as it was thrust into me with savage gusto as he sought to thrill me with its unwavering rigidity before letting go of his juices. Feeling experimental, we fucked in positions that were new; looking for the ultimate dirty fuck. After numerous explosive orgasms, I was sore, in fact…burning. And with that abrasive pain I felt my sexual pleasure reach new and dizzying heights.

CHAPTER 11

*W*e were awake early. Simon got out of bed before me and he was in the shower by six forty five. I leaned against the door-frame, eyeing his muscular body, delighting in the cock that was responsible for my stinging lower parts. Nice though the thought was, I couldn't possibly have partaken in any early morning horniness if it had been on offer. Grinning cheesily at me the instant he was aware of my presence, he started to smear the soap around his nether regions and quickly tried to hide his wince of pain. I laughed out loud.

"Feeling battered are we? I'm glad it's not just me then!"

I walked away and left him to freshen up, still chuckling in my amusement. I dressed in the towelling robe and climbed back into bed to enjoy a five minute read, while Simon finished his morning ablutions. The five minutes turned into twelve and when he re-appeared his skin looked raw.

"I had a bit of a problem getting the temperature right. It was too fucking hot or bitterly fucking cold, nothing midway. Get them up here today to sort it, Helen. It wouldn't be good if you got scalded."

I suppressed a laugh, not at his predicament but at his crimson looking skin. And trying to be a smart arse, all I could offer was;

"You should have stuck with the cold water then, you rampant bastard."

He all but leapt across the room and dived on top of me. He tugged on the belt and parted my gown, playfully planting kisses on my boobs and down my stomach towards my bush. He laughed.

"You love me being rampant, dirty bitch. Are you ready for me again?" He growled.

I pushed him off.

"Not a chance at the moment, sleaze ball." I chuckled and after a sudden thought, came out with, "Sleazy Simon…the… lecherous lawyer."

He laughed, grabbed a pillow, and aimed it at my head. Failing miserably, it came to a halt, like a torso sitting propped up in the solitary bedroom chair.

"Name calling, Helen, how could you stoop so low?"

He hesitated, eyes to the ceiling, clearly trying for the counter attack. With an over dramatised look of lust, he narrowed his eyes and, in his sleaziest of voices, growled at me.

"Raunchy   Rushforth…the…nymphomaniac   number-cruncher."

He guffawed at his own wit. I rolled my eyes at him.

"Seriously? Number-cruncher? Is that the best you can come up with?" I was scandalised for a moment, then I couldn't help but join in with his raucous laughter.

The moment of hilarity didn't lasted, though. I blinked, and in that nano-second, he rapidly assumed his serious lawyer look.

"So, I've got to dash. Would this afternoon be good for you? I have meetings this morning." Before giving me the chance to reply, he added, "And where, my hotel or back here? No, forget that, here would be better."

"Well I have a meeting myself this morning. It could go on for an hour or two. Does one thirty sound okay?" He glanced at his watch before answering. "Yes. That could work for me. I should be able to make it. Listen, Helen, what we'll be doing this afternoon, is running through some of the things the defence may hit you with. Of course, we're not sure what sort of crap Anthony will have filled his Counsel's head with, but I'll warn you it will be anything that is going to make him look to be the victim in all this. It will be an attempt by him to get the jury on his side and make you out to be the bad bitch. He won't have painted a nice picture. Do you follow?"

My head swam with the scenario, or more appropriately, the reality, and my stomach grumbled loudly, the fear kicking in, since he stated the probabilities and possibilities so bluntly.

"I get the gist."

"Right, I must get back to the hotel and change my clothes. Happy meeting, whatever it is." A flash of suspicion shot across his face. "Hey, you haven't got a new client you've failed to mention have you?

"Get out, Simon. I wouldn't be so stupid as to wander down that avenue again, I promise you." He smirked triumphantly, and was gone.

Rather than shower (which according to Simon, needed some urgent maintenance), I opted for a leisurely soak in the bath using the complimentary lavender crystals from the hotel's luxury toiletry selection. Half an hour later I was pleased that I'd done so; the soreness of my inside and my folds were more comfortable, having benefited from the lavender infused bath water. I towelled off and plonked myself in front of the dressing table to apply some make-up.

Dressed in an Austin Reed charcoal-grey suit with a beautiful lacy top I bought in Paris, I lingered in front of the full-length mirror, appraising my image and trying to decide which of the meagre choice of footwear I'd brought would look best with the suit. There was nothing though, that could equal the look of my black court shoes with the two inch heels; sensible, not too frivolous.

At quarter to eleven I arrived at Covent Garden tube station and walked the last few streets to my destination, the Radisson Blu Edwardian on Mercer Street. It had been easier than I first imagined, with just one change at Piccadilly Circus. Never had I seen such a beaming smile like the one he greeted me with as I picked him out amongst the guests milling about in the main foyer. That much clichéd term 'from ear to ear' could have been devised just for him. Arms open wide, he stood up to greet me and my heart melted with the genuine affection I felt for him. His hug was further welcomed by me and he continually planted kisses on my cheek, as if to prove I was there and not about to disappear.

"Helen, it feels wonderful to have you here, at last. Shall we go to our room straight away? It's more private."

His expression showed excitement and eagerness, his eyes shining in anticipation. A feeling of warmth enfolded me and my stomach danced and fluttered in delight.

"Yes, that's fine. I've been dying to see you, you'll never know how much. But if you don't mind me saying so, you're looking a little stressed. I hope you're not worrying. It will be fine, I promise."

That word, again; promise. Said oh too easily!

Stop promising things, Helen!

His eyes sparkled wickedly and he rubbed his hands together vigorously.

"Good. I'm more than ready for this. Let's go."

My higher end estimation of the time it would take to finish our meeting was spot on. Exactly two hours later, I walked briskly and business-like back down Long Acre to Covent Garden tube station to catch my first train and I would hopefully arrive back at my hotel room before Simon turned up. Having been indulging my mind in a re-run of the last two hours I hadn't paid enough attention to my whereabouts. I had a slight distraction as an old lady waiting to cross the road with her husband, stumbled on the kerb and jolted me away from my thoughts. I noticed that everyone (a slight exaggeration) seemed to be staring at me as I charged along the pavement. Had I suddenly grown two heads or what? Then it came; the dawning. My face must have been cracking with the supercilious smile that I plastered across it. I made a conscious effort to remove it and placed my lips back together; straight-faced but grinning inwardly as I wondered how many hours it would take for the smirk of satisfaction to disappear from his face. I only had a couple of minutes wait for a train and I arrived back at my hotel room just three minutes later than the one thirty-ish appointment with Simon. He arrived ten minutes later, out of breath and thirsty. He helped himself to my gin, cheekily holding up the bottle to offer one to me. I nodded eagerly, but minded myself to take it steady. It wasn't the most brilliant idea on an empty stomach.

"Let's get started then." he said, handing me the glass. "By the way, good meeting? You seem happy enough."

"Yes, the best."

I took a large gulp from the glass and almost spurted it out in disgust.

"Fuck!" I spluttered, "Do you have to be so pissing tight with the tonic, Simon? The tonic is cheaper than the large measures of gin you help yourself to."

"I thought you liked everything stiff, Helen?" He raised his eyebrows up and down like one of the Marx brothers, imaginary cigar in hand. To think that I had, until recently, thought the guy to be devoid of humour, corny though it might be, it showed through once in a while.

"Anyway, enough of this stupidity and innuendo, let's get this case on its wheels."

There came another snigger from him at his latest pathetic play on words. Seriously? Four hours it took us, running through my statement, running through the questions I was likely to face. He asked me if I would feel intimidated in Anthony's presence, and not forgetting his drug-dealing, drug-pushing cronies. He even staged a sort of trial run where he posed as Anthony's defence lawyer launching a verbal attack on me. I stammered my reply, rehearsing my part, and he banged on the coffee table, throwing alternative wording at me.

"You're fucking stuttering, Helen; a sign of weakness. They'll hone in on that weakness if you let them. Confidence…never let it waver."

He continued to throw suggestions at me.

"That sounds a little ambiguous, Helen. Let me think on that one for a minute."

We repeated, corrected, repeated, corrected, and finally he was satisfied that I was confident enough that my answers contained nothing that could be blasted apart.

"But don't forget, sweet thing. This has been a rehearsal with me; your friend, fuck buddy or whatever. It's going to be a different ball-game in the morning…though you might not get called tomorrow. A judge, his defence, a jury of twelve, his family, all their families, everyone in the Public Gallery and of course the press, fucking scum of the Earth."

I slumped deeper into the sofa, feeling beaten before I

even entered the courtroom and I wasn't even (thankfully) the accused.

"Great. That has been most comforting, Simon. You bastard!" I glared at him.

"You'll thank me when it's all over, sweet thing. I promise."

"Don't you start!" I warned. "Making bloody promises. I've been doing too much of that lately. I must stop."

After my fourth large measure of gin, the effects descended without warning – one minute sober, the next, I was off my face.

"I'm calling...room shervice, Shimon. I've got to...eat shumsing shoon. Your G and T's have got me where I'll shoon be flat on my back. Do you...erm...want shumsing?"

I thrust the menu into his hand, giggling and slurring uncontrollably in my gin-induced euphoric haze.

"Yes, you flat on your back. No! I stand corrected by myself. You on your hands and knees, bare arsed and begging for it, as is the norm with you, Helen. You need something else besides food, sweet cheeks."

I watched with blurred vision as two of him wandered into the bathroom and returned with two glasses of water and both were thrust into my hand at the same time. "Drink this, my little number-cruncher," he ordered. "And when you've finished I'll get you a refill. Now drink!"

"But...but   you've...already   brought...two, havven...havvenchoo?"

I was aware of screwing up my face and scowling. A little after the event, something registered. Number-cruncher? What the fuck sort of terminology was that? He tutted at me like an old spinster of a school ma'am, and before I finished the last couple of sips of water, he snatched the glass and returned much later with more water; or so I thought.

"DON'T go to sleep, Helen. I want you to drink this…and our meal will be here shortly. You were nodding."

I downed the water greedily and ran my tongue around my lips slowly. I felt parched. By the time our meals arrived, my drunkenness started to wear off. Trying to put the imminent court appearance to the back of my mind, I tipsily focused instead on that morning's meeting, how well it had gone and the excitement it brought me. Better still was the promise of further exciting times to come. I could feel my face colouring up; the excitement of keeping a secret that not even Simon was privy to.

As we ate, Simon was quiet. I knew he was dying to find out about my meeting and rather than come out and ask, I think he was rather hoping I would volunteer some information. When he thought I wasn't looking he'd glance across the table and watch my face every time I raised the fork to my mouth. At one point, as my knife cut a section of club sandwich, he placed his hand over my knuckles.

"Helen, you are beautiful. I love to see you smile, it enhances your beauty. You really do seem happy today. I'm pleased."

He was fishing. I knew it. The devious bloody lawyer in him couldn't resist. Throw the fish a nice treat and it'll take the bait! My stomach back-flipped as he paid the compliment; looking deep into his eyes it brought about the familiar dampness in my panties. I wanted to fuck him… once we finished eating and let our food settle. For now, I was content to throw back a compliment or two, and put an end to his nosiness.

"Thank you, Simon. And what female would not be happy and have a fucking great smile on her dial after she's been fucked senseless all night? AND woken up that sore that she couldn't sit on her touché the remainder of the day, huh?"

Oh fuck! That lusty fucking smile of his! I wanted to open

my legs to him there and then, but keeping a grip, I neatly placed my knife and fork on the plate and stood up.

"Where are you going, sweets? You haven't finished eating."

"I have. I've had enough and these trousers are cutting me in two. It's been months since I wore them and I must have put some weight back on. Besides, I don't like sitting around in a good suit. I'm going to throw something else on."

It was an excuse. I needed to rid myself of the sopping panties I'd thrown in the carrier bag full of washing in my bedroom, not to mention having a squirt of perfume and re-applying my lipstick. Feeling like the slut that I had been... still am, I changed my top for a seductively red number and a new full-length skirt with a side-split that reached halfway up my left thigh. I deliberately left off the clean thong I placed on the bed.

He'd finished eating and in my absence had sneakily poured himself another generous measure of gin and highly likely, he would have carefully added nothing more than a splash of tonic.

"Helen, I won't be staying tonight. I've still some work to do so I thought it best if I get back to the hotel. Around tennish, I think."

"I imagined that's what you'd do, Simon. That's fine."

No problem. I'll get what I want before then. I'll make sure of it.

I sat next to him and sipped the half glass of wine that was left from when we'd eaten. He made to stand, offering to pour me another of his gins but I declined. I was sober and wanted to keep it that way. I wanted to enjoy what was to come with a clear head.

He grabbed the remote and switched the TV on. I assumed he'd been hoping to catch the latest news headlines. I watched with him for a while before becoming distracted again. He always looked hot in his suit, handsome, intelligent; sexy as fuck. I remembered what I had waiting for him under my skirt. The top of my thighs were damp. Still very excited after events during the morning, I was on cloud nine and greedily wanted more thrills. He turned and smiled as the news credits rolled.

Fuck me, I want him!

"Do you want it on or off, Helen?"

That was the perfect cue for my purpose. I shuddered in delight and a little more moisture escaped my folds.

"Off!" I raised my legs off the floor and onto his lap, tauntingly so. "And what would you like on or off, Simon? Hey?"

With a flourish, I peeled back the front of my skirt from its slit, opening my legs slightly as I did so. I watched his eyes, the hungry look as he peeked down with longing at the pouting lips of my pussy, wet and waiting for him.

"Fuck!" He stared in fascination as if seeing it for the first time. "You've already got off all that is necessary, sweet cheeks."

He didn't meet my gaze; he couldn't tear his eyes away from what I offered on a plate. Abruptly, after a couple of minutes, he'd stared long enough and resolutely moved his hand from the remote to run his thumb over my clit. Nerves jumped throughout my body, I sat up straighter and pulled off the red top, flinging it recklessly into the air. I tensed as the clit massage was causing me to glow with need. Teasing him further, I unclipped my bra, exposing my breasts for him, but he flicked his head up only fleetingly, intent on giving the pleasure to my lower region.

I fondled my own breasts and leaned back again to enjoy not only his actions but those of my own volition, tweaking and pinching my nipples until they stood erect and further sensitised. Swapping finger for thumb, he eased two fingers into my depth and swept the thumb time and again over my burning clit. My mind raced ahead as every nerve in my warmth was alight and ready for further stimulation. He thrust the fingers in and out, bending them and finding my G-spot instantly. I arched my back, gripping tight to the back of the sofa in ecstasy, my breasts abandoned as I exploded around his invasive, deep probing fingers.

I screamed his name as the throes peaked and, pussy-watch forgotten, he analysed my expressions, reading my eyes as I panted and gasped, cheeks burning with pleasure. I couldn't speak. I was breathless, so I communicated with my eyes and I nodded to him 'I want more, much more.'

"You are fucking insatiable, sweetie."

His eyes searched mine. He wanted to see my reaction to every touch; every time he placed a finger on my body. I met his gaze and made a complaining groan as he pulled his fingers free.

"Si…mon! No!"

I cried in frustration, wanting him inside me by whatever means he was offering.

"Wetness; lots of wetness, Helen."

With admiration, he smiled at his glistening fingers and placed them on his tongue, savouring the taste as he sucked on my juices, and looking for some reaction from me out of the corner of his eyes. My answer was to get back to work caressing every last inch of my breasts, my nipples more sensitive than usual. I jumped as I brushed over them lightly.

In a deft move that seemed to happen at lightning speed, he rolled the top of his body to face me and slung my legs, knees bent, resting over his shoulders. Supporting my back-side mid-air, he let his tongue glide over my clit, before thrusting it deep inside my warmth, twirling it around then tasting my inner coating, lapping greedily. I jerked violently as I was swept away in wave after precious wave of a multiple orgasm, rocking my world and blowing my mind. I closed my eyes tight, loathe to let any small distraction, anything in my vision, intrude on my concentration and enjoyment of every second. Recovering quickly, it was his cock I wanted. Down below I still tingled, ached to feel his fat length fucking me brutally.

"Fuck me, Simon! NOW!" I appealed, my throat sounding hoarse, somewhat gravelly.

"Your wish sweet thing. I don't know how long I'll last, though. Get on your hands and knees, like I mentioned earlier, Helen."

He lowered my legs from his shoulders and as I shuffled around ready to stand, his lips dropped hard onto mine. He demonstrated his urgency, shoving the full length of his tongue to the very back of my throat, almost making me gag with the move.

"Deep and then deeper still, I'm going to fuck you with my full length, sweetie. Hard, deep and…rough."

Surprised to find that I was still wearing the long skirt, I lowered myself onto the carpet while Simon hitched it up above my waistline. Ready for him to ram hard into me, I growled with impatience, but he appeared in front of me to tantalise and taunt. Almost in my face, he waved his solid cock in front of my eyes, slowly massaging its thickness and length, base to tip and back again. I licked the drool from my mouth, murmuring, grumbling my need. I opened my mouth to take him in as he brushed it past my lips, but he was adamant.

"No! Not this time!"

He snatched it away and moved off to approach me from behind. As I waited, the anticipation was almost tipping me over the edge. My every nerve was ablaze, tendrils creeping through my stomach and the glorious beautiful ache that only the desire for sex can summon, was there, awaiting fulfilment.

I gasped in shock when the first thrust came, caught unawares, expecting him to needlessly prolong my impatient wait, such was his style. As he said he would, he pounded hard and deep, one hand on my waist and the thumb of his other pushing hard onto my anus, a promise of secondary penetration. His breathing was laboured and heavy, deceivingly further away than I imagined it to be, the silence of the room causing the illusion. He started grunting with the effort as he thrust harder than I thought possible. He pulled out and I heard the rip of a foil pack.

"Hu...uh? What..."

"Condom, my cock...is raw. FUCK IT!" He snarled. "I'm... nearly...there!"

I faltered with the force as he stuffed into me with venom, my arms weakening as I let go, breathless yet energised at the same time. I felt him place both hands onto my waist this time, to give stronger support to my position. I pushed back at him with his thrusts to take him deeper and I felt the perfect pain as he throbbed deep inside and gave me his all, every last pumping spray of his seed.

"Helen...Helen...You're going to...fucking kill...me...one of...these days." He gasped, as he clung tight, still pulsing inside me.

We were spent. Our energy depleted; last night's colossal sessions and little sleep, the in-depth court rehearsal had been wearing for us both, intense meetings we attended individually, it had all taken its toll. Though he said it would be ten, he left at nine-thirty. I remembered he had further work that needed his attention and I hoped it wouldn't take him too long. He had a demanding trial to attend and needed a decent night's sleep; alone!

Much as I needed the same, it never materialised. I slept only fitfully and the periods of unrest were filled with the words and the warnings he'd given. 'Confidence!' 'Never waver!' 'Don't let them sense the tiniest shred of weakness.' 'You were suffering from O.C.D.' 'Don't mention the words, mental illness. It will be misconstrued, ripped apart.' 'Grief! Use your grief to your advantage.' Those words and thousands of others seemed to tap painfully in my head. Meanwhile, I tried to remember the things I hadn't to say. The words tangled and jumbled and served to cause me confusion as I tossed and turned, exhausted, worried and panicked. I dozed some more and then I was in court, accused of murdering my David, my parents faces showing a vicious hatred of me from their seats on the jury. I sat up sharply, awake, shocked and frightened, tears threatening. I drank some water, nodded off again, and this time it was Simon who shimmered his way, vapour-like, into my nightmare. He was naked and standing in the dock with a hard-on so small it was hardly discernible. He was accused of 'perverting the...' I never heard the full charge. I sat in the public gallery cackling and jeering 'Pervert. Pervert.' Then the judge demanded 'take her down' and it was me who was led down the steps, fearful and afraid for my sanity.

I woke up in a sweat, having slept through the alarm. It was seven fifteen and my stab at the number of minute's sleep I managed was between seventy five and ninety five. My head didn't feel as if it was joined to my body, or if it was, it was surely by sinew alone. I hauled my arse from under the duvet and dragged my feet through to the bathroom, holding my head with both hands, determined to keep it in position, lest I should lose it completely. Staring in disbelief at the horror vacantly watching me, mouth agape, I turned on the cold water tap and filled the washbasin. She looked up at me again, blackened eyes, hair like a wad of black steel wool. How the hell was I expected to make myself look presentable within two hours? I plunged my head face down into the icy water, optimistic of a double whammy; the double throb that coursed through my head had to go as well, it must!

Five minutes it took me. I plunged, popped up to take a breath each thirty seconds, and then plunged some more. I scooped the water over the back of my head, slowly massaging its area in tiny circles, tingling with the cold, but rejuvenating and calming away the brain pain until all that remained were minor niggles. I showered and made coffee, propping myself up in bed and enjoying the fix of caffeine; a celebration in honour of the headache that had now deserted me.

My mobile vibrated on the dressing table with an incoming call as I tended to the black circles around my eyes. As expected, it was Simon. I groaned a 'good morning' that I was unquestionably not feeling. His voice was effervescent, loud, and everything that wasn't me.

"Helen," he boomed "How are you? Up and raring to put your hubby where he belongs? Sorry! EX-hubby!" His laugh rang even louder in my eardrums.

"Oh fuck! Did you have to ring and mention that?" I moaned. "I was just starting to come round. 'Shit' isn't an apt word for the night I've had."

"Huh? Why?"

"Trust me, Simon, when I say, you're better off not knowing."

There was silence from his end. I sighed into the mouthpiece, heavy with exasperation.

"That good? Well, I just called to say I'll meet you on the steps as discussed. Listen to me. Don't worry too much, sweetness. You probably won't be called today."

I lost it, fully lost it at his words and bellowed down the phone hoping it pained his eardrums like he deserved.

"YOU MEAN...TO FUCKING TELL ME...THAT I MIGHT... HAVE TO...MIGHT HAVE TO GO

THROUGH...THIS FUCKING LOAD OF CRAP AGAIN...TONIGHT? WELL...FUCK OFF, SIMON!"

"All right, sweet cheeks! See you shortly."

I snorted loudly, but to a connection that was dead. He'd gone.

CHAPTER 12

*S*imon was waiting for me when I arrived. He led me inside and away into a private room out of the spotlight, away from all who wandered the building. He folded his arms around me before kissing me softly on the cheek.

"Helen! You look tense. I've got your back in there, relax."

The enormity of the nightmare hit me with such force during my ride over in the cab. Every little detail came flooding back, the photos I covertly snapped of the cars that came to and driven away from our house, the packets of substances I discovered, first in the greenhouse and later, in the tool-box in the garage. Dropping the envelope into the police station doorway that night…and making my escape to Paris after watching Anthony being driven away in the back seat of the one of the police cars in attendance. At that time, my O.C.D. reached a plateau, but the medication had calmed me, my grief for David the much bigger factor. I took it all in my stride as without any qualms whatsoever, I stitched up the husband I used to love.

I was rid of the medication I was prescribed. My self-weaning (which went against the advice of my French G.P.) had amazingly worked but I sat day after day in my Paris apartment, using alcohol as my crutch to see me through the dark times.

"Simon, I..." I sobbed. "I can't believe it. How the fuck did I ever get caught up in all this?"

I sat with my head in my hands, tears and snot threatening to wash away my foundation and mascara. Simon thrust a hanky into my hands.

"Let it out, Helen. It'll do you good."

My stomach felt empty and sickly, snarling at me in disgust, starved of its morning sustenance.

"You should have had something to eat, Helen. It would have settled that rumbling; given you some strength."

"Nothing could give me strength today, Simon." I snivelled. "I feel so...so...desolate."

He eyed me in concern, gave me a weak smile, and I took that as my cue to spew out my feelings of hatred, my bitterness for the situation the bastards inflicted on me, the innocent bystander.

"That scum!" I gestured to the building at large. "All that... that SHIT in our garage – his garage!" (I corrected.) "Packets of the fucking stuff ready to be pushed at innocent people, ruining fucking lives! Getting the prost...the girls who walk the streets hooked on the fucking filth. Getting beautiful young girls so hooked, they have to...start selling...their bodies to fun...fund the fucking...le..lethal habit. M...men too...over...overdosing...dying..."

Another wave of violent sobbing racked my body, such was my shock on contemplating the damage that had already been done with the drugs that passed through the greenhouse before my dark discovery in the corner of our, his garage.

He sat next to me and moved in close, arm about my shoulders.

"Helen, you're exhausted. That's why you're being over emotional. Take a few deep breaths for me, sweetie. You can...*will* get through this."

He searched my eyes as he guided my breathing. I followed each breath he took, holding it in before matching his release of air, pausing before taking in the next lungful, and I soon felt calmer. He was my rock. I trusted him implicitly.

"Consider this, Helen. Those twats gathering in there as we speak...they're only small-time dealers. Yeah, that's right."

He nodded as my mouth gaped, eyes widening in disbelief at his revelation. I was so naïve. Satisfied that I'd calmed down, he asked,

"Did you bring anything to occupy you, Helen? Time drags in these places, believe me. I'm going to have to go now. I'll come and see you or, more likely, get a message to you; let you know if you're going to be called today or not."

"I...I've got a magazine and a paperback in my bag."

I experienced a feeling of utter panic in the knowledge that I had to sit in the room alone, but I didn't want him to see it. I covered it well. He gave me an encouraging smile as he got up to leave. With a groan of frustration I plucked the book from my handbag and stared at the pages, not recognising, not understanding the printed words that I tried hard to focus on, as they appeared and then morphed and faded away like the patterns of a kaleidoscope.

For three hours I sat, thoughts running amok in my head and...wishing I'd disappeared without a trace all those months ago. Wishing I threw my cell phone into the Seine, or better still, that I never set foot in France. More attractive would have been a cabin in the Australian bush, miles from anywhere; contact with civilisation... minimal. I should have hidden away forever, leaving behind the life that became my living hell.

I got up and started to pace around the tiny room, jumping in fright as, with my back to the door, there came an urgent rap on the wood and it creaked open behind me.

"Mrs Pawson?" A young girl leaned in through the door and handed me an envelope. "A message from your lawyer, Mr..."

I snatched the envelope from her hands eagerly.

"Thank you!"

Fingers trembling, stomach flipping nervously, I read the short message from Simon. 'Helen, Go home and get some sleep. You won't be called today. The defence are stringing it out, trying to clutch at straws. You'll be needed tomorrow without fail. I'll call you later. Simon.' Though it was hard to glean any satisfaction from a sudden fit of temper, I slung the paper at the wall in anger. Three fucking hours of tearing my hair out and he told me to go home. The hotel, he meant. I didn't know where my fucking home was these days. My face burnt with fury. Sweeping up my bag, I rushed out of the building and didn't look back.

Having had two 'Simon measures' of gin and tonic, I flung myself onto the bed where, fully-clothed and shoes still on, I slept away the afternoon and into early evening. In my dream I heard a rapping sound, and suddenly woke to realise the rap was on my door. I leapt off the bed and rushed to the door, keen to stop the noise that was increasing in volume and adding to my headache. Simon pushed his way past me and I launched myself at him, into his arms.

"I thought I'd pop by..."

I knocked the wind clean out of his very upright sails.

"...instead of ringing," he finished, with a gasp.

I forced my lips hard onto his (the door still wide open) in delight.

"Hel-len!" he warned, leaning over my shoulder to push the door closed

Forcing my tongue between his lips, I met with his teeth and my tongue prized them apart. I wanted to lose myself in him, him to lose himself in me, craving to leave my hell behind and be consumed in the inferno that was our relationship. I felt the dampness begin to pool between my legs and I grasped the waistband of his suit in one hand and the other crept down his chest, over his stomach and started lowering his zip. A few seconds later, after a sharp intake of breath, his hand folded tight over mine. He exercised his willpower with admirable certainty, his voice not wavering.

"NO! Helen, no! There'll be no fucking tonight. I can't! Because if we do it just the once, you'll want more. I'll want more! You'll have me fuck you all night, if I let you. My mind is made up. I'll stay for a drink or two, but no touching, no pleading eyes. You are going to bed alone...to sleep! Not negotiable, sweet thing. I'm going back to my hotel."

I was gutted but thought better of arguing my point. I'd never seen him so adamant. I scowled, wondering what the hell I was going to do about the tingle that was creeping deep from the ache in my groin upwards into my stomach. He filled me in with the afternoon's events in court as we sipped our way through his two promised drinks.

"Take a couple of painkillers, Helen. With the drink they should knock you out for the night. I need you fresh and raring to go tomorrow. No tears and no anxiety. I want to see a positive Helen Pawson...Rushforth, sorry, in the morning."

He'd seen me squirm in anguish at his slip-up, his use of my ex- marital surname, and sheepishly grinned his apology.

It was a first; to see Simon and not having sex. Still smarting a little at the rejection, I offered only my cheek as he got ready to leave, but caved in with his parting shot as he held me tight to his body.

"Your part in court will be over tomorrow, Helen. I can guarantee they won't call you again. I'll fuck you tomorrow night – it can be your celebration that it will be the last you'll ever see of him."

Some consolation that is! I still have the court appearance to get through, you bloody idiot!

"I'm going to hold you to that, Mr. Lechy Lawyer man."

He smirked. I opened the door and watched him stride purposely down the corridor towards the lift. A lump formed in my throat as I realised there was going to be no change of heart, no turning round and coming back to take me brutally to my other world.

I hate it when men are right...and he was right. I took a couple of ibuprofen after he left and washed them down with another 'Simon measure'. Talk about one's head hitting the proverbial. When I opened my eyes at half past seven the next morning, I could barely remember lying down on the bed. There had definitely not been those 'waiting for sleep to come' moments. The tablets and booze knocked me out stone cold, and now I was wide awake, refreshed, a determination to get this thing done and over with, and not forgetting what was on offer much later in the day. I was quite excited and...positive. I nodded to myself in the bathroom mirror and spoke out loud, watching my reflection as the doppelganger uttered the words with me.

"Positive, Helen! When did you last feel that?" I grinned like a pantomime cat. I would certainly meet with Simon's approval today.

The morning passed by slowly and I'd done my bit at last. I didn't have too long to wait and, as I took my place in the witness box, Simon gave me an encouraging smile as he thankfully, prompted me when, on a couple of occasions, I faltered. I put across the stories of my marriage with relative ease, all things considered. My difficulty arose as expected, with the explanations that were necessary regarding my O.C.D. and, more significantly, the grief of losing my parents. There was more to come though, as I tentatively mentioned the devastation I felt after losing my lover. Simon requested, out of respect for David's family, that his name not be disclosed in public. As it bore no relevance to the case, it was granted.

Anthony's face, on hearing that I'd had a lover, showed an expression of pure malice. Losing control, he shouted out in front of the whole court. "You fucking cheating cow! Who was he? You bitch! Double fucking standards."

I opened my mouth, the words already on my tongue, about to mention the rape, but Simon's eyes narrowed and he shot me a dark warning glare. The judge rapped hard and shouted a warning to Anthony.

"Mr. Pawson, any more disruptions from you, particularly not ones relevant to this hearing, and you will be taken away and charged with contempt of court. Do you understand?"

Anthony's lawyer approached him and whispered something. Anthony nodded back at him. His defence turned to the court announcing;

"My client understands, Your Honour. There will be no further disruption and my client has asked me to convey his apologies for the outburst, Your Honour."

My elation was short-lived as I knew I would shortly be cross-examined by the defence. More than anything I wanted to give Anthony a gloating grin of satisfaction, but my stomach churned nervously. I wasn't free to go at that point.

Late afternoon I celebrated by splashing out on some clothes and scintillatingly sexy underwear in Knightsbridge, sauntering around stores, happy that hopefully, I'd seen the last of Anthony Pawson. Simon turned up again after I'd eaten. He praised me for keeping my wits and standing firm during my torturous cross-examination. He expected the case would be over in the matter of two to three days.

"Do you want to be there for the final verdicts, Helen? Then there'll be the sentencing to follow?"

"I most certainly do *not*!" I voiced most emphatically.

"No matter! I'll keep you informed anyway, sweetie."

Before he arrived, I tried on some of the new underwear and chose to wear a matching bra, thong and suspender belt in a rich purple silk colour. Rather than his favourite black stockings, I wore a neutral colour with lacy tops. Frivolous, as I'd felt when I was shopping, I purchased a maid's outfit with the intention of jogging his memory back to our first time. Celebrating in style, court case put to bed for the night, we followed suit shortly after. With the maid outfit lying on the lounge floor in a scrunched up pile with my thong, he told me to leave the stockings on as they made him extra horny. As I lost myself in the dirty sex play and orgasms, I smiled, amused, wondering how the fuck stockings could make him any more rigid and throbbing than he already was. My rock; my rock hard lawyer! By the early hours, we collapsed in a heap onto my bed, spent, sore…but satisfied.

CHAPTER 13

I enjoyed a pleasant few days following the traumas of the 'pre-court blues' which led to the day my presence was required in the witness box. I hadn't heard back from or seen Simon since over taxing his sexual energy, so there must have been nothing worthwhile for him to report back. He mentioned that he was possibly going to commute from his Essex home for a few days and catch up with his wife and family.

Not having heard from me since my parents' funeral, I spent the first Saturday visiting aunts and uncles and one or two cousins. Calling them first to forewarn that I would be visiting had saved me time and a few different house visits. Dad's siblings and my cousins gathered at Uncle John's house in Brentford, and Mum's family all assembled at Auntie Sheila's home in Virginia Water. I had been looking forward to the visits but with a tinge of sadness at the thought of my absent parents. I knew it would be an emotional day all round. Following our mutual tears after I arrived and then listening to their tales of shock on receiving Anthony's call about the accident, the mood lightened up somewhat. Happy and funny family memories came pouring out and we shared more than a few laughs, particularly when I heard about some of the scrapes my father had gotten into as a young boy. I came away from both homes vowing to keep in touch and not to shut myself away again.

On the Sunday, I was mentally exhausted and indulged in what was, for me, an extremely lazy day, refusing to shift my backside from under the duvet until well past noon. I ate, courtesy of room service, a delicious brunch, which arrived with an equally scrumptious pot of coffee. I did nothing more exciting than lie on the sofa and watch an old black and white movie, 'Tread Softly Stranger', which starred the inimitable Diana Dors. The film wasn't really my thing, but it was the first time I saw the sexy and beautiful Diana star in something other than the few pop videos she'd done up until her untimely death in 1984. I lost interest in the movie towards the end and, stifling a yawn or two, I went for a long soak in the bathtub.

The only problem with soaking for any length of time is that you always have time to take down and dust off some of the memories that come back to haunt you. To me, time spent in the shower usually involved a determined scrub down and soaping the body, washing my hair and getting out as quick as possible, without those extra free minutes to dwell on certain thoughts. I suppose that, having done the family visits the previous day, it was the trigger for my child-hood and school years to become the focal point of my thought dredging. School holiday time had always been centred around family life, visits to southern seaside resorts with cousins, staying on the farm that was owned by an aunt and uncle of my mother, and the family barbecues. At other times we would be out of the country, just Mum, Dad and I, enjoying a bit of culture, visiting theme parks, water parks, and not forgetting the laziness of time spent on the beach. I ached to be able to live a re-run of those times and have my parents back, for a while at least.

The not-so-comfortable thoughts were the years I spent in private schooling and the persistent, unrelenting taunts and torment I was on the receiving end of; by a gang of obnoxious females who thought they ruled the school. The other girls, who were far from being bullies, were intimidated to such an extent that none would dare to come to my assistance for fear of any reprisals. I stayed tough, barely shed more than a solitary tear, concentrated on school-work and enjoyed the attention of the boys, which was no doubt the underlying reason for my victimisation.

The water all too soon became tepid and just as I was poised on a re-cap of my uni years, it seemed an ideal time not to add any more water and get myself out and dried off. With no further plans for the day, I didn't bother getting dressed and sat around in the towelling robe flicking through the T.V. channels. I just settled into a Dimbleby documentary and my mobile rang…it was Simon.

"I'm on my way up, sweet pea."

Genuinely surprised by the call, I was suddenly overwhelmed with excitement. My stomach clenched tight in anticipation. Because he left London to stay in Essex for a few nights over the weekend to spend time with his wife, I hadn't expected him to return until Monday morning, in time for the final days of the case.

"Okay, then. Is this a flying visit or are you staying?"

A knock came on the door and I rushed over to open it. He beamed as he stood in the doorway, mobile phone to his ear and spoke directly into it as he continued to grin at me.

"Well, now that depends very much on what is on offer, Helen."

He pressed the button and disconnected the call. A quick peek around him showed that there were no staff or hotel residents in the corridor. Grinning back at him playfully, my eyes connected with his and I pulled on my towelling belt allowing the front to fall open. I gave an excited gulp as my breasts were partly revealed along with the results of my afternoon's bush trim. That wild exhibitionist move on my part induced a seeping of moisture into my folds and my heart started to race. I'd never been so daring. His eyes looked hungrily at my body for a second, and then he placed his hands inside the open gown and onto my hips. He swiftly pushed me backwards into the room and kicked the door shut with a resounding slam.

"Fuck me, Helen. Do you always have to be so fucking welcoming and accommodating?"

His lips met with mine as he peeled the gown back from my shoulders. Thrusting his tongue into my mouth and his fingers inside me at the same time, I sensed his urgency.

"I need to fuck you wild now, Helen. I need this, no messing. So take your pleasure while you can."

I needed no further bidding.

"Fuck me then! I need your cock, Simon!" I pleaded.

As I raked my fingers through his hair, my warmth accommodated his throbbing length with relish, and clenching my muscles tight around his girth, I came in a gush as he thrust deep into me. He groaned out loud, aware that his orgasm was ready to explode and urgently rubbed hard on my clit bringing on my second flow just in time. My body arched expectantly and, squeezing my warmth around him again, I milked his cock as it twitched his release.

Our bodies flopped together as our breathing calmed and he sighed heavily in my ear, fondling my breasts longingly.

"I…I didn't get the chance to enjoy every inch of you." He gasped in disappointment. "But anyway, in answer to your earlier question, it looks as if I'm staying…doesn't it?"

I growled naughtily at him and eyed my watch as I

pushed his damp sandy hair back from his forehead; he'd been in my room no longer than ten minutes. The whole night lay ahead of us...

It was late Monday afternoon by the time I heard the phone vibrating away in my handbag. I met up with Catherine earlier and we headed to Selfridges and had an enjoyable lunch in HIX restaurant. We were currently in a queue in Christian Louboutin, patiently waiting to pay for our purchases when my phone started to buzz. I frantically scrabbled around in my bag desperately trying to find the phone. As my hand closed around it, the ringing stopped and I groaned.

"Important call, Helen?" asked Catherine. "You look pissed off about missing it."

I looked at the screen, distracted somewhat as I answered her.

"It was Si...my lawyer. My ex-husband is in court to..."

It rang again and my finger fumbled on the button in my haste to take the call.

"Yes, Simon? Tell me."

I held my breath as I waited to hear the verdict.

"Are you ready? Anthony has been found guilty of possession, and aiding and abetting. The other three have all been found guilty of possession and dealing."

"Good. How long?"

"Sentencing will take place tomorrow. I did tell you, if you remember."

He told me on a couple of occasions, but it hadn't seemed important at the time. Besides, I had other things to look forward to in his presence; the mind-blowing sex that was happening on a very regular basis.

"You'll have to call me tomorrow night then. You haven't forgotten that I'm flying back to Paris tomorrow afternoon?" Silence. "Simon?"

"Yes, I'm still here. How could I forget that? I didn't need that unwelcome reminder, sweetie."

Aware that Catherine stood eagerly at my side waiting to hear Anthony's fate, I wanted to end the call quickly.

"Well thanks for letting me know, Simon. And I'll hear from you tomorrow night?"

"Yes, you will. Bye, Helen." Then lowering his voice, knowing I was spending the afternoon with Catherine, he added, "And you'll see me tonight for my goodbye present, too." I grinned.

"Thank you, goodbye, Simon."

Just as promised, he came to my room again that night, not staying to sleep, but we certainly made the most of the five hours he was with me. He left, totally unaware of my future plans or that he would be seeing me sooner than he imagined. He discussed with me the possibility of flying out to Paris for a few nights in a month's time and I hadn't dismissed the idea yet. He was also not aware of the troubles that constantly churned over and over in my mind the last couple of days; my relationship, if it could be deemed as such, with André. As my short time in England was rapidly coming to a close, I knew that many decisions needed to be made. I had almost made the most important one.

Once I took my seat on the plane, I fought hard to hold back the emotion. The pull of London and its attractive benefits; the promise of the new lifestyle that awaited me, tugged at my heart strings. My days of feeling imprisoned in the apartment in Paris were now casting a big shadow over me. Whilst it had been the right decision at the time (an escape from two years of hell that had been my destiny), it was over. It was a means to an end, nothing more. The initial devastating grief had passed, and while I would probably always display waves of O.C.D. from time to time, I felt that I'd done well. It was time to shed the loneliness, break my news to André and return to London to start again.

I dumped my case in the hallway with my decision firmly made. I dialled the number. This was to be an extremely important call for me. The voice at the end of the phone was ecstatic with my news. Plans would be put into action immediately by both of us. I made a booking to fly back to London, unsure how long my business would take I hadn't troubled buying a return ticket. Sometime later, the call came from Simon.

"He got four years, Helen. The other three got fifteen, fifteen and twelve years."

"Okay, so tell me, how long will Anthony end up serving?"

Do I really want to know?

"With good behaviour? Eighteen months to two years."

Not fucking long enough for the bastard! He should rot!

I paused to consider my feelings.

"Helen? Helen?"

"I'm here."

"Helen, it's a good job you're in Paris out of the way. The families were livid; just young men and all that…"

I butt in quickly, cutting him off. "Simon, I'm coming home, back to England, tomorrow."

"No, Helen, listen…you can't. Stay where you are, it's safer for you. The families will be gunning for you. You'll have to watch your back if you're here."

He sounded annoyed but I was determined to get my point across and, besides, nothing was going to change my mind.

"Why? Why will I have to watch my back?" I challenged.

"You have provided fucking damning evidence that has put those scumbags where they deserve to be, behind bars. But don't forget, they have friends. They are sons, they are brothers, and one of them has a wife and child. The wife is from a…a family that…shall we say, has friends in high places, people who will stop at nothing, Helen."

Batting that information backwards and forwards in my brain for a few seconds, I remained defiant.

"And no amount of threat is going to prevent me from living where I want to live, Simon; from doing what I want to do with my life. My mind is made up. I'm sorry if that doesn't meet with your approval. I'm flying back tomorrow. I'll be spending two or three days house-hunting. Well, as long it takes me to find one."

We didn't speak much after that…an icy silence developed. He called to give me the news of the sentencing and after I blurted out my news, it seemed as if he couldn't end the call quick enough. Rather snappily, he made an attempt at goodbye.

"Well, if there's nothing else, I've things to do, Helen."

My face flushed with anger, not to mention the bitter disappointment I felt in my heart as it pounded in my chest. Simon had always been a tremendous support to me and I couldn't help but feel that now the court case was over, so would our relationship of sorts. My days as a call-girl to the clients he'd introduced were in the past, he knew that. So what was there to hold us together now that his services as a lawyer were no longer needed by me? I reminded myself that he was the one who needed my help with the case.

I cried myself to sleep that night, sad for the relationship that wasn't. Another small portion of my last few years would be abandoning me.

CHAPTER 14

*T*rying at any cost, to avoid any long discussions with André, I struggled to make an excuse when I saw him. He called in for a brief catch-up on arriving home from work. I used the court case as an excuse for my weariness and overstated how much time I spent in the courts being cross-examined by Anthony's defence. I also over-dramatised how much the constant to-ing and fro-ing around London had taken its toll on me.

I took a deep breath, knowing that he wouldn't be impressed as I blurted out that I would be returning to England the following morning to attend to some urgent business matters.

"But why didn't you get this stuff done while you were over there?" He demanded to know.

Shit! I don't need this!

"Because I ran out of time, that's why! My return ticket was already booked and besides, I left some paperwork here; things I should have remembered to take with me. Yes, I had weekends to myself, but it wasn't possible to do my business on a weekend."

There was disappointment in his eyes, and something else…suspicion. He paid close attention to my face and my body language, searching for some sign of a lie.

"But I need to spend time with you, Helen."

Hopefully, my eyes would not betray my feelings.

"I know. I'm sorry but that time is going to have to wait until I come back. I'll only be away for three or four days this time. I need to wash that case full of clothes tonight and repack it."

I nodded in the direction of my hall where the suitcase still sat and waited for him to digest what I was saying. Rather petulantly, he looked from me to the offending suitcase two or three times. I could tell he was dying to say more but presumably thought better of it. He finished his coffee and got up to leave. At the door he turned round and spat out moodily.

"I'll see you when you get back then, whenever that's going to be." He let himself out and I heard him grumble something under his breath as he crossed the landing; words I didn't manage to catch.

Throwing some of the clothes from my case into the washer, I left the rest in the laundry basket – it could wait. Instead of being bothered with washing and ironing it was easier to select fresh clothes from my wardrobe. In no time I was good to go. I spent what was left of the evening, hours in fact, searching the internet for a new home. I browsed through loads (it felt like hundreds) of properties in the Greater London area through numerous estate agent websites. After checking their site maps for the locations, along with a large number of fabulous and appalling interior and exterior photographs of the houses, I finally settled on seven that held my interest. I printed off each of the properties details from the estate agents' sites. I planned that, before I left for the airport the next morning, I would make the relevant calls for appointments to view when their offices opened at nine.

I wouldn't be able to gain access to my money for a few weeks as I had invested all the inheritance from my parents' estate, but in the meantime I could rent something short-term until I had a completion date on one of the houses. Another option was that I could arrange a short-term period in a more modest hotel room. I wasn't too bothered which one, as long as I could escape Paris. There was also the other *big* reason I had to move back quickly following my meeting a few days back with a certain gentleman. I needed to tell Simon about it.

CHAPTER 15

*B*efore my cab came to collect me for the run to the airport, I made my nine a.m. phone calls to the estate agents and secured a Saturday morning appointment to view a large bungalow in Richmond. I was filled with regret the minute I ended the call. The property was literally a stone's throw from my childhood home. I just felt that not enough time had passed since I sold what had always been my family home. I hadn't even been able to face visiting the house after my parents' deaths. I was still with Anthony at that point, so I sent him over to fetch all their personal belongings. I shuddered trying to imagine how I would feel living close to their old house; inadvertently looking out of the front window of that bungalow expecting them to drive past and then experiencing the heartbreak again on the realisation that it was never going to happen. I made a mental note to cancel the appointment before Saturday came around.

My first appointment was for the day after my arrival in London. I checked out its location in Maida Vale very carefully, more with regard to access for the underground system, than for any other reason. Interestingly enough, Maida Vale was situated on the Bakerloo line and perfect for the commute that I would be making most days of the working week. The big bonus was that the property was only a short walk round the corner to the station; a street called Elgin Mews. I was looking forward to viewing the property, but something niggled constantly at the back of my mind. It seemed too good to be true, but I would know soon enough.

I still had a bit of a heavy heart, having not heard back from Simon. As upset as I would be if things came to an end, I was determined not to let it affect me too much. I was about to start my life over and it would either be with him or without him. My determination faltered though when I kept checking my mobile for missed calls or texts every two or three minutes.

How can there be a missed call when the bloody phone has been in your hand for the last few hours?

By six o'clock, twenty four hours had gone by without any contact from him. I ordered my gin and tonics from room service as I hadn't brought my own supply this time. I was at a loss, not quite knowing what to do with myself. I felt empty and so sure that this was it between us. Time and again I paced the room feeling like I wanted to vomit and also, the beginnings of a stress headache; that pressure that also caused my ears to buzz. I wanted to speak with him. I needed to know whether this was the end or not. I wasn't able to phone him and I screeched my frustration as I threw the phone onto the table. Phone calls were verboten! He might be with his damned wife for fuck's sake. A text message then! Snatching up the phone again, I tapped out a simple brief message, 'Simon, phone me please'.

I stared at the message too long, thinking perhaps I didn't want to know the direction we were headed. I pressed the backspace, quickly deleting the lot.

I crawled into bed at ten, feeling sorry for myself. I also let a certain element of doubt creep into my head. I already made a certain commitment and was about to make even more. I hoped to hell I was doing the right thing. The only thing I knew for sure was if I didn't go ahead with these plans, I certainly wouldn't return to Paris to live. I would be running once more, something I was becoming accustomed to.

During that midway point between awake and semi-comatose, I reached out for my phone as it vibrated on the nightstand. My finger automatically connected with the green 'answer' key. I didn't open my eyes or look at the screen. I croaked my greeting.

"Yes?"

"Helen, where the fuck are you?"

His tone had my dozing hackles up immediately. Time to let the sarcasm ooze! "Bed!"

"Bed? Where?"

I was tempted to reply 'bedroom' but I knew he'd see red, although the impulse was immense.

"Hotel!"

"Which hotel? Come on, Helen. Don't play fucking games with me. I was looking out for you. Listen, we need to talk."

I took a deep breath to calm myself before it ended up as a full scale war between the two of us.

"I'm viewing houses for the next few days."

"Do you need some help?"

"And what would be the point in that, Simon? Besides, how the hell could you be seen viewing properties with me?"

"I could help in other ways, not with the viewings," he admitted. "Look, I've not called to argue with you, Helen. Your mind is made up and I know I can't do anything to sway you. We still need to talk though."

Recognising the fact that he wasn't about to give up, I caved in.

"Okay. I'm in the same hotel as last week, room 701."

"Good. I'll be there before seven tomorrow night. Happy house-hunting."

The first property, the cause of my excitement; the mews cottage in Maida Vale, certainly ticked all the boxes. It was beautiful. According to the agent who took me along for the viewing, it had undergone a major refurbishment three years previously. It boasted three bedrooms, one with an en-suite, walk-in shower room, a house bathroom, lounge, kitchen diner and a dining room. An integral garage had the main garage door opening out onto a delightful cobbled street. It was tastefully decorated throughout and I fell instantly in love with it, and sorely tempted not to bother viewing the other six.

In the afternoon, having been driven to St John's Wood by a different agent, my heart lurched when we pulled up in a street that overlooked the row of mews cottages where David had lived…and where we had… I gave myself a shake, literally, and refused to dwell on the matter any further. Although his house was now jointly owned by Catherine and Ruby and was on a long-term let, I knew I couldn't live this close, even though I had nothing against the girls. Before the cottage was leased, Catherine had offered it for my use, but I turned her down, although I had been thrilled by the kind-ness and generosity she'd shown. When the agent parked up in front of the property, I couldn't bring myself to get out of the car. I stared back and forth between David's old house and the property we parked in front of. She watched me carefully as my eyes went from one house to the other.

"Helen, do you want to go in and inspect the house? You seem to be in a quandary."

She sounded a little impatient. I hesitated before giving my answer.

"I am so sorry. The property looks lovely from the outside, but I've realised that it would be too much to live this close."

I briefly explained the personal reasons behind my sudden lack of interest, and pointed out what had been David's mews cottage. She softened and averted her eyes when she realised I was getting a little emotional.

"Have you seen any other properties yet, Helen? Anything that you really like?"

Deciding to be honest with her, I explained about the mews cottage I was in love with.

"Yes, I have actually. It's in Maida Vale, Elgin Mews South. It's a stunning cottage."

"We happen to have something similar in that area, but it's Elgin Mews North. Would you like me to phone the vendor now and see if it's okay for us to pop over from here?"

"No, thank you. Not today. Can I give it some thought and get back to you tomorrow, though?"

I felt terrible for wasting her time. Maybe I would think about it later and view the house she mentioned, but I wasn't sure yet. I also started to feel distracted and worried about Simon's visit that night. My neck and shoulders were feeling tense and aching badly and my stomach was in knots. I didn't know how I would manage to get through the evening if what I expected to happen was about to become reality. He said that we needed to talk. For the life of me, I couldn't possibly imagine what else it could be. I would have to accept it and get on with my life. I had to. It wasn't as if Simon was ever going to play a big part in my life. Our friendship was always about sex from the first day I met him.

Sitting on the side of my bed, I read and re-read the

printed details of the properties I viewed online. Without hesitation I ripped up the ones for Richmond and St. John's Wood, leaving an extremely overpriced two bedroom flat in Knightsbridge, a four bedroom terraced house in Kentish Town, and two properties in Ealing, both detached. Flicking through the papers time and again, I was confused. A lack of concentration to take in what I read, trying to work out the pros and cons of each, was giving me a headache. I started pacing again, unsettled about the whole house thing and becoming increasingly nervous about Simon's visit. I sat, stood up again, sat once more and fidgeted, arranged and re-arranged the magazines and other bits and pieces I placed on the coffee table. I hoped he wasn't going to be late.

As he promised, he arrived well before seven. I opened the door to let him in and immediately walked away without any sort of greeting.

"So, it appears I'm still in the bad books?"

Clever of you to have worked that one out!

I slumped down onto the sofa, fixing him with a glare, posing an unspoken question. He tried again.

"How did the house hunt go? Is it over yet? Or are there more to see?"

I could feel the anger rising from my toes up to the roots of my hair, burning me up. I made a quick decision to go on the defensive, tell him exactly how it looked, to save me the hurt of having to hear the words come from him. I started blurting it out, no holds barred.

"You see, that is the question, isn't it, Simon? Is it over yet? Well why the fuck else would you come round here to talk to me? What else could it possibly be? I don't do clients anymore, so that's finished with. You've had my help with the drugs case. What is there now? It's all gone, hasn't it? No more reasons for us to stay in touch!"

He hadn't even had the chance to take a seat. He stood

there, mouth open in amazement, looking as if he'd been knocked on the head with a hammer. He tried to speak but was genuinely shocked by my verbal attack.

"Helen, I..."

"No. Hold it right there. Is that why you want me to fucking stay in Paris? How easy that would be for you."

"HELEN! SHUT...THE...FUCK...UP! Let me get a FUCKING word in, WILL YOU?"

I jumped, suddenly worried that half the guests in the hotel would have heard his outburst. I put my hand up to my mouth to stifle a return volley of abuse. He waited a few seconds to be sure I calmed down.

"Right, Helen. Let me speak now, please? I accept that you want to come back to London to live, I really do. I only wanted you to stay safe because I care. I want to help you with your search for a home. I don't want this to be the end for us. I love...what we've got. You're very special to me. But I can't offer more than being your shag buddy, if you accept that?"

I started to shake. Relief coursed through my body and I allowed my shoulders to sag.

"Really?"

"Yes, really."

I panted, struggling to get my head around the sudden turnaround.

"That is all I wanted, Simon. I was hurting to think that our friendship was finished. Business done, as they say. You're a terrific friend...and the rest. I was afraid...to lose that."

He nodded to show me he understood.

"Just a couple more things, Helen. Hear me out, please? I don't know how long I can do this. I'm not getting any younger and I'm making the most of it...you know what I'm saying? I'm sure you'll eventually meet someone else and when you choose to call it a day...well, I'll be happy for you... I think. I mean, are you for real? Look at your body, Helen. I can't think of one man I know who would willingly give up access to that...to you. It's not just your body. You are a beautiful person, beautiful and intelligent. You have everything."

I cried then. He came and sat with me, holding me tight. Nothing further was said; subject closed.

"What will you do, Helen?"

The question came out of the dark as we lay there waiting for sleep. We had sex earlier. It eased the earlier tension of the evening. Once was sufficient for both of us, and we were content to sit in bed afterwards to discuss the property details I showed him. He advised me to go ahead and view them all or, at the very least, take a look at the mews cottage in Elgin Street North. I had no printed details for that one, only the mention of it by the lady agent.

"Look at some of the others, as you advised."

"No, not the properties, sweet cheeks. What will you do once you've moved back?"

I yawned, sleep ready to hit me, eyes starting to feel heavy and I mumbled my words as I gave in to my drowsiness.

"Well, I think I can tell you now. The meeting I had last week? You remember? It was Ted Hopkins who I met with. I'm going back into practice. The staff don't know...ye..."

I was aware of nothing after his lips brushed the tip of my nose.

"Night..."

I already made up my mind that I would put an offer in for the cottage in Elgin Mews South. I made appointments and turned up for the viewings in Ealing, Kentish Town and Knightsbridge. The two in Ealing were with the same agent and we went directly from one to the other. Both were oversized detached properties with five bedrooms each and far too big for me, so I discounted them straightaway. They were attractive family homes and, considering the market, were excellent prices for couples who had three or four children. The other cottage in Maida Vale was a good deal smaller than mine, or more appropriately, the one I had set my sights on. The kitchen was smaller, the bedrooms were smaller, and it didn't have the en-suite; no match for the one I wanted.

The Knightsbridge flat and Kentish Town terraced property didn't come up to standard either. The photographers had cleverly focused on the positive and had done a sterling job of hiding the negative; raising the camera in a lounge to hide a very tattered and worn carpet, lowering the camera in a couple of bedrooms to hide the badly stained ceilings. They were shabby and I was thrilled; I didn't want to like anything else. Butterflies in my tummy and shaking nervously with excitement, I couldn't wait to get back to the hotel. I poked among the magazines laid on the floor at the side of the bed, searching for the details for Elgin Street South. Trying to control my attack of the shakes and assume a more business-like voice instead of that of an excited child, I dialled the number of the estate agent and left my offer...£30,000 lower than the asking price.

It was a long, painful, nerve-racking wait for over thirty six hours. At one point, convinced I was going to be unsuccessful, I was tempted to call back and concede; offer them the asking price. I called Simon for his thoughts.

"Helen, don't be so fucking stupid. Wait it out. They do this deliberately to see how desperate people get, see if people's impatience will get the better of them."

"But there have been lots of viewings and they have had other offers."

"I'm sure the agent would have told you if the other offers were higher than yours. Stop panicking."

I was so frustrated. I wanted to tell him he didn't have a

bloody clue what he was talking about. Basically, he wasn't telling me what I wanted to hear, 'go ahead, Helen'.

By four thirty on the Friday afternoon, I had the call, my offer had been accepted. Ecstatic didn't even cover it. I made a quick call to inform Simon. He finally managed to get a word in when my squealing, high-pitched voice had quieted.

"I'm thrilled for you, Helen. I was right again, by the way, in making you wait it out, wasn't I?"

"Yes, yes."

Realising what was to be done next, I hurried Simon off the phone and called Bill Douglas (who was still dealing with David's estate). I instructed him to act for me in the purchase of Elgin Mews.

On Sunday, after having had only a couple more hours with Simon since we had officially become 'fuck buddies', I caught the train to Heathrow. It was time to return to Paris and face the music. I had no idea how long it would take for the house to 'complete'. Ted Hopkins wanted me to start back at the practice in two weeks' time, but I knew there was plenty to keep me occupied in the meantime. First and foremost, I didn't know where I was going to live until I could move into Elgin Mews, so I needed to get my arse into gear and make a few calls. Then there was André. That wasn't something I relished the thought of and it started to prey on my mind, marring the euphoria that I was enjoying...and I resented the intrusion.

CHAPTER 16

I was sickened, disgusted with myself. Once again, I took the cowardly way out. I rolled over in bed, for the umpteenth time. I'd been tossing and turning, running scenarios through my head; a short story being dramatised in so many different ways, so many different places, some of the best Hollywood actors playing the role of André. The ending was always the same though; he was used, cast aside, hurt. No matter how, where, and why it was happening, Helen Rushforth always played the starring role... the bitch!

The idea came to me during the flight. You've got to avoid him like the plague. I hadn't even left CDG airport after my flight landed. It was after ten on Sunday night and he would no doubt have heard the door to my apartment if I returned to the apartment. I walked out of the terminal building and got a cab to drive me further round the airport to one of the hotels in the vicinity. My plan was to travel back into Paris on Monday morning and check into another hotel. During the day, whilst he was at work, I would be able to go into my apartment without him knowing.

Had André been the sort of arrogant, selfish, womanising guy that I so despised, it would have been easy. I pondered on how come I let myself be sucked so deep into a friendship, a relationship like ours, without figuring out sooner the way it would come to an end. He did nothing wrong to deserve what I knew had to be done. How do you say to a guy so lovely, 'Sorry, you've been an amazing friend to me, helped me, cared for me and fucked me, but I got it all wrong? The fucking was on my terms, when I wanted, but I've never really been attracted to you.'

I cried again. Not for myself. I cried for André, for the hurt that he was going to feel. After all, I'd been there myself, quite a few times.

I checked into the Paris Rivoli Hotel next morning, just a five minute walk from the apartment. Each day I visited the apartment for a few hours to do what needed to be done. Simon called me during the Monday afternoon.

"Helen, please tell me you haven't sorted out a rental property yet? I think I've sorted something for you."

"Where…and how come?" I asked eagerly, hoping to hell I could return to London that very night.

"It's a friend's flat near Hyde Park. Actually, the guy was one of your…clients…"

"What the fuck? Simon, how the fuck could you do that to me? He'll be coming round thinking…"

I was bloody furious with him, jumping in like that.

"Helen, credit me with some fucking sense, will you? He doesn't even know it's you. He's going abroad for three months, so he won't be around to ever find out. By the time he's back, you'll be nicely ensconced in Maida Vale. What do you think?"

Although I felt a tad suspicious that everything seemed to be going too smoothly, I still couldn't control the excited lurch in my stomach or the smile that threatened to remain on my face for all eternity.

"Well it sounds good to me. How soon could I move in?"

Please let it be tomorrow!

"Ah, that's where there's a slight downside. He doesn't leave for another week or so. You'll probably have to slum it in a hotel for a couple of nights, but you're used to that anyway."

He'd been so good to me. I couldn't let him hear the disappointment that I was feeling, my chagrin that the flat wasn't available yet. Putting on the most animated and cheery voice I could muster, I ended the call.

"Simon, that is fantastic. Thank you so much. How did I ever cope without you in my life?"

I could visualise him with a big grin at the other end when his reply came.

"You didn't!"

Two days later I heard from Bill and the estate agents, both calls within a few minutes of each other. The completion was expected to take place in four to five weeks. I thudded around my apartment punching the air and singing and dancing in the process. I started to empty my wardrobes of the best of my clothes. I filled two large suitcases and then set to work on emptying the fridge of the 'out of date' dairy items and threw out a loaf of bread, green with penicillin. I pulled dust sheets (always used by my parents between their visits) out of the hall cupboard and covered all the furniture in readiness. I shouldn't need to visit the flat again, until it was time to return to England…and finally do the dirty deed; break my news to André.

Back at the hotel, I was lost. Overcome with boredom, I tried to read a book. I couldn't settle though, so I painted my nails and took the varnish off again, unsatisfied with the colour. I showered until I got sick of showering. I gave myself a manicure and painted my nails yet again. Devoid of company, I even got dressed in my finest and went downstairs to the restaurant to eat. Afterwards, I sat at the bar in the cocktail lounge and made conversation with the young, English barman, Ian, working in France to improve his language skills. He was charming and polite and...way too young. I watched in fascination as he skilfully mixed the odd cocktail or two for the rather sparse clientele.

As my pleasant and impromptu evening came to an end, he hit me with a bolt out of the blue.

"Helen? I hope you don't mind me asking. What is the difference between waiting it out in this hotel and waiting it out in a hotel back in London? If that is what you're desperate to do, if that is where you want to be, then I know what I'd do. You say you have nothing to keep you here."

I stared at him as if he was totally crazy. My head felt so befuddled I couldn't quite grasp the logic. He had a grin plastered all over his face, so pleased with himself, and waiting... waiting for his suggestion to hit home. Finally, it got there and I still stared at him incredulous. I held my arms out and he came from behind the bar and allowed me to hug him.

"Ian, you are a bloody genius. I've been waiting about, putting off the inevitable, stalling with something that could be over and done with tomorrow."

He coloured up as I kissed his cheek and wished him well with his ongoing studies.

"Good luck with the André thing!" He shouted after me as I left the bar. It was my turn to colour up, guiltily, as I nodded in his direction.

Feeling uncomfortable with my guilt and the deceit of what I was about to do, I returned to the apartment for eleven o'clock the next morning, Friday. I was collecting the two large suitcases I left ready, intent on getting out of Paris without a word to André. I couldn't face it. I couldn't bear to look him in the eye and have to endure the hurt; witness the hurt in his eyes and watch him crumble before me... cowardly though it was.

I conducted a last check around the apartment, remembering to switch off the fridge and leave the door open. Without a backwards glance, I turned my key in the door. I knew I would come back one day but it would take a while. In two punishing journeys, I hauled my heavy suitcases down the staircase into the entrance hall. Such was my urgency to get away, I trembled with nerves. I called a cab company and was told someone would be with me within ten minutes. I moved my cases to the kerbside and, shifting from one foot to the other, I wrung my hands together, anxiety taking over. I looked up and down the road in desperation, not knowing from which direction the taxi would approach.

My body sagged with relief when the cab finally pulled up alongside me. The driver, obviously having seen the size of my suitcases, climbed out of the driver's side and walked around to open up the boot. I already pulled the rear passenger door open when I noticed a blue car about to pull up behind us...André's blue Citroën. My bloody heart skipped a beat as he shot out of the car towards me. Suddenly frightened, I didn't know whether to get in the cab or stay where I was. What the fuck was he doing here? He was meant to be at work!

"Helen! You're ba...ck!"

His eyes left me and fixed instead on the cab driver who stood with one hand gripping the handle, ready to heave the first heavy case into the boot. I watched in horror as the truth registered in his eyes, mouth agape, he staggered backwards a few steps.

"You're not...you're fucking leaving, aren't you?"

I couldn't answer. The words wouldn't come. I nodded,

shame seeping through my head and swamping in the pit of my stomach.

"You're a coward, Helen! You didn't have the fucking decency to be able to tell me. No! I came back to collect some paperwork, for God's sake…to find you getting ready to fuck off to…wherever you're fucking off to…"

He paused, seemed to be thinking for a second, then,

"…or is it…who you're fucking off to be with, Helen? I bet that's it."

The driver looked from one to the other of us and looked at his watch, clearly agitated. His mouth started moving, hurling sentence after sentence of rapidly spoken French, which I couldn't translate fast enough, but by the look of his steadily building anger, it was directed at me in particular. I got the picture. He had other fares waiting and was not at all happy to be kept waiting. Desperate as I was to get away, I didn't want him to drive off leaving me stranded with André and my heavy suitcases, which still sat on the pavement. I looked at André and appealed to his better nature, hoping to hell he wasn't planning on keeping me for half an hour, wanting an inquest into what went wrong.

"André, get him to wait…please!" I begged.

I fished my purse out of my shoulder bag and quickly snatched 100 euros and thrust it into the driver's hand. André did as I asked and as the driver seemed appeased, I gestured for him to carry on loading the cases into the car.

"Why, Helen? Answer me that!"

I searched my mind for the words, thinking of a way out…to soften the blow…but they didn't surface.

"Because I…I didn't want to see the hurt in your eyes. I know! I know hurt, it's been a best friend throughout my life, André. It's accompanied me everywhere. I have loved you though…but as a friend. I'm sorry! The rest didn't follow suit as I expected it to. It would have been wrong of me…it was wrong of me to get involved and let it continue."

Then I suddenly remembered his accusation as I stepped into the cab.

"I'm going back to England; back to my career in accountancy. That is all! There is no-one else in my life. I've not cheated on you, André."

I moved to pull the car door closed and had to snatch my arm quickly back into the car. André slammed the door shut with a resounding thud and turned on his heel, shoulders slumped. I turned my face away from the window, shedding a silent tear. I didn't dare look back as the driver pulled away from the kerb. I'd seen enough…I felt like the biggest dollop of shit ever. It would be a long time before I could ever get the image of his face out of my mind.

I hadn't even booked a flight, but I was prepared to sit around at Charles de Gaulle until a seat became available. It wasn't too long before a staff member of British Airways walked urgently across to where I was sitting.

"Miss Rushforth? We've just had a last minute cancellation on the next flight, business class. It leaves in twenty five minutes. Could you come over to the desk now, please, if you wish to take the seat? Check-in is about to close as they have just commenced boarding."

By the time my bags had been checked in and my credit card charged with the cost of the flight plus the great chunk of excess baggage fee, I really had to fly. Fortunately, with most of the scheduled flights boarding or shortly due to take off, passport control was quiet and my hand luggage was screened successfully. I ran the last four hundred yards or so to the gate. They were waiting only for me. Everyone was already seated when I boarded the plane…and all eyes were on me, all curious to see who had been the guilty party causing the five minute delay to the expected flight time.

CHAPTER 17

F or the last four days, I'd been in Paris on business
for the company I work for. It was a punishing sched-
ule; meeting after boring meeting, seminars, audio visual presenta-
tions, lunches involving a far from sensible intake of wine, early
rising and less than five hours sleep each night. Along with fellow
employees from our overseas branches, I did the essential sight-
seeing after finishing each day's business itinerary. Our nights had
been a constant round of pubs and clubs, stumbling back to our
hotel between one thirty and two in the morning. The daily process
was repeated from seven each morning, regardless of the thick
heads, nausea and hangovers from Hell.

I was relieved when my cab pulled away from the hotel. In a
few hours I'd be back in London, then home to bed. I needed to sleep
away the weekend in my own bed. No more booze. I already had
my monthly quota in the last few days. No more buying short after
short for the lone females perched on barstools, in the hope that it
would get me laid. Back to eating just one sensible portion of one
course, instead of the three courses that left us all feeling bloated,
stinking of garlic and farting like troopers, letting rip the rancid
odours that had the capability to empty a pub.

I arrived at the airport in plenty of time and, unlike me, I couldn't be arsed with having a beer, browsing the duty-free or roaming around. All I wanted to do was check in, get through passport control, then hopefully, find a quiet place to sit and nod off until the flight announcement system requested the passengers of my British Airways flight proceed to the appropriate gate number. Once at the gate, I plonked my backside again for the normal half hour wait until boarding, maybe forty winks would be in order if I found another opportunity.

The time dragged and lethargic as I was feeling, I hadn't been able to catch even the shortest of catnaps. People were bumbling around me, throwing their carry ons into vacant seats and wandering off expecting me to keep watch over their belongings, despite the constant warnings about unattended baggage, while they went off to buy up all the bargains the duty-free shops had on offer. Toddlers exercised their lungs in protest at being shackled forever into their pushchairs, drunks (even at ten in the morning) staggered around asking directions for the umpteenth time to the 'smoking area'. I sat and unwittingly become hypnotised by the 'departures' screen, as the flights out rolled on and jumped up the screen until at last it was there... my gate number appeared. We started boarding almost immediately on arriving at the gate, which was a plus. I could stow my rucksack, take my seat, and not have to move again until we landed at Heathrow.

Before the managing director's P.A. booked the flights, I sent her an email asking if she could try for a seat with extra legroom (economy class, the norm for a mere departmental manager). She did her best, for which I was grateful, the front row of economy, the only downside being that it was an aisle seat. I sat, fingers crossed, fervently hoping that the person who'd booked the window seat wouldn't show. It seemed that luck was maybe on my side...

...but, surely, most of the passengers were on board now. Club Europe passengers (probably being served champers now behind the black curtain) had boarded first, along with parents and children

and the wheelchair bound. I was puzzled as to why the doors were not yet closed. A blonde-haired stewardess picked up the wall-mounted phone and spoke briefly before hanging up. Looking towards the back of the plane, she held up one finger, indicating to her colleagues that one passenger was still to board.

Fuck! No doubt it would be my absent neighbour, which would totally scupper my chance of moving over to the window seat. Great! I hoped it wouldn't be some boring old fart with verbal diarrhoea, wanting to brag about every holiday destination they'd ever been to. Or worse still it could be an aviophobe, hanging onto their paper sick bag and gripping the arm of the seat for grim death. Feigning sleep seemed to be my best option.

As we waited, my eyes started to feel heavy and were ready to close when a movement caught my eye. The stewardess backed away from the door giving a cheery 'good morning' followed by 'can I see your boarding pass please?' Eager, or rather, curious, to see who would be my dreaded travelling companion I craned my neck to get a better view of the latecomer. I gaped in astonishment to see Helen...Helen...I racked my brain but I couldn't even remember her bloody surname. Whatever her surname, she gave the stewardess an apologetic smile, mouthing 'sorry', I assume for having held up the flight for two or three minutes. Fuck! What the...how the hell would she feel when she saw me sat there? Utter panic moved in on me. I had no wish to make eye contact if she started to approach. Looking down to the vacant seat on my right, I grabbed the paperback and magazine I placed there a few minutes ago. Then I had a much better idea. I glanced back down the aisle, scanning all the rows on both sides, looking for another vacant seat. I spotted not one, but a pair of adjacent seats, four or five rows back on the left hand side. I had to make my move pretty sharp, before the doors closed and the cabin crew started with the safety spiel. Swinging back round to gather the rest of my belongings, I chanced a look...to see her long, black-stocking clad legs and tiny, firm arse step through into first class and the stewardess pulled on the curtain, keeping the privileged from the eyes of us mere 'economy class'.

Heart still pounding from the shock of seeing the bitch, I couldn't wait to get off the ground. In spite my earlier silent rant about the dedicated and desperate alcohol dependants, I couldn't wait for the arrival of a tasty trolley dolly offering teas and coffees, but better still, spirits. I needed a Jack Daniels. I knew sleep would be impossible once I'd seen her.

I wondered what the hell she'd been doing in Paris. Perhaps she had also been there for business reasons. I imagined she would have stayed in a hotel more luxurious than that booked by my employer. I closed my eyes as the pilot accelerated down the runway. Although I'm not fearful of flying, I dreaded that transition from when the buildings flashed past so quick to the illusion that you're almost stationery as the plane starts its ascent; as if the speed has gone. It was too weird a sensation for my liking.

I got my Jack Daniels ten minutes after take-off; it seared my throat but soon coursed through my body and I welcomed the warm, calming effect. The trolley dolly was pleasing on the eye too. Her wedding ring indicated she was off-limits, but she appreciated the attention as I shamelessly flirted with her. She wore far too much make-up though. 'Natural' was a word that didn't exist in the vocabulary of female cabin crew; unlike Helen. She was a natural beauty and on the occasions we came into contact, her make-up was always subtle; she was perfect. A bitch, but a perfectly sexy and beautiful bitch!

I tried to get comfortable after finishing my drink, but couldn't find a decent position for my neck. Eventually I settled, but thoughts of Helen plagued me. She was looking more stunning these days. Out of all the women I've had over the years, Helen provided the best sex I ever experienced in my life. She certainly knew how to fuck. My mind ran away with me, along the road of filth and soaring heat that was Helen. I hated the bitch. I jolted back to the present, semi-hard and sweating profusely, despite the chill of the *air-conditioned cabin. A seat belt announcement came on. We would soon be approaching Heathrow; ten minutes to landing.*

As we taxied towards the terminal building, a queue in the aisle quickly formed. The snapping of people unfastening seatbelts started the second the wheels touched down on the runway, regardless of the warnings from the cabin crew and the lights that remained on. The overhead storage compartments were being opened, and bags were dragged down over the heads of the more patient travellers who remained seated, sensibly heeding the warnings.

As 'first class' were disembarking first, I tried to catch another glimpse of her. But with the others crammed like sardines up to the point where the stewardess held them back, my view of her was blocked. She was very tall and I swore she was one of the first to leave. Suddenly, my mind was made up. I would approach her at baggage reclaim. I wanted to see if she would come to some arrangement with me. I wanted to fuck her again. I really needed to get my hands on the bitch and...I was up for the challenge.

With everybody pushing forward in their desperation to be first in the queue at immigration (it would serve them right if their case was last out onto the carousel) I was second to last off the plane. My eyes scanned the queue as we waited; passports in hand, like an obedient herd of sheep, but I couldn't see her waiting in line. Once clear, I rushed to baggage reclaim, finding a vantage point from where I could see those who entered and those dragging their wheels towards Customs. I waited patiently, every now and again checking on my case, which completed its circuit of the carousel for the umpteenth time. She didn't show. I crossed my fingers and tried to look nonchalant as I strode through customs, willing the officers to select anybody but me for their rubber-gloved delve through yet another case full of dirty washing and souvenirs.

Outside in the London sunshine, I struggled with my suitcase through the little groups that gathered both sides of the main door, greedily drawing on their first cigarette for the last three or four hours...the long-haulers even more so. They were in seventh heaven, cigarettes in mouths, lighting up, desperate for the nicotine fix they'd been denied.

I looked towards the taxi ranks; no sign of her there. She wasn't even waiting at any of the pick-up points, the courtesy bus stops. But with my delay in getting off the plane and the time I wasted in baggage reclaim, she had a good head start. She could have been half-way home (wherever home was) by that point. Fuck it. I resolved to track the bitch down, but how I was going manage that I didn't have a fucking clue.

I went straight home to bed. I whispered my last words before I drifted off.

"Beware, Helen...I'm coming to get you!"

CHAPTER 18

*W*hile I was sat around waiting for a seat on a flight bound for Heathrow, I sent a text to Simon letting him know of my decision to return to England and that it was imminent.

Hi, Sat at CDG waiting for the next available seat on a flight back to H/Row. Had to get out of here, couldn't wait 2 wks. Going to book a hotel when I get there. H x

It took only ten or fifteen minutes for a return text from him.

Hi back,

On landing, call my friend, Harry. Will text you his number in a min. He lives 2 mins from H/Row. He's a friend, Harry. Drives me sometimes. Forewarned him. He'll be there for when you get through customs. No hotel needed. The flat is free now. He won't be back. Harry will take you there.

See you soon. SS the LL x

What the hell? I stared at the last part, SS the LL? There was a little bit of a delayed reaction before the light flickered to life in my head, but eventually I got there. With too many passengers milling about, I had to hold my hand over my mouth to prevent a guffaw escaping as I recalled the mad moment of name-calling we had. With the serious shit that Simon dealt with on a daily basis, I was shocked to realise that some things at least, implanted themselves firmly in his grey cells. It was rare that any humour surfaced, but at least it proved that a sense of humour was present within him.

Three hours later as my plane taxied towards the terminal building, I switched on my phone and made the call to Harry, who confirmed he'd be there outside, to meet me.

I entered the large arrival hall without so much as a hint who to look for. Simon hadn't given any thought to mention what this guy looked like. I searched the faces of all the drivers and guides holding their boards up with passenger names on. I couldn't see any of them bearing a board with my name scrawled across it so I presumed that Harry would be outside with his car. I started to head for the exit, and a giant pair of hands appeared on the handle of my trolley and pulled it out of my grip. I turned to my right to see who the hands belonged to; an oversized bear-like guy in his fifties with a shaven head and earrings in both ears. He glowered, but not in an unkindly way.

"We need to 'urry, Miss Rushforth. I'm 'Arry, by the way, and I'm parked illegally right outside the main door there," he nodded towards it, "with my engine running. Let's do this."

For an older, large guy he took off like a bloody greyhound and I was running to keep pace with him. Once outside, he tugged on my sleeve to get me to follow him to a Toyota Rav 4, which sure enough straddled the kerbside, engine ticking over like he said.

"Get in the car, I'll deal with these." He barked, looking around us worriedly.

He flung open the boot of his car and started throwing my heavy cases in. I stood open-mouthed at the ease with which he hauled them off the trolley and launched them into the boot. He noticed my amazement.

"Piece of piss with my muscles, lady! Now, GET IN THE FUCKING CAR! We've gotta go!"

By the time I yanked open the rear door and sat down, he was fastening his seatbelt with one hand and releasing the handbrake with the other. I looked out of the window, scanning the area as we pulled away, mainly to see if anybody in authority spotted us. I couldn't see anyone in pursuit, but the trolley I'd used was left abandoned by him where the boot of the car had just been.

Once en-route, he didn't speak for some time until he made a stop (again, parking illegally and on a corner of all places) to call into a pizza place.

"Do you want anything getting, Miss Rushforth? They do an excellent pepperoni in here…but then I suspect you're an 'am and pineapple type of person?"

"No thank you, Harry. I'm not hungry…but you're right about the ham and pineapple."

He gave me a strange look…a look that gave the impression he thought I was the strange one. Hesitating as if he wanted to say something else, he suddenly thought better of it.

"Alright, I'll be two minutes."

The deafening slam with which he shut the car door almost scared the crap out of me; even though I expected it, my heart leapt into my throat.

The two minutes he promised somehow dragged towards fifteen before he emerged from the place with his pizza box already wide open in one hand, his other stuffing a portion of said pizza into his mouth as if he hadn't tasted food in months. I was eager to be on the move and get to the flat, worn out with all my recent comings and goings. All the while he'd been waiting for his pizza I sat fretting about how

André was coping after what I just did to him. Another worry I had was whether someone was going to come along and tackle me about the car being abandoned in the carefree manner which Harry seemed accustomed to doing. I couldn't resist when he finally got back in the driving seat.

"You were ages. We're illegally parked and I…"

"I'm back now. We're going. Nobody's said anything to you, 'ave they?"

"No, but…"

He obviously had enough of the conversation. He ignored me and started the engine, pizza box sat in his lap.

We pulled up half way down Chancery Lane some twelve minutes later. Harry hauled both suitcases up to the first floor landing where he deposited them outside a door marked 1c. His hand fumbled in his pocket for keys…and found them. I stood back as he opened the door and pushed both suitcases into the hall with his feet. He dangled the little set of keys in the air and dropped them into my open palm.

"Thank you, Harry. You've been so kind."

He smiled back at me, revealing a couple of gold upper teeth to his right side.

"No problem, Miss Rushforth. 'Ope you get settled in okay."

He was heading to the staircase and I shouted after him.

"Wait. Don't I owe you some money?"

Looking like the cat that licked the cream off the trifle, he smirked rather too knowingly.

"No, Miss. Your…erm…friend…Simon…took care of expenses."

I can't say I was too surprised by that revelation.

"Oh…I…" I stammered.

Then, grinning like a total moron, he came out with his parting shot. "I expect…'e'll be dropping in on you soon enough. 'Is office is just around the corner."

It took a few seconds for me to recover from what Harry was insinuating. I was speechless. I wondered if he was implying something...or had Simon hinted to him what there was between us? No, surely Simon would have kept quiet. He was the one who had so much to lose. Realising that Harry made a swift exit (whilst taking advantage of the looks of shock and horror that must have been plastered all over my face) I went in to explore my temporary home.

CHAPTER 19

I only just closed and locked the door behind me when I heard Simon's voice booming out my name. I didn't even flinch. If I'm honest with myself I was half expecting it.

"Helen! At last! I've been waiting ages. Come here. This hard-on of mine is not going away of its own accord."

To hear a voice boom like it did from a supposedly empty flat should, by rights, have made me jump out of my skin. Due to the fact that Simon organised both the flat and my transport from Heathrow, it didn't exactly come as a surprise to realise he would be there to form his one-man-welcome-party. I laughed before I even entered the lounge.

"So…you're here? Why doesn't that surprise me?"

I pushed open the lounge door to find him sprawled over one of the black armchairs, head propped on a cushion, his legs dangling over one arm. He even had the television on, though the volume was muted. Looking smug, he replied cockily,

"Because you're incredibly hot…which means I can't get enough of your delectable body, my little nymph. I also thought you might like to use my body too. I haven't got long though. I've somewhere else I'm meant to be right now."

I knew it wouldn't be the answer he was expecting, but what the hell.

"Too right I want to use your body. There are two heavy suitcases in the hallway that need to be in a bedroom. How many are there...bedrooms?"

Clearing his throat, he formed a childlike pout with his lips.

"Oh! That wasn't the use that I had in mind."

Since he didn't reply to my query about bedrooms, I walked around the furniture and opened both doors off the lounge. One door opened to reveal a recently fitted, space-age kitchen. All white gloss doors and black granite work-tops, not unlike my kitchen in Elgin Mews. I loved it. The second door led to a small inner hall, with three doors off; the bathroom and two bedrooms. I was thrilled with the place and, coupled with my delight to be back in London, I had a sudden attack of excited butterflies and breathlessness.

I stood in the doorway of the larger of the two bedrooms which appealed to me the most, and shouted out to Simon,

"I'll have the cases in here please, Simon."

He appeared almost instantly, dragging the largest of my suitcases behind him.

"Ah, I thought this would be the bedroom you'd choose, and I was right. It's more...you."

"Sorry, Simon, I'm making use of you while you're here. As for raunchy, dirty sex, do you mind if we leave it for today? I've hardly had a wink the last few nights and I'm ready to sleep for England."

He hauled the suitcase onto the bed.

"I assume that's where you'll want it if you're going to be unpacking everything, madam?"

My mind raced ahead. The flat was ideally situated for

my base for the next few weeks...I noticed that Simon appeared to be waiting for me to say something, suddenly I remembered...

"Oh. Yes, thank you."

Unable to stop myself, I started rambling.

"I have a couple of weeks before I start work. I'll do all my jobs this week and then rest up for the second one. I need to buy furniture and curtains for my cottage. I've got some of my belongings in storage as well. I'll have to arrange for that to be delivered when I get a completion date. I could also do with a couple of new suits for the office. I'll need a new car as well. I'm going to..."

He stifled a fake yawn as I reeled off all I had to do, and then butted in.

"Excuses, excuses, Helen! Why didn't you just come out with it and tell me truthfully, that you don't fancy a fuck today? I'm a grown man. I can cope with rejection you know."

He smirked and once I'd done my damnedest to convince him that it wasn't a ploy to get out of shagging, he guffawed, big belly laughs. I roared at him.

"YOU BASTARD!"

He walked away, his laughter continuing until he returned from the hall with my last suitcase.

"Well, since there is nothing more exciting on offer than either helping or watching you settle in here, I'll be on my way. I shouldn't really be here anyway. I've got several bundles of case notes to read through."

Turning crimson, I felt guilty, but hot dirty sex was the furthest thing from my mind for a change.

"Give me a couple of nights to get rested and more settled, Simon. Then I'm all yours. I'll be more than ready for you, I swear."

His smile suddenly vanished, and he was back to looking serious as he disappeared into the bedroom with the case.

"I was only joking, Helen...about the sex. I didn't come round here with fucking on my mind, honestly. Although...I wouldn't have said no had it been on offer. I just wondered if there was anything more you needed me to help you with."

"You have been extremely kind to me, Simon. I can't thank you enough for everything you've done, but honestly, I'm fine. I'm just going to order a takeaway and then once I've had food, I'll crash for the night. I'll need to get some food in tomorrow."

He gave me a big bear hug and I rested my chin on his shoulder for a minute or two. I couldn't imagine my life without him now. I thought back to the first time we met. Never could I have imagined having the type of relationship with him that we now had. I moved my mouth to his and kissed him passionately. He was the first to break away. We said our goodbyes and he left. Strangely enough, I didn't feel any sense of loneliness after he'd gone.

I hardly had time to breathe in my first week back. By the time the first two or three days were over I was thrilled with everything I managed to achieve. I purchased an ex-demo Mercedes, sixty three miles on the clock, and a few thousand cheaper than if I'd ordered brand spanking new. Accompanied by the estate agent and an interior designer I went to visit the cottage so the designer could take window measurements. The curtains wouldn't be done in time for my move, but luckily, the owners were leaving most of their curtains anyway. I ordered some new furniture and purchased a few items of clothes for work. I was shattered but happily looking forward to my week of rest.

Simon visited me at the flat late one afternoon and although he hadn't stayed the night, we indulged in one of our wild sessions of sex and debauchery. I bubbled with excitement when I told him about my new car and his face clouded over with worry.

"Helen, you've got to be very careful when dealing with car salesmen. How do you know you've got a good deal? You should have come to me. I know people who would have sorted you out a decent car and more than likely at a lot less than you've paid."

"Simon, will you stop it please? You can't sort my life out for me. Believe it or not, I'm a big girl and very independent, I might add."

He stroked my hair as we lay facing each other with our heads on the pillows.

"No, you're not big. You're perfect, sweetie. Anyway where is the car? I'd like to take a look." I sighed with frustration at his over-protectiveness.

"You can't see it. It's still at the showroom and they are keeping it there for me until I move into Elgin Mews. There's no point having it while I'm here. It would cost me a fortune in parking."

With a grunt, he agreed that it had been a sensible move on my part. He was with me no longer than three hours and by seven he returned home to his wife.

Early on in my second week, I received a call from my solicitors. The vendor's solicitors had been in touch saying that they were hoping for a completion date in about ten days. For me, it meant that, barring any problems, I should have been able to move in on the Saturday after my first full week of work. I was overjoyed. Nearer the time I would be able to organise delivery of my furniture which, fortunately, was all coming from the same store. I would also need to arrange to get delivery of my belongings… personal things that I put into storage before I left for France. I couldn't resist sending a text to Simon, passing on my good news.

CHAPTER 20

he voice at the other end of the phone sounded very young but nevertheless, professional.

"Good morning. Hill, Young and Co, how may I help you?"

"Good morning, could I speak to Helen please?"

I asked in a confident and business like voice, but screwed my face up, gritting my teeth at the same time in mock disappointment as I waited for the reply, which would bear the expected bad news. I didn't have to wait long.

"Sorry, sir, but perhaps you have dialled an incorrect number? We don't have anybody here called Helen."

She genuinely sounded sorry, I was impressed.

"Oh... are you a firm of accountants? Helen is an accountant."

I offered, even though I knew it to be a pointless remark.

"May I suggest that you have the wrong practice, sir?"

She laughed politely.

"There are plenty of us around to try."

"Look, I am really sorry to have troubled you at all. My memory is shocking. I could set off right now and drive straight to Helen's office, she does my accounts each year, but trying to remember what the business is...and I don't have the phone number in my address book."

I lied and she giggled again.

"That's no problem, Mr... er, I hope you manage to track her down!"

"Thank you...thank you very much."

"Have a good day, sir. Goodbye."

She hung up. I managed to replace the receiver without slamming it down in my annoyance. 'Patience, buddy!' I remonstrated with myself, first smacking my forehead and then pulling my hair in frustration.

It was only the first call, and I had a feeling that my search was going to prove to be like looking for a diamond lost on a beach. I had (it seemed) hundreds of accountants phone numbers left to try and I would keep going until I tracked her down. I had to! The main problem I faced was that I couldn't remember Helen's surname, even though I was unable to forget anything else about her. It was months since I last saw her. Giving myself a bollocking for allowing my mind to start wandering, my eyes drifted up and down the list of phone numbers looking for a likely choice to call from so many. I decided not work through the list in order as, knowing my luck, it would probably be the fucking last number I tried. Random, then! I closed my eyes and raised my pen high in front of me and stabbed down at the list. Opening my eyes, I glanced at the ballpoint squiggle next to... Arnold Crowley Associates and, sighing, I reached for the phone once more.

"Arnold Crowley Associates, Good morning!" Came the throaty voice I associated with someone who smoked forty a day.

"Good morning. Would it be possible to speak with...um...Helen, I think her name is?"

"Well, you could if she worked here. Sorry, I think you've been given the wrong number, sir. We don't have a Helen." she croaked.

I hadn't really expected there to be, but I still shook my head in desperation. A little too snappily I managed,

"Oh, shit. Sorry. I'm sorry to have troubled you. Goodbye!"

Four calls, one cappuccino, and a whole packet of Jaffa Cakes later I was still as far away as ever from tracking her down and feeling totally depressed. Abandoning my desk, I grabbed the cup and saucer and empty biscuit packet and slouched through to the kitchen. My couple of days off from work would be over tomorrow (Friday) and I really hoped to find her before the weekend. The accountancy firms would all be closed on Saturday and Sunday. Once I was back to work on Monday, the opportunities for making personal calls would be few and far between. I could, of course, use my cell phone at lunchtimes, but that wasn't very practical. I usually had one or two colleagues with me when I went out for lunch each day and there was no way I wanted them to have the slightest hint of what I was up to.

Having washed up my few breakfast pots, mid-day, I sat down to watch a little daytime TV until I was ready to go to the gym. I was meeting my friend, Taylor, at two o'clock and was looking forward to our catch-up, a work out, and a pint or two. Taylor was a doctor at the National Hospital for Neurology and Neurosurgery. The only reason we'd been able to organise a trip to the gym was because he was also taking some long overdue annual leave. Grabbing the remote, I flopped onto the sofa and switched on the telly. Flicking through the channels, I settled for an old documentary, 'Big Cat Diary', but even my love of lions, cheetahs and leopards could not hold my attention for more than five or ten minutes. Helen was still well and truly on my mind and I was becoming obsessed with my need to find her.

"Bollocks," I shouted out to no-one in particular. "One last call for today!"

I shot up from the sofa so fast that Bella, my Persian, almost flew through the air with the sudden fright. She ran off to take cover in my bedroom.

"SORRY, BELLA! I didn't mean to scare you like that!" My

voice was too loud for her though, and I saw her back end scuttle away under my bed.

Back at my desk, I picked up a black marker pen, looked up at the ceiling and performed yet another downward thrust at the list of accountants. A large black splodge tarnished the letter 'P' of K.M.T.P, one of the larger accountancy practices in the London area. Hmmm, somehow I was doubtful, but I picked up the phone regardless. With my hand shaking as I tapped out the number on the keypad, I listened carefully as it started to ring out, and I crossed two fingers of my left hand.

"Good morning, K.M.T.P?"

"Ah, could I speak to Helen, please?" I cringed inwardly as I uttered the words, "Helen...erm...I can't remember her last name..."

"Oh, you must mean Helen Hartman? Hold the line please." As a swift afterthought on her part, she added, "Who shall I say is calling?"

I spluttered guiltily as I said the first name that jumped into my head, "Erm, Peter...Peter Newton."

Still wide-eyed in self-disgust, I chided myself. Just what the hell are you doing? What the fuck are you planning to say to her? I felt panic rise in my stomach as Beethoven's 'Moonlight Sonata' tunefully found its way down the line. So much for the supposed soothing abilities of classical music; well, unless you were annoyed as fuck, as I was.

"Good morning, Mr Newton." I jumped, startled to hear a voice breaking into my moments of turmoil. "How is it that I can help you today?"

I hesitated, not knowing what to say. The voice did not belong to Helen...at least, not the Helen that I was searching for. The words were rehearsed, and spoken by...maybe a young trainee, fresh from college. The accent was from somewhere up north. I quickly hung up.

"Fuck it, FUCK IT!" I rapped the desk with my fist in anger. "Helen, where the FUCK do you work?"

A quick shower and change of clothes later, I headed out to meet up at the gym with Taylor. I was relying on it to chill me out; an intense work-out in which I could vent my frustrations on the weight equipment and most definitely the punch-bag.

CHAPTER 21

*S*leeping *through my alarm clock, and getting up an hour and fifteen minutes later than I planned, the time soon reached nine thirty. I'd wasted half an hour. My last day's leave, Friday morning, and my last chance to do what I needed to do. Standing in front of the kitchen sink, I quickly shovelled cereal into my mouth, ready to add my bowl to the previous night's dishes and eager to get back to my detective work once more. I was on a mission.*

Slurping the remainder of the milk straight from the bowl, instead of using the spoon, I laughed out loud, rather rebellious, glad that my mother...or anyone else, for that matter, couldn't see me. My mother's wrath, particularly where abominable table-manners were concerned, wasn't for the faint of heart. Placing the bowl and spoon directly into the sink, I clumsily snatched up my second cup of coffee of the morning, which I brewed five minutes earlier and slopped it messily onto the kitchen floor. Watching the contents of the cup and holding it more carefully so as not to repeat my clumsiness on the lounge carpet, I made a beeline for the desk.

I decided that I would work my way through the list from the beginning this time, instead of picking randomly at them with a pen. I already crossed out the first few calls I made yesterday. Waiting for the last shreds of sleep to release me from their grasp, I sipped at my coffee, my attention being sought by a young robin. He was staring in at me, chirping from the tree a few yards away from my living room window. I muttered quietly at him,

"At least you don't have my problems to contend with, you cheeky little bugger!"

As if totally understanding the challenge that lay ahead of me, he nodded his head in my direction a couple of times then flew off, probably in search of some additional breakfast delicacy, fresh from beneath the tiny square of lawn.

With the reason for my distraction gone, I spoke out loud to myself,

"Right, get focused you idiot, no more talking to damned dickie birds who know Jack shit."

Heeding my self-bollocking, I scanned my seemingly infinite list, determined to get cracking. Sighing heavily, I picked up the handset and tapped in the first un-ticked number on the list.

Six calls later and still I hadn't managed to discover which fucking firm of accountants Helen worked for; that's if in fact, she was still involved with accountancy at all. I was sighing every few seconds and it did cross my mind that I might never find her. I was just about to replace the handset in the charger when the phone rang in my hand. I answered rather warily in case it was somebody from the last number that I called and then hung up when it was answered at their end, as I was getting too agitated. Maybe that person had done a last number redial.

"Hello, son...you sound rather...tense. Is everything alright?"

"Oh hello Mum! Yes, I'm fine, thank you. Didn't mean to sound tense, I'm just trying to get a few jobs done since I'm back to work on Monday. I keep getting interrupted. Sorry, no offence meant... not to you, at least!"

"Well, that's reassuring, darling!" she laughed, sounding relieved.

It was over half an hour she kept me chatting. (It was actually her that was doing the chatting, not me.) Mainly it was about my father; things he hadn't done that she asked him to do, things he had done that she wasn't too happy about. I couldn't keep the smile from my face. Some things would never change, especially where Mum and Dad were concerned. The conversation shifted from my dear father to their forthcoming holiday, a month in the States. She was worried about the timing of the holiday, since my sister would hopefully have a one-week-old baby (in addition to her two-year old daughter,) by the time they were due to leave.

"Maybe I shouldn't be going," she fretted "She's going to have her hands full. I should be here to help."

I didn't know what to say to her by way of reply, so I said nothing. She was obviously still waiting for my views on the matter and the fact that I hadn't put forward any comment, brought on a new edge to her voice.

"Are you still there, darling?"

"Yes, Mum, I'm here."

"Are you okay? You're very quiet, darling. Are you depressed or something?"

More sighing on my part.

"I just didn't know what to say to you, Mum. You've had me being tense and...now, depressed. I can assure you I am neither, I swear. Just got a lot on my mind work-wise, that's all."

I needed to wrap the call up and pretty soon. Time was ticking on and I had more enquiries to make if I was to achieve my desired result before five o'clock. I was digging in the depths for an excuse to end the call, but fortunately, my mother saved the day. It saved her from being offended had I made any excuses.

"Oh, well if you're really sure you're fine, Son, I will speak to you soon. I must dash, my hairdresser will be arriving soon and I want to wash my hair quickly so that I'm ready for her. I'll say bye for now."

"Yes, okay! Bye Mu...um," But she'd already gone!

Finally, I could get back to business. Within the next fifteen minutes, half a dozen more wasted calls meant that six more phone numbers had been crossed off my list and I was feeling extremely irritable. Returning from the kitchen with a packet of crisps and a Fosters from the fridge, I decided I would go for a random number once more. After all, working the list in order hadn't been very productive. Bella grouched at me for moving her off my writing pad, voicing her displeasure at being inconveniently shifted from her latest sunny position on the desk. As I picked up the handset, I noticed she left a little clump of fur on my pad. I picked it up and, for want of any better ideas, I noted the name of the company the fur was deposited upon. I grinned.

"Are you trying to tell me something, Bella? Is that the one I should call next?"

She turned and blinked at me; fixed me with one of her disgruntled, feline glares, and haughtily stalked off to my bedroom again, flicking her tail several times in disgust.

For lack of any thoughts on which phone number to select next, I decided to dial the 'fur-clump' number, bemused by my crazy idea. The phone had barely rung once and another friendly voice greeted me.

"Hopkins Partnership. Good morning, can I help you?"

"Ah, good morning, could I please speak with Helen...erm... erm, I'm sorry I'm trying to remember her surname." I lied, once again.

Still exuding a most pleasant tone of voice, she offered,

"You must mean Mrs Paw...sorry, it's Miss Rushforth now."

Damn it all, that was it! Her maiden name. Married, she'd been Helen Pawson...and she was now Helen Rushforth again. I assumed she must have divorced or something. Wow, this was going to be so easy for me. Suddenly my depressing, big black cloud had a sparkling, silver 'hope-filled' lining.

The receptionist's voice disturbed my thoughts and I was brought back to the present.

"Sorry, Sir, but can anyone else help you? Miss Rushforth is not..."

I didn't need to, and certainly had no wish to, speak with anyone else if Helen wasn't available. I didn't even wish to speak to her, it was too soon. 'Don't be rude this time,' I chastised myself. 'No hanging up.'

"Sorry I will have to call her back some other time. I've just been summoned into a meeting. I'll say goodbye for now."

Lying was becoming second nature at the moment. I replaced the handset carefully and 'high-fived' the air, ecstatic. I gave myself an invisible pat on the back. Finally, I had almost everything I needed. I now knew the address where she worked, her phone number at work, and her full name. A little more detective work, then I should be able to find out where she lived. "GOTCHA, Helen! GOTCHA!"

CHAPTER 22

*T*ed Hopkins agreed to keep my return to work a secret from the staff. I was harbouring a few mixed emotions about seeing the girls again. Although I considered most of them to be my friends, I still couldn't help but feel nervous. I was not only ill when I last saw them all, I had been grieving as well. My O.C.D. was also at its worst after the tragic death of my parents, and the staff at The Hopkins Partnership didn't know about David. Being a multi-millionaire, they would no doubt have read about his death in the national newspapers, but wouldn't have had any inkling about my involvement with him. Even though I didn't personally tell the staff that I was leaving, they all knew that I was grieving for my parents, and that I was suffering with my mental health issues. I left the office quietly one morning, leaving Ted to break the news to them. I had been so emotionally wrung out. I wouldn't have known where to begin explaining my reasons to everyone. I knew the girls would have tried to convince me to stay and offer their help, but at that time I needed to be alone. Nobody could have helped me and what I did by running away to France, had been the best option for me.

From the flat, I walked to Chancery Lane tube station and changed trains once at Tottenham Court Road. As I stepped onto the platform at Embankment, I smiled to myself, remembering Leanne, the effervescent young trainee who took a fancy to my car. I bet she'd still be trying to recover from the shock of seeing my old Mazda parked in her parents' drive, then opening the envelope to find the registration document and keys. I'd known that she wasn't in a position to purchase a vehicle on her trainee's salary, and I needed to get rid of it. Ted hadn't mentioned in our telephone conversation, or during our meeting, whether Leanne still worked at the practice. In fact, he hadn't mentioned any one of them individually.

I pushed a few stray hairs behind my ears as I walked from the station towards the office with in-flight butterflies taking up residence in my stomach. I was feeling more than a little apprehensive and worried about what my friends would think of me now; leaving all those months ago without saying so much as a goodbye, not confiding in them when, since my early days in practice, we had been so close. I could feel my heart racing and even though I wasn't rushing, I felt like I was gasping for breath, having a mini panic attack.

Breathe, Helen, breathe!

I slowed my pace to a saunter and forced myself to slow my breathing. Inhale…slow, hold it a second, exhale…slowly. I repeated these words over and over in my head as I carried out the exercise in rhythm with every step. It worked. My breathing calmed down. I turned the last corner. Holding my head high, but with shaking hands, I strode the last twenty five metres towards the office with false confidence.

Timidly peering around the door after I quietly eased it open, I saw two ladies stood with their backs to me…

Gemma, the office manager, and the temporary receptionist Ted mentioned (who was covering for Cindy, still on maternity leave). Almost in a whisper, I said, "Good Morning, ladies." Gemma's head spun round so quickly it's a wonder she hadn't done herself a permanent injury. She stood open-mouthed for what seemed like an age but was actually seconds, and then screeched at the top of her voice,

"HELEN!"

She almost leapt across the floor and flung her arms around me, still squealing

"Helen, what are…are you back…?"

And stopping mid-sentence, she darted to the glass door, which lead to the other downstairs and upstairs offices, bellowing,

"GET DOWN HERE, EVERYBODY! NOW! COME AND SEE WHO'S HERE!"

She turned back towards me once her shouts induced the frantic opening of doors throughout the office, along with footsteps in the office directly above us. She addressed the receptionist,

"Christina, can I introduce you to Helen…Helen Pawson? She's Ted's part…"

I flinched on hearing the Pawson name and quickly interrupted her,

"Gemma, I'm no longer married to…we're divorced. Would you mind telling everybody that…"

"Did I hear my name mentioned?" asked Ted calmly, as he entered the room, footsteps in the background, thundering down the stairs almost drowning out his words.

"Helen, welcome back!"

"…my name is Rushforth again?" I managed at last, but my words seemed to get lost in the excitement and commotion.

Gemma could have been watching a match at Wimbledon. Her head darted quickly between Ted and I, and back again, and again. She looked awestruck.

"You mean...you mean...you *are* back here, Helen?" she struggled. "To work, I mean?"

Unable to speak and not quite knowing what to say, I nodded slowly. She did a little jig.

"Whoop, whoop!" I laughed loudly at her enthusiasm and Ted saved me the bother of a reply,

"Yes, Gemma...and...everybody, we are fortunate enough that Helen...erm...now Miss Rushforth, has decided to...join us again. I have known for a few weeks, but decided that... you...didn't need to know until now."

There were more excited shrieks from Gillian, Janet and Leanne as they pushed forwards for their hugs and kisses. I was overwhelmed. Not having seen her along with the gang, I wondered where Nina was, but figured she was maybe taking some annual leave. I felt a cosy, warm feeling envelop me...that and more nervousness as I spotted a few new faces giving me the once over...one or two not sharing the same enthusiasm as the others!

As Gillian, Gemma, Janet and Leanne clustered around, relentlessly throwing questions at me, Ted decided it was time to get things back to business.

"Right, there will be time for your catch-up chats later perhaps, so if everybody would kindly return to their work, please?"

He turned swiftly to address the faces that were unfamiliar to me.

"Those of you who have yet to meet Helen, never fear, I will be round to introduce each of you in due course. In the meantime, Helen and I need a little chat. Could we have a pot of coffee with two cups please, Christina? Could you bring them to my office?"

It showed the respect each staff member had for Ted as

they all made their way back to their offices without further ado. I followed him through to his vast office, experiencing a lump at the back of my throat as I remembered my last visit…soon after the death of my parents. Once he closed the door behind me, he turned and swallowed me up in his arms.

"I know…I know, Helen. I can see it in your eyes. You're remembering the last time…you…" He left the words unsaid. "It's really good to see you. It was my lucky day…the day you agreed to come back, Helen."

I loved Ted so much. I could never have wished for a better boss…and these days, partner?

"No, Ted. It's me who is fortunate… that you waited for me whilst I sorted myself out. I need to work, to do something. Maybe you will have realised that I am fairly wealthy now with my parents' money…and…" I hesitated, and sighed heavily, "…other funds too. But money means nothing to me without those people that I love. Having the rich bitch life is not for me, Ted and it never could be. There's only so much shopping and holidays I could take, especially with my past… mental ailments. My mind needs… stimulation…"

Ted was quick to butt in.

"…and we will be giving you plenty of that, Helen. I will explain shortly, but there are…one or two matters that I need to make you aware of."

Oh, no, not problems I hope? Not when I've just come back, please!

I could feel a little panic set in and I held my breath. My palms felt tacky all of a sudden as I dreaded what was to come. Perhaps I made a mistake in coming back. Hoping that I was giving him the impression that I was patiently waiting for him to continue, I wished he would just hurry up and put me out of my misery.

"You might already have noticed Nina's absence, Helen? She has been very ill and hasn't been here since…about a month after you left. She…was diagnosed with throat cancer."

That fucking 'C' word again. I felt the tears threatening and I experienced a vile wrench in the pit of my stomach as I instantly thought of David. Then, just as quickly, I remembered where I was and my mind jolted back to the devastating news about Nina.

"Oh, my God, Ted. I…poor Nina, I must…"

"Her oncologist is optimistic, Helen. Nina is in remission already and at her next six month check-up, they expect her to be in the clear. It was caught in the early stages, fortunately. She has been very positive and cheerful from the off. She'll hopefully be returning to work over the next month or two. I expect it won't be long before she's calling in here when news of your return reaches her."

He gave a cheeky grin.

"Perhaps she'll join you all on the obligatory girlie night out to celebrate your return? I imagine the girls are making arrangements even as we speak."

I laughed.

"Right, Helen – staffing matters. You will have noticed some new faces already? Don't worry, I shall introduce you shortly. Christina, who I understand you have met just now, is a temporary receptionist covering Cindy's maternity leave. We also have Darren and Danielle, who are both permanent and fairly new additions. They are trainee technicians and have already been out as part of the auditing team. Now, I…"

The barely audible tap on the door brought the conversation to a halt. Ted didn't respond immediately so I called out,

"Come in."

It was Christina delivering our coffees. She hit me with a warm, infectious smile as she placed the tray on Ted's desk, uttering,

"Sorry to interrupt, folks; essential caffeine fix, as requested."

Amused, I smiled back. Ted also grinned. "Thank you, Christina."

As the door closed behind her, he added,

"She's a character, that one. I would like to keep her on after Cindy comes back. We could use her elsewhere."

Pouring coffee for us both, I became aware that Ted was watching me carefully. Knowing him as well as I do, I knew he was waiting for my reaction to his news so far. Although I planned to keep quiet to hear him out, I was a little bewildered as to why he had taken on extra staff and I was feeling more than a little worried. Where the hell was all the extra money going to come from? He held out his hand for the coffee and I looked him in the eye as he took it, but his eyes were revealing nothing. My curiosity piqued.

"Why are you being so...mysterious, Ted? So...damned... infuriating," I scolded, as he sipped at his coffee, still staring at me with a rather intense look.

"Okay, okay. I'll get to the point now," he said, holding up his hands in defeat. "We have another new member of staff and another partner...I..."

"Ted...what the...?"

I could hear the tone of my voice as it raised an octave.

"Right. Don't butt in, Helen. I have decided to cut my hours down. Semi-retirement, let's say. I need to spend more quality time with Hilary that has been lacking a bit for ages and yes, the golf is to blame. The problem is...sorry, was... that we are going to be very busy. We picked up a couple of new accounts. One in particular, is a big client; Hire It, PLC. They have come to us from K.M.T.P. Apparently their client fees almost doubled over the last two years, so, as you can imagine, they weren't particularly happy. I asked the client who was their main contact at K.M.T.P. so I called him...

offered him a good package. He is to be the main man for their account at our end…and our new partner. His name is James Mortimer. I'll introduce you shortly. There's someone else as well; you'll meet her in a minute. Come on…let's have a tour of the newbies."

And with that, he was up and opening the door before I had time to gather my thoughts.

Someone else? I wondered why he was keeping the 'someone else' under wraps for a while longer.

Following behind as he made his way up the stairs, I plucked up courage to ask the question (though I dreaded his answer) I was dying to ask since the minute I walked through the front door.

"Ted…my office..?"

"…is still your office, Helen. It's been left exactly the same. Nobody has used it since you last sat in there. You surely didn't think I would let someone come in and take over your office? Not when I was expecting you to return…be it now or five years' time?"

A sense of relief flooded over me and I exhaled slowly. It was strange coming back, but how could things ever have been the same if somebody had settled into my space?

"I'm flattered and grateful. Thank you, Ted."

"We decorated some of the unused offices on the second floor. Danielle and Darren are sharing one of them. Stuart and Kate have moved up from the first floor and Jim has taken over their office. Here we are now."

He tapped lightly on the door and, without waiting for a response he entered the room with me following in his wake. The guy looked up from his computer screen and made a move to stand up.

"Jim, sorry to interrupt…can I take this opportunity to introduce you to Helen? Helen Rushforth, Jim Mortimer."

It was the guy with the heavily-gelled, blond hair who I

spotted propping up the door frame in reception. His eyes roved up and down my body a few times, although I also noted he emanated a superior, yet bored façade.

Looking me up and down again as he did in reception half an hour earlier, he held out his hand and smiled, but not with his eyes.

"I'm pleased to meet you, Helen. Ted has been singing your praises for the past few months, as have one or two others. I'm looking forward to working with you."

I bristled immediately; my dislike of him instant. There was something mocking about the way he said, 'Ted has been singing your praises', and then again with the way he added, 'as have one or two others'. Fingers of suspicion started to tweak in my brain. He wouldn't know sincerity if it cropped up and bit him on the arse. His eyes were very dark, piercing...and cold. Returning the smile I didn't feel, I displayed my manners, nevertheless.

"Likewise, James."

He glared at me for my use of his full Christian name and I reaped some satisfaction from the fact. Yes, there was certainly something about him that made me extremely uncomfortable, and, dislike him though I did, there was something sexually attractive about him...in an arrogant sort of way.

He gave me a long lingering look and abruptly turned to Ted, ignoring me completely. I felt as if I'd been dismissed.

"Can I discuss Findlay & Gray with you this afternoon please, Ted? There are one or two aspects that we need to go through, regarding all their bank accounts."

"Sure, Jim. Just give me a buzz when you're ready." He moved to hold the door open for me. "Right, Helen, I'll take you to meet the others."

I was relieved when Ted closed the door after us. I was glad to be out of there. The guy made me feel uncomfortable;

those eyes and that thin-lipped expression. I somehow doubted I would enjoy working with him as a partner. An unsettling tinge of regret about my return was creeping up on me...along with the fact that I couldn't keep the thoughts...imagining what it would be like to be fucked by him...out of my head.

On the second floor, I was introduced to Danielle and Darren in their recently decorated office. I was impressed with their good manners and enthusiasm for their work. They met in college and, seemingly, were working well together. Danielle took in every inch of me, probably admiring my designer clothes. She was a stunner with her emerald eyes, petite nose, lustrous red locks, and a winning smile. Instinctively, I knew that Darren was besotted with her. She gazed at me...he gazed at her in admiration. That was something to keep my eye on. If they became involved, they wouldn't be able to attend the same audits; it just wouldn't be professional. Perhaps she didn't see Darren in the same way, though.

Once out of Danielle and Darren's office, but before we passed Stuart and Kate's office, Ted took me aside and all but whispered,

"Observe carefully in the next one, Helen. I would value your opinion in a little while."

Without further comment, he turned and walked on ahead down the corridor, leaving me totally puzzled as to why he warned me to watch carefully, and feeling disquiet about someone I had yet to meet. He didn't trouble to knock this time. As if it was intentional, he abruptly barged into the room ahead of me and boomed in a very business-like tone,

"Linda, I would like you to meet Helen, my valued partner, who has just returned from some much needed time-out. Now that Helen is back with us, Jim will no longer be your line manager. You will report directly to Helen."

Just as James Mortimer had done, she made an attempt to smile at me, but it never managed to reach her eyes. Not making an effort to get up and shake hands, she remained seated and rather grudgingly muttered hello. I guess she was somewhere in her late fifties. Her auburn colour almost covered her wavy locks, but there was an inch of grey root growth. The make-up was sparse; her thin foundation barely covering the maze of fine thread veins on her cheeks. She was thin-lipped and her grey eyes narrowed; her dislike of me shone through without even the slightest attempt by her to hide the fact. I noticed back in reception that she looked at me as if she had a bad taste in her mouth. It surprised me to hear Ted speaking to her in an abrupt, unfriendly manner, it was not his usual style. We made our excuses and left her to the mountain of work stacked up on her desk.

Ten minutes later and, thanks again to Christina, we sat enjoying our second cup of coffee. Just as I wondered how long it would take him to get back to the point, he spoke,

"So…Linda. Your opinion please, Helen?"

I raised my cup to my lips, sipping slowly, which gave me time to think how best to word my answer. I didn't know the woman after all. I figured it would be unfair to judge after being in her company for less than five minutes.

"Okay, do you want me to be truthful, or should I lie to you, Ted?"

He raised his eyebrows in mock surprise.

"That bad, huh?"

"I shouldn't judge on first impressions, but I can't say I'm greatly enamoured. I found her lacking in manners. She wasn't impressed with being told that I'm to be her line manager. Obviously, I can't comment on her work. Time will tell, I suppose."

"I have no complaints about her work, Helen. My personal thoughts are that she is not going to be with us very long. The choice will not be hers to make. She's only been here a matter of weeks and already she has attempted to cause some dissension amongst the other girls."

I was scandalised by that knowledge and opened my mouth to start protesting, but it was needless.

"It's all sorted now, but a word of warning, she can make out like she's your best friend and she will turn the knife in your back at the same time. The girls have now seen the situation for what it is… fortunately, I might add. No harm was done in the end, but let's just say that Linda doesn't have any friends here…except Jim, maybe. And I'm not even a hundred percent sure of that anymore."

Somehow, I wasn't at all shocked by that revelation; that James and Linda were, or had been friends.

Our conversation ended shortly afterwards. Finally, I was able to settle myself in my office and start picking up from where I left off. So I'd been back in the office less than two hours and I already made two enemies. Whilst I familiarised myself with some of the client folders on my desk and prioritised my workload, my thoughts kept straying to Linda-what-ever-her-name was and James Mortimer, and the hostility that I felt so strongly from both of them.

Welcome back, Helen!

CHAPTER 23

J 'm fucking furious! It's the second time it's happened. Two weeks in a row I left work early to wait in Villiers Street, just a few yards from where Helen's office is situated. I kept watch from a safe distance and planned to follow her. The trouble was I couldn't follow someone home from work if they weren't at bloody work, could I? Last week it was six o'clock when the last couple of lights went out in the offices, but she hadn't appeared. This week, everyone was gone by five forty five; the whole building was in darkness when I arrived, a little later than when I made the previous visit. She may not even have been at work. Either that or she left early. There were other possibilities, of course; she might have been out of the office to meet a client. Being a qualified accountant, I couldn't imagine she would be going out on audits; that job was, more often than not, left to the accounting technicians. She could even be taking some annual leave; it could be that, or she may be ill. I didn't like to think of her being ill. But then I was assuming a lot; thinking that perhaps she hadn't anybody to care for her. She was an extremely attractive woman for heaven's sake and, for all I know, maybe she did have a boyfriend.

The only thing on my mind was to try and find out where she lived. I realised that the only way I would ever find that out, and whether there was a man in tow, was if I followed her home from work at some point. I already tried a few different requests through directory enquiries for the Greater London area, but as I only had her name and no address to go on, I'd more or less been told to bugger off. My thoughts though, were that she must have opted to be ex-directory.

There was still so much that I didn't know. I didn't know whether she drove in to work and if that was the case, where would be most likely for her to park her car. Maybe she commuted every day. With the nearest underground station, Embankment, being not too much of a hike from her office, that seemed the most sensible option. I certainly didn't have a clue, but I was intent on finding out.

Annoyed to have wasted my time yet again, I resolved to leave it for a couple of weeks; maybe I'd choose a different day of the week next time.

It's fortunate for me that I don't work too far away from her office. Dear Helen, so near in some ways, yet at the moment, she may as well be at the farthest end of the universe.

CHAPTER 24

*M*y house purchase didn't go ahead quite when I hoped it would, during my first week back at work, and I felt bitterly disappointed. Having been a touch too optimistic, I jumped the gun and organised for the belongings I had in storage to be delivered on the first Saturday. Once I found out from my solicitors that completion had been delayed due to the next link in the chain, I had to contact the storage company and the person delivering my belongings, to postpone everything for another week.

As it turned out it was a blessing, for me at least, and after my earlier anti-climax, I ended up feeling relieved. There was a delay of roughly six days in the shipment of my new furniture. Had the completion taken place when I hoped it would, I would have been unable to move in anyway with no bed to sleep on.

The exchange of contracts and completion finally happened at the same time; the Wednesday during my second week back at work. After the call came telling me it was all signed and sealed, I left the office for a couple of hours to go and collect the keys, *my keys*, from the vendor's estate agent. I was happier than I had felt in months when I walked out of the agent's door. I had a good feeling about the house and now that I was back working, it felt like a new beginning, a chance to start afresh. I was tempted to visit the house one night after work, but after speaking with Simon, I talked myself out of it. There wasn't really anything to be gained from doing so. What could I have hoped to achieve, except for the satisfaction of walking round each room with a dirty great smirk on my face, knowing that it was all mine? Another factor that helped keep me away was that the place was empty. I didn't want to see it devoid of furniture and possessions; looking bare. It was a home, my home, and as such should be full of my belongings; have my mark, my personality and love within its walls.

After the initial drag to the week, Saturday morning arrived faster than I thought it would. I was wide awake and raring to go. By five thirty I'd showered and had breakfast. I packed my suitcases on Friday night so the only remaining job was to give the flat a good clean and empty the fridge, which, fortunately, I hadn't kept fully stocked. Harry, thanks to Simon stepping in again, came across from where he lived near Heathrow to transfer me, the suitcases, and my box of groceries from the Chancery Lane flat to my new address in Elgin Mews. He arrived at the flat just before eight, bustling about as I expected and in a rush to get there. I was pleased that he actually managed to drive me straight to Maida Vale without the need to stop off somewhere for an all-day break-fast. As he heaved the suitcases out of his boot, he stared in amazement at my cottage.

"Lovely place you've got yourself 'ere, Miss Rushforth. You'll 'ave to show me which of the bedrooms you want these suitcases dumping in."

"I will, Harry, as soon as I get the door open. And please, will you stop calling me Miss Rushforth? I'm not the formal type. My name is Helen, as I'm sure Simon has already told you."

I felt useless, hot and bothered, and shaking with excitement as I stood at the front door. My hands trembled uncontrollably as I tried a second time and failed, to get the key in the keyhole. Harry, waiting impatiently with his rush to get back on the road, snatched them out of my hand.

"'Ere, Miss Rushforth, let me do that, or else I'll still be 'ere when your furniture comes. I don't wanna get roped in to 'elping with that as well."

He turned the key with ease, and opened the front door. Standing back and gesturing for me to enter first, he joked,

"Don't s'pose you want an old fart like me to carry you over your thresh'old, do you, Miss Rushforth?"

I howled with laughter, but stopped in my tracks for a moment, checking his expression out, unsure as to whether he was joking or somewhere akin to being serious. Frowning at my laughter, and once more, giving me the impression that he thought I was strange, he asked,

"Did I say something fucking 'ilarious or what, Miss Rushforth?"

His face was a picture. I started laughing again, regardless. He was very comical when he wasn't being exasperating, like persistently calling me Miss Rushforth when I asked him constantly to use my Christian name. Heading for the stairs, I nodded to the suitcases, which still sat on the pavement. A steady drizzle had just started to come down.

"Right, follow me then, before my cases get wet. You're in a rush to get off, remember?"

He picked up one suitcase and deposited it inside the front hallway. On his way back to retrieve the second, he grinned up at me, as I leant over the railings halfway up the stairs.

"Pity there ain't the right man 'round to do it for you, eh?"

"Wh-at?" I was baffled.

"The right man…to carry you over the thresh'old! Pity 'e ain't around, isn' it?"

I had no doubt as to who it was he was referring to. He was making insinuations about Simon and I, just as he'd done when he ferried me from the airport to the flat. Choosing to let it pass, I pointed to the bedroom that would be mine and he'd soon done the couple of journeys up the stairs with the two cases. He left a short while later, having refused my offer of a can of Diet Coke. It was the only drink I had available to offer from my meagre box of groceries.

The girls who kindly offered to help me, arrived shortly after nine in my old Mazda. Leanne, who passed her driving test while I'd been living in France, had picked up Gemma and Christina, who both lived not too far from her parents' home. They came armed with a carrier-bag full of assorted cleaning sprays and cloths, three bottles of wine, a massive arrangement of fresh flowers, and half a dozen 'New Home' cards from most of the staff at work. The previous owners must have been particularly fastidious, however. Every cupboard to every last corner was immaculately clean, so there was very little for us to do. My belongings arrived just before ten and, as we then had my television and some drinking glasses, we sat on the carpet in a corner of the lounge and started on the wine.

We lost track of time as we guzzled the wine and watched old pop videos on one of the music channels, Christina expertly singing along and mimicking some of the groups and solo artists. In the parts of the songs where she didn't know the lyrics, she kept us all amused with her own, frequently rude, versions. What with our raucous laughter and the volume of Christina's singing reaching sound-barrier level by the minute, I almost missed the rapping on the front door. Gesturing for the three of them to hush up for a minute, I rushed to open the front door, thinking it must be my furniture delivery.

"Miss Rushforth?"

The question was asked by a young, spotty guy (who barely looked old enough to drive) as he read my name from a clipboard.

"Ye-es!"

"I have a delivery for you."

He marched off to a small white van, the back doors already wide open, and returned with a fabulous basket of flowers, adorned with purple ribbons, and a bottle of champagne. There was only one person they could be from.

Without a word to the girls, but fearing that my very crimson face would give me away, I walked straight through to the kitchen, not missing their questioning looks and raised eyebrows. At that stage, we were already giddy from the amount of wine we consumed, but I felt a sinking feeling in the pit of my stomach. Questions were about to be asked and I had to try for the most miraculous 'fobbing off' that I could possibly manage.

"Ooh! I would say someone's got a boyfriend," Christina sang out drunkenly in her best operatic voice.

They all gathered around me in the kitchen, waiting for me to pull the little gift card from its envelope. I hoped they wouldn't notice my sigh of relief as I read Simon's words and luck was on my side.

"What does it say? Come on, tell us, Helen," urged Leanne. "And who are they from?"

"Okay, okay!" I smiled as I read the words out to them, thankful that Simon knew I was having help to move that day, and would have purposely kept it low key.

"It reads, 'Happy New Home, Helen. Kind regards, Simon x'. There, are you happy now?" Christina and Leanne were eager to know more, though.

"Spill, then! Who the fuck is Simon?"

All eyes were on me, as they waited for my answer to Christina's question.

"Sorry to disappoint you, ladies. Simon's just a friend. He's the lawyer, the one who prosecuted Anthony. And…I am pleased to inform you all that he is in his fifties, balding… and very happily married."

I laughed like hell, both at their faces and at my own ingenuity. They all stared at each other in disbelief…and disappointment too, but totally oblivious to my relief. I knew I'd succeeded in throwing them off course with the truth, but I left out the fact that Simon was, in fact, outrageously sexy and attractive.

My furniture arrived early afternoon, which provided a welcome distraction for Leanne in particular. The two hunky delivery drivers flirted shamelessly with her and she soaked up all their compliments and attention like a sponge, her boyfriend temporarily put to the back of her mind. Perhaps it might have had something to do with the fact that she was drunk; we all were. We had done all there was to do. My storage boxes had been emptied, all furniture was in its place, the only thing left for me to do at my leisure was unpack the clothes from the suitcases.

We ordered a pizza delivery late afternoon and after eating, started again, drinking the night away until ten thirty. I had to call for a taxi to come and collect the three of them as Leanne was incapable of driving. Before I waved them off, she slurred her reminder to me that she'd be around the following day to collect her car.

It was a strange feeling after living in flats in Chancery Lane and central Paris to be laid in bed late at night and not having to listen to the city centre traffic and constant sound of sirens as they passed by. I knew I was going to love living in my new house and that it was the beginning of the healing process!

On Sunday morning, I was sat in the kitchen, enjoying a couple of slices of toast and a coffee, when I heard knocking on the front door. Wearing nothing but my shower robe, I felt a little reluctant to see who was there, but the knocks became more urgent. I checked my appearance carefully in the hall mirror before unlocking and opening the door. I was a little bewildered to see Harry standing there, holding of all things, a pet carrier from which came a desperate, feline howling.

"Harry! What the hell…?"

Raising the basket up to eye level, he held it in front of my face, giving me a wide grin as he did so.

"This is for you, Miss Rushforth. I 'ope you like cats? I figured you could use some company, living 'ere all on your own."

I peered into the basket to get a better look. It was certainly a handsome creature, a plain grey Persian with amber eyes. It was adorable and at a guess I would have thought to be no more than a year old. I was thrilled, particularly with Harry's kind thought for me, worried about me being alone.

"Yes. I love cats, Harry. I've never had one though. My mother was always allergic to pet hairs, so we couldn't. What is she called? Where did she come from?"

He given me that look again; that 'crazy woman' look that was becoming all too familiar.

"'E's a male. 'E's come from my 'ouse. Our cat 'ad a litter last year and we never got round to getting rid of the little buggers. Figured we could do wi' one less. You'll like this 'un. 'E's a loving little fella, just what you need."

I shook my head at Harry, while giving him a big grin at the same time. His sales patter, well I had to hand it to him.

"You still haven't told me his name, Harry. I need to know his name if I'm going to keep him, don't I?"

He scowled back at me, but his expression gave him away. The corners of his mouth were twitching with the hint of a smirk.

"Puss…'e's called Puss. Answers to it anyway."

I poked my finger into the cage, eager to see the cat's reaction to me. His answer was to rub his neck against me and purr almost as loud as he'd previously been howling.

"Thank you, Harry. You are so thoughtful. I will have him and I'm going to name him Harry, after you. But I'll have to go out, I haven't got any…"

"Now, why would you wanna call 'im after me?" he asked, but he anticipated the rest of what I'd been about to say. "Got everything in the car you'll need, Miss Rushforth. Litter tray, litter, food and bowl. Just didn't wanna bring it all to your door, in case you didn't want 'im. I ain't got a bed for 'im though, so you'll 'ave to sort that yourself."

He thrust the handle of the pet carrier into my hand and rushed off to his car. When he returned with two carrier bags full of Harry's supplies, I was eager to get back inside and let my pet explore his new surroundings.

"Harry, why don't you come in? Have a cup of tea or coffee? You can see how Harry reacts to his new home."

It was there on his face again, that look. I couldn't help but wonder what it was about me that made him think I was strange.

"I've somewhere to be, Miss Rushforth, but thanks anyway. And why would I wanna see? I know exactly 'ow 'e'll react."

Seeing that he was ready to make a move, I put the cat

basket down and leaning towards Harry, I placed a kiss on his cheek. His eyes widened in horror as he flinched.

"Steady on, Miss Rushforth. All I did was bring you a cat."

Then he was gone, red-faced with embarrassment. I picked up the bag of cat supplies and took my new fur baby to explore. By mid-afternoon, we'd bonded.

CHAPTER 25

*I*mpatient, I looked at my watch yet again. It was five thirty. For fuck's sake, are normal office hours not nine to five, like mine? Just two minutes had passed since I last checked. She was more than a little late leaving the building and it occurred to me that perhaps she hadn't turned up for work at all.

As I was casually doing a reccy of the area for a place where I could keep out of sight, I noticed the lights go off in one particular office, thirty or forty yards away from her place of work, but on the opposite side of the road. Two minutes later, some guy (probably the manager) emerged from the business and into the doorway. Glancing out into the street, he thrust his hands deep into each coat pocket for a few seconds and quickly selected a key from the bunch he retrieved. In one fluid movement he inserted the key and turned it in the lock. I paused in front of the estate agents window next door under the pretext of looking at the dozens of properties on offer. As I watched him in my peripheral vision, he stepped onto the footpath, pushed his collar up around his neck and strode rapidly down the street away from me, head down and hands back inside the protection of the pockets. Without even one backwards glance from him, once I figured he was a safe distance away, I quickly abandoned my pretence at house-hunting and stepped smartly into the wide porch-way, the door now sporting the tiniest 'Hours of Business' sign that I've ever seen. In the matter of a few seconds I backed myself into the darkest corner, where the nearest street-light cast its shadow, and the waiting commenced...

Ten minutes later...

Perhaps I missed her after all. To the best of my ability I tried to recall the faces I saw leaving the office. I hadn't exactly had the best opportunity of seeing any one of them too clearly from my position. It was freezing cold and the wind was biting to say the least. One or two of the female staff left the building with hoods up, partially hiding their faces. Others had donned a new-fangled type of scarf, a versatile one that can be worn in many different ways, and these too, served to partly conceal their profiles. Two of the female staff ventured off in the opposite direction, but I wasn't concerned. I knew just by their height alone that neither one of them was her. Of the pair of them, one was wearing a short white coat and she barely reached five feet in stature, while her colleague was maybe just a couple of inches taller. They linked arms and pulled each other closer in a futile attempt to ward off the ensuing chill. Shortly after they were out of sight, two guys also left the office, a couple of minutes apart from each other. Their faces illuminated only by the dim street-light, my view wasn't perfect but one looked to be late thirties/early forties and the younger one I guessed to be an eighteen or nineteen year old trainee. I shivered again. I would give it ten minutes more. Then I would return home, eat, and hopefully it wouldn't take me too long to thaw out. My new log-burning stove was a godsend.

I could still feel the droplet of moisture poised at the end of my nose. It had been threatening to trickle down into my recently grown moustache for the last fifteen minutes. Rather reluctantly, I removed a handkerchief from the tepid warmth of my pocket and promptly dabbed at the offending clear, watery dewdrop...just as the lights were extinguished in her office building.

First out onto the street was an older man, stocky in build. Even though I was roughly thirty yards away and it was dark and dismal, I guessed that he would be retirement age, if not older. He turned his back to the street (and me) and spoke to somebody who was not yet out of the door...then suddenly, she was there beside him. I was mesmerised. I was aware of my gaping mouth and how it must make me look totally gormless. But I was in awe and...why was I holding my breath?

I assumed the guy to be her boss. The minute she joined him on the pavement he stepped forward and turned the key in the lock. She spoke to him briefly as she stood in wait... straight, tall and beautiful as ever. She wore no headwear to protect her from the cold, only a scarf draped loosely around her neck. Her beautiful, long, dark hair was twisted around and held up in place by a single clip instead of the way I always remembered; loose and flowing. No long coat covered the legs that went on forever; she wore a short, dark-coloured jacket. I didn't see one hint of a shiver from her as they chatted for a couple of minutes. He touched her arm in an affectionate manner and, finally turning away from her, started walking down the street in my direction. Fuck! I hadn't expected her to start walking in the opposite direction. It could only mean one thing; she was heading towards the tube station and not the car park. Damn it all!

I crossed the street quickly and as I stepped onto the pavement in front of the boss guy (well, he was her partner really, her senior partner) he looked up, nodded his head at me and uttered,

"Goodnight. Freezing isn't it?"

I was shocked and did a swift double-take. Such a rare occurrence, a pleasantry in London!

"Oh. Um..yes, it is rather. Goodnight." I managed to stammer.

Recovering from this unexpected, brief exchange with a total stranger, my eyes scanned the footpath ahead of me and there she was, just turning the corner where I assumed, she would then cross the road and head down into the Embankment tube station.

I upped my pace until I was striding it out. I couldn't let her out of my sight. Not only was my guilt at what I was doing starting to stress me out, I had another dilemma playing on my mind as I stumbled on the kerb in my haste; Northbound or Southbound? Northbound or southbound? Five minutes later I was stood feet away from her on the northbound platform. My last minute stab in the dark had paid off. I somehow couldn't imagine that Helen's destination would have been Lambeth or Elephant and Castle, and on this occasion I was right.

Considering it was technically still rush hour, there were not too many people about but even if she looked across, I doubt very much that she would recognize me. A bad fashion decision I know, but I was wearing one of my baseball caps with the peak pulled quite low over my eyes. My moustache, designer stubble and a long cashmere coat completed the image of...yes, a total prick! But I didn't care, as long as she didn't realise she was being followed, and by whom!

I had no idea at which station she would get off the train. I was totally winging it. I knew nothing...other than the fact that I didn't want to lose sight of her. It was so tempting...knowing that she was only twenty feet away from me... to approach her. I managed to control the urge and turned instead to face the wall. Looking up at the London Underground map, I tried to determine in which area she lived.

After a couple of minutes or so, what had been distant sounds of shouting and chanting were rapidly getting louder, coming from along the walkway towards the platform. Four youths wearing 'hoodies' staggered noisily onto the platform and propped them-selves up, backs against the wall. I broke into a nervous sweat. They were too near to her for my liking. They'd clearly been drinking or snorting coke, maybe even something more sinister. An overwhelming need to protect her swept over me. I edged my way along the wall, so that I could be close at hand should her bag suddenly get snatched or worse still, if they started to show any sign of being intimidating towards her. As it turned out my worry was needless. They were drunk, yes! But threatening? Definitely not! It seemed as if they were oblivious to both their surroundings and the few passengers waiting to board the next train.

The temperature on the platform must have been a few degrees below what it was at street level, due to the icy draughts from the gaping mouths of the tunnel. I was feeling chilled to the bone and at this stage hadn't a clue how much longer it would be before I could return to my flat. The sudden tell-tale screech of the rails alerted us all that the train was approaching. Hanging back a little, I watched as Helen carefully moved forward towards the edge of the platform. I couldn't be in her line of vision at any time. I had to be cautious in case she recognised me. Amazingly, the small gang of drunken youths had manners, as they politely waited, two on either side of the door, for Helen to board. Though I did manage to catch them eyeing her body appreciatively and exchange knowing winks, I couldn't really blame them for that. Once they boarded, they veered off to the right of the door just as she turned to search for a seat to her left.

Feeling a tad uncomfortable...and sneaky, my eyes never left her as she walked almost three parts of the way down the carriage. Ignoring a vacant seat on her left, she settled for a pair of empty seats a little further along on the right which faced forwards, and thankfully meant that she had her back to me. As I was ready to flop down on the seat that she decided against, I received a withering glare from the lady passenger already seated; a classy looking, seventy-something-year-old, who evidently had no intentions of moving her shopping bags and Louis Vuitton handbag to allow somebody to occupy the seat. I nodded my appreciation as the bags were snatched moodily away the instant my butt was about to make contact. Her stony look bore into me; a feeble effort to summon my guilt, I fancy. Choosing to ignore her, I plucked my paperback from my pocket and opened the pages to where I last left my marker. However, this was not a time when I wanted to lose myself in James Herbert's 'Nobody True', no matter how enthralling I was finding it.

I glanced towards Helen, my heart pounding in my chest. As she sat, her knee-length skirt had ridden up her thighs and she was busy straightening it, shuffling her cute butt on the seat and pulling down at the hem, covering her thighs to look more respectable. She was immaculate as always. It was difficult for me to look away from those beautiful legs, those perfectly shaped calves...nice slim ankles...those soft, warm breasts...I remembered them well. I was feeling hot and ...rapidly getting hard...uncomfortably so. I looked back down at the open book, its words blurred. The thoughts of what I wanted to do to her first and foremost in my mind; visions of what I would love her to do to me were also plaguing me. I closed my eyes, focussing on those thoughts. Despite being chilled only minutes earlier, I was suddenly feeling hot and sticky. In my mind I was pulling down her panties urgently, fucking her right there on the floor of the carriage, surrounded by curious and disgusted commuters. She threw her head back and screamed, but I was confused. Was she screaming at me to get off? Or was she screaming because she wanted more? But although I couldn't make sense of it all, I carried on fucking her regardless...until...

...Oh fuck! I stifled a groan as my hard-on gave an unexpected couple of twinges and spurted cum. Fuck! What the fuck am I doing? I looked out of the corner of my eye at my fearsome neighbour but she continued to look straight ahead. Maybe my groan hadn't been as audible to the passengers as I first thought. Perhaps...hopefully, they would think I was yawning. I'm an adult for fuck's sake. I was thirteen years old when I last shot my load in this manner. One of the sexiest girls in my class wrapped her legs around my waist during our swimming lesson. Cross with myself at my juvenile lack of control and inexperience, I snapped at her, 'Get off me, you fucking stupid bitch!' Unaware of my plight and looking stung, she bit back instantly, 'Tosser! Go fuck yourself then!' I was the colour of beetroot the rest of that day and embarrassed for weeks.

Never have I been so thankful for my long cashmere coat, not even when I'd been out on that freezing street some fifteen minutes ago. I was furious at myself and I glanced around, paranoid that other passengers' eyes were burning into me, as if knowing what just occurred. Nobody batted an eyelid at me, nobody had a clue, not even those now stood in the aisle ready for our arrival at the next stop. As the train jerked to a standstill, my travel companion gathered her bags off the floor and threw me another corker of a scowl as she stood.

"Oh I'm sorry! Sure!" I said, as I backed into the people shuffling down the aisle.

She moved off, mumbling something inaudible as I settled back into the seat. Still ready to burst a blood vessel at my stupidity, I thrust my novel back into the depth of my coat pocket. Whilst my hand was in there, I took the opportunity, through the lining, to clutch at the front of my trousers and boxers to try and re-adjust myself, although there was nothing I could do about the swamp of stickiness.

Feeling a little less uncomfortable, as the train doors closed with a hiss, I glanced across towards Helen...or more appropriately, Helen's now vacant seat. Fuck it! Whipping my head around quickly, I was just in time to see the back of her disappear into the tunnel towards the escalators. Shit! I didn't even know where we were. The second before the train entered the blackness again, I got my answer as I caught sight of the sign displayed on the platform wall; Maida Vale. How could I ever have imagined anywhere but?

CHAPTER 26

With her purse out in readiness, Gillian was the first to arrive at the bar.

"What are you all having to drink? I'll get the first round in."

While everybody had to think what they were having, I knew what I wanted, so was first in with my order.

"G & T for me, please, Gillian."

"Prosecco please." (Christina was the wine drinker; I knew that from the day she helped me move in to Elgin Mews.)

"I'll have a Fosters, please," Leanne piped up.

"Make that two Fosters then, Gillian," added Janet.

Gillian finally caught the attention of the tall, skinny barman after taking our drink orders; the rest of us, on spotting a table in the far corner, went off to claim it, before Gemma returned to the bar to help carry the drinks back.

It was our first Friday night after-work drinking session since I returned to work a month ago. As the rest of us settled into our corner in the Lamb and Flag, a favourite pub of ours from my pre-France days, waiting for Gemma and

Gillian to return with the drinks, Christina was just getting warmed up. She hadn't even got a drink at that point, but even though it was the first time I'd been in a pub in her company, it was obvious that she didn't need drink to have a good time. She exercised a great deal of self-control at work when she had to be professional, but being a natural enter-tainer and someone who loved to shock, she found it diffi-cult to rein it in. She fished around in her purse for some change and, dancing en-route, made her way over to the jukebox, totally oblivious to all the attention she was attracting from the other clientele, who watched her in delight.

Though Leanne and I had been sat for less than a minute, we soon had to get up and remove our thick coats, as it was far too warm in the area we chose to sit. Folding my coat carefully, ready to place it over the back of my chair, I had my back to everyone in the place. Leanne hissed loudly at me to attract my attention.

"Helen. Helen. Pssst! Look! Look at Christina."

I glanced over in the direction that Christina had headed and I was gob-smacked to see her 'dirty dancing' to 'Do You Love Me' (from the film) with a young guy who I guessed would be no more than nineteen; less than half her age. The pair had a rapidly growing and appreciative audience. Half a dozen young lads who seemed to be mates of the wannabe Patrick Swayze, were riotously egging them on as they watched the pairs' suggestive, but nonetheless, accomplished moves. Gemma and Gillian appeared again as they made their way back to our table with the drinks and their jaws dropped in astonishment the instant they caught sight of Christina and her young dance partner. They stopped dead in their tracks, totally mesmerised. After a minute or so, the track ended and, carrying our drinks, they had to pick their way back to our table rather carefully, through the small crowd that had gathered. Everybody in the pub broke out into rapturous applause and Christina was given a fierce hug and a thank you from her new found friend. She was still moving raunchily as she came across to join us all, with her great cheesy grin. We all laughed as we gave her our own private round of applause and she treated us to some celebrity-like bows. I felt so full of affection for her. She certainly knew how to put the 'joy' in enjoyment.

When all the hilarious chit-chat about Christina's dancing finally calmed, Gemma suddenly focussed all the attention back to me.

"Now I have a proper chance to ask, how are things, Helen? You've been back a month now, so how do you feel about everything? Are you glad to be back in London, and working with us all again?"

Her question caught me completely off guard. I'd been so busy since moving into my house, that I hadn't really done much in the way of analysing my thoughts. I stammered as I tried to find the right words, and hoped they would understand.

"I have...never been happier. I...I wish..."

Gemma quickly cut in, "You shouldn't have gone, Helen. We would have helped you, every one of us. Being out there by yourself..."

Wondering how I ever managed to tear myself away from this amazing bunch of ladies, I gave her my most truthful answer.

"In some ways, I really wish that I hadn't disappeared over there and lived like a hermit all those months. I missed every one of you desperately, even though I didn't stay in touch. I felt I needed the break. Maybe it would have been more beneficial to me if I had stayed in London...who knows? I would have all my friends around me, wouldn't I? But I got there in the end...managed to get over...things. I'm back...and feeling so much better now. I'm happy that I'm working with all you ladies again, and happy with my new house."

My eyes glazed over as I started to get over-emotional, and the gin had played its part, as always.

"Well, we're all so happy that you're back; you've no idea. There's nobody happier than Ted though, especially as he's going into semi-retirement."

Not too long after that exchange, Christina and I returned from the bar with our third round of drinks, when it was Gillian's turn for the questions. She had such a serious expression on her face as I was about to sit down and I wondered what was coming next.

"Helen, I've been meaning to ask you...has Ted told you about Linda Brownlow? How she tried causing trouble between us girls before you came back? She almost had Leanne and me at each other's throats, through her bloody lies."

Leanne nodded in agreement, and from the look of anger I could see in her eyes, I could tell that the very mention of the woman brought back hurtful memories.

"Yes. He did mention it...but he wasn't specific about who was involved. He also told me that now I'm back, Linda is to report directly to me, not James Mortimer."

To Gemma, whose office was situated nearer to Linda's room, it seemed to come as quite a surprise.

"Really? Well, that doesn't appear to have worked then. She's in and out of Jim's office all the bloody time," she grumbled, then as an afterthought added, "and I'm not too keen on him either. There's something about him..."

Following mine and Gemma's revelations, there were plenty of disgruntled mumblings between the other three; grumbling that the woman was blatantly going against Ted's instructions that she report directly to me. It left me in no doubt as to their individual feelings about Linda.

I knew I had to be careful about how I went about the rest of the conversation. James was after all, a partner of mine, and Linda was an employee. I couldn't appear to be unprofessional in front of the girls by coming out with any derogatory remarks. I hoped I was on neutral ground, when I finally commented,

"I somehow can't see Linda wanting to report to me. It seems she appears to have some sort of problem with me. Which, if that is the case, then she's going to keep running to James, isn't she?"

Before I uttered those few words, I hadn't realised it would be like igniting a bomb. It prompted a major rant to start between Gemma, Gillian and Leanne. Comments flew back and forth between the three and I couldn't keep up, my head was spinning.

"She's jealous!"

"But why would…?"

"Jealous of what, though?"

"Jealous of Helen's position…"

"Her looks, her clothes…"

"Helen is her employer…"

"…and she has no right…"

"She shows no respect for anybody…"

All the time their opinions were being hurled back and forth, Christina was observing and listening to what the girls had to say, but remained tight-lipped until their venting ceased. Right out of the blue, she was ready to have her say.

"Well, it could be jealousy. But I think not!" She turned to face me once more. "I'm sorry, Helen. But she fucking hates you. I've seen the way she looks at you, when you're around. Sorry, but its pure hatred!"

Gemma, Gillian and Leanne gaped at her, eyes wide open, mouths open wide, before they turned towards me to gauge my reaction, perhaps to see if I was offended by Christina's honest though rather blunt, statement. Blunt though it may have seemed to them, Christina did nothing more than state exactly what I felt the first time I met Linda Brownlow; that she detested me. With Christina's worried eyes also on me, I stared back at each one of them in turn. I hadn't been offended in the least, but I was shocked. I was dismayed to have somebody tell me they actually witnessed Linda's intense dislike of me; what I had thought all along, to be something that existed only in my head.

"But...why? How could she hate me when she only just met me?"

I voiced the questions just once, but looked at each of the four in turn, hoping to see answers in their eyes, waiting for them to whisper their feedback. But they had no answers for me.

We only stayed in the Lamb and Flag for a couple of hours that night. Throughout my journey home on the tube and for the rest of the night, the thought kept coming back to haunt me; why did Linda Brownlow hate me so much. It was not only the girls who couldn't answer. I couldn't think of one possible reason why the woman could despise me.

CHAPTER 27

*T*owards the end of my second month back at the office, a Wednesday, I was under pressure in Ted's absence, (a month touring South America), to produce some urgent, projected figures for one of our oldest clients. The company was considering the buy-out of a considerably smaller, but failing business. I had stacks of accounts on my desk that had been prepared by the technicians and which needed signing off. Thursday and Friday were already ruled out for catching up, as I had various meetings to attend. Even though I would have loved nothing more than to go home and curl up with a DVD and a bottle of wine, desperate times called for desperate measures. The signing off of the accounts wouldn't take too long between my meetings and, as I needed to get the projected figures to the client for Friday, I planned to stay behind for as long as it would take for me to finish up my spreadsheets. I could give the figures to Christina the next day so she could prepare the presentation pack for the client.

I sent an email to all the staff to inform them of my late night work, requesting that the last person to leave the building should not activate the alarm. Around twenty minutes or so before six, Gemma brought me a latte.

"Right, Helen, you're by yourself, I think I'm the last. Don't work too late. You've got a couple of busy days ahead."

"Thanks for the coffee, Gemma. I won't. I should be done by about eight. Goodnight."

Picking up my cup and saucer from three hours earlier, she beamed.

"See you in the morning then. Goodnight."

I heard the main door close a couple of minutes later, followed by the sound of her heels clipping on the pavement as she passed by outside my office window, heading for home. I pushed my own wave of longing to the back of my mind.

The peace and quiet once the phones stopped ringing was total bliss and I made good progress. I was hard at it and had already completed the projected manufacturing profit and loss account and done the fixed and current assets of the balance sheet; I was only left with the current liabilities to do. Seven fourteen was the time according to the computer, so I looked forward to being on my way by twenty to eight at the latest. After a quick trip to the loo, I returned my empty cup to the kitchen before once again, settling into my chair for the last hurdle. Carefully scanning my Excel document before continuing, I jumped sharply as a voice boomed from the open doorway behind me.

"Did you think I needed some company, Helen? That's nice."

Bloody James Mortimer! Recovering quickly from the shock, I was furious with him. Not only for startling me; I didn't need him hanging around holding me up. I wanted to be home.

"FUCKING Hell, James! What do you think you're doing,

frightening me half to death? I thought I was here alone. I'm busy. These projections need to be out tomorrow."

With a ridiculous smirk on his face, he shuffled over and stood behind my chair.

"You should manage your time better, Helen. Then you wouldn't need to stay after hours."

Supercilious bastard! I ignored his comment and started tapping away at the keyboard, in the hope that he'd get the message. A couple of minutes passed and he hadn't moved. He leaned over my right shoulder.

"Are you spying on me, James? Come to see if I'm doing my job properly? Trying to find fault with my work?" I snarled.

My head started spinning and I couldn't focus on my drafts.

"Helen...Helen, come on now, the name's Jim! Why so formal? Lighten up a little. We've known each other for a few weeks now."

His amusement was evident, but came with that unmistakable mocking tone that I had now become familiar with during our working week.

"I prefer to keep things formal. Jim is too informal, so I call you James. I don't like you. Why would I want to be informal where you're concerned?" I candidly pointed out.

I tilted my head to the right to look up at him, and served up what I hoped would be one of my special glares. Unperturbed, he held my glare, and while doing so, let his right arm fall over my shoulder; his hand shooting straight down my top and into my bra. He gripped hard on my breast, and there was a hint of his breath and lips close to my ear.

"Oh, I knew the instant I met you that you didn't like me, Helen."

His words were like a hint of breeze that would barely

disturb the leaves on a tree, so delicate that I hardly caught them.

"Wha…what…the…f…fuck …do you think you are doing?"

Looking away from his piercing dark eyes, I let mine follow the progress of his hand as he tightly squeezed my nipple and played it between his thumb and forefinger.

"You may not like me, Helen, I accept that…and yet…you want to fuck me? You would love me to fuck you, I know you would."

"I…don't…I…you…how dare…?"

I was burning with rage at his arrogance and his assumptions; though the words had been correct. The heat was overwhelming me, encasing me in flames, the tendrils of which I felt at every nerve-ending. I was powerless. Unable to move, unable to protest, I stared down at my keyboard, oblivious to the screen displaying my recently created spreadsheet.

"Don't deny it, Helen."

He spun my chair around to face him, and pressed the front of his trousers in with two splayed fingers, clearly displaying the outline of his hard-on.

"I've seen you glancing at my cock several times, Helen. Look at me." He pointed to his face with one hand and abruptly lifted my chin with the other. "Look at me, Helen. Read my eyes." Although he raised my face upwards, I averted my eyes and avoided his intense stare. "The eyes, Helen. NOW!"

Feeling like a naughty schoolchild, I obeyed. I hated this guy and couldn't understand why I wanted him so much. Yes, he got that bit right; for now, at least. I looked into his dark eyes, just as he commanded. Mixed thoughts were running through my mind, thoughts that he was going to…maybe, hurt me. Thoughts that I wanted to fuck him until I hurt him and I relished that idea. I didn't like him, that was a fact, yet I was confused. Suddenly aware of the dampness in my panties, I wanted to take them off. However, he took control.

"Stand up now. I'm going to take your clothes off, Helen. Nice and slowly. I'll make it fun."

As if in a trance, I rose from the chair, still staring directly at him. In one swift movement, he grabbed at the hem of my silk top and, forcing my arms upwards, he tugged until my head and arms were free and he let the top fall to the floor. He moved closer to me and pushed my breasts together, then gently covered the lace of my bra with his mouth, his tongue taunting each of my nipples in turn through the delicate fabric. Though he continued holding my breasts together, I sighed in disappointment when his mouth no longer played on the sensitivity of my buds. Seconds later, his tongue lightly swept up and down the cleavage he created, and I wanted his 'hard-on'…his skin touching mine…inside and outside. Instantly, I ached for some close up contact; needed it so badly that my head was in a spin and yet his lower body was not even pushed against me, just his strong hands and tongue were the only connection.

I lost track of time…imagining…over-thinking… wantonly experiencing a pre-run in my mind…an imminent fucking marathon. Those thoughts alone were sufficiently exciting enough to increase the dampness already penetrating the soft fabric of my panties. Come on, action, I'm ready and waiting! After what I guessed had been five minutes of having that evil tongue sliding up and down my cleavage, he slid his hands around my back to first unclasp my bra and then to unzip my tight pencil skirt. Clenching my stomach with excitement, and biting my lip simultaneously, I felt his hands on me again, easing my skirt over my hips with a deliberate light brushing of the skin down the outside of my thighs as he lowered the garment this time, rather than letting it fall. Then he was behind me, his hot lips kissing my right butt cheek unexpectedly and I jumped, then groaned as he bit into my skin.

He moaned and whispered as he kissed, sucked, teased and nipped at my rump with his teeth.

"Very nice, lovely, Helen."

My impatience was such that I started to fidget, roughly twirling strands of my hair around, first my fingers, then my thumbs, sighing loudly with each passing minute. I didn't have much longer to wait; he edged his thumbs into the top of my thong and slid it lazily down to my ankles. In those last few seconds, I closed my eyes tight. Still playing out a blisteringly hot and deliciously sticky scene in my mind, I licked my lips as I parted my legs slightly and pushed my bottom towards him. Playfully slapping my bottom and both thighs, he ordered,

"Close your legs, Helen. You're too forward. I'm going to teach you to be patient."

"Please...I..." I urged.

"Not quite...yet. I've told you already, honey, it has to be...slowly."

My spine tingled with a new excitement as he taunted up and down my backbone with his fingers and tongue, so subtle, nothing but a hint of contact between us. I gasped as every nerve ending was awakened.

"Bend over your desk, Helen. I'm going to switch off the light."

Pushing my chair aside, I positioned myself eagerly as I heard the flick of the light switch. My office was thrown into semi-darkness; just a subdued amber glow from the street-light behind the window blind and the blinking patterns of colour from my screen-saver. As he had done nothing but torment me, I resolved to exercise a little patience. I closed my eyes once more. Though the office heating was off and I was totally naked, I felt clammy. It seemed as if his hands scorched me each time they skimmed over my skin.

"Listen, Helen! Hear it. Use your senses, feel each pent up nerve waiting… patience."

His breath was hot on my neck, his lips journeying on my shoulder, and I was becoming oblivious to the traffic and distant police sirens that sounded so noisy earlier. I could hear his steady breathing along with my own heavy, rapid breaths, then…the unmistakable sound of a zip.

I didn't trust myself not to beg, so I repeated the words over and over in my mind, inwardly urging him on. 'Please, don't make me wait any longer. Please don't make me wait any longer. Fuck me, right now'. Somehow, I knew he'd make me wait.

Then he was there again, rubbing the length of his hardness over my bottom first, each cheek in turn. I badly wanted his cock inside me. Rough, fast, slow, rough, thrusting, pumping… He pulled away from me…for…it seemed like an eternity, making me wait, playing that game. Bastard!

"James…" I pleaded.

"All in good time…patience, Helen!" he growled back. "Soon though - soon. Part your legs now, sweet thing…not too wide."

My stomach ached for him. I was ready, tense with anticipation of my release that was to come, hopefully soon. Waiting, waiting patiently. Ah! He was working the top of my legs with his cock, between my thighs, rolling it up and down and it felt wonderful...hot…throbbing. I moaned loudly with my pleasure…and frustrations, as he taunted me. Rubbing the end of his dick very high up, I gripped my thighs together, feeling sure he was planning to slam hard into me when I least expected it. Opening up for him a little, his hardness fell away. His finger swiftly traced over my labia from front to back and I shuddered. Not quite, but almost at the point of orgasm.

"Now? James…please?"

Shit, the bastard had me begging! The last thing I wanted to do! The contact stopped again.

"Helen, I've told you. Just…wait. Eyes closed…hear, smell, feel, wait."

I raised my shoulders from the desk. I felt slightly drunk, fuzzy headed…and puzzled. Jolting myself to reality, I understood that I'd been holding my breath too long. I took a couple of deep inhalations and lowered my head slowly, listening carefully, still waiting…

"Wait…wait…" he whispered, barely audible now.

I had to hand it to him. It was his ultimate torment. Rather abruptly, my thoughts of being fucked real hard had gone and I was aware that I could hear breathing…only…it was just…mine. Only mine! There was no breathing from James.

"James? What the fuck are you doing?" I asked, cautiously.

A door slammed somewhere in the building. I rapidly pushed myself upright and hurried over to flick the light back on, feeling more than a little nervous. I dressed quickly, noticing the time, ten minutes to nine. Tears welled in my eyes. I gave a cursory glance around the office; all was in order. I couldn't even muster enough regret for my almost-finished spreadsheet. I would catch an earlier train in the morning, nothing lost. I scooped up my handbag, jabbed at the light switch and strode nervously along the corridor into reception. As I prepared to arm the alarm system, my eyes were drawn towards the lime green 'post-it' note stuck to the inside of the front door, 'Goodnight, Helen!' Bastard!

I gave him the benefit of the doubt when I realised he'd gone. He was married, after all. Maybe he just couldn't bring himself to do it. At least that is what I told myself as I dressed. But no...this was all a fucking game to him.

Struggling to find sufficiently appropriate words, I screamed out,

"YOU FUCKING...PIECE OF...FUCKING SHIT!" as I struck out at the front door two or three times with my foot; scuffing the paintwork with my heel.

I took a couple of minutes to calm myself and regain a modicum of dignity before locking up and stepping out on to the pavement. Hurriedly approaching the end of the street I shivered, not due to the cold drizzly night, but more from feeling unnerved. Somebody was following me. It had to be him. Spinning around in a confrontational manner, I expected to see him close behind, ready to whisper maliciously into my ear...but he was nowhere to be seen.

The only person coming in my direction was a guy wearing a long coat and a baseball cap, head down against the drizzle. Although he was at least fifteen yards behind me, he seemed to shrink back in alarm at my move and crossed over to the opposite pavement. Feeling a flush of embarrassment at my own stupidity and thankful for the darkness, I turned the corner and almost ran the last few metres to the station.

Pure anger, both with James and with my recklessness prevented me from sleeping that night.

CHAPTER 28

At five twenty five, irritatingly much later than my self-imposed rule of being there by five fifteen, I took up my position in the same place. I even started to think of the look-out point that I frequented, as 'my doorway'. It occurred to me that if anybody witnessed my presence in the shadows over the last couple of months, they might have regarded it as suspicious behaviour. It was a sobering thought that the police might consider that I was casing any of the local premises with a view to burglary. Making a mental note to start looking for an alternative watch post, I fished the mobile phone out of my coat pocket as a ruse. Just pretending to text or surf the net while I watched her office; it was fairly commonplace to do that these days and almost fool-proof.

Had I possessed any foresight or had some friendly angel tap me on the shoulder and eerily tell me that I would need to stick around here for hours...then I really wouldn't have bothered. Unfortunately...or fortunately, whichever way one might choose to look at the matter, I don't believe in angels, friendly or otherwise, and my foresight is...well practically non-existent.

Settling down for the evening 'watch', it appeared that some of the office staff may have already departed for home before my arrival in the street, as since I arrived, I only witnessed two ladies leave the building. One of the women was met outside the main door by, who I assumed to be her husband or boyfriend not long after five thirty. They linked arms, crossed over from their side of the road and walked past 'my doorway' huddled together against the cold. From a little snippet of conversation as they passed me, I gathered that they were discussing the evening's TV listings and their night's agenda of programmes they intended to watch.

Lady number two emerged from the building maybe twenty minutes or so later. She didn't hang around to lock the door and hurried in the direction that Helen normally takes to the Embankment tube station. There were still lights on in two of the offices; one each on the ground and first floors. So, my logic kicked in; at least two staff must still be working. Hopefully one of them would be Helen...unless of course I was too late to witness her leave the office earlier.

I paced up and down my six foot wide porch, thinking long and hard about whether I should stay where I was and keep watch. The other options I seriously contemplated were: should I join my colleagues in our usual 'after work' local just two or three streets away? Or...would it be more sensible to make my way home? Each option had its merits and its downsides. Going home meant food washed down with a few beers from the fridge, warmth and entertainment courtesy of 'the box'; its downsides, having to cook for myself and...being alone. The upside to the local would involve a few fresh-from-the-pump beers, food which didn't require me to cook it and some company. The cons outweighed the pros, though. I would have to endure the idiots who couldn't stop talking about work and Charles Parker's incessant bragging about his bank balance (ironically, he was always the one who happened to be missing when it was his turn to buy a round of drinks). Add to that the endless, boring discussions about football...footballers...football results...and football league tables, and that was that option quickly disregarded!

'Right then, mate,' I asked myself out loud, 'is it home? Or remain here keeping watch?' Choices, choices! So I could freeze my backside off here or go home. It wasn't too hard at all really, to come to a decision. The big reward by staying put; I would get to see Helen, hopefully. My mind firmly made up, I settled myself into a corner of the porch yet again, mobile phone at the ready.

A rather boring, uneventful hour passed by, in which the main action happened to be...me blowing on and rubbing my hands together for a little warmth, me stamping my feet for a little warmth...and then...I knew I was going to have to do something and quick. My bladder finally reached 'fit to burst' stage and there was no way I could stay in situ any longer until I found somewhere where I could have a much needed piss. It was ten minutes till seven. I stared over at the building. Both offices were still lit. With my need to urinate becoming more urgent with each passing second, I turned to my left and walked off in search of a toilet. A dark alley would have sufficed, but preferably no further than six feet away. Trying not to think about my desperate need to pee, I busied my mind fretting about whether Helen would be gone before I returned.

Having walked a couple of blocks to find that, due to one or two drunks and people taking short-cuts, there was no privacy in any of the few dark alleys I passed, I found myself face to face with one of my earlier options; the pub, our local venue, currently playing host to my colleagues and their mundane banter. Annoyingly, I had to walk past them all to visit the gents, and after the ultimate relief and sheer satisfaction of having peed, I was about to exit the pub when Tim Falshaw (our football-obsessed, lunatic colleague), waved a freshly pulled pint in my face.

"Got you one in, mate," he boomed.

Great! Exactly what I didn't need!!

"Cheers, Tim, I'll have to owe you one. I've made other arrangements and must dash as soon as I've downed this."

I apologised, feeling guilty at being economical with the truth.

"Ah, right!" He winked knowingly. "A blonde, I'll bet!"

I played along jovially.

"Or it could even be a redhead, Tim!" I joked, laughing at both his and my own suggestions. My thoughts quickly returned to that long dark hair, those long legs...

Taking up my post again some time later, and feeling warmer and more comfortable than before I went walkabout looking for a lavatory, I was relieved to see that the staff were still in Helen's building, both lights still burning. It sure was a late night for somebody. I came to a decision; if Helen did not appear out of the offices by eight o'clock, I would head off home to my flat. I was feeling ravenous and craving something to eat, anything at all. An interesting observation suddenly had me fully alert. The upstairs office light went out and not before time. My hunger for food was instantly replaced by the need to catch a glimpse of Helen. After all, it seemed like forever.

My boredom and tiredness quickly forgotten, I eagerly awaited further movement...but disappointment followed.

It was just after eight o'clock when the downstairs office was suddenly plunged into darkness...and yet, no staff emerged from the building as I waited a further half hour; a half hour that had dragged by. I was frozen and shivering again. Even my eyes were stinging with the cold. I'd given up on the mobile phone and stuffed my hands back into the coat pockets. I was relieved that pedestrians were few and far between, and those who did pass by didn't even trouble to look in my direction. Had they shown any interest in me at all, it might have looked less suspicious if I'd unrolled a sleeping-bag beforehand and feigned homelessness and maybe a drink or drug-induced slumber.

Almost rigid with cold, and with my eyes fighting to stay open, I jerked in surprise at the sound of a door slamming a little way off. Momentarily disorientated, I shook my head in an attempt to ward off the fuzzy-headedness. Then there was action at last. Someone just left the office. Someone in a hurry. It was a guy, the same guy who I noticed before on a couple of occasions. I pushed myself further back into the darkness of the corner as he swiftly headed in my direction. I looked him up and down as he neared, taking in as much detail as I could. He was dressed immaculately; I guessed at early forties, but most noticeable was the self-satisfied look on his 'handsome-bastard' face.

The downstairs office light came back on...but only briefly. Just before nine she stepped into the street, beautiful as always. Something was different though. Her demeanour was a little jumpy. That tall, confident, 'cat-walk-like' stride was lacking. It seemed... no, I was certain that something was wrong with her.

Leaving my humble hidey-hole, I tilted the baseball cap to shade my eyes. Taking up a steady pursuit as she made her way to the corner, I wondered what could have happened to upset her. It had to be something to do with him; the guy who left a short time ago. Had a meeting or something not gone too well? Or, and I felt a pang of jealousy at the possibility, was Helen romantically involved with him, and they just had a ding-dong of a row? I felt an acute surge of anger overwhelm me.

Keeping a safe distance behind her, and my identity a secret, was as always, essential. Ahead, she suddenly spun round on her heels looking...confrontational. I stopped dead in my tracks, fearing that she would recognise me. Keeping my head tilted down and chin tucked into my scarf, I slowly took a step back, horrified for a few seconds. In reality there was no way she could have known that it was me, particularly with the distance that separated us and only the dull amber glow from the street-light. However, one thing I did not mistake was the shock register on her face. Shock because the person following her was not who she expected it to be. I gave her a slight nod, raised my right arm briefly (pacifying, reassuring her that I didn't intend to do her any harm) and crossed the road, hopefully helping to allay her fears.

Time to call it a night! I didn't want to push my luck any further. I was rather unnerved when she turned to face me. The *question was, over the last few weeks, had there been times when she suspected that she was being followed? Or maybe I was being a tad paranoid. I couldn't help but feel that the key to Helen's unusual behaviour had been him; the guy who worked in her office. He had to be the one who caused her to be so distraught.*

CHAPTER 29

I was furious with James Mortimer. I couldn't understand what possessed him to do that to me. The humiliation, not to mention the sexual frustration, also played heavily on my mind.

After arriving home from the office, all I was able to think about was getting laid. I needed to get my thoughts off the degradation I suffered because of him. I resorted to sending a text to Simon. It was the safest way for me to contact him, just in case he happened to be with his wife. My words were simple, 'fancy a chat?' Within three minutes of sending the message, my mobile rang. I flushed with plea-sure…and anticipation, hoping, although the chance would be slim, that he would be available. He happened to be at the gym when he received the text; getting dressed after his workout and shower. My mind quickly conjured up a sexy image of his body and I smiled to myself, memories of our last fucking session almost making me blush. I also felt a little disappointed, because it seemed the prospect of me having sex that same night was not good. Having exchanged pleasantries for a few minutes, he told me that he would be staying in the city the following evening and asked if I would care to join him; exactly what I'd hoped for, but a day late. I didn't hesitate to say yes though, and my panties were soon feeling damp, my heart beating faster than normal, as I tried to form an image in my mind of what lay in store.

As I turned the corner into Villiers Street the following morning, my heart sank when I saw him. James Mortimer was walking towards the office from the opposite direction. He was roughly the same distance away as me, which meant we would probably arrive on the doorstep at the same time. Even though a few metres separated us, I still managed to see that smug grin appear on his face the minute he spotted me. I felt the ruddy heat in my cheeks as I flushed with embarrassment…and the shame. Never before had I felt so ashamed of myself for being taken for a ride by such a twat. My determination suddenly surfaced, along with the unabated anger and I strode out the last few metres at a faster pace, arriving on the doorstep seconds before him. Once over the threshold, I paused in wait, with the door still ajar. Without even turning to face him, I saw the shadow he cast from behind me; he was at last on the step. With a satisfying slam right in his face, I kicked the door shut and hot-tailed it to my office.

Sitting at my desk shortly after, I berated myself for behaving in such a blatantly juvenile manner. Every few minutes though, the thoughts of spending the forthcoming night with Simon kept me in a horny sort of dream world, and for the biggest part of the day, I managed to push my anger to the back of my mind.

After an hour or so of banging away on my keyboard I completed the previous night's spreadsheet and answered a dozen emails. I was still stewing in my anger with James Mortimer so I tried to let my mind wander instead, to my plans for the evening. It seemed pointless going home to Maida Vale only to have to return to Knightsbridge, so I threw some make-up, toiletries and spare undies into one of my larger handbags before setting off for work. Simon told me he wasn't expecting to arrive at the hotel before seven o'clock, so I would stay at the office until he called me to let me know when he'd be there. I was hoping and praying that I wouldn't have unwanted company in the office after five thirty; him, the new partner. As it turned out, it was my lucky day. He had a late afternoon meeting with a client in Sussex, so hadn't returned. It was ten minutes gone seven when I received the call from Simon and almost the second he was off the phone I called a cab to collect me.

Since we discussed our 'relationship of sorts' a few weeks ago, he had, to save any possible embarrassment for the pair of us, started to use a different hotel in Knightsbridge for his business use, which alleviated some of my worry. There was a few occasions in the past when I had to sneak around in the corridors of the hotel where I used to work during my darker days; the same one where Simon would frequently stay. I was always terrified of being seen by the staff who knew me.

The taxi dropped me off at the hotel by seven thirty and we spent a fantastic night together. The sex as usual, was delicious and disgustingly dirty. I had rid myself of the previous night's frustrations, sexual and otherwise, by being overly aggressive. I'd also taken along a vibrator and that provided additional orgasms to the ones that Simon expertly brought about, as well as helping prolong his release too. Each time he came close to letting go, he withdrew from me and went back to using the battery-operated toy. During our first round of shagging, I noticed his raised eyebrows a few times, while I was riding him with a little too much exuberance. He flinched a number of times and asked,

"Has someone been rattling your cage at all, Helen? You're being a bit rough with the old boy tonight."

His comment brought me back down to earth. I have him my apologies and made a determined effort to put my anger behind me and enjoy my time…and sex, with him; the main reason for my being there.

"Oh, it's nothing, Simon. Just work."

He grunted, a little peeved, before bursting into laughter.

"Next time I phone you, I'll ask if you've had a good day before I invite you over for sex, should I? You would tell me, wouldn't you, if it was me who made you cross in anyway?"

It was my turn to grin.

"No. You never have," then swiftly, I added, "not yet. But that isn't to say you won't at some point. So beware."

We had a very hot night, with the emphasis being more about fucking and orgasms than getting much in the way of sleep. Even though I'd had less than three hours sleep, I awoke feeling remarkably fresh, extremely satisfied and… sore. He joined me in the shower and was onto me in a matter of seconds. I closed my eyes in pleasure as he kissed and nibbled at my neck from behind. Anxious to ensure that I made up for the amazing sex he gave me throughout the night I turned towards him and knelt down. I looked up into his eyes and avariciously tasted the head of his throbbing length, my palm rubbing tauntingly up and down each solid inch. He gripped my head and held firm, tangling his fingers through my hair and gnashed his teeth at me, goading me in delight.

"Oh, fuck…Helen. Grrr!"

Cupping his scrotum, I swept one finger teasingly over his puckered rear entrance and tongued his cock before taking his full length in my mouth. With every nerve in my body rocketing with desire, I managed to curb my selfishness and looked up into his face. I wanted to watch his eyes light up and hear him roar in ecstasy as he let his seed gush into my mouth. I moved my mouth back and forth faster, taking him deep into my throat and almost gagged as he thrust forwards into me, my teeth grazing his skin. He groaned almost continually, but then without any warning he withdrew.

"No! No! Not like this, Helen. I want…I want to be… inside you. Go, lean over the bed."

Before I had a chance to move or respond in any way, he seized my wrist. Leaving the shower running, he dragged me towards the bed and lowered me face down over the side. He shoved two fingers hard inside me, and playing my clit with his thumb, increased my aching dramatically.

"Fuck, Helen, you're so wet, sweetie. Are you ready to let your juices flow some more? I'm going to fuck you like a madman."

He rammed hard into me, I was unable to answer. He knocked the breath out of me as he pounded away and both of his hands crept around my thighs to stroke my clit. I arched my back and bucked as my orgasm hit. Every nerve end tingled, my stomach lurched and I screamed out in pure joy. I wiped my hand over the beads of perspiration on my forehead. I was struggling to breathe too. Simon tensed behind me and I could tell he was nearing his own climax. With one arm around my hip, he expertly circled his thumb over my sensitive bud. With his other hand, he lingeringly slid a finger into my anus and it was that lazy move that took me over the precipice again. I clenched around his cock just in time to feel the twitches of his release, and he let out a rapturous moan before letting his body flop onto the bed. It took a little while before our breathing steadied.

Within the hour, I'd been back into the shower, put my make-up on, dressed, and was on the tube, making my way to the office. Simon was also en-route, but to court.

James Mortimer passed me in the corridor at one point during the morning and I couldn't help but make sure that he saw the self-satisfied grin on my face as his eyes met with mine.

CHAPTER 30

Since being humiliated by James over two weeks ago, the two of us had come into contact on no more than three or four occasions. The first time had been when I kicked the door shut in his face the following morning. But the other two or three occasions I saw him, had literally been just that! It hadn't even been necessary for us to discuss any business matters. It was purely coincidental that he happened to be in reception a few times when I was passing through. Luckily there was always another member of staff around at the time. Therefore, there had been no opportunity for any snide remarks from him...or myself, for that matter. I couldn't seem to put what he did to me in the back of my mind; how belittled he left me feeling. I didn't trust myself to utter even one word to him, for fear of spewing out the tirade of abuse that was never far from my lips. Thanks to my own stupidity, my professionalism was already totally undermined, without adding to it.

Friday came around and I had two meetings to attend. I was in Croydon by ten o'clock visiting a client. He was somewhat concerned about his personal, rather than business tax matters, largely due to his rapidly increasing portfolio of rental properties, and thankfully, I'd been able to relieve him of some of his worries. Once free of that particular meeting, I hot-tailed it over to King's Road in Chelsea, to meet up with a new client Jilly Greaves and her business banking manager to put forward a business plan for the expansion of her business. At Jilly's request, I was tagging along for a little moral support, although I had my doubts about the bank being willing to offer her any further funding.

Throughout the meeting I was content for Jilly to do all the talking and she did so rather admirably, with conviction and oozing confidence. Meanwhile, I sat and observed, carefully watching the face of her business manager as his eyes meticulously scanned her paperwork and asked numerous questions of her, especially with regard to whether she'd considered alternative sources for the funding. The patronising, almost sympathetic, smile on his face strengthened my suspicion that the meeting was going to be a complete waste of time.

Jilly and I followed the bank visit with a chat over lunch, throughout which, I was honest about my thoughts on the extra funding she was hoping for. She started her business little more than a couple of years ago and during that twenty four month period, the profit had more than exceeded her expectations and as a result, made her overly optimistic. Somewhat tentatively, I explained to Jilly that growing too big, too soon, often has a detrimental effect on a business. Noticing that she frustratingly raised her eyes to the ceiling, I realised this was not what she wanted to hear, though I was rather shocked at her next revelation.

"Helen, I just dispensed with the services of my last accountants because they told me exactly what you have just said." She lowered her eyes and gave me an apologetic smile. "They disagreed with me, just as you have now done."

"Sorry, Jilly. But I can't say I'm sorry for giving you what I feel is my best advice." Nervously, I took a deep breath, and added, "I must get back to the office. It's your call, Jilly. No doubt you'll be in touch?"

I didn't bother to wait for her answer. I picked up my handbag and folio and, as her eyes focused on something beyond my right shoulder, I left her with her thoughts, fully expecting that The Hopkins Partnership's new client, was already an ex-client.

Almost before I was through the front door of the office, Christina greeted me with,

"Hey, Boss. Whatever you've done, you nailed that shit. I only just put the phone down. Jilly Greaves called and said I was to give you her heartfelt apologies." Without pausing for breath, she carried on, "She said to tell you that she's not happy, but that you're right. She's going to call you on Monday. I don't think you've lost her."

Though I was taken aback by the way Christina addressed me, I was also highly amused. I couldn't help but smile...and it had nothing to do with the call from Jilly. I was still getting to know Christina and hadn't really had that much to do with her since my return to the business, but I'd heard excellent feedback from the other staff.

"Bloody hilarious..."

"...she knows her job inside out..."

"...unique..."

"...even the clients think she's ace..."

I felt that a mild ticking off was in order, though. But I had no desire to offend our 'unique' temp.

"Christina, just a couple of little matters..."

A look of horror swept across her face; one of those what-the-fuck-did-I-do-wrong type of look that soon disappeared when she saw me smiling in amusement.

"...first of all...please don't call me Boss. It's Helen.

Secondly, I have no wish to pop your bubble. I like that you're bubbly, but please be aware, that any comments like 'you nailed that shit' would not have been appropriate had there been clients in the office. Staff, in the privacy of the office, maybe…clients and Ted, definitely not. Okay?"

"I'll consider myself well and truly scolded, Bo….Helen! But I'm always careful when people are around…well… mostly." She looked at me rather sheepishly.

"There's no scolding, Christina. Let's call it a little friendly advice, shall we?"

And with that, I left her gazing at me in surprise as I moved away from her desk through reception and down the corridor to my office.

For the next two or three hours, I worked away steadily and undisturbed, to reduce the pile of paperwork in my 'in' tray until I noticed my email inbox. There was two emails waiting to be read. I could see that the first one was nothing more than trash and the second was from…James. Anger immediately started building in the pit of my stomach just from seeing that bloody name of his on my computer screen. Feeling as if he was invading my personal space as he had done over two weeks ago, I opened the email, eager to see what he wanted. After that, I could get the email along with his name, wiped from my screen as fast as I could.

Hi Helen,

Could you please bring me down the old Wright and Butler file from the archive room? I wouldn't know where to start looking and I'm told they were your clients and that you would know exactly where it is archived.

Regards

Jim

In the few seconds it took me to read, my blood was at boiling point. What the fuck? Asking me to bring him an old client file as if I was his office junior! Inwardly seething and with my hands shaking in anger, I rapidly banged at the keys as I composed my snotty reply.

James

This is a small task that you could have given to Christina, or one of the trainees, to do. I have more urgent matters to deal with than searching for an old client file that is surely of little importance, particularly at this time on a Friday night.

Helen

After hitting 'send email' I fiercely slammed pens and paperwork around my desk for five minutes, all concentration for my work utterly lost. I decided that it would probably be in my (and everyone else's) best interests that I leave the office earlier than usual. Doing a rapid 'U' turn, I straightened up the skew-whiff paperwork that I'd taken my frustrations out on. A dull pounding began in my head, and I silently cursed myself for letting that idiot cause me such stress. As I picked up my pens and rulers to place them neatly back into my desk tidy, I groaned as yet another email hit my inbox and I was incensed to see that it was from him again. Tempting as it was to delete it and bugger off home, I went ahead and opened it.

Hello again Helen,

Christina left work early with a headache. Most of the techies are out on audits and I'm not troubling any of the accountants I've been upstairs to the archive room but my search was in vain. I really had no wish to trouble you, but we may get the Wright and Butler account back. I am meeting with them Saturday morning (tomorrow) and I want to have some background knowledge before the meeting. That's why I need the file as a matter of urgency; otherwise I wouldn't have wanted to put you to any trouble. Sorry to ask again, but please could you help?

James

"Fucking hell!" I cursed out loud.

My plans for an early escape from the office were in ruins, but my earlier anger eased off a little. It was now a major irritation and I tutted and grumbled, punching hard at the letters on the keyboard as I sent him my brief and smart-arsed reply.

Fine! Give me ten or fifteen minutes.

I purposely stayed at my desk to wait ten minutes or so. With no intentions of letting James think I jumped to it instantly on his say so, I was determined to make him wait, although I didn't want to hang around the office any longer than was necessary. Roughly eleven minutes after I pressed 'send email' I grudgingly made my way up the two flights of stairs to the large archive room, which was in effect, the attic. It ran the full length and width of the building, with row upon row of racking down the higher centre area, which formed five aisles. Under the lower parts of the eaves, at the back and front of the building, there was a row of two-tier filing cabinets. Old accounting records of previous and current clients were stored up there, along with the archived accounting and payroll records for The Hopkins Partnership itself. Buff coloured client folders when full, were placed in archive storage boxes, on which the contents of each were labelled. Fortunately for me, I knew exactly where I would locate the file of Wright and Butler; second shelf up from the floor, and in the furthest corner from the door.

When I opened the attic door, the tiny skylight in the roof provided nothing but blackness; daylight had been gone for maybe fifteen minutes. I flicked the light switch and the one pathetic pendant fitting in the centre, with its gloomy 40 watt bulb, provided not the best illumination for searching through old records. I made a mental note to get one of our young men to replace it with a higher wattage bulb as soon as possible. As my eyes adjusted to the meagre lighting, I carefully made my way over to the racking in the far corner. Scanning the labels of the half dozen storage boxes on the second shelf up, my eyes finally accustomed to the dim light, I eventually pulled out the one with Wright and Butler listed on its contents label. I removed the lid and rifled through the buff folders until, halfway down the box, I found what I was looking for.

"There you are," I said, speaking out loud to the inanimate folder as I pulled it free and placed it out of the way until I shoved the storage box back.

I was just about to grab hold of the folder again when the attic was suddenly plunged into its normal night-time blackness.

"Oh, fuck!" I groaned out loud, as I was left fumbling around for the bloody folder. Not forgetting who caused my unwanted predicament, I grouched to myself sulkily. "Bloody James Mortimer and his damn file!"

Trying to grope around in the dark for the folder was pointless, as I couldn't even see my own hands. It niggled that I would have to go downstairs and waste even more time to get either a torch from the kitchen, or a new light bulb. I scoffed at myself as I started groping my way along the racking trying to suss out where the outline of the doorway was.

So stupid, Helen! You'll need the torch anyway if you're going to change the bloody light bulb!

Carefully feeling my way along with both hands out to the side of me, I came to the end of the aisle. Suddenly, I was pushed rather roughly into the end of the metal racking. I screamed out loud as whoever it was, pushed the weight of their body hard in to mine. I jumped sharply as he whispered softly in my right ear,

"There's nobody to hear you, Helen, only me."

I should have bloody realised. I cursed myself inwardly before venting at him.

"JAMES! GET-THE-FUCK-OFF-ME! THIS-INSTANT! I screamed at him, totally outraged one second, then with my voice shaking, I became anxious.

"The staff..." He cut me off in a split second as he spat out his reply,

"...have all gone home, Helen...early. I told them all to go and start their weekends early. They've worked hard this week." He laughed, I assumed, with pride at his own resourcefulness. "It's just you and I, Helen...oh, and some unfinished business in the dark...like last time."

He pushed his body hard against mine again and I struggled, trying to free myself, but his strength and bodyweight held me tightly in position; the hardness of his length, pushed tight between the cheeks of my backside. With one hand fiercely gripping my right arm, he pulled it out from where it had been trapped in front of my body. Forcing my fist open first, his free hand grasped mine and pulled it into position near the metal upright of the cabinet. Something brushed across the back of my knuckles towards the direction of my wrist and, once there, was pulled tight, forcing the silver beads of my bracelet to dig into my skin.

"James...let me...fucking...out of here." I screeched at him. "Your folder...is somewhere over there," I don't know why, but I nodded in the darkness to the general area where the file sat. He wouldn't have been able to see my head movement anyway. "Just let me go home. You're...hurting me."

My stomach churned. My head was in pure turmoil. I didn't know whether to feel angry, or scared...or turned on. He laughed, manically, as he pulled roughly on my left arm and began to repeat the process.

"Soon be done, Helen. Then we can start enjoying ourselves...in the dark."

As a second restraint swiftly swept over the back of my left hand and tightened, the turbulence in my mind turned into absolute fury. I realised what the restraints were; cable ties! Cable ties that we used for archiving hole-punched documents to free up lever-arch files; cable ties that were evidently placed in situ in advance... already looped loosely around the metal upright ...waiting for the intended victim; me!

"YOU...FUCKING...BASTARD!" I screamed at the top of my voice. "YOU DIDN'T EVEN NEED...THE...THE... FUCKING FILE!"

With his weight still holding me firmly against the shelving and the length of his cock still throbbing against my arse, he let his hands rub suggestively up and down the outside of my thighs.

"YOU...PLANNED...this...whole...
BLOODY...CHARADE!"

Withdrawing his hands from my thighs, he eased them between our bodies, and in that restricted space, he unfastened the zip at the back of my skirt. I tensed.

"DIDN'T YOU? I bellowed. "FUCKING ANSWER ME, JAMES!"

Not expecting it, I almost died as his voice suddenly hissed in my right ear.

"Yes. I did plan it, Helen. Of course I did. Because you still want me to fuck you to hell and back, don't you, Helen? And I still want to fuck you; rough, hard...and make you cum a thousand times over. Make you beg for more...and more...and..."

As my skirt fell to the floor around my ankles, I subconsciously parted my legs a little, while I started raging at him once more.

"It was cruel and heartless, what you did to me last time, you twat! If you're planning on...pissing off...and lea..."

He cut me off before I could finish, "You're an impatient bitch, Helen. You needed to exercise some patience and self-control. But you've earned a little treat tonight."

I inhaled deeply and closed my eyes. His promise of a treat caused an ache through my core and I was feeling damp below as he pushed my panties down, urgently. I wanted him...desperately, and I hated myself for that; for needing him to fuck me senseless.

"I can feel suspenders again, Helen. You know, I really wanted to fuck you badly that other time. You'll never know how bad, but I exercised self-control. You could learn a lot from me, sweetie." Stroking two fingers over my folds, he taunted me, edging closer to my entrance and then away again, stroking through my pubic hair. My mind was also suffering and the tendrils of my earlier dull headache were back, creeping into my forehead. Fearing an action replay of that night in my office, I couldn't help but remain tense. In my mind I was fighting so hard not to want him, but my body was already on fire and wanting that action; needing to cum, time and again and wanting his cum to put out my flames.

Suddenly, the pressure on my body was gone, his fingers had gone, and for a few seconds I thought he'd done it again; played the same trick as last time. Then, in a matter of seconds, I heard shoes being kicked off, a zipper being lowered. My every nerve was taut and my insides churned with longing. His bare cock felt warm as it waited, poised rock hard, throbbing against my buttocks, and his fingers stabbed into me, opening me up and swiftly explored my depth. He massaged furiously over my clit and I tingled and shuddered in anticipation.

"You're nice and wet for me, Helen. Are you ready for me to make you wetter still? Your cum and mine, sweetie."

Oh fuck! I was on the edge.

"Yes, I'm ready. James…just…FUCK ME!" I begged.

"Not yet, Helen! You're going to cum for me a few times before I fuck you for real."

As he eagerly worked on my clit and continued to jab inside me with his fingers, I arched my back in anticipation, but it was his tongue that tipped me over the edge when it provokingly licked at my rear entrance. In ecstasy, I moaned out loud and my body quivered in pleasure as I 'came'.

Barely giving me a chance to still from the peak of my climax, I gasped with greedy longing once more as he guided his pulsating length of muscle between the top of my thighs, rubbing my labia, its head cavorting in my wetness. His breathing became as laboured as mine as he bit into my neck and whispered behind my left ear,

"Slide your wrists down the metal, Helen. They'll move a little lower down to the next shelf."

Panting with expectation, I did as he asked, thinking that maybe my move would speed up the proceedings and I would soon have him filling my tingling, wanting depth. Feeling more comfortable once I had done so, and without the restraints digging painfully into my skin, I was able to concentrate fully, enjoying the feel of his thumb working frantically at my clit again.

"Are you ready to explode again, Helen? Another treat? You're a lucky lady this evening, wouldn't you say?

"J… just do…do it!" I stammered, as I arched my back expectantly.

We lost contact momentarily as he backed away to give me space.

"Bend over, make it…easier," he stuttered, and I could tell his need was growing, though my mind promptly flitted back to his boasting, about how he could exercise strict self-control.

"Right. I…I'm ready," I whimpered in a needy manner as I

leaned forwards, and the cable ties suddenly loosened a little more, moving freely about my wrists.

His hands groped in the dark and as he found me again, his right arm soon circled my waist, his hand thrusting upwards and under my bra. He pinched tightly on my hard nipple as his left hand guided his cock back between my legs, towards my wetness. From the pit of my stomach I ached for it...craved it, and I bit into my bottom lip. I thrust my rear towards him and, in full control, groaning loudly, he eased only the head into my opening, pulling out again instantly, pausing and repeating again, in a rhythm of his own choosing. In answer to my increased moans of pleasure, he rapidly abandoned his gropes at my breast. With a new urgency, he raked his nails down my front to thumb once more at my swollen button. I cried out noisily, feeling drunkenly giddy as my body shook violently with an orgasm so intense...mind-blowingly intense.

"AAARRGGHHH!" I screamed, causing him to pause in his actions.

"Helen? Wh...what's the matter?" he urged, sounding worried. "JA...JAMES! BACK OFF, QUICK! GIVE ME... GIVE ME...SOME SPACE!" I squealed desperately. "CRAMP...CRAMP...IN MY CALF! SORRY!"

"Okay! It's...okay, Helen."

Immediately sensing the space he considerately put between us, I silently crouched low, my recently freed hands groping in the blackness and deftly locating my skirt and panties on the old carpet. Using the metal corner for impetus, I pulled myself up and charged for the door and, as I reached the stairs, I heard his ear-splitting bellowing,

"YOU FUCKING BITCH! I'LL FUCKING GET YOU FOR THIS!"

Still in my heels, it was difficult trying to jump three or four steps at a time, but my decision to get my revenge was now worrying me, and I was genuinely fearful that he would catch me. I only had seconds to spare. My heart was pounding as I reached the first floor landing, but I still couldn't hear him taking the stairs.

I want to get to the front door. I need to get to the front door. Oh fuck!

Panic had taken over. All I could think about was getting out into the street, safely. Muttering to myself to be careful, I all but launched my body down the height of the last staircase. As I landed almost in a heap on the ground floor corridor, I saw the light from my office door. My handbag and coat! Must get my handbag and coat! Fuck, I've still got my skirt to put on! I stumbled toward my desk and snatched up the coat and handbag just as I heard his first footfalls on the top staircase. Figuring it would be unwise to get trapped by him in my office, I ran down the corridor and through to reception. I was gasping for air in my panic.

"HELEN! FUCKING WAIT THERE, DAMN YOU!" he shouted as I heard him striding across the first floor landing, about to make a start down the main staircase.

I unlatched the front door and opening it halfway, I stood out of sight behind it, stepped into my skirt and smartly tugged it into position. Venturing out from my makeshift dressing room, I stuffed my knickers into my bag and hurried over the threshold into the night air. Satisfied to be out of the confines of the office, I paused on the step to put my coat on, taking a deep breath or two as well, in an attempt to stem my panic-stricken gasping. I pushed my right arm into the sleeve of my coat and reached for the doorknob, ready to pull it closed behind me. Just as the door almost clicked into position, it was wrenched out of my hand and he grasped at my wrist, squeezing it painfully.

I looked into his eyes, smiling in a self-indulgent manner and held his gaze. With a quick backwards tilt of my head towards the street, I indicated the passers-by on the pavement; it was still rush-hour. He snarled at me through gritted teeth, keeping his voice low.

"I'll fucking get you for this, Helen. You need teaching a lesson or two, you bitch!"

Feeling rather smug at my revenge and not forgetting my very recent, much needed, sexual relief, I replied cockily,

"You need one or two lessons yourself, James! The first subject should be… the correct way to use cable ties. Perhaps I'll show you next week."

Giving him the broadest smile I could muster, I snatched my arm out of his grip with venom and quickly made my way down the street towards the tube station, without a backwards glance.

Before I turned the corner, I could hear him shouting down the street after me.

"HELEN!"

I carried on walking. I was on cloud nine.

"HELEN, I NEED THAT FILE FOR TOMORROW!"

I smirked.

Really? Then go find it yourself, you bastard!

CHAPTER 31

ork-wise, the run up to Christmas was a busy one. Four of our bigger account clients were having their annual audits, we had meetings galore to attend and the end of year self-assessment rush for the self-employed had already begun. At least three of the staff needed more than just two or three days off sick, which, thankfully, hadn't been at the same time during this busiest of periods, when they succumbed to a nasty flu virus doing the rounds. Luckily for me, it hadn't amounted to anything more than a head cold. It started with a sore throat on waking and by bedtime, I was sneezing constantly and my head felt like a kettle drum, but I managed to drag myself out of bed and go into work the next day. By the time we were due to leave the office the same night, I already felt much better.

With the exception of Linda, who after a unanimous decision, was not invited all the girls, myself included, went out for our obligatory girl's pre-Christmas bash to Mahiki, the exclusive night-club in Mayfair. This was held on the last Saturday before the office closed for the two-week holiday period. It was my annual treat for them all. In keeping with the Caribbean theme we drank cocktails all night, danced, and indulged in a little 'spot the celeb' contest, of which there had been more than a smattering. Nina also came along to join us after a little coaxing, but only for a couple of hours. She put on a good show of enjoying herself but hadn't been able to indulge in the cocktails because of her chemo three days beforehand. Christina, who was temping to cover Cindy's job as receptionist, very graciously told Nina how she hoped she would be feeling much better soon and could return to work. We all knew how much Christina enjoyed working for the practice, but her kind words for someone she only just met had been genuine and totally unselfish that I couldn't help but feel a strong affection for her.

On the twenty third of the month we closed the office at one o-clock; the start of our Christmas/ New Year break. This happened every year without fail, and straight from the office, Ted, myself and every member of staff went to a nearby restaurant, Champagne Charlie's, for our Christmas meal. There were more of us than ever with the new staff members, the new trainees and...bloody James Mortimer and Linda Brownlow. For that reason alone, I was dreading it; fearing any snide remarks, wondering if he would delight in fixing me with his gaze and his smug bastard grin. I knew that he was still smarting from my little payback stunt in the archive room. As things turned out, he was on his best behaviour in front of Ted, and other than approaching me a couple of times to ask what I would like to drink from the bar, he mainly tended to steer clear of me and any conversation that I happened to be involved in.

It was a pleasant and fun-filled afternoon and most of the staff exhibited copious amounts of Christmas spirit in addition to drinking it. Linda, just as I expected her to, almost remained tight-lipped throughout. She sulkily jabbed at the amazing lunch with her fork, eating only a small amount of turkey and the roast potatoes. She grudgingly replied when spoken to but never voluntarily joined in with the conversations and hilarity. By two forty-five she disappeared without a word to anyone and without even wishing one of us a Happy Christmas. After four o'clock, all the staff started to drift off, and there was kisses, hugs and festive greetings galore until the only ones remaining were James Mortimer, Ted and his wife Hilary, who joined us every year for the party, and me. Ted and James eventually started talking shop and I prayed that I wouldn't get drawn into their chat, as it would have been too much like hard work to be civil to him. So it was rather convenient when I met up with Hilary in the ladies' powder room, for me to tell her I was overly tipsy and that I was about to leave for home. I wished her all the best and asked her to pass my best wishes on to Ted. After a little hesitation, I thought it appropriate to ask her to convey those wishes to James too, though it nearly choked me to do so. I made a discreet escape.

I finished my Christmas shopping a couple of weeks beforehand, not that I had much to do. I had no family to buy for other than Catherine and Ruby, David's daughters, who I now considered to be my family; sort of stepdaughters. I spent an exciting day in the city looking for presents that I knew they would love, along with some pretty unusual novelty items. Of each of Mum's and Dad's families, my aunts and uncles stopped buying presents a good few years ago when their grandchildren started arriving, so there was no need to buy for them. The only other presents I bought were for my closest friends at work: Gemma, Gillian, Cindy, Nina, Leanne, Janet, and this year, Christina. We'd always done it. Never anything too expensive, just a token gift for around ten pounds. We had, as always, exchanged our gifts on the last morning at work, but we all agreed to take them home for opening on Christmas morning.

At their request, Catherine's and Ruby's presents were under the tree at my house. During our telephone call a couple of weeks ago, I asked if they would like me to mail them to their home address. As I expected, both girls were spending the holidays at home with their Mum and step-father. I was thrilled when they agreed to come across to stay with me for a few nights. They were due to arrive the day after Boxing Day.

Christmas Eve arrived with one or two snow flurries, and as there was no reason to leave the warmth of my cottage, I indulged in a very rare, lazy morning in bed. I went downstairs to the kitchen around eight thirty and made a pot of coffee and 'nuked' a couple of chocolate croissants in the microwave for a few seconds. After giving Harry his breakfast, I made my way back up the stairs with a tray, making sure I left the bedroom door open for him. Once he feasted, he would be sure to make his routine early morning appearance for some fuss and attention.

For the first hour or so I made myself comfortable propped up on the pillows, and read a novel I started a few days ago. With Harry having made himself at home on my bed and constantly craving attention, I struggled each time I needed to swipe across the screen to turn the page. The second I removed my hand from his fur, he nudged at my arm persistently until he got my undivided attention again. After a time I gave up on my attempts to get back into the story I'd been reading. Snuggling back down into bed, I concentrated on trying to increase the volume of his louder-by-the-minute purring as I stroked him lovingly with both my hands.

Eventually, Harry fell asleep. He was usually shattered anyway after his night-time wanderings and when he finally drifted off to sleep, his purring was replaced by hilarious little snorting noises. As I carefully manoeuvred my hand away from the snoring little beast in case I woke him from his slumber, my thoughts turned to David. Thinking back to my grief-stricken months, it occurred to me that had he not had cancer and died that November just over a year ago, we could have been preparing for our *second* Christmas together. However, I was stuck with facing my second holiday period alone, except for the company of my furry-faced friend. I silently indulged in more than a few tears and oodles of self-pity for half an hour or more. I imagined myself browsing through the best stores in London or Geneva searching for the perfect gift for him. More than that, I pictured his handsome features and that sexiest of smiles as he opened his gifts from me and I felt his hot sensual lips on mine as he thanked me for each and every one. I finally gave in to some loud sobs that wracked my body, feeling my devastation all over again. As Harry, from his curled up position with paws over his eyes, removed one paw and carefully scrutinised me with one eye open, I hauled myself out of bed and into the en-suite, determined to shake off my misery and make the best of Christmas; alone.

As it was unnecessary for me to venture outside, which due to the freezing cold weather I was relieved about, once I showered, I threw on some old grey jogging bottoms and matching grey fleece and poured myself a gin and tonic. I planned, while in the shower, to get comfy on the sofa and see what Christmas films were having yet another airing on television. Drinking alcohol and stuffing my face with chocolates also formed part of the itinerary, along with some phone calls to convey my festive greetings to some friends.

With the remote in one hand and a G & T in the other, I flicked through the channels and as I wasn't the least bit interested in Home Alone Two, The Great Escape, Jumanji or the special Celebrity Christmas Family Fortunes, I switched off and opted for some music instead. I decided to shift my butt through to the kitchen to prepare my Christmas dinner for one. When I did my last food shop, I literally given myself a pat on the back as I purchased fresh vegetables, a free range chicken (I hate turkey) and all the trimmings; intent on cooking rather than selecting an easier option. Singing along with the lyrics to the seasonal songs on the radio, I chopped my vegetables, prepared home-made stuffing and wrapped a couple of chipolatas with bacon in readiness for the big day. Slightly inebriated, I danced between the worktops as I worked, trying to force a Christmas spirit that I didn't feel.

Taking my place on the sofa once more and with Paul McCartney and Wings 'Mull of Kintyre' blasting out, my thoughts quickly turned to Mum and Dad; they'd both loved that song. Mum told me years ago that they spent their entire honeymoon exploring Scotland and some of its islands. I closed my eyes as memories of family Christmases came to the fore. My first pony, Beauty, had been the main present when I was five years old; my pile of presents under the tree that were sneakily taken downstairs after I was shooed off to bed each Christmas Eve; the fabulous Christmas Dinners when aunts, uncles and cousins attended; Mum's scrumptious mince pies. How I ached to experience those happy, seasonal days just once more. To have my father poised, ready and waiting with his camera to capture my expression with each parcel I opened. It was that horrible knowledge that they were gone forever and along with them, Christmas had died as well. This time it was a gin-induced grief that visited me. Oblivious to the festive background music, my heart broke all over again as I grieved for my parents. I snatched a handful of tissues and, face down into a cushion, I sobbed uncontrollably for the second time that day, occasionally dabbing at the stream of tears that threatened to soak the cushion.

At some point during my tear-sodden indulgence, I must have succumbed to more than just a doze. When I finally came to, it was dark outside and approaching half past six. Mince pies! I haven't bought any mince pies! Where that thought suddenly sprung from I had no idea, but rather abruptly, I dashed into the kitchen and switched on the oven in readiness, feeling that I mustn't let Christmas pass without baking mince pies. Luckily I purchased a couple of jars of mincemeat a few weeks back and I scooped it into a bowl and added, as Mum always did, a couple of tablespoons of brandy. Not quite sober, I had to really think hard what to do next, so I voiced the instructions out loud for a couple of minutes to gain some concentration. 'Grease and flour a tartlet tin, twelve.' I rummaged through my baking tin cupboard and found said item and completed the greasing and flouring. 'Okay! Get things ready for pastry making.' I opened and closed cupboard doors gathering all the necessary items together. 'Mixing bowl – check! Rolling pin – check! Pastry cutters – check! Flour, butter, cup of water – check!' I preferred to sit when baking, so once the ingredients and utensils were to hand, I sat on one of the two stools at my low-level, centre island (which also served as a kitchen table), and set to work.

While I kneaded the dough, it suddenly came back to me where the sudden urge to make mince pies h stemmed from. During my earlier reminiscing of my parents' Christmases, Mum's delicious mince pies had sprung to mind. I had never tasted mince pies to beat them wherever I had been. With Mum's words ringing in my ears I started mixing the pastry. 'You need cold hands, Helen…and never take too long over mixing…don't over-rub the fat in, darling.'

With the two mounds of pastry expertly rolled out to the

perfect thickness on my floured granite top, I placed the cutters carefully to make sure I got twelve bigger rounds for the bases of the pies and the twelve smaller rounds for the lids. I was just about to start pressing each base into the greased tin when my doorbell rang a couple of times.

"Fuck!" I cursed.

I wasn't expecting any visitors so I was puzzled. Everyone I knew would almost certainly be involved in family gatherings somewhere, so I expected it to be my scatty, but likeable, new neighbour, Cassie, who I quickly learned was not very skilful at compiling even the simplest of shopping lists. Heading to answer the door with my hands still clogged up with pastry and flour, I wondered what festive item she 'simply couldn't be without, darling.' I laughed as I flung the door wide open, and in a mock grumble, uttered,

"NO! You bloody ca…can't….."

My voice petered out; astonished to have a Christmas gift bag almost thrust in my face by Simon, the last person I expected to see.

"Merry Christm…FU…FUCK ME, Helen!" He stuttered. "Fucking hell. I can't believe it! Only you could look as stunning in jogging bottoms."

After standing there rigid with shock, eyes and mouth, wide open all I could manage was a barely whispered,

"Si…Simon?"

CHAPTER 32

"*D*o I get invited in then, sweetie?" he asked as I remained in a daze, unable to take it in; the fact that he was on my doorstep on Christmas Eve. "Or do you expect me to stand here in the...it's fucking snowing, you know...freezing my bollocks off?"

My vision was so blinkered to see Simon standing there, I hadn't even noticed the snow until he mentioned it, but for a second or two my eyes focussed on the street-light over the road. Yes, it was snowing. Big flakes were coming down thick and fast, and it was sticking to the cobbled road. I suddenly remembered my manners.

"Of course, Simon. Come in."

He stepped into the hallway and once he placed the gift bag on the floor, he turned around and kissed me ever so gently on the lips before I even closed the door. The way his lips whispered over mine sent my head into a spin.

"Wh...what are you doing here, Simon?"

Ignoring my question, he held me away from him, appraising me from top to toe and chuckling with laughter.

"Flour in your hair, flour on your nose and..." he dabbed

on the right-hand side of my face a couple of times, "…your cheek…it's even on your clothes, sweetie. Yet you still manage to be a ravishing sight to behold and so…sexy!"

Releasing my arms, he encircled my waist and pulled me tight up to him, kissing me in a more demanding and needful way. I could feel the early stirrings of a hard-on, as he pulled me hard against his crotch. A heady feeling came over me. I was hot all of a sudden, and remembering the last time we met up, I could feel my dampness down below. I wanted him. But it crossed my mind that I didn't know how long he called in for. Maybe he called just to drop off the gift bag for me? Reluctant to let my need grow for fear of being left disappointed, I regretfully pushed him away and announced,

"I'm making mince pies."

And with that said, I didn't leave him much option but to follow me as I walked down the hallway and back to the kitchen.

"So…what exactly are you doing here, Simon? And on Christmas Eve too, of all nights?"

I enquired again, as I picked up one of my rounds of pastry and pressed it down firmly into the tin. Keeping my back to him, intent on doing something to rid myself of the desire that burned within my lower regions and the vulgarity of the scenes that ran through my mind, I peeled another pastry round from the floured granite. Without any warning, I jumped, momentarily startled as he swept my hair to one side and kissed my neck softly. His hands delved into my waistband and pushed my jogging bottoms down urgently. Arching my back expectantly, I sighed and closed my eyes.

"I'm here…to give you your…Christmas present, of course," he eventually growled, as he nibbled provocatively at my neck.

He'd shoved my joggers down as far as mid-thigh, and with a few smart moves between our bodies, his fingers swiftly unfastened the metal buttons of his flies. The fire inside of me that I just tried so hard to extinguish, took hold once more. I groaned with longing when I felt his solid length slap onto my rear as it was released from the confines of his denims and underwear. His arms reached around to my front. Hands edging upwards and into my bra, he tweaked at my proud and sensitive buds. I shuddered with excitement.

"Turn to face me, Helen."

He lowered his hands to my waist, his fingertips inadvertently tickling the sides of my ribs, and guided me around to face him, his brown eyes sparkling with wickedness. I felt his thick, throbbing cock at the top of my thighs and could contain myself no longer. With my fingers unfastening the buttons of his shirt with skilful speed, I disturbed his probing fingers as I leaned into him and tried to yank it down over his shoulders and arms. It snagged on his watch for a second as I carelessly tugged it free and threw it across the kitchen floor. Every glorious nerve in my body was alert, tense and waiting, my heart pounding, and I gasped in anticipation.

"God, Helen! You are just…so fuckable!"

He snarled, wantonly. And with that he hoisted me into a sitting position on the worktop and swiftly wrenched my bottoms and panties over my feet and dropped them to the floor. His mouth crashed onto mine, his tongue darting in and out between my lips, and I sensed his urgency as he fumbled to unfasten the zip of my fleecy top.

"Simon! I want you now…fuck! Let's go up." Struggling to breathe, with my heart beating like a bass drum, I pleaded with him.

My eyes roved over the sexy masculinity of his broad chest and bending my head down, I tongued each of his nipples in turn and watched as they too became erect. He panted heavily as I nuzzled in and appealed to him more urgently.

"Si...Simon, upstairs..."

"No! It's here and now, sweet thing," he wheezed as I felt the head of his cock nudge eagerly at my wetness and I cried out to him pathetically, impatient for more.

Supporting me with his hands, he leaned over and lowered my back onto the work top, and as he did so, his rigid muscle edged into my opening. Squeezing his fingers between our lower bodies he made his first contact with my clit whilst he slowly pushed further into me and it tipped me over the edge before I had a chance to savour the moment. My body continued to judder in the throes of orgasm as he didn't let up with his increasingly powerful thrusts. Spurred on by my cries and evident sensitivity to his each and every move, he ground his hips deep into my pubic area, forcing even further into me.

Thoroughly engrossed with the way every inch of me tingled inside and out, I gave a deep sigh of enjoyment as he lowered his head and covered my right breast with his mouth. He taunted my nipples playfully. I was vaguely aware that his right arm reached way beyond my head, but it didn't occur to me to wonder what he was doing as I was busy concentrating on his touch, and the ripples of pleasure coursing through my depths. Seconds later, he lifted his head from my breast and gazed deep into my eyes as he sharply thrust two fingers toward my tongue.

"Taste it, Helen. Let me watch you...suck and lick."

Opening my eyes to look at him, trying to grasp his true meaning, I sucked greedily on his fingers, and tasted alcohol. In an instant he withdrew his fingers and smeared more of the sweetness onto my lips before pushing them back between my teeth. Holding his gaze, I saucily sucked the mincemeat off his fingers greedily, and he was frenzied, his eyes burned with crazed lust, and I wanted him to fuck me harder.

He reached over towards the bowl again and brought his fingers back to smear more of the festive mixture around my lips and into my mouth.

"Suck. Sweet, Helen! Suck me...hard!"

My heart felt as if it almost stopped with the intense, unanticipated eroticism of the moment, but it was me; I was holding my breath. As I held his gaze, I sucked hard and clenched tight around his cock and couldn't miss the fierce inferno that raged in his eyes. I sensed that his need to spill was nearing critical. Then...he'd watched for long enough, and his mouth came down hard on mine, our tongues danced together and we shared the taste in wild abandon for each passing second as he plunged faster and faster, deeper into me with his rigid muscle.

"FUCK!" He yelled out loud "Oh...FUCK!"

I reached out and grasped the cheeks of his arse, stilling his movements, squeezing tighter on his length, which remained buried deep within me. I was desperate to feel his throbbing and reach my own dizzy, mind-blowing orgasm as he exploded. I screamed out loud as I came, accompanied by his noisy, vocal grunts of pleasure as his release still pumped inside of me.

Still grunting in his delight, he pushed his arms underneath me and pulled me closer to him before letting his bodyweight rest on top of me. While our breathing slowly returned to normal, his head seemed to be jerking against my breasts. I lifted his face up to meet mine and was amazed to see that something was suddenly amusing him as he sniggered up at me.

"What? What's so funny, Simon?"

I shrieked as his infectious chuckle made me smile. Without answering at first, he pulled one arm out from behind my back and dangled a sticky, sorry looking piece of pastry in front of my eyes, and laughed out loud.

"Your back is covered in rounds of pastry, Helen. There's mincemeat around your face and your mouth and you've still got flour on your nose."

I huffed at him sharply, feigning irritation, before hissing at him hysterically.

"Well answer me this, Mr Shag Buddy; how the hell do you come to have mincemeat on your left ear, huh? And you've stolen some of my flour; it's stuck to the sweat on your forehead."

With both hands free, he pushed himself back up to stand, both of us still snorting in raucous laughter. He grabbed my hands and hauled me up to stand in front of him. I turned slightly away from him to pick up my joggers and panties and he doubled up again, hands on his knees, howling.

"It seems your pastry is as fond of your arse as I am, Helen."

And he reached out to my backside and peeled off four sad rounds, holding them up for a second for affect, then jumped over to my waste bin to dispose of them, his denims and boxers still around his ankles.

I rushed upstairs afterwards to have a quick clean up, and get into my dressing gown. Walking into the lounge, I hadn't expected him to have made himself comfortable so quickly but he was lounging on the sofa, denims back on but still bare-chested, and with a glass in his hand, which he raised to me in greeting.

"I've poured one for you, sweetie. Don't worry."

"I wasn't! So, would you now mind explaining to me why you are here on Christmas Eve and not with your family?" I asked firmly. "Not that I'm complaining, you understand."

"As I told you earlier, Helen, I came to bring your pres…"

I stopped him mid-sentence with a scowl in his direction,

imagining they had some row or other, and I was desperate to know why and what about.

"Okay, okay! I'm teasing. We were due to go over to our daughter's house today, in Bristol. It is essential that we stay for four nights apparently. Some 'do' or other arranged at her husband's parents' home."

He paused and took a few infuriatingly lingering sips of his wine. I raised my eyebrows, fixing him with one of my special scowls.

"Yes, Miss Impatient. If you would stop glaring at me, I'll spit it out."

I carried on scowling, but he set out to explain it anyway.

"Well, my wife is staying the four nights. She drove over to Bristol this morning. I stayed back here to do some work. I have a large case due to commence in court next week so I needed to get my papers in some sort of order. I'll be driving over there first thing tomorrow morning…when I leave here. My wife already took my luggage."

I could do nothing to suppress the broad smile that must have lit up my face. He beamed at me, obviously delighted at my reaction to his news.

"Now…come on!" He urged as he pulled me up off the sofa. "Your oven is still on. Have you plenty of ingredients left?"

Without waiting for me to answer, he ploughed on regardless, and hurried through to the kitchen to make a start.

"We've baking to finish, and I'm rather partial to a couple of mince pies with a nightcap."

I watched, totally dumbstruck, as he cleaned up the mess we made and deftly set about mixing more pastry and rolling it out to perfection. I filled the bases and placed the lids on them as Simon washed up the baking utensils. Within forty five minutes I removed a perfect tray of mince pies from the oven and joined him in the lounge.

"And talented pastry chef to boot, huh? I'm impressed, Simon."

He grinned up at me, as I sprawled next to him on the sofa, my dressing gown parting and seductively exposing my nether regions to him. His eyes lingered a few moments and I don't know if he realised it but I saw the longing as he swallowed, then ran his tongue around his lips, perhaps in anticipation.

"In addition to what other talents, may I ask?" He queried.

"Well, there's…"

"Oh shit, hang on." He got up and rushed off to the hallway, returning with his gift bag, which had been forgotten by the pair of us during our messy and blatant eroticism. He gently placed the bag in my lap as he walked past me to sit back down. Peering into the festive gift bag, I counted three parcels in all. There were two small packages and a larger one; an Ann Summers' gift bag. Suddenly feeling guilty that I hadn't bought even one gift for him, I apologised most profusely.

"Simon, you shouldn't have. I feel guilty and so sorry. I didn't expect anything. We are not really in a relationship, if you know what I mean?"

"Helen, don't say another word. Nothing you could ever buy me could match up to the pleasure I feel every time I fuck you, sweet thing. Nothing could equal that pleasure when I look into your eyes and watch the expressions on your face as you cum all over my cock. Nothing…" He cut his sentence short as he watched me picking at the sticky tape that held the Ann Summers bag closed. "No. Not yet, Helen. You can open that one before we take a shower together later. The two smaller ones you must keep until morning."

Feeling like a naughty child, I placed the bag on the carpet, eyeing him sheepishly.

Even after we'd sat around for a couple of hours or more, I was still struggling to get over the surprise at him even being there with me, let alone the fact that we already had sex amongst some mince-pies-in-progress. However, it was lovely not to be alone. He was a fantastic lover and an interesting guest whose company I always enjoyed. With my subject of accountancy being so unappealing to many, I seldom discussed it outside a work environment. However, listening to some of Simon's tales about courtroom dramas was fascinating. He regaled me with some basic and funny details about his cases, but ever the professional that he was, no names were ever disclosed by him and I would have expected no less.

After a few glasses of wine and almost three hours of stimulating conversation, Simon went through to the kitchen and returned with two plates, two mince pies on each.

"Here you are, sweet thing. Eat these first then I will let you open the Ann Summers' bag."

One mince pie was enough for me, tasty though it was. I offered the extra one to him while I picked off the sticky tape which held the bag together. I opened the bag to discover a glittery, silvery blue, 3-way vibrator, which besides the usual vaginal penetration, offered a clit stimulator plus anal penetration. I ogled it shamelessly as I removed it from its gaudy box and examined every inch.

"This looks like being some erotic and dirty fun."

"Well when you bought the last one, I was quite disappointed. For a lady, like you, Helen, it was just so boring, and you are definitely not boring. Anyway, this one is waterproof as well. So...care for some dirty fun in the shower, Miss Rushforth?"

He held his hand out to me, but I didn't take it. I

unscrewed the cap of the vibrator, looking to see what size batteries were required; 3 AAAs. Fuck! I knew I didn't have any and I cursed in my frustration.

"Oh, fuck it! I don't have any…"

"Helen, look in the bag…they're at the bottom."

Sighing with relief, I groped in the bag to retrieve the batteries. I noticed the bulge in his denims was expanding as he watched me fondle the phallus, and I shuddered as the wanting ache in my groin resurfaced. Snatching the vibrator from the sofa, my stomach flipped in excitement as I headed for the stairs.

"Seriously, Helen, did you honestly think I would purchase a vibrator to use on you and forget about the fucking batteries?" He tutted and teased in his almost sarcastic manner as he followed close behind me, slapping my arse on each step.

Rushing to get into the shower room, I was hoping I would have time to finish shampooing the baking ingredients out of my hair, before Simon joined me. I left him sat on my bed inserting the batteries into our new sex-toy. I hadn't forgotten the comment he made downstairs about it being waterproof. I presumed that he intended to turn our shower into adults' play-time. Although he purchased it for me, he would also be getting his satisfaction from it. The way I saw it, it was for our mutual benefit, therefore 'ours', but I had no doubt that he would have expertly argued the point, if I gave him half a chance. He was a barrister, after all.

The few glasses of wine I had since our shag in the kitchen had made me light-headed and somewhat giddy, and although I giggled when I first saw the vibrator with its extra protuberances, I hid my real feelings. I couldn't seem to rid my brain of the thought of being doubly penetrated by the damned thing, and have my clit stimulated at the same time. I was so excited, and the top of my thighs grew deliciously damp before I entered the refreshing flow from the shower head.

Simon seemed to take forever to join me. Pleasantly drunk, greedy for more, and without a care in the world, I could think of nothing else but 'coming'. I needed to cum. Not able to think straight, it didn't occur to me to call out to Simon to hurry up. I was on fire. My stomach was churning with the need to be fucked. One way or another, I wanted satisfying. I'll do it myself then! It was only a drunken thought and not something I often resorted to, but desire taking over, I made a lather of shower gel in both hands and leant forward; my forehead on the cold tiles. Thinking only of my self-gratification, I smoothed the creamy lather down towards my clit with my right hand, taunting it gently with my thumb. I felt like I was floating. I rubbed over it a few more times and then moved on to stroke the folds of my labia. Then I roughly pushed two fingers into my depth; my body jerked in ecstasy. I poked them in and out of myself, and it felt dirty. Somehow it felt wrong, but I didn't care, to my heart and my body, it felt right. It was heaven. I was also fondling my breasts with my free hand, and it was like an electric charge that touched every last nerve, both in my breasts and in my warmth. I knew I was going to cum, and for once it was of my own volition.

Opening my knees outwards, to gain deeper access with my fingers, I almost stumbled clumsily as my hand was suddenly wrenched from between my legs, and Simon growled manically in my ear.

"Let me help you with that, you fucking horny bitch. Phwoar! I've loved watching the masturbation scene you just laid on for me for the last few minutes, but I'm going to fuck you now, sweetie, first of all with this!"

Without wasting another second, he plunged the quietly humming vibrator deep inside me. Each orifice, along with my nub, felt such immediate intensity that I 'came' instantly…and explosively. My back arched and my legs would have buckled beneath me if he hadn't quickly grabbed me in his arms.

"Fuck me! You were there before I touched you, sweetie. I should have watched you make yourself cum first, and used this later."

My breathing took some time to calm after the orgasm and I turned to watch as Simon seductively soaped his body and stared at me intensely. I could see the fire deep in his eyes as he started massaging the length of his cock, soft slow moves at first that became faster as he gripped himself firmly and groaned at me in pleasure. I looked on, eyes wide and completely mesmerised.

"Oh, yes. I can wank as well, Helen. But I'd rather stuff it into you and feel your wet, pulsing pussy gripping me hard."

Taking my elbow to assist me, he said,

"Get on your hands and knees on the tiles, sweetness. I'm going to fuck you hard from behind and I want you to scream out when it hurts."

Trying not to slip, I lowered myself to all fours, eager for his cock, but I wasn't quite ready when he slammed it inside me with as much brute force as he could manage without his knees giving way. He knocked the breath out of me and I screamed. I screamed again with the next, and every other thrust he made. He was drunk and I didn't understand where his power was coming from. I struggled to breathe, but it was mind-blowing. Hurting, yet feeling alive and revelling in my hurt, I gripped hard on his thickness to feel every throbbing inch of him filling me to the core. Every nerve in my depth tingled in sweet pain as his length rubbed abrasively with each thrust into my clenched depth.

I'd been to heaven and beyond and I wanted him to feel it too, to send his cum deep within me. I screamed out to him.

"FUCK ME HARDER! SIMON!!"

He grunted some more but I was so sore I couldn't feel his cock twitching. I knew that when he gushed, it would induce me to cum once more, but it would sting. Pleasure and pain; I wanted it immediately. Seeing the vibrator in the corner, I reached for it and switched it on. Propping myself up with just one hand, I tilted my head so he could see my face. Switching on the vibrator, I ran my tongue up and down its length as I looked into his eyes. Once I had his attention, I shoved it hard in my mouth and sucked lovingly. It tipped him over the edge; he was there, matching my screams as our juices mingled.

Ten minutes later we were in my bed, our bodies spent, and it took all of three minutes before Simon was breathing heavily in his sleep. I was feeling a few degrees nearer to sober so I tried to read for a while and, as I was switching my lamp off, I spotted the vibrator on the cabinet at his side of the bed. My eyes were soon heavy and my last thought, before drifting off, was to wonder what he had planned for me when Christmas morning arrived.

CHAPTER 33

J awoke with a start sometime just after six in the morning, when I heard the toilet flush in the en-suite. I quickly pushed myself up and put one foot out of bed, ready to go and find a weapon. For a worrying few moments I genuinely thought that someone had broken into my house. Then I spotted the vibrator and events of the previous night came flooding back and I smiled to myself, indulgently. The bathroom door was ajar and the next thing I heard was Simon brushing his teeth. Luckily for him, before I rushed into the shower the previous night, I'd put a pack of new toothbrushes next to the wash basin.

Thinking that he was preparing to make an early start for Bristol, I waited for him to come back, ready to use the bathroom myself. He winked and slapped my butt playfully as he passed. Planning to make a pot of coffee and heat some chocolate and almond croissants for breakfast before he left, I grabbed my thick shower robe from the peg behind the bathroom door when I freshened up. I was surprised to see that he was back in bed, still undressed, and he patted the mattress next to him with a cheeky look in his eyes and a wide grin to match.

"Come here, sweet thing." He growled. "I want to wish you a Merry Christmas."

I hesitated; tempted. But it was playing on my mind that he should have been with his family today of all days, and I felt a little angry that he put me in this position, and he appeared to show no guilt for being in my bed. I was stood with my hand on the door knob, ready to go downstairs

"Well, I'm wishing you a Merry Christmas too...from over here." I added a little too late. "Anyway, I thought you were getting ready to leave? I'm on my way to make coffee and croissants."

He raised his eyebrows and his smile disappeared, a question playing on his lips.

"Do I sense some annoyance on your part, Helen? I detect a certain tone to your voice. I don't know, you tell me...what you're...what's eating you up?"

I brought my hands up to cover my face and I closed my eyes for a minute, thoughts swirling around in my brain. I was stumped. I didn't know how to explain.

"Helen?"

I opened my eyes and met his. I couldn't read what he was thinking and it concerned me somewhat. Worry? Was he worrying about what I was about to say? Or perhaps it was rejection, simply because I hadn't immediately jumped back into bed with him.

He snapped at me then, and I flinched.

"Helen? Tell me please. What is the matter? I'm not a fucking ogre. I need to know if I've said or done something wrong."

My stomach churned as I met his eyes again. I knew there was no point in delaying any longer, so I took a deep breath before blurting out exactly how I felt.

"Okay! Okay! I'm feeling guilty as shit, Simon. That's what! Here you are with me, naked in my bed, and its Christmas morning and you want to fuck me. What about your wife? She's probably missing waking up next to you right now; waiting with the family for you to arrive, so they can give you your presents. You should have gone to Bristol yesterday. Then I wouldn't have to feel like shit on Christmas Day. I would have been okay alone if you hadn't come round last night. I wouldn't have had to feel like this."

I was aware that my voice had risen to a level that sounded almost hysterical. He lowered his gaze, sighing heavily. I stood there, nervously clicking both thumbnails against both the nails of my forefingers, feeling uncomfortable and not knowing where to look; my face flushed with embarrassment. He looked up at me again, his expression softened, and he held his hands out for mine.

"Helen, come here please."

With a little more encouragement, I moved towards him and as I placed my hands into his I sat down next to him on the side of the bed.

"Can I ask you something, sweet thing?" I nodded my head once, not trusting myself to speak. "In all the time we have known each other...and answer this honestly, please. Have you ever felt guilty about our fucking? Have you ever, honestly, given my wife a second thought when you've been fucking me in my hotel rooms?"

I shuffled my backside around, a tactic to try to avoid his stare, but he placed his hand on my cheek and gently pulled my face closer to his.

"Helen?"

"I...er...NO! I bloody haven't! Have you?" I lashed out, feeling my guilt had just become a bigger burden during the last minute.

"So why now, sweetie, when it hasn't bothered you

before? Explain that to me please. And I'll answer your question in a minute when I've said one or two other things you need to know."

He was being very patient towards me. I suddenly started to see my outburst as rather pathetic, and I knew before I even let my answer escape my lips what his reply would be.

"It's Christmas, Simon. It's family time."

Yes, pathetic!

"When people are married with a family, Helen, every day should be a family day. So are you saying that for three hundred and sixty four days of the year it will be okay for me to fuck you, but Christmas Day is different and I should be with my wife? It doesn't quite work like that, sweet thing."

The way he put forward his argument did nothing at all to help the overwhelming turmoil I felt. I understood what he was trying to say, but I still wanted to argue the point; put him right. I was so irate, my head started pounding. The ire was more at myself than with him, and I felt furious that I bothered mentioning it at all.

But I…"

"No, Helen. Let me explain some more please and then I'll answer your question at the same time."

I opened my mouth to speak, but he placed two fingers over my lips, silencing me.

"Before you came in to my life, I had been unfaithful on a handful of occasions. I think, deep down, my wife knows, although she has never hinted at it, or voiced any suspicions."

Somehow, that cold hard fact didn't surprise me, although he may have noticed I was startled by his honesty.

"Yes, I know I'm a bastard." He stated those words with conviction. "Over the years, Mary…hasn't been very forthcoming in the sex department. She's not keen on sex and when we do…do it I am sure she sees any sex other than the missionary position as dirty. She won't try anything else. I

270

know that doesn't excuse what I've done, both in the past, and what you and I are doing now. I know it's wrong. Now let me put this to you, Helen. The day I met you, I was the one who started it all. Look at what I got you involved in for a while."

He paused a while, half expecting me to butt in. It was hard for me not to make some comment, but I resolved to let him continue. With no reaction or remarks from me, he carried on.

"I was the one who chose to come here to you last night. You didn't make me do it against my will. I pushed my presence onto you. You have nothing to feel guilty about, so stop it, please. You asked if I feel guilty, Helen. Yes I fucking do! Every time! Every time in the past, and every time I fuck you. Yes! I feel the guilt! I love my wife. She is very precious to me. I have needs that are so very different to hers, but it will never stop me feeling guilty. I'm the one who has to live with it. If you decided to end this arrangement of ours today… well, what I'm saying is that before long there would be someone else. I…yes, there would. It's the way I am, Helen."

There was far too much emotion in my head, and part of me felt slightly pacified by what he said, yet I was still troubled with guilt. Simon had only spoken briefly about his wife and during that time I found another reason to feel guilty. Things should have been different for me. I should have been spending my second Christmas with David. He should have been the first person I thought about the minute my eyes opened. David, and my parents, should have been here with me. I wanted to cry, but I couldn't just then. Lost in my thoughts, I stared at my hands in his and felt positive disquiet about that moment.

He shook both hands to snap me out of my reverie.

"Do I take it this matter is now dealt with?"

I nodded, but without much conviction.

"Yes. I suppose it must be."

"Are you going to come back to bed then, sweetie?" He pointed to the bedside cabinet. "This present didn't make much of an impression on you last night, did it?"

It was barely conceivable what he just said. My anger returned in an instant. I felt the colour rising, but I had no desire to get caught up in further in-depth conversations. Faking a smile, I played along but all I wanted to do was get him out of my house, as fast as I could.

"I would have loved to, Simon, but to be honest with you, I don't think I can. I have just been to the loo and my bits are stinging like a bitch. Any more, and I don't think I'd be able to sit down for a couple of days."

He looked crushed, but just as I had done, he made an effort to conceal it with a smile.

"Okay, that's fine. Let's face it, I have enough to feel guilty about already, without having your sore pussy on my conscience as well."

I let the sarcasm pass over my head and left him to get dressed in peace.

At breakfast was almost total silence between us. He sat at the counter drinking coffee but I drank mine on the move, as I made a show of involving myself in further preparations for Christmas lunch. I could feel his eyes piercing into my back, or maybe I just imagined it. I prepared my vegetables the day before so in no time at all, I struggled to find another chore and found myself hovering, wondering what to do next. Almost before I knew it, his arms were around my waist, and with the softest, most caring tone I ever heard from him, he brushed my hair behind my ear and whispered,

"Helen, please come and sit. Let's not be like this with each other."

He led me over, and eased me onto the chair next to where he'd been sat, and reached over for the coffee pot.

"I'm sorry, Simon. It is not my intention to be so... My parents should be here. David should be here. I..."

My eyes glazed over and then I was full of regret. Going over my words, I felt so callous. Pining for another man's company when I was with Simon...but I had loved David. I still did.

"Again, it is me who should be apologising, not you. I am just so fucking insensitive. Forgive me?"

I caved instantly. His apology was genuine; his eyes negating his tough, lawyer front.

"Of course, I forgive you, Simon." To put him at ease, I leaned forward and kissed him on the lips, lingering a little and holding his face in my hands. "How could I not?" I asked. "Particularly as I need you to show me exactly what that vibrator is capable of...the next time I see you."

Gazing deep into his eyes, I willed him to read me; to know how I felt about him. I needed him to know that I still desired him and desperately needed our arrangement to continue. He gave a sigh of relief, and returned my kiss enthusiastically, and for once, it was without lust and innuendo.

"Well, I guess that means it will have to be soon." We smiled knowingly at each other, as our foreheads met.

He was ready to leave by seven thirty, and it was with mixed emotions that I followed him to the front door to see him off.

"Drive carefully in this snow, Simon."

"I will. Open my other presents once I'm gone and enjoy them. We'll speak soon, yes?" I nodded. He kissed my cheek before pulling me in for a bear hug. Suddenly, he broke free from our hug and held one hand up behind his ear, as if listening to something.

"Think I can hear your mobile bleeping, Helen. No doubt

somebody is sending you an early Christmas greeting. Now, remember what I said. I must go."

I opened the door for him and feeling the frigid air, closed it quickly once he crossed the threshold into the wintry morning. I didn't wait around to watch him crunch his way through the snow, before turning the corner to where he parked his car in the neighbouring street. Finally, I was able to let go of my watery Christmas Day grief. I returned to the kitchen where, head in my hands, I sobbed freely into my coffee. The lack of a comforting pair of arms around my shoulders, having nobody to tell about the strong grief I still felt, added to my sense of feeling utterly lost...and lonely. For a while, I wished I accepted one of the half dozen or so invites I'd had to spend the day elsewhere. Disposing of my lukewarm and tear-diluted coffee down the sink, I poured a large glass of Vinho Verde and wandered through the lounge and back upstairs to join Harry, who would no doubt be settled on my bed.

Waking abruptly from what was a deep and dreamless sleep, I thought for a second that the day had passed me by. The digital numbers on my alarm clock soon contradicted that thought, though. It was ten past nine. I'd only been asleep for about seventy minutes and strangely it seemed like twenty four hours or more. For such a short slumber, I felt remarkably refreshed; my head much clearer and more posi-tive than I demonstrated earlier. The half glass of wine I was drinking earlier graced my cabinet and I was disgusted at my stupidity.

After tipping the remains of the wine down the loo, I showered and while I dressed, I remembered that there were several phone-calls I needed to make. Due to the surprise visit by my 'shag buddy', my plans to make the calls the previous night had been scuppered. The gift bag from Simon was sat between the cushions on the sofa, with the two small presents inside that I'd intended to open before he left. There were also several presents (from the girls at work) under the tree for me to open, amongst the ones that awaited the arrival of Catherine and Ruby.

As my fingers worked to unpick the curled ribbon on the first of Simon's presents, I gave a regretful sigh. I felt sorry that my selfish outburst pushed him into making some revelations that he maybe wouldn't have thought appropriate to mention otherwise. He loved his wife, she was precious; I knew that now. Yet I could have lived without him actually voicing the fact. The fact that he did speak it, hadn't exactly made me happy. I peeled off the snowflake wrapping paper to find a bottle of Jean Patou's eau de parfum, 'Joy', along with a short message he scribbled, 'Helen, I thought I would give you a little of the large amount of what you bring to me – 'Joy'. My love, always, Simon x'. His second gift also had a note attached, 'Here's what you love best…to go with your second best…gin!' It was a novelty ice-making mould to make ten cock-shaped pieces of ice. Although I shook my head in despair of the man, I couldn't help but feel amused by his Christmas gesture.

It was after my solitary lunch when I eventually picked up my mobile to give my festive greetings to Catherine, Ruby and my friends from the office. Simon had been right about my mobile phone bleeping with a text message as he left. There were three texts in all by the time I got around to checking it out. Gemma and Cindy had left their widely distributed, one-for-all texts, simply saying 'Merry Christmas xx'. When I clicked to open the third message, I was stunned to see Christina's lovely, cheery face with an arrow over her nose…a video message. I pressed the button to play and I watched enthralled as Christina sang to me, East 17's 'Stay Another Day' using her own hilarious lyrics and being a good deal less than complimentary about Linda and James. In keeping with the season, she was wearing a white parka-type coat, fur-trimmed hood over her head as the band had done during the making of the video. With her husband driving, Christina was doing the filming from the front passenger seat of their car, with her eighteen-year-old daughter and fourteen-year-old son sat in the back. During most of the filming she was looking straight ahead, but every couple of lines, she gave a sideways grin into the phone. When it came to each chorus, her son and daughter harmonised in the background, sounding like true professionals. In between the choruses they covered their mouths, trying to conceal what would have been their rambunctious laughter. Clearly they were enjoying their contributions to the unscheduled Christmas message.

As the song drew to a close, and her kids skilfully faded out the final chorus, Christina beamed into her mobile, 'Just for you, Helen…just for you.' I didn't know whether to laugh or cry…so I did both. The complete thing was priceless, but more than anything I was touched by the gesture; how this lovely lady had gone that extra mile just for my enjoyment. Although I never actually voiced my opinions regarding Linda and James to the staff at work (I left that, to the rest of the staff), Christina's message without a doubt, acknowledged that she was aware of the issues.

With the amazing video fresh in my mind, I dialled the first number and I was still laughing when the call was answered. Heidi, David's first wife, had picked up Catherine's mobile first, and before handing me over to her, she chatted pleasantly for a couple of minutes. She explained that Ruby hitched a lift with the parents of her best friend, Emily, to visit her in hospital. Emily had been rushed into hospital on Christmas Eve with appendicitis. Once Catherine and I exchanged our snippets of news, I made quick calls to Ted and Hilary, Gillian, and Leanne. Knowing that Nina and her husband, Paul, had gone to her parents for the Christmas break, I sent her a quick Christmas text. Her treatment had lowered her body's resistance to common ailments and she'd suffered flu-like symptoms for the past couple of days. At least she would be looked after.

With the phone calls all made, I finally got comfortable on the sofa with a gin and tonic and spent most of the day reading. It was rather unusual for me on Christmas Day, but I wasn't once tempted to switch on the television to watch the umpteenth rerun of one outdated film or another. Only due to a random heart-breaking chapter in my book, did my mind start to wander and I found myself succumbing to another tearful few minutes, dreadfully missing my parents and David. All my Christmases had been spent with my parents except for the two years since their untimely deaths, but where David was concerned, I grieved for what I never had, and yet sorely missed; buying a Christmas card for 'The One I Love', the excitement of searching for presents I knew he would be thrilled about, sharing a festive drink and a kiss, making love in the firelight; all the things that fucking cancer robbed me of.

I went up to bed just before midnight and, unable to sleep, my mind played havoc with me. I was not one to feel jealousy, but I felt such strong envy of my friends, at home with their husbands or boyfriends and families; people to share with, care for, laugh with and cry with. Surrounded by strangers in France, I hadn't entertained such thoughts, but now that I was back in the midst of friends and colleagues, I realised that being alone was becoming an issue for me. And I felt vulnerable. It was a long time before sleep folded me in its arms.

CHAPTER 34

After the girls arrived and settled in, the morning after Boxing Day, I asked them if they fancied a ride out into the countryside. They were delighted at the chance for us all to do something together, other than the usual post-Christmas activities of, being couch potatoes, watching too much TV, and eating far too much chocolate and other unhealthy nibbles. I didn't have a clue where to take them, or what they would enjoy doing, but just as we were about to get ready to go out, Ruby made a brilliant suggestion, much to my surprise.

"How about Epping Forest, Helen? It's somewhere I've never been and yet, I've always wanted to go."

I tried to hide my look of disbelief at the fact that Ruby wanted to do something other than drink or get stoned.

"Yes, we can do that if you want, Ruby. I have been to Epping, but not since I was about eight years old."

Catherine was full of enthusiasm at the suggestion as well. Her eyes shone with excitement and, beaming at her sister, she gave the plan her seal of approval.

"That's a brilliant place to go, Ruby, from what I've been told."

I'd been looking forward with nothing other than dread, to the girls coming to stay for four days. Although I was extremely fond of the pair of them, I hadn't been able to form a bond with Ruby and couldn't rid myself of the unpleasant memories of those couple of days they spent with me in Paris. Catherine, as always, had been a pleasure to deal with, but Ruby was a nightmare from start to finish. After advice from their mother, Heidi, Catherine cut short her own week with me. She was needed to accompany (or, more truthfully, chaperone) Ruby on the return flight to London.

From the day they arrived, things seemed different with Ruby this time. She'd graciously flung her arms around me, and kissed me on the cheek when I answered the door to them. There was no trace of the troublesome teenager who was responsible for all the havoc in Paris. With her make-up toned down considerably, she still looked older than her sixteen years, but definitely not the twenty-something-looking female I remembered meeting for the first time at Charles de Gaulle airport. I was pleasantly surprised to see the changes in her. Catherine also looked much more relaxed and I wondered if it was anything to do with the new persona that Ruby exuded.

After Ruby's request to visit Epping Forest, the three of us got ourselves suitably dressed up for the sub-zero temperatures outdoors with thick coats, hats, gloves and warm boots. Before leaving, we heated some soup and filled two old Thermos flasks, which had belonged to my parents and stuffed them into a backpack. Rather than bother using the car, we took the tube into Oxford Circus and used the Central line to Theydon Bois, which was the easiest option for our plans to walk The Oak Trail. The already stunning scenery was further enhanced by the thick, white, sparkling frost. Not only had the trees been thickly coated, the ground was hard with a firm, white crust. We crunched our way around the trail, revelling in its beauty, and were surprised at how many families had also chosen to leave their homes, post-Christmas and venture out into the fresh air and winter wonderland.

Catherine immediately linked arms with me when we set off on our walk and it didn't take Ruby long to follow suit. I was so thrilled to be in their company, enjoying quality time with them and where Ruby was concerned, it was a relief to see her looking relaxed, being so amiable, and without even a glimpse of the self-destruct button she had on display in Paris.

The next few days passed by far too fast and the weather stayed sunny, although it hadn't been sufficient to raise the mercury much above zero. It didn't stopped us from going out each day, though. We hadn't planned ahead for the other three days. Each day we set off for the City and ended up doing whatever took our fancy. We visited Hampton Court Palace, Canary Wharf (where we ate at Smollensky's American Bar and Grill), The Royal Observatory, and The London Eye. The second night of their stay, we took a taxi in to the City where we went to see 'The Woman in Black' at the Fortune Theatre and afterwards we sauntered along the streets to Carluccio's in Covent Garden; Catherine and Ruby's favourite Italian. It was difficult for me to keep a smile from my face as I thought about how delighted David would be, if he was watching over the three of us, seeing us bonding, and especially the pleasure it gave me by having his flesh and blood, if not him, close to me.

When meal-times came around, usually early evenings, on the nights we ate at home, Ruby was keen to show off her culinary skills and begged me to let her take over the kitchen.

"Please, Helen. You won't regret it. I've already seen what's in the fridge and…"

I was overjoyed to see her passion for an activity that I would never have connected her with. I agreed wholeheartedly, and was pleased to let her demonstrate her prowess in the kitchen and do something that she was evidently passionate about.

Catherine and I deliberately stayed in the living room out of her way. I didn't wanted her to feel like she was under any pressure if we stayed to watch. Catherine poured a glass of wine for herself and me and then, as she played with the remote, looking to see what TV had to offer, she passed comment on the sounds of activity coming from the kitchen.

"You wouldn't think so, but she really is a whizz in the kitchen. We've all told her so, at some time or other."

I smiled, genuinely enjoying the way things were going, and feeling satisfied that at last, I was learning more about Ruby.

"Catherine, I can't tell you how lovely it's been to see Ruby looking more settled…and not drinking. She's like a different person. Maybe something was on her mind last time. How has she been at home lately, behaviour-wise?"

She studied the TV guide for a minute longer and then switched it off while she pondered over her answer. A little hesitantly, and showing concern in her eyes too, she finally spilled forth her thoughts.

"She…has…been better, I think, since the fiasco in France." She twisted her hair around her finger. It looked as if she was considering her next words carefully.

"She thinks highly of you, Helen, considering she never really spent much time with you. Did you say something to her? She doesn't get drunk these days. I…have some…reservations though. I don't know. Sometimes, it's like she's almost…too quiet. Like something's brewing; the calm-before-the-storm type of thing."

I somehow doubted that the brief exchange that I had with Ruby that day at the airport was responsible for her improvement. All things considered, I didn't want to be the one responsible for any change in Ruby's behaviour. I wanted it all to be her own doing; that she finally saw the light and was mending her ways because it was what she wanted. I suddenly realised that Catherine was all agog, waiting for me to answer her earlier question.

"No. I don't think it was anything I've said to her, Catherine. All I did was to tell her that I went through some tough times like she said she was going through. I promised her that one day, I will explain certain…events in my life, to her. That was about it, I think."

It seemed as if our conversation about Ruby was over. Catherine finished off her glass of wine and lay on her tummy on the carpet. She started fussing over, stroking, and playing with Harry, who every now and again gave her an affectionate little bite as he watched her hand move gently over his fur, time and again. Chuckling at him and his antics, she abruptly turned around to face me. With her smile gone, she was looking deadly serious.

"You should really get another one, Helen. Harry would love the company; a little friend for him to play with."

I shrieked, but only jokingly. Seeing that I didn't dismiss the idea completely, she started laughing again. I couldn't help but join in…and it was something I would give some thought to, now that she planted the seed. After all, he was adorable…and good company.

After roughly an hour and a half in the kitchen, Ruby called Catherine and I into the dining room, where she was eager to show us her beautifully decorated table. I was fascinated by her finishing touches; the whole effect was stunning.

"Wow! Ruby! Where did you learn to fold napkins that way?"

She did her best to look casual, keeping a smile from appearing on her face, but I could tell she was thrilled with my compliment.

"You can both sit down. Dinner will be served in two seconds."

She flitted back to the kitchen, and before Catherine uncorked the fresh bottle of chilled wine that was left on the table, Ruby was back with two plates of food.

"It's Middle Eastern spiced lamb koftas with crunchy salad leaves and minted yoghurt. I hope you're going to like it."

She smiled as she placed the plates in front of me and Catherine, before scurrying away again to fetch her own plate back to the table. Our plates of food were well presented and looked truly delicious. The meal would have been simple enough for her to prepare, but I could tell that she put her heart and soul into it.

"Ruby, this looks amazing, honestly...I..."

She laughed.

"You'd better taste it first, Helen, before you pay any compliments."

While she watched me, I cut into one of the koftas and took a forkful. It tasted delicious, and the amount of spice she used was just right for my taste-buds.

"I'm loving this, Ruby, you've got the koftas just perfect."

She was delighted. Catherine also praised the food and Ruby flushed with pride, but hardly touched her own meal. She poked the food around with her fork but obviously wasn't hungry enough. I wondered if perhaps her appetite had gone once she finished preparing the meal. On occasions that happened to me when preparing food; by the time the food was ready, my appetite had gone.

For dessert she served up a luxury bread and butter pudding, which she told us was made with chocolate croissants, a shot of brandy and fresh cream. It was one of the most scrumptious desserts I ever tasted. Yet again, I couldn't help but notice that Ruby pushed the food around her plate with disinterest. Catherine, who devoured her serving of the dessert greedily, had also noted Ruby's lack of appetite.

"What's wrong, Ruby? Don't you like it? It's lush!"

As if she just remembered we were sat at the table with her, she looked up at us, a little surprised.

"Oh! Oh, yes! I normally like it. I'm just a bit fed up with food at the moment. I think I ate far too much on Christmas Day and Boxing Day, and I've felt a little bloated ever since."

It was a fair comment.

On the last night of the girls' stay, Catherine went to bed by nine thirty, leaving Ruby and I watching a few back-to-back episodes of 'Friends' on Freeview. Just like Catherine had done earlier on in the evening, she was laid on the floor petting Harry. When the credits rolled after the episode, she sat up and asked,

"Can we switch off the television please, Helen?"

The question surprised me. I laughed.

"I thought you couldn't get enough of Chandler, Ruby?"

I switched off the TV anyway as her eyes were almost been pleading with me. She joined me on the sofa and I was shocked to see her eyes glazed over with tears.

"Helen, this is the first time I've had a chance to talk to you alone. I've wanted to apologise for my behaviour in Paris. You were so kind to me and Catherine, offering to have us to stay with you and I behaved like a total twat."

As I watched the tears trickle slowly down her face, I suddenly felt so terribly sorry for her. She looked pale, tired and...vulnerable. I held her in my arms for a while, until she pulled away, readying herself for more.

"There's no need to apologise, Ruby. I've forgotten about it already, and you're forgiven."

She screwed her face up and looked at me dubiously. I was helpless to know what to say to convince her.

"No. I behaved abominably. There's no excuse, Helen. I was doing similar things at home too. Mum and my stepfather despaired, but I couldn't stop myself."

I waited for more tears to flow, but she seemed to be digging deep for some inner strength.

"Then why, Ruby? Why did you behave like you did?"

"I get down. I think I've always felt a lot of pressure...to be more like Catherine. She's always been prettier, always been more intelligent. She's always had the nicest personality. She was Dad's favourite; she's Mum's favourite. It's hard work trying to follow in her footsteps...she..."

"Ruby, David didn't have a..." She cut me off in an instant.

"...she's always been the most popul..."

"Ruby! Listen to me, please! I can tell you that David definitely did not have a favourite. He loved you equally. And, furthermore, you do not have to try to be like Catherine. That is not what people want from you. All you have to do is be yourself. Stop striving to be like Catherine. She is beautiful. You are beautiful. But you are beautiful in different ways. You are being too hard on yourself, and it has got to stop."

Looking like the young girl that she is; just a teenager with plenty of growing up still to do, she had a guilty look on her face when she spoke again.

"I have stopped, Helen. I think I've seen the light. I'm just concentrating on my studies now. No more wild parties or heavy drinking."

She rested her head on my shoulder then, and I hugged her close. It couldn't have been an easy situation to be in;

feeling as if you were second best. Never having had a brother or sister, I had no first-hand knowledge of sibling rivalry.

"Well promise me one thing then, Ruby? Don't overdo the studying. You have been looking so pale and tired this week. I recognise the signs. I used to be flat out when I was studying for my qualifications. It's good to take a break now and again but you still need a social life."

We sat there in silence for a long while, her head still resting on my shoulder, my arm protectively around her. I was scared to move, suspecting that she'd fallen asleep; she had looked worn out and I didn't want to disturb her. I jumped, startled a little, when she spoke.

"We went back, you know…to Paris. Catherine, Mum and I went during the October half-term. Four days we were there for. We stayed in a hotel just around the corner from your apartment."

I was stunned and struggled to find something to say. I felt the goose-bumps on my arms and shuddered as if someone walked over my grave, remembering my little scene with André.

"Oh! And did you get to see all the tourist attractions this time?"

I couldn't see her face. I hadn't meant it to be a dig at her, but I imagined she was feeling a little guilty about the week they had meant to be staying in Paris with me. She knew that I had various activities planned for each day of their intended stay in Paris, and it was cut short due to her behaviour.

"Yes, we did most of them." She looked at me rather sheepishly. "I got the Saturday afternoon to myself to… mooch around, though."

"Nice. Did you do anything interesting? I bet you went shopping?"

Without replying to my question, she stood up, stretched, and announced,

"I'm tired. Goodnight, Helen."

I got the feeling that she regretted mentioning Paris; that she was feeling bad.

"Goodnight, Ruby. Sleep well."

I cried when they left the following morning. I walked around the corner with them to the tube station, and we all indulged in a very emotional goodbye, particularly where Ruby was concerned. I was however, feeling much happier in her company. It was certainly the breakthrough that I hoped for.

CHAPTER 35

The house seemed really empty and deathly quiet for the first couple of days after Ruby and Catherine returned home. It was amazing for those few short days to hear their laughter, enjoy some fun with them and to get out and about; something I should have been doing more often. I thought back to André in Paris, and my shock after he first met Catherine and Ruby; when he referred to them as my younger sisters. I was quick to put him right and explained that, although they weren't my sisters, I thought of them as surrogate stepdaughters. The truth of the matter was that I had no wish for them to think of me in a stepmother role, and was now regarding them as exactly what André once thought them to be; my younger sisters. I hope that David was happy with me in that role.

I was still stunned that they wanted to spend time in my company because it was David's wish that they should get to know me; it hadn't necessarily meant that they would want to. After all, they hadn't even been aware of my existence until the end, when David became really ill. It didn't necessarily follow that they would be willing to meet me, let alone get to know me. I was delighted that we were all eager to do as David wanted.

For the first couple of nights after their visit, I curled up in bed and before giving way to sleep, I felt such a lovely feeling of warmth throughout my body and mind. For the first time since my parents died and David, not too many months after them, I thought of the girls as my family. I stressed to them both during those four days, that whenever they felt the need, they should call me, or visit me. I also added that I had every intention of being there for the pair of them if they needed me. I only hoped that if they ever did decide to visit, they would not do so unannounced. I could imagine Simon's and my own embarrassment if they happened to call round on the off chance.

I received a text message from Simon on the morning of New Year's Eve, asking if my visitors had departed for home, immediately followed by him asking if I would be available for the afternoon. I was somewhat relieved he only mentioned the afternoon, as I'd made arrangements to join my cousins (on Mum's side of the family) for New Year's Eve celebrations in the City, where the idea was to finish up in Trafalgar Square with all the usual revellers. I was looking forward to it, as it was something I had never done, in all the years I lived in London.

I sent Simon a rapid reply to his text; hopefully, one that would have his blood racing.

Hi

Yes, I'm here. Don't wait until pm. I am gagging for it. Get here as soon as you can.

Love H x

Within seconds, his second text bleeped its arrival. My face broke into a smile as I read it. My message had had the desired effect. My pulse started racing as I read his horny reply.

Dirty bitch. Be ready, but without the mince pies this time. Our toy is waiting eagerly, I'll bet. Be with you in half hour.

SS the LL x

Our shagging session on Christmas Eve seemed like forever ago, and though I'd been crazily busy with the girls since then, my need was instantly awakened at the mere mention of sex. Although I hadn't been wearing any panties (only my towelling robe) at the time, I could feel a hint of warmth and dampness in my folds, not to mention a few premature twinges inside my depths. My head started running away with the usual dirty thoughts. I decided to take a shower. I wanted to answer the door to him with my hair wet and no make-up. Simon liked 'natural'. The only things I would be wearing were a short silk kimono and perfume.

He was on me the second he closed and locked the front door behind him. Not one to take his time, he grabbed my hand and almost dragged me up the stairs. Putting my selfish need behind me, I was in the mood to make him wait; prolong things a little.

"I'm going to undress you today, Simon – slowly."

As we stood at the side of my bed, he untied the belt on my robe, and let it seductively drape open. His eyes roved every inch of my nakedness, but as he made a move to fondle my breasts, I caught both of his wrists in my hands.

"No! No touching! Not until I say you can! You will have to be content with looking for now."

I was burning up, excited by my dominance. I intended to make it torturous for him, and although there was nothing I wanted more than to get physical, I was going to make him exercise some patience; the tactic I stole from James Mortimer. Deliberately pushing my naked breasts against his chest, I played my fingers over his tie, before undoing his perfect Windsor knot. I gazed into his eyes as I played and took pleasure from seeing the glint, his eyes burning with desire. I held both ends of the tie out to my sides and flexed each of my arms in turn, easing the tie to and fro across the back of my neck, before throwing it across the room. I could see his frustration gathering; he swallowed nervously. I gulped, and my breathing felt constricted.

"You're a bitch, Helen!"

His arms by his sides, I noticed his hands clenching into fists and opening again. He was trying hard to control his temptation to let his hands roam my body.

"I know!" I simpered. "And don't you dare move your hands. You have to be good if you want to fuck me." My sexual tension was increasing. My fingers fumbled nervously with the buttons of his shirt, but eventually they were all unfastened. I peeled the shirt over his shoulders and pushed it down his rigid arms, but it hung from him; his cuffs hadn't been unfastened. Faced with his beautiful hairy pecs, I couldn't resist taunting his nipples with my tongue. His chest hair tickled my cheeks. I imagined sitting astride his chest, and feeling that hairy chest prickling my groin. I closed my eyes briefly at the thought.

"I will let you undo the cuffs of your shirt…while I enjoy myself…but be warned…" I whispered.

I marvelled at my willpower as I placed kisses on and tauntingly licked every square inch of his chest. I wanted him badly, needed his cock inside me, letting him do everything he wanted to do to me, doing everything I wanted to do to him. He groaned with need, his shirt cuffs undone, and hands by his side once more.

"Come on, Helen. I…I need…to fuck you…sweetie. Let…let me…"

I stopped his words with my mouth, my wanton arousal developing fast as I kissed him briefly on his lips. He thrust his tongue urgently to the back of my throat, but I fought him back. Finding strength from within, my tongue aggressively forced his to the back of his throat. I tasted his spearmint breath. Although I wasn't quite ready to give in to it, my core tingled in anticipation and I opened my legs slightly.

I pulled away from the kiss and glared into his eyes, making the moment deliciously intense for both of us. Holding his gaze, I watched his reaction as I unfastened his belt and slowly lowered his zip. I revelled in his heavy breathing, his gasps, and his slightly parted lips. It was paining him. He ached to touch me, but although he accepted defeat for that moment, I could see he was excited by his temporary subservience.

I resisted the temptation to look down at his enormous, hot length as I unleashed it and allowed it to slap hard against his stomach. My whole abdomen lurched excitedly, as he gave a great moan of longing, and I felt my natural lubrication, the wetness of foreplay.

"Oh…oh…Helen, please."

"Won't…won't be too…too much… longer now."

I started to pant along with him, gasping for breath, finally getting impatient, unable to wait much longer. Just another few seconds, I promised myself, as I moved my head down his chest and licked a trail, a moist path of saliva, from the centre of his chest to where the tip of his cock was waiting, poised and throbbing just below his navel.

In the blink of an eye, so swift that I left him wondering whether it happened or not, I swept my tongue across the head of his stiffness. I repeated the move a few more times, meeting his eyes as he looked down, watching my actions, and he silently conveyed his desperation. His hands moved to and quickly rested on my head, and although I spotted the movement, I didn't stop him. He ran his fingers through my hair and twisted it around for a moment. Not wanting to wait a second longer, I took the full length of his pulsing cock into my mouth, letting him thrust gently between my teeth. Without releasing it, I reached down to unfasten and remove his shoes, leaving him to step free from his lower clothing.

Before I had the chance to realise what happened, he threw me face down onto the bed and parted my legs with his.

"What...what do...you want...Helen?"

My head was in a mess; I couldn't think straight. I was on the verge of orgasm and I didn't care how; I just wanted to cum.

"Any...anything! Just...do it...now!" I begged.

I felt one of his hands part my thighs, and with the other, he guided his rigid length to nudge at my pussy, before plunging hard into me; hard and deep.

"That's just to tip you over the edge. Cum for me, sweetie."

I screamed out loud with my short-lived but intense release. I felt as if I was soaring high in the sky. It was a moment of eroticism and pleasure where only I existed, me and my ultimate enjoyment; no-one else, not even Simon. I drifted on its waves. I was stunned to hear his voice as I slowly descended back from my oblivion.

"Was...that nice... sweetie?"

"Beaut...iful."

My own voice sounded dreamy. I felt his cock slide out of me and I jumped when, unexpectedly, I was being penetrated in both openings. The pulsing movements of the vibrator had my body on edge all too soon. The dildo and its anal protrusion rotated deep within my front and rear warmth and the third performed arousing circular moves over my clit. The damn thing was taking me to the edge faster than I wanted. In my mind, I wasn't ready to cum again, but my body as usual was on fire, nerves alert, and sumptuously tingling. I gripped tight onto the duvet and pulled myself away from the beastly toy, hoping to stem the imminent orgasm that threatened, but I was too late. My body juddered in spasms of ecstasy, and I felt too wet. I growled at Simon in disgust.

"Simon, take…the fucking thing…away. It's too…intense."

"What's…the matter, Helen? Are…you okay?"

"No! I don't want…to cum…every other…minute."

I rolled over to face him, my breathing gradually returning to normal, and saw his concern.

"I want…to feel you. I want to enjoy your cock, fucking me hard, deep, rough, slowly, and…dirty. I want your cock, Simon."

His mouth crashed on to mine, and before he shoved hard into me with both his tongue and cock, he growled at me.

"That's good! Because…I've wanted to fuck you for the last…since I stepped through your door."

I gasped in delight, my breath pushed out of me as he rammed deep and held it. I could feel his throbbing girth, setting my nerves off again. He bit into my breast and twirled his tongue around my nipple for a few seconds, before he pounded into me, grinding his pubic bone into mine for deeper penetration. It was more pleasurable to me; having deep, internal contact with his skin, his muscle and his deliberate moves, not rigid plastic and a battery. There was that touching of souls, an orgasm brought on with intent and meaning, instead of being artificially induced.

"Helen…turn over! I want…to fuck…your arse…." he ordered.

I jumped up, and standing at the bottom of the bed, bent over it, legs apart, keen to get him back inside me. Reaching around to my folds, he moistened his fingers in my juices first, before pushing them inside my rear. Once happy that the tightness of my anus would accept his length, he guided it carefully, inch by inch, letting me gradually grow accustomed to the intrusion. I finally relaxed. He pushed some fingers inside my wetness and thrust into both openings. I bit into my bottom lip with the pleasure…and the pain. His moves were gentle at first, but as he thumbed at my clit, he gathered speed and groaned loudly. My stomach flipped, my body jerking with the thrill of the double penetration, but suddenly he bent his fingers inside me, and my head couldn't accept what was happening. My eyes crossed, everything went out of focus as he caught my g-spot. It spiralled into another fiercely intense release. He continued to thrust into me simultaneously, prolonging my orgasm, and my clit throbbed painfully in response. My body was still calming as, shortly after I had, Simon cried out with the violent release of his deposit.

We stayed in bed all afternoon, although we only indulged in sex one more time. A short while after round two, Simon went downstairs to the kitchen and returned with a bottle of white wine and two glasses.

"What day does your office open again, Helen? I'm staying at the hotel one night next week. I don't know which it will be yet, but I can let you know, if you want to join me, that is?"

I let my shoulders slump at the mention of work and I groaned in dread. He raised his eyebrows, as if to query my mutterings.

"Sorry…if it was my suggestion that prompted such a look of despair on your face, Helen."

"Sorry, Simon. It wasn't that, and you know it. It was just the thought of the office opening that caused it. Work! I'm dreading it. I'm not looking forward to going back if I'm to be truthful."

Immediately I said it, his face clouded over with a look of

concern, ready and alert for me to volunteer more information.

"I thought you loved your job, Helen? What's gone wrong?"

"Yes, I do love it. It's...I don't think I've mentioned her to you before, but Ted employed a new member of staff before I returned from France. She's called Linda Brownlow. For some reason, she hates me. I knew it the minute we were introduced...and the rest of the staff have noticed it as well. The trouble is...I don't know why. I don't know what I've done to her. She was told, by Ted, that she has to report to me, as a line manager. She won't do that, though. She keeps reporting to James Mortimer, the other...prick, who Ted has taken on as an extra partner."

He looked as puzzled as I felt.

"And you don't know her? You never saw her before, I take it? Are you sure it isn't jealousy, Helen? After all...you..."

"NO!" I emphatically cut his words dead, not wanting to hear all the reasons once again; the list of reasons the girls reeled off to me that night in the Lamb and Flag.

"It's definitely not jealousy. I have a feeling I have seen her somewhere before, but I don't know exactly where or when. I'm totally mystified."

Deep in thought, he gazed at me for a minute or two, perhaps waiting to see if I could come up with an explanation. In the meantime, I was hoping maybe he could give me an answer, some justification for Linda's hatred of me.

"Helen, my suggestion to you is to do some digging. Find out whatever you can about her. First of all, look at her employee file as soon as you can. Maybe there's something on record; where she's worked previously, where she's lived. See if anything comes to light, if there's a possibility that your paths have crossed somewhere before the Hopkins Partnership. There's got to be some explanation, surely?

Check up on that guy as well; James whatever-his-name-is. See if there's a connection between him and her."

Thankful at last, to have something I could work with, I sighed as I smiled at him.

"And what if I can't find anything; any clues? What do I do then, Simon?"

"It depends how far you want to take it, sweetie. Do you want to accept that maybe you haven't laid eyes on her in your life before? Or do you want to dig further and find out something you maybe wouldn't want to know?"

I rubbed my eyes, suddenly feeling exhausted with the whole situation.

"Oh, I don't fucking know what to do, Simon. I don't know the right way to go about it, but I have to know why she hates me. I can't just let it go." I snarled with frustration.

"There is another way, of course, sweetie."

He paused, and screwed his face up in a grimace, preparing himself, I thought, for some backlash from me, should I not like what I was about to hear.

"You could always...ask her...what the problem is."

He ducked, arms covering his head for protection. I knew why he made the move; it was to throw some light humour into the weighty conversation. I couldn't help but laugh, but I knew the topic would continue to play on my mind.

By late afternoon, Simon left and returned home to Essex, to join his wife and family for the New Year. After a soak in the bath, I got ready and headed out to meet my cousins at King's Cross station, ready to see the New Year in in style.

CHAPTER 36

The festive season was finally over. Spending New Year's Eve in central London with my cousins, turned out to be an amazing night, from what I could recall, but not one that I was in a hurry to repeat. I can't remember ever having drunk the volume of alcohol that I consumed in just one night. After having eaten what could only be described as a mediocre meal in a restaurant in Covent Garden, we made our way from pub to pub and, as planned, were in Trafalgar Square in time to see the New Year in, amongst all the other revellers. I can't remember anything after that, but when I spoke to my cousin, Tara, late on New Year's Day, she seemed to remember the four of us ended up in a nightclub, but exactly where and how was totally beyond her. Goodness knows how we'd managed it, but we somehow got to the right place at the correct pre-arranged time to be collected by her father, my uncle. Another thing she remembered (after a brief nap in his car), was that it was around six thirty in the morning when he safely delivered me to my door.

It was dark outside when I woke up. It took me a few

minutes to realise exactly where I was. I reached out to switch on the lamp that was nearest to the sofa, and on raising my head from the cushion, the movement made the room spin around. Delicately lowering my head onto the cushion in the hope that the dizziness and nausea would go away, I was desperate to close my eyes, but not before I'd seen what time it was. I looked over to the DVD player under the TV and it was just after twenty past five in the afternoon. I slept away most of New Year's Day, and was still fully-clothed, though I must have kicked my high heels off after I came in through the front door because I was shoe-less. I racked my brain trying to remember what we had done and where we had been after Trafalgar Square, but my head hurt too much for thinking.

Stop thinking! Stay still!

For ten minutes or so, or it could even have been longer, I tried not to think, or move. I felt battered...and ill. There was also a horrible pressure on my bladder and it was growing urgent. I desperately needed to pee. I groaned loudly, before forcing myself to sit up, resentful of the call of nature that I needed to attend to.

I swear blind I almost fainted. Everything seemed to go black for a few seconds, and I felt as if I was going to lose consciousness. Just as quickly, the feeling passed, and I tentatively pushed myself to stand, fearing that I wouldn't make it to the bathroom in time if I didn't hurry. I discovered where my shoes ended up as I made my way towards the staircase; one was deposited between the sofa and the kitchen and the other was in the hall, behind the front door.

After warily negotiating each stair, it'd hit home that I was unsteady on my legs and sadly, still intoxicated, I managed to make it to the bathroom. The instant I parked my backside on the loo and started peeing, the vile acidic taste of vomit rose into my throat. I sobbed in fear as I retched, my throat tensing and stomach lurching, putting up a fight against the inevitable; my most hated sensation of choking. Fortunately, I finished my pee, before having to quickly kneel, head over the loo and let nature take its course. Three times I threw up before I dared to stand and go for a lie down on the bed. When I felt sure that nothing else was due to come up and a tad closer to feeling human again, I showered and brushed my teeth.

I remained in bed for the rest of the day, only once venturing downstairs to the kitchen, but only long enough to make myself a couple of slices of dry toast and a cup of coffee. I also took a jug of water and a glass back upstairs with me. I propped myself up and read for a little while, making sure to sip the water regularly to keep myself hydrated. Though I'd always had a phobia about vomiting, once I got it out of my system I felt much better. I was also thankful that I still had the next day, Sunday, to myself, to ensure I was fully recovered before the third of January arrived and and we would all be back at the office, with our busiest month facing us.

CHAPTER 37

*T*he holidays had flown past at lightning speed and the third of January arrived all too soon. Much as I loved my job and looked forward to the post-Christmas catch up with the girls, my biggest dread was bumping into Linda Brownlow and James around the office.

Since I always had a tendency to be over-sensitive, which stemmed from being bullied in school, I found it very difficult living with the fact that certain people out there in the big bad world hated me, particularly when, racking my brain as I did, both then and now, I never found any conceivable or valid reason for them to do so. As a result of the bullying at school, I shed a lot of tears during those years. Rather than let myself get upset over Linda Brownlow, I intended to stay focussed on finding out what the Hell I had done to deserve my current status; being hated by her.

Ted and his wife, Hilary, as they informed me before the Christmas break, had gone away to some exotic holiday destination for the whole of January, so he wouldn't be in the office for his usual couple of days a week. It was inevitable therefore, that at some stage I would end up needing to be involved in a meeting or two with James Mortimer; yet another reason for my trepidation.

On the first morning back to work, the train was crammed. I hadn't been able to find myself a seat, and the constant jostling by other commuters when they were getting on and off at each stop, succeeded in adding severe irritation to the other unwanted emotions I was harbouring. My walk from the tube station to the office would have more appropriately, been called a 'stomp', with the anger I exuded.

Thankfully, the morning quickly disappeared and I calmed down by the time the girls and I gathered in the kitchen at lunchtime. Lingering longer than usual after our lunches, we listened to what each other been up to during the Christmas holidays. Christina, as usual, caused uproar amongst the others, when she re-played on her phone, the video I received from her on Christmas Day; her East 17 tribute with her own ingenious lyrics

Because we were busier than usual, Monday and Tuesday passed by before I barely had time to take a breath or blink. The fact that I hadn't laid eyes on either Linda or James had been a mega plus. Halfway through Tuesday afternoon, a text message (which he more or less told me to expect) came through from Simon.

Hi Sweetie,

I'm staying at usual hotel on Wednesday night. Care to join me again? If so, will text you room number when I've checked in.

Love S x

I replied immediately.

Hello,

Of course I'll join you. I can't wait.

Love H x

At last, the distraction I was waiting for. Something to look forward to that would take my mind to a different place; a sanctuary from the stress I was feeling. With my excitement building, perhaps a little too prematurely, my mind started to stray to thoughts of what I would wear. Thinking back to the last time I visited him in the hotel, I wouldn't bother going home after work. It was more convenient and saved a lot of time to take a cab from the office around seven o'clock.

With my mid-afternoon thoughts of sex doing me no good whatsoever, especially with dreaded enemy, James Mortimer, too close to hand, I gave myself a severe dressing down, so that I could hopefully find some fragment of concentration from within. Somehow, I was lucky enough to summon a few shreds and I successfully immersed myself into work once more. Sadly, it only lasted for half an hour at the most. It was hearing Linda Brownlow's voice in the corridor that suddenly nudged me into remembering her personnel file; I needed to take a look at it, and the sooner the better.

I went along to Ted's office and grabbed an armful of personnel files, including those of Linda and James. At least if someone walked into my office and saw me with ten to fifteen files, it wouldn't look as if I had singled out just the two payroll members. I perused Linda's folder with interest, eager to find something. There were three positively glowing employer references from her most recent positions. She had worked as a purchase ledger clerk for a plumbing supply company for five years, a book-keeper for an accountancy practice in Surbiton for two and a half years, and accounts office manager for a well-known corporate insurance company for well over ten years. Her CV told me that she was born in Guildford, in Surrey in 1954, making her fifty seven, which was thereabouts the age I first thought her to be. Attending Boxgrove Primary and Guildford High Schools, she achieved seven G.C.E. 'O' levels, and gone on to finish her education at Guildford College. The only other points of interest were that she was married, with two older children who were not dependents. There was nothing at all to throw any light on matters; no place of employment that I ever had any dealings with. One suspicion of mine before opening the file, was that she had maybe previously worked for a company where our team had done audits, but it turned out not to be the case. I sighed heavily, the puff of air wafting a few loose papers across the desk. I snatched them up in frustration and stuffed them haphazardly back into her file. My nerves were frayed. My feeling that I saw her somewhere before had now been shot down in flames, unless of course, I'd come across her in day to day life; a random face in a supermarket queue at the tills, one that I'd never forgotten. A feeling of defeat suddenly overwhelmed me and, placing my elbows on the desk, my head slumped in my hands. I closed my eyes, to do some thinking.

When I heard voices in the corridor, it snapped me back to the present. Half expecting a knock at the door I forced my eyes open, but whoever had been chatting, the voices quietened and moved off into another office. I was holding my breath but was finally able to exhale, with relief. Rifling through the employee folders once again, I found the one for James Mortimer. I started sifting through all the paperwork, even though I'd been told by Ted, more or less everything I needed to know about him. The only notable knowledge I gleaned from the file was that he'd been born in Bromley in 1968, and achieved his qualifications at the London School of Economics (which had been my uni for just short of two years). I already knew that he was married, but hadn't realised that he had one son who was still a dependent. Before starting work for the Hopkins Partnership, he'd only ever been employed at K.M.T.P. since leaving uni. There was no evidence to connect him in any way with Linda Brownlow. Feeling totally pissed off, I threw his file onto the stack and promptly returned them all to the filing cabinet in Ted's office, more determined than ever to get to the bottom of the matter.

Simon called me sometime around six thirty to let me know his room number. As I was the only one left in the office, I had the 'ladies' to myself for re-applying my make-up and quickly getting changed into some sexier clothing. I carefully folded my suit and packed it into my laptop case along with my toiletries, before calling a cab. At five to seven, the taxi pulled up outside the office. I hurried out into the freezing cold, eager to get into the warmth again...and eager to have sex...and Simon's arms around me.

CHAPTER 38

I hadn't had much chance to follow up on Helen's movements for more than two weeks. What with the pre-Christmas, then the post-Christmas and pre-New Year arrangements I had, and the usual things like family parties, various corporate functions and catching up with my social life, the time had gone. It seemed that it had commenced in low-gear, gradually picking up in speed, until New Year's Eve approached, and then shifted into Mach 3.

I also thought I would be correct in assuming that Helen's office would be closed during the festive period, so any attempt by me to track her down at that time would have been futile.

As I made further plans to continue my persistent trailing of her, my mind kept going over and over the stressful thoughts that plagued me continually. I became paranoid thinking about what she was doing for the holidays, whether she spent the time alone or with family and friends. Remembering the guy from her office, who evidently upset her a short while ago, I tormented myself with visions of him fucking her. I kicked out in rage at a base-unit door as I rinsed my dishes when that old monster, the green-eyed one, took over, causing my far-from-rational thinking. I managed to calm myself down, by repeatedly telling myself that they'd fallen out over a business matter.

No matter how many times I remonstrated with myself about the office guy, I let other, equally monstrous, imaginings into my head. I was obsessed with her, continually punishing myself with the fact that somebody had to be fucking her. If it wasn't the man she worked with, then there had to be somebody else; but who? Helen Rushforth was sure to have someone sharing her bed, even if it was only a couple of times a week. She wasn't the type to go without sex for weeks on end.

With a pre-Christmas backlog of work keeping me at the office until after eight, I was unable on Monday and Tuesday, to go and... stalk (yes, I acknowledged exactly what it was that I was doing) Helen, once more. Before I knew it though, those couple of days of hard work and longer hours paid off. My backlog was dealt with, and Wednesday night I was able to leave work at four thirty, along with everyone else.

As usual, I watched all the staff as they one by one, left the building between five and six o'clock. The man who I thought caused Helen to be distressed that night (the one who I also thought was shagging her) left the office around half past five, and before the majority of the women. She was the only person who hadn't left work. I cursed her, wishing that just once in a while, she would have the decency to work normal fucking hours.

The weather, which I came to accept as normal; icy temperatures, frequent sleet, snow and biting, cold winds, was certainly living up to its reputation. I felt as if I was almost rooted to the spot; it was so bitterly cold. I let my mind drift for a while, as I stood waiting, to thoughts of how it would feel to suffer from hypothermia. How did people cope when they were lost in mountain fog for hours at a time, perhaps with an injury as well, and having to suffer the effects of exposure? Was it painful? Nudging myself back to the present, I moved out of the shelter and stamped some circulation back into my feet. I tramped up the street, crossed the road, and came back past her office, before crossing back to my porch-way. There was still one window that was lit up in Helen's building, the same one on the ground floor that I noted had a light on each time I'd known Helen to work late. Evidently, it was her office.

I didn't know how many times I'd already looked at my watch, but I looked at it yet again; twenty minutes before seven. It was the coldest night I'd experienced in a long time and I was struggling more than usual. My vision seemed to be suffering in addition to everything else. My eyes were stinging. There was nothing tumbling from the sky; no rain, snow or sleet, but my sight was so blurred that it seemed as if there was moisture of some kind descending. I knew I couldn't cope with the sub-zero temperature much longer. Seven o'clock. I would give her until seven and then get myself home. To stay out any longer than a further twenty minutes would be foolish.

I moved about some more, stamping, and then shifting from one foot to the other and holding it for a minute, believing I was protecting each foot in turn from the cold that struck upwards through the concrete of the step. I was finally distracted from that preposterous act when the light went out in Helen's office; some movement at last, maybe. Seconds later, another window was lit up. It was adjacent to the main door so I presumed it would be a reception area for clients. She must definitely be due to leave soon. I welcomed it; I needed to see her, needed to 'want' her and needed to get out of the cold. It would give me something else to focus on; an alternative something to become fixated with, instead of being as I had since just after five; preoccupied with the cold.

When there was less than five minutes to go until seven o'clock, a black cab passed by me, its rear lights glowing red as the driver applied the brakes. It stopped right outside Helen's main door. Fuck it! It looked as if I wasn't going to get more than a glimpse of her. Another fucking wasted night! Within seconds, she'd locked the building and was opening the cab's rear passenger door. She had with her, some type of small suitcase on wheels; it could even have been a laptop case, the type that people use as carry-ons when flying, but I was too far away to see it clearly enough.

The cab pulled away; time for me to torture myself yet again. My suspicions reached out from within, grabbing at my throat until my breathing felt restricted. I faced the door I'd been leaning against and slowly banged my head against it a few times in frustration. Not knowing where she was going and with whom, was driving me to distraction.

For the first time, since starting out on my mission, I questioned my actions; I asked myself what I was hoping to gain from relentlessly stalking her. After all, if I was not going to achieve anything, what was the point in carrying on? I had to remind myself that all I succeeded in doing was, more often than not, almost freezing my nuts off, and persistently punishing myself with thoughts of Helen...and other men fucking her. I needed to seriously think about where this was headed.

CHAPTER 39

I climbed out of the cab and moved over to the driver's window to hand him the fare that was displayed on the meter. Without a word, he took the money from me and the electric window started to close before I turned towards the hotel entrance. I was just about to set foot in the hotel foyer, when I heard a shout. "Miss?" I hadn't been expecting anyone to address me, so I ignored it and carried on walking in. I jumped, instantly startled, when I felt a gentle tap on my shoulder and turned around to face a rather portly, old gent with heavily-lidded eyes.

"Sorry, Miss, but was that your cab?"

His finger pointed out of the main door indicating the taxi that I'd used. It was still parked at the kerbside, the cab-driver frantically beckoning me over to him.

"Thank you very much. I'll go and see what he wants."

Realising how it must look, I quickly added,

"I did pay the fare, honest."

He smirked in his amusement before continuing to head towards the reception desk. I hurried back outside, wondering if I'd done something wrong.

"Didn't I give you enough money?" I asked the driver worriedly as I approached his side window.

"Yes, Miss, you did. But I think you may have left something on the back seat?" He turned to point in the direction of the left-hand, rear seat. "Is that yours?"

Looking through the rear window, I spotted my laptop case on the empty, nearside seat, where I placed it beside me when I got into the cab. I was momentarily, horrified. I'd never before left anything on a bus, train or any other form of transport. Realising how lucky I'd been, I heaved a sigh of relief.

"Thank you so much. I would have been utterly lost without that tonight." After I opened the door and grabbed the laptop case, I delved into my handbag, finding a ten pound note in a small, inside, zip-up pocket, which I gratefully thrust into the cab-driver's hand. "Thanks again."

"Look after your things better, young lady, or it could cost you a small fortune."

He didn't smile, probably thinking that a friendly nod would suffice. Still looking at me, with his deadpan expression, he put the car into gear and moved away.

By the time I reached Simon's room on the seventh floor, and he closed the door behind me, I felt as if I was about to explode. He pulled me close towards him. Moving in for a kiss, he stopped and stared deep into my eyes, his smile gone.

"Helen, what the fuck is the matter? Your whole body is as tight as a drum. Too much tension. Has something happened?"

I gasped, struggling to catch my breath. I couldn't comprehend what was happening to me, and my eyes were wide open in terror. I was unable to answer him, as genuine fear engulfed me.

"Come on, Helen...breathe. We've done this before

remember; we did it that first day in court. In…hold…out…
hold…keep repeating it. Come and sit."

He led me over to the sofa and persuaded me to sit,
before kneeling at the side of my legs. He patiently helped
talk me through the breathing exercise.

A short time later, I'd calmed down somewhat and Simon
poured us both a glass of wine.

"I think…you've just experienced some sort of panic
attack, sweetie. Now, when you're ready, do you think you're
calm enough to tell me what's gone on today?"

He sat at the side of me and held my hand, smiling
encouragingly. In my head I was still trying to make sense of
what just occurred, but I was baffled.

"That's the problem. I don't know. Nothing significant
has occurred today to bring on something like…like that. I've
had a decent enough day at work, though I did get a little
stressed at one point. I searched those employee files, you
know, Linda Brownlow and James Mortimer. I couldn't find
anything to link them both, and more aggravating for me, is
that there is nowhere, from checking her CV and papers, I
would ever have met up with her."

He shook his head at me slowly. It seemed to me as if he
was lost for words, or maybe he couldn't believe that I'd
allowed myself to get into such an anxious state. No words of
wisdom came, no lecture about letting things get to me, but
he smiled once more.

"Simon, your silence is ominous; it's speaking volumes.
That was no valid reason for me to get stressed, was it? The
only other thing that…almost happened, was that I left my
laptop case in the taxi just now. Fortunately for me, he was
an honest cab-driver. Yet again, that's not an obvious cause
for my tension. I just don't know why. I can't fathom it."

I sipped at my wine, trying to read his eyes, warily
watching his lips, wishing he'd say something. The wine had

the desired effect, working its magic, soothing my nerves, and it was Simon who now looked as tense as I felt earlier.

"Helen, do you think that maybe you are getting a little too fraught about this Linda person? Because, for fuck's sake, I know you're not the type to stress over a bloody laptop case, sweetie."

"I'm not going to let it get to me, Simon, but...I still intend to do some more investigations. There is a reason... there has to be, and it's waiting to be found...but it's certainly not jealousy. Now, can we drop the bloody matter, please? I'm over it."

He tentatively gave a sigh of relief, though gave me a look of doubt, as if he wasn't fully convinced. After taking a couple of good gulps of his Merlot, he muttered grouchily as he shuffled up close on the sofa,

"Yes, we'll drop it, sweet thing, if it makes you happy. Are you sure you want to stay tonight? Maybe you aren't in the right frame of mind?"

Feeling seriously affronted, I glowered at him before launching into all the reasons, all the excuses I had for wanting to be there with him.

"Simon, I have come here tonight hoping to leave all that shit behind me. I'm escaping for a night, and...I will be in the right frame of mind, thank you very much. And particularly after I've had another wine or two."

He leaned into me and kissed me on the cheek.

"Well, I'd better get pouring then, hadn't I, sweet thing? Drink those last few dregs and I'll get you another. "

He switched the television on, but although I feigned interest in a wearisome, traffic-cop documentary, I was still mulling things over, wondering what steps I could take next to delve into Linda Brownlow's background. It didn't take long before he lost interest in the programme, and perhaps noticing I was in deep thought, he stared at me intently.

"Helen, you are not fucking watching this programme. Let me guess. You're... No. Let me make a suggestion. Do some proper research. Births, deaths and marriages, that's what you need. Find out how long she's been married, see if she's been divorced, there may be another surname she's had, an alternative that you could look up."

All of a sudden, I didn't want to think about the woman any more. I had to get her out of my head. She, or it, had become my new obsession.

"Simon, can I ask you something please? It's a bit of an unusual request for me."

He looked at me curiously. "You haven't said what you think...to my suggestion. Is this question of yours relevant, honey?"

I considered not asking him at all. I had no idea how he was going to react, and I felt a little nervous. My stomach was fluttering and I could feel, or I could have imagined it, that there was a lump blocking my throat. I had to force myself though. I knew it was what I needed. I hesitated before letting the words, my immensely ambiguous words, roll off my tongue.

"No, it isn't relevant." I paused, taking a deep breath, deeper even than the ones I took earlier, to steady my hyper-ventilation. "Simon, could we not have wanton, dirty, selfish getting off, tonight, please? Will...will you...make love to me, please?"

When I saw the look that appeared on his face, I felt disheartened and my stomach suddenly had an empty, sickly feel about it. He just stared back at me, open-mouthed. My interpretation, rightly or wrongly, was that he was possibly a bit unsure, and fearful as to what my request was implying. For an instant, I thought about just getting the hell out of his hotel room. I'd embarrassed myself and I could feel the colour creep into my cheeks.

"Helen? You're...what...are you saying? I..." he stuttered, "I can...can do it...love-making...but...is this...?"

Just as I envisaged, he was getting worried. I touched his lips with my fingers, silencing him. I had to make it right, and quickly. I couldn't afford to lose the bit of normality (if that was the right word) that our relationship offered; his company, the sex. I didn't want to lose those things...or him.

"Hold it...right there. I'm not saying anything, other than I want gentle, loving sex, not just fucking for the sake of fucking and getting off. I want to be held, to feel like you actually care for me, rather than using me. I'm aware that we both use each other for our sexual gratification, and as brilliant as that has always been, it's not what I want tonight, Simon."

I watched the panic drain from his expression, and a look of relief replaced it. I didn't wish to see anything else, any other emotion in his face, so I looked away from his eyes, before adding,

"You needn't worry. I don't...love you...or anything deep like that."

He had nothing further to say on the subject. We did nothing all night except cuddle up on the sofa, until we were eventually laid in bed. Lying face to face, we talked for a while, made jokes and smiled at one another. It was a warm and comforting...togetherness. There was no pressure, sexual, or otherwise. I didn't know if he felt the same, but I remembered that was the normal way of life for married couples. In the early days, during my marriage to Anthony, we talked before making love. Things had even been that way for a while during my relationship with Gavin, when I'd been at uni.

We kissed for a short while before he even touched my body. The kisses were passionate and I closed my eyes, feeling the warmth of his lips on mine, without our usual probing of tongues. My heart melted and it felt good. The love-making, our first ever, followed on; naturally, and beautifully. There was plenty of tenderness in his exploration of my body; stroking my arms, stroking the outside of my thighs as he buried his length deep into me. That extra special touch, being carried out in a loving caring manner. We moved perfectly together; gentle, considerate, exploring, but there was something lying low, something that was being left unsaid, and I pushed the thought quickly to the back of my mind, hoping it wouldn't surface again; a 'for-one-night-only' moment.

I gratefully accepted his tongue, and let mine dance with it, as our mutual need grew. Together, we toiled urgently, pushing our bodies even closer, to reach the orgasms that we individually craved. He fell asleep, holding me tight, arm about my waist, and once his breathing deepened, and he was firmly in sleep's grasp, I cried, silently, so he wouldn't wake and query the tears. I couldn't understand why I cried; or perhaps I understood only too well and was afraid to acknowledge the fact.

His parting words to me, as he left me applying my make-up the following morning came out of the blue.

"St. Catherine's Index. That's what you need for births, deaths and marriages, sweetness. You can also research these things online. Google it! Text me if you find anything of interest. The sooner you put this to bed, the better. I want to know. Have a good day, sweetie."

After placing a smacking kiss on my lips, he rushed out of the room, and smirked back at me while he tried to straighten the knot on his tie.

CHAPTER 40

*I*nstead of using a taxi again, the journey from Simon's hotel to Embankment was only three stops on the tube, and after the previous night's incident, I took more care not to let go of my case. After Simon left for an early start, and I finished my make-up, there hadn't been any reason for me to hang around, so I arrived at the office at five past eight; the first one there.

With Simon's parting shot still ringing in my head, and no staff at the ridiculous hour, I didn't go straight to my office. I dumped my case in the corridor and climbed the two flights of stairs to the second floor. Still deep in thought, I walked to the end of the corridor and, for only the third time since Linda joined the partnership, I entered her office. Curiosity and my obsession got the better of me. I didn't go into her room with the intent to nosy into her desk drawers or check out the browsing history on her computer. Just what I hoped to gain, I had no idea, other than an illogical feeling that her office might have some clues to offer.

Besides the faultless cleaning of our twice-weekly service, it appeared that Linda was also doing her bit to keep the room immaculate. She didn't, unlike most of the staff I know, have the usual assortment of office paraphernalia littering her desk, such as tape dispensers, staplers, calculators, paper clips and bull-dog clips. Other than her computer screen and keyboard, one psychedelic pen pot, a three-tier set of letter trays and her telephone, the only item of a personal nature which graced the desk was...a framed photograph of her register office wedding. Listening out for other staff members arriving, I picked up the picture to take a closer look. Dressed in a pale grey suit, she held a small bunch of pink and mauve freesias and her new husband's arm was around her waist. He beamed proudly; his smile more than compensating for his lack of stature. Most interesting from my point of view though, was that, from studying her face carefully, the picture must have been taken at least eight to ten years ago. After replacing the frame precisely where she left it, and at the same angle, and feeling guilty at my intrusion into her space, I hurried back down the stairs.

I turned my computer on, but quickly abandoning it, I wandered over to stand near the window, my thoughts totally not on the work I should have been getting back to. As I stared out, I noticed that the early morning drizzle that I had the misfortune to walk in from the station, had turned quite heavy, and umbrellas were out in force. I also noted that a few staff members hurried past my window towards the main door. Soon, I could smell the unmistakable aroma of filter coffee as it drifted down the corridor from the kitchen.

Sitting down at last, I sighed heavily as I browsed through my numerous Excel documents trying to locate the one I needed. When I finally opened the spreadsheet, my eyes couldn't focus on the rows and columns of never ending figures. The only image I could see in front of me was that of Linda's wedding. I knew I was going to need some more information before I could take it further, but I needed someone to help me. She certainly wouldn't want to answer my questions, not that I was about to ask her anyway.

A soft tapping on my door disturbed my thoughts.

"Come in, Christina!" I shouted.

"Mor-ning, Hel-len!" She almost sang as she entered; my cup of coffee in one hand and some paperwork in the other. "How did you know it was me?"

I gave her a teasing grin. "Well...a) you're always first in my office with the coffee, and b) there is only you who can do a knock on a door that is far quieter than your voice."

She gave me an over-dramatised look of being seriously insulted. I laughed.

"Well...you did ask."

She positively guffawed with laughter. One of the many things I had quickly discovered about Christina was that because she possessed such a loud, raucous laugh, everyone always knew whereabouts in the office she was at any given time. She certainly brightened the days, especially the dark and dismal ones.

"By the way, thanks for the coffee, Christina."

She ignored my thanks, and evidently, like me, she wasn't in a rush to start work. She parked her bottom on one of the chairs in front of my desk and started chatting. I wasn't paying much attention though, as she rattled off some of the woes, of having a pubescent, teenage son, a love-struck daughter, and a workaholic husband. An idea suddenly came to me. Only mildly sorry about butting in, I asked,

"Christina, would you help me with something, please? I...I need to know something about Linda. Would you mind? But you must keep it to yourself, at least, for now."

Always eager to please, she grinned.

"Of course I will. What is it that you need to know?"

I lowered my eyes, not wanting her to see that I was

frowning. In the space of those few seconds since I asked her, I wondered if I was doing the right thing; I was having doubts about my own idea and fiddled nervously with my pen.

"All I need to know is how long she's been married. There's a wedding photo on her desk; bring the subject up, see if she'll volunteer anything."

I was taken aback when she resolutely stood up and made her way to the door.

"Right, I'll be back to you within the hour. Her mail will be ready to take up shortly."

I soon got my head buried into the work, and my short-lived doubts were pushed out of my mind. For the first time in days, I felt hopeful, and certain that, in Christina, I'd chosen the right person for the job. None of the other girls would have been willing to converse with Linda anyway. They made their feelings about her very clear. She had, after all, tried causing bother between Gillian and Leanne at one point. Also, Christina was such an effervescent and instantly likeable character, that even Linda Brownlow would find her pretty hard to ignore.

Thirty five minutes passed before Christina suddenly flung my door open, and victoriously (and dramatically, as was her way) raised her arms in celebration, as she silently mouthed the words,

"It's done!"

I hurried over to where she remained, hysterically poised in 'freeze frame', mouth and eyes wide open. Grabbing her arm, I pulled her in, out of view in case anyone happened to come along the corridor. I closed the door and whispered,

"Tell me then!" I struggled to contain my excitement as she smirked triumphantly and took a long deep breath, deliberately prolonging her moment of glory ...and my wait.

"Come on, Chris…" I started, but cutting me off, she spewed it out in an instant.

"She's been married nine years in April…Guildford Register Office…his name is Roger…honeymooned in Guildford…four bridesmaids, all from Guildford…one best-man…and her…"

"Christina!" I warned, trying to hide my amusement.

"Sorry! Forget the last bits then. Nine years ago this coming April at Guildford Register Office they got married. Husband, Roger. Will that help?" I was thrilled and couldn't resist giving her a hug.

"You're a bloody star, Christina."

For the next hour, I toyed with the thought of taking the rest of the day off and heading out to do some research, but decided against it. But while I was browsing on Google, searching for some of the genealogy sites where you could buy a number of credits and do the research yourself, I discovered a few small businesses that would do all the legwork for a fee. I didn't think twice and dialled the number for a researcher whose business was situated not far from Somerset House; swiftly…before I changed my mind.

Expecting to wait for two or three days, I was stunned to receive a call back with my search result by three thirty the same day. He explained that the information I provided made his job 'a piece of piss'. For a professional person, I think he could have phrased it in a more pertinent manner, but keen to hear his findings, I kept my thoughts to myself. My stomach fluttered in anticipation as I waited for the surname.

"Registered in Guildford…April two thousand and two… Roger Austin Brownlow, married Linda Anne…Glenton. Glenton is the surname you're looking at, Miss Rushforth."

It felt such an anti-climax and I sighed heavily as, for a

second, I failed to realise that the guy was still on the line, and I'd not made any comment or even thanked him.

"Oh, I'm sorry about that. I'm a bit shocked, to tell the truth. I don't really know of anyone with that surname. But thank you for your time. Thank you!"

I was beaten, I felt sure of it. I heard of the surname before, but I couldn't recall ever knowing a 'Glenton'. The more I pictured Linda's face though, my conviction that I had seen her before was getting stronger. I sent a quick text to Simon to keep him updated.

Hi,

Just to let you know that Linda's previous s/name was Glenton. No wiser. Bitterly disappointed.

Love H x

CHAPTER 41

The minute I pressed 'send', it crossed my mind that I probably wouldn't hear back from Simon until early evening, as I knew he'd been due in court that afternoon. Hearing my mobile ring, some seconds later, as it vibrated across my desk, I picked it up, in the expectation that it would be one of my clients calling. I was amazed to see the display 'Simon calling…'

"My God, that was quick for you. Have you nothing better to do?" I asked him, cheekily.

There was an ominous silence for a moment; he hadn't even treated me to one of his usual cheery or suggestive greetings.

"Simon?"

He cleared his throat, nervously.

"Yes, I'm here sweetie." Another silence followed. I waited. I could feel perspiration on my forehead, and for some reason, was suddenly scared. "Helen, are you really certain that Linda's previous name is Glenton? Did you do the research yourself?"

Oh shit! Now what?

"No. I paid someone; a small company that researches family history for people. I didn't have time. Why? What's the matter?"

"Oh! Well, that being the case, if indeed she was Linda Glenton, I know exactly why she hates you. And you have seen her before."

Trying to keep calm, I realised that he wasn't deliberately trying to rattle me by making me wait, but I couldn't help getting annoyed. I was worried and all sorts of ideas were playing on my mind.

"SIMON! Just tell me. Stop playing games." I snarled at him.

"Okay, okay! You have seen Linda Glenton previously, Helen; in court, at the trial. Her son...Daniel, I think, yes... Daniel Glenton was one of the drug-dealing little scroats. He's the one who got twelve years. You helped get her son banged up, Helen. That's why she hates you."

It felt as if my heart was pounding on my chest wall. So I knew at last. I had my answer, and it was a valid one. What mother wouldn't hate the person whose evidence resulted in her son being incarcerated? An overwhelming feeling of sadness took over me. I felt sorry...and upset for the woman upstairs whose only contact with her son, for the next few years, would be limited to maybe once a week. I didn't blame her for hating me, but I hadn't wished to hurt her, personally. All I had initially set out to achieve was to get some justice, get my revenge on Anthony.

"Helen? Helen, you have to be...very careful how you handle this now. She has as much right to be an employee of your company as the rest of the staff. But I'm worried for you. Of all the businesses in and around London, she fucking ends up with a job there; where you are. I don't like it. I'm concerned about you...as should you be too."

My thoughts already started running away with me. I was

way ahead of him though and barely heard more than an odd few words that Simon muttered.

"Don't worry, Simon. I'm on it. I know exactly how to deal with it. Promise. I'll speak to you soon."

Just before I disconnected the call, I heard him shouting down the phone.

"HELEN! HE-LEN! DON'T DO ANYTHING RASH...YOU WI..."

After arriving home from work, I made a call to Ted, but it went straight to his voicemail. Leaving a brief message for him, I explained the Linda situation and my intended action, asking him to get back to me as soon as possible. Feeling drained, confused and guilty, and furthermore, wondering what effect the matter would have on the Hopkins Partnership, I tried to rack my brain as to where Ted and Hilary had gone on holiday. The time difference could mean either they'd already be in bed, or they were a few hours behind the U.K.

It was almost three hours by the time he got back to me, and it wasn't the call; the chat that I'd hoped for. He sent a simple text.

Helen,

Deal with the matter as you see fit. I trust you to do what's right. Just keep it from going to a tribunal, please.

Love Ted and Hilary xx

I didn't even bother going to bed that night. I knew what had to be done and I would do it. But I was fearful of what Linda's reaction would be.

CHAPTER 42

*T*he thought irked me considerably, but I hadn't been able to get away from the fact that I would have to involve James Mortimer and one of the other girls in my meeting with Linda. As Christina was the only staff member aware that I'd been about to do some research, she was undeniably my best choice. James, as she always gravitated towards him, would be there as Linda's moral support.

Having given the staff time to finish their mid-morning coffee, and after confirming with Christina that James didn't have any clients with him, I asked her to grab an extra chair from reception and come through to my office. She arranged the chair she brought, and the two chairs already in my office, where I asked her to place them, facing me; her chair to my right, and the other two on the left. I waited for her to sit and gave then I gave her a brief run through of what would shortly be happening. For the first time since knowing her, her face was without its infectious smile; mouth down-turned. She looked vaguely embarrassed, an unwilling observer to the imminent…meeting?!

My hands shook as I picked up the phone to call James. I

was clearing my throat as he answered.

"Helen! What a delightful surprise. I knew you must be missing me. What can I do for you? Or what could you..."

With my eyes on Christina, watching to see if she showed any sign of having heard his suggestive words, I cut in rudely with my most severe, but business-like voice.

"James, could you come down to my office, straight away?" I snapped.

"Ooh! Guess who sounds needy! Can't you wait until our employees have gone home, Helen?" He taunted.

"Five minutes, James! We're having an urgent meeting."

I slammed the phone down in anger before I was tempted to come out with a few scathing and inappropriate remarks in return. Whether Christina was being discreet, or she hadn't actually heard anything James said, I hadn't a clue. She was staring with over-acted interest at her most recent, fluorescent, stick-on fingernails. My heart went out to her. Confrontation was not something she, or I, were comfortable with and I could see the disquiet that I felt, mirrored in her eyes.

James knocked once and strode cockily into my office, a lewd grin plastered across his face, until the second he spotted Christina, who fortunately, hadn't seen the salacious look he gave me. His expression clouded over rapidly and he glowered at me before asking,

"Helen? What is this?"

I didn't know whether Ted ever made any mention of Anthony's court case to James, so I spent a few minutes explaining about the drugs haul and the resulting court proceedings, before mentioning Linda's son and his involvement.

"So, is it your intention to dismiss her, Helen? Because I'll warn you now that..." He stopped mid-sentence, as his eyes followed my hand to the phone.

She answered after five or six rings, her voice cold.

"Hello, Linda. Could you pop down to my office now, please? I've called an urgent meeting." She grunted her reluctant affirmation.

Trying to look cool and unconcerned, she marched into my office and sat down stiffly, but I could see the tension etched into her face. She folded her arms defensively. Other than the tension, her expression was totally blank.

"Linda, I've called this meeting…just between the four of us today, because we've been in a situation…for the past few months…that cannot be allowed to continue. Christina is present to observe; a witness that this matter is dealt with fairly. James is present in the role of…your former line-manager…and…moral support for you. I have requested that they both keep every aspect of this meeting confidential."

My stomach was churning and I could hear the strain in my voice as I stammered the words. I paused to take a couple of deep breaths before continuing, and to see if she wished to comment. Rather than meet my eyes, hers were fixed on my left shoulder. I continued.

"I have not been blind to the fact that you have been very…cold towards me, since my return, Linda. And I have spent…many hours…trying to find some answer…some…reason for your attitude towards me. Yesterday, I discovered…the basis for your…iciness."

There was a flicker in her eyes, and she looked directly at me, waiting but defiantly staying silent.

"As you no doubt already know, I am the witness, Linda; the one whose statement was responsible for your son being sent to prison. And that is why you have alienated yourself. Am I correct?"

Her eyes glazed over, but then her determination and defence mechanism kicked in.

"Yes. But I…"

I couldn't drag it out any longer than was necessary. I wanted it over; a clean slate, for both our sakes. I held my hands out, indicating that she was to stop.

"Linda, let's make this quick, and then we can sort things out. Please answer my next questions honestly. Did Anthony Pawson tell your son that I was a partner in this business? Did you apply for this position, knowing that fact?"

Her face crumpled, and then she cried, but was vehement as she sobbed her answers.

"No! No, Helen, I swear. Anthony Pawson...and Daniel, my son, didn't have...conversations. They...did business...they were not friends. Daniel had...no knowledge of...Anthony or...his private life. I..."

I could feel James's eyes burning into me, but he remained silent. Christina was very quiet, eyes fixed in the direction of Linda's knees. I sighed.

"Are you certain about that, Linda?" I snapped, already believing her, but just to dispel any lingering doubt.

"YES! I promise. When I applied for this job, I didn't have a bloody clue. I heard your name mentioned once or twice after I started here, but it only actually registered with me, who you were, on the day you came back. I recognised your face...from seeing you in the witness stand. Honestly!" She pleaded.

I leaned forward, elbows on the desk and put my head in my hands, relieved that it was over; glad that perhaps we could move forward.

"Are...are you...going to sack me?"

I looked up at her again, incredulous that she thought of me as...ruthless.

"No, Linda. I'm not going to sack you. As an employee, you have rights. Your work is, from what I'm told, impeccable. But the situation cannot continue, as I mentioned earlier. I don't expect you to like me, Linda. In your position, I wouldn't like me either, but you have to learn to put it aside. Our personal feelings must not affect the atmosphere in this office, at any time. We have to work together in a professional manner. Do you understand what I'm saying?"

She sobbed new tears, perhaps relieved that she wasn't about to acquire the status of 'jobless'.

"Yes. Yes, I und...understand. May I go now, please? I need to...get myself...together."

I nodded. Thankfully, James left with her, accompanying her back up the stairs.

Christina stood up to leave shortly afterwards, but as she reached my door, the spare chair she brought firmly in her grip, she finally voiced her opinion on what she observed.

"She won't stay long now, Helen. I'll bet she'll be job-hunting tonight. I'll give it a couple of months and she'll be out of here. Trust me!"

"Hmm! We'll see. It depends whether at her age, she wants the hassle of trying to compete with much younger job applicants."

Linda kept a low profile for the rest of the day. The next morning, James stormed into my office and thrust an email right up to my face.

"Well done, Helen. A new staff member needed. You've lost us an excellent book-keeper."

I couldn't see to read the piece of paper that he held, completely out of focus, two inches away from my face and I struggled to comprehend what he just said.

"Linda's resignation...by email. She's not coming back."

While I was shocked that Christina's prediction had been partly right, I was mortified to have treated Linda so fairly and yet I had to cope with James Mortimer's snide remarks. I knew I would always feel sorry for Linda. Her son rightfully deserved his prison sentence...but it was Linda who would always have the shame to endure...that, and the hurt.

CHAPTER 43

I finally found out, just a few days ago, what I spent the last three months trying to achieve. I now know exactly where Helen Rushforth lives. So many times I've followed her, even travelling on the same train as her some days, and then discreetly getting off at her stop, Maida Vale. But somehow, I was never able to pluck up the courage to pursue her that bit further; to see precisely where she lived. I feared that if I settled into the routine that I allowed to develop, that she might soon catch on to the fact that someone was stalking her. I came so close at times... then backed off at the crucial moment. I knew I couldn't approach her in public, not that that was what I intended to do anyway.

The idea came to me in the small hours, when sleep was too distant and unwilling to take me into its grasp...I would be there at Maida Vale before her. Tired though I was, the next night after leaving work, I caught a train that I hoped would get me to her home station at least half an hour before she arrived.

My plan worked a treat. Leaning against the wall outside the station, I opened up the Daily Telegraph on the pretext of being engrossed in the days expected but nevertheless, depressing stories. As things turned out, I had a shorter wait than anticipated. She emerged from the entrance hall on my right, and passed directly in front of me, the newspaper obscuring my view, before appearing again on my left hand side. After walking only a few yards, she took the first turn to her left. As I traced her steps and kept the distance between us to roughly ten yards, I noticed it was an arched access she'd taken, which led into a pleasant and undoubtedly expensive, residential street called Elgin Mews South. Staying safely out of her view on the corner, I watched her as, half way down on the right hand side, she approached what I presumed was her door. I only stayed long enough to be sure that it was her house; watching her as she plucked a bunch of keys from her handbag and entered the property.

Happy, for once, to have achieved something positive for such a minimal amount of my time, I called at my local for a couple of pints before heading off home. I was ready and looking forward to planning my next move.

CHAPTER 44

Simon sent me a text early Friday afternoon, asking if I had any plans for the weekend. The only entry in my diary was an appointment with a beautician nearby for a manicure and facial at ten o'clock on Saturday. I only made the appointment because a shopping day in the city with Leanne, Christina and Gillian had to be postponed because some of Christina's relatives were paying a visit. Wondering what Simon had in mind…and hoping that it was the same as what I fancied, I sent my reply.

Hi Simon, What did you have in mind? I have one appointment at ten on Saturday, the rest of weekend, free. Love H x

I kept the phone in my hand, waiting for answers, but no reply came. It was almost two hours later when it rang. I was in Gillian's office at the time, so I made my excuses and returned to my office, before daring to answer it.

"Hi, what kept you?" I asked him." I've been waiting to hear back from you for ages."

There was a bit of attitude in my voice. He hesitated

(knowing him, he'd be looking for a smart-arsed retort) before calmly giving his stern reply to my little dig.

"Witnesses, Helen, witnesses. That's what kept me." He paused for a few seconds, perhaps giving me the chance to digest his response and feel a little remorse for my initial outburst. "My wife and daughter have gone to Prague for the weekend. Somebody's having a hen-party, by all accounts. I'm free as from tonight, but it's up to you. Are you up for some weekend frolicking? If not, well...I'll do something el..."

Bloody annoying prick!

"Oh, Simon, stop getting arsey. Yes, I'm free, barring an appointment at the beauticians around the corner, ten o'clock tomorrow morning. I'll be about an hour. Or I could cancel it. So I take it, you're coming to me then?"

I couldn't be sure if I heard it properly, but it sounded as if he was breathing heavily before answering,

"If you're sure? Can you cope with me for a whole week-end, Helen?" He snorted loudly. "I know you can cope with plenty of sex, but can you manage with a full weekend of me?"

It was my turn to keep him waiting for a few seconds, allowing myself time to come up with something witty.

"Well, that's a leading question. I may have to gag and blindfold you...but that won't be while you're fucking me! See you when you arrive, lech!" I sniggered down the phone, grinning to myself as I disconnected the call, not allowing him to come back at me with an equally snide retort.

I rushed through my paperwork for the rest of the after-noon, eager for the working day to be over, and bursting with enthusiasm at the thought of two days full of scintil-lating sex; dirty dealings of a sexual nature with my lecherous lawyer. I hadn't seen or heard from Simon for quite a few days and I couldn't wait to have him between my thighs again. I lost myself in some hard-core musing and soon my panties were pleasantly damp. I closed my eyes and allowed my thoughts to wander some more, and my fingers to trace over the silk top I was wearing, my nipples standing to attention at the caress. My heart started racing wildly when the phone rang at five minutes to five, making me jump. It was Christina calling me. She apologised profusely for putting the call through so late in the day. One of my clients, apparently, did not want to be fobbed off. The call could have waited until Monday morning as there was nothing I could do, but the client felt the need to get a few things that he was concerned about off his chest before the weekend. He chatted for over half an hour and I had to keep steering him back to his original worries, fearing that if I didn't keep him on track, he would talk forever. I cleared my desk and switched my computer off while he was speaking, so when he said his final goodbye, I grabbed my coat and handbag ready to leave.

I heard footsteps coming down the stairs, just as my hand was poised on the door-knob, so I hung back a few minutes, hoping that whoever it was would get out of the door quickly. I hadn't wanted any more delays. After a few minutes I heard nothing else, so switched off the light in my office and hurried through to reception. It was just my luck that James Mortimer had been about to open the front door, and he swung round on hearing me enter the room. Leaning casually against the door, he smirked in delight.

"Helen. How lovely to see you. You've turned into a bit of a hermit, haven't you? I don't see you from one day to the next. You're shutting yourself away in your office all the time. Are you avoiding me, Helen?"

My hackles were up immediately, but my stomach lurched as I realised everyone else must have left for the weekend and it was just the two of us. I needed to be assertive and not let myself be intimidated by him.

"No, James, I haven't been avoiding you. I've been very busy. Please stop playing your silly games, now. I have…a… some guests coming for the weekend," I looked at the wall clock, "and I need you to move aside now and let me out of the door, please."

With his lascivious grin not fading in the slightest, he stood aside and gestured to the door, which he held open for me.

"Well, go then, Helen. I wouldn't want you to be late for your…erm, guests, or guest, is it?"

"Guests, plural!" I lied, as I moved to pass through the door.

As I was just about to pass him, he pushed the door almost closed and whispered in my ear,

"You can't hide away or run forever, Helen. It will happen – we will go all the way. We'll have full sex…you know that already, don't you? You still want me to fuck you, so stop denying yourself, Helen."

I looked him in the eyes, and saw them twinkling with wicked delight.

"You are fucking deluded James! I'm going home. Good-night!" I snapped. I snatched the door out of his hand and didn't look back as I rushed out into the bitter night and down the street towards the tube station.

The Friday night with Simon was amazing, and by the time I was getting ready for my beautician's appointment, I felt as if I was in some form of sexual stupor. Our sex lived up to its usual standard; dirty, creative, mind-blowing orgasms, vulgar language and sore body parts. One troubling factor for me though was that, at times, when I closed my eyes, it was James Mortimer's face that smirked at me, and I imagined fucking him for real, riding him as if my life depended on it. These visions induced a new aggression into my sexual activity and, although Simon hadn't made any complaints, I sensed that in my exuberance, I'd hurt him.

As I was getting ready for my appointment the next morning, Simon showered and got dressed.

"I've decided to look up an old friend while you are out, Helen. I never usually get the chance with being home in Essex most weekends. He lives near Hampstead Heath, so I think I'll drive over there. I'll bring something back for lunch, shall I? I should be back around midday and I'll cook something nice for us tonight."

He leaned over to kiss me as I was putting the final touches to my make-up; the make-up that my beautician would soon be removing. My heart melted at his thoughtfulness.

"Thank you, Simon. That will be great. I'll look forward to it. If it's as good as your mince pies...well..."

I heard him chuckle as he was going down the stairs. "Bye, Helen." The door slammed behind him, so he wouldn't have heard me shouting it back to him.

He was as good as his word. He arrived back about twelve fifteen with hot sausage rolls and some delicious cream cakes from a traditional family bakery near Swiss Cottage. I prepared a little salad to go with the hot rolls, while he sat and related two or three strange tales from his school days that, Charles, his friend brought up while they'd been reminiscing.

After he helped me tidy the kitchen, we settled down for a quiet afternoon. He slumped in front of the TV, glass of wine in hand, to watch some rugby match or other, and was reading his newspaper in between his spells of shouting out loud during the more exciting parts of the action. I, as was becoming a regular habit, was pinned in position with Harry on my lap, petting him while trying to read, when an urgent, loud rapping at the front door made him shoot off me in horror, fur on end and tail like a lavatory brush. Simon jumped as well, almost losing his grip on the wine glass. He glanced at me nervously and I watched his eyes quickly scan the room for anything that might give our game away.

The knock came again within seconds, only much louder than it had been before. I felt nervous, but mainly for Simon and I found myself shaking. I searched his face for some hint of what he wanted me to do about the intrusion. He nodded in the direction of the door.

"You'd better get that, Helen, before the door gets taken off its hinges."

Taking a deep breath, I tentatively turned the key as the third round of rapping became almost deafening. I shouted out, niggled at the impatience of the would-be caller.

"Just a second - just a second!"

I almost staggered backwards in shock, when I opened the door to see Ruby stood before me, rivulets of mascara-streaked tears marring her beautiful, young face. She launched herself into my arms, sobbing her heart out. As I hugged her to me, trying to console her, I spotted a huge suitcase on wheels just to the side of my front door. Her sobs increasing, it seemed she was too distraught to offer an explanation.

"Come on, Ruby. Let's get you inside. We can't do this on the doorstep."

Releasing her, I pulled her gently over the threshold and hauled the suitcase through the door after her.

"Helen…would it…be okay for…for me to…to stay…just for…a few days."

A slight panic came over me and, wondering what I was going to do about Simon, I was at a loss for words as her request spun around in my head.

"I…yes…you can stay, of course you can." My stomach

churned with panic and I could feel myself colouring up guiltily. I only hoped Simon had heard our conversation, and had some plan in mind. "But before I let you stay, Ruby, I… I'm going to need to know why you're here. I'll make some coffee. Come through to the kitchen."

I pushed open the lounge door to see Simon putting his jacket on, getting ready to leave. Taking a quick look at Ruby's tear-stained face, he smiled kindly at her, before saying to me,

"Helen, it's been lovely to see you, if only briefly, but I can see you two girls must have plenty to talk about. I'm going to make myself scarce and leave you in peace."

Ruby's face clouded over; the tears that had not yet dried up, about to be joined by more.

"I'm sorry. I…I've spoiled your afternoon."

Touching Ruby gently on the shoulder, he said,

"My dear, I have no clue as to your problems, but I'm sure that by this time tomorrow, things won't look so bad." He kissed me on the cheek. I noted the disappointment in his eyes even though he was trying hard to conceal it. "I'll let myself out. You girls can go and talk. Is it okay for me to use your bathroom before I go please, Helen?"

With Ruby heading into the kitchen, her back to us, he managed to give me a wink. I interpreted this to mean that he would go upstairs and remove any evidence of his presence in my bedroom and the bathroom.

"Did you really need to ask?" I winked back at him and mouthed 'thank you'.

Ruby sat staring into space as she drank her coffee. I was concerned for her, and various thoughts flitted to and fro in my head; wondering if she was drinking heavily again, or worse still, her mum had kicked her out.

"I'm not going to push you, Ruby. Just…talk when you feel you're ready."

We sat there for ages and two or three times she opened her mouth, but whatever it was, she was finding it difficult to come out with the appropriate words. Then suddenly, a scary thought came to me and I had to ask her,

"Ruby, does anyone know you're here? You haven't run off and…and not told your mum, or Catherine, where you were going, have you? The trouble is, if they don't know, I'm going to have to tell them where you are. You do know that, don't you?"

She managed a wry smile and nodded.

"I…I wouldn't do that to you, Helen, I promise. They… knew I was coming here, but they…I told them…you invited me. I'm sorry. I've brought clothes for college. I can…get there from here…can't I?"

I looked at her in disbelief, not understanding why she'd told everybody that I invited her. I stared at her, waiting for more, but she turned her face away. I hadn't even been sure if I could believe what she was saying, or whether her mother really knew where she was. I got up to put more coffee on to filter and the second I wasn't looking directly at her, she finally blurted it.

"I'm pregnant, Helen."

I dropped the two cups before managing to reach the kitchen sink and spun round to face her, my mouth wide open.

"Oh, Ruby! My God! What…oh, my God. Who…does your mother know? Or Catherine?"

She started blubbering again, so I sat down next to her and took both her hands in mine. Shit! I didn't want to be in this predicament!

Forgetting about coffee, I poured myself a large glass of wine, the last of the bottle Simon opened earlier. Ruby helped herself to a bottle of water from the fridge and we went to sit in the lounge.

"Nobody knows except my best friend...and... now...you."

My heart was racing and I felt a cold shiver run through my core, like somebody walked over my grave. She was so naïve. I don't think she realised she had put me in a very awkward position.

"I've come to you because I need your help, Helen. Will you help me? Please?" she pleaded.

"I...I don't know, Ruby. How many weeks are you?"

I half expected her to say that she only missed one period, and was floored to hear her utter the truth.

"Twelve, I think. Nearly thirteen. I've done two tests. They were positive...both of them."

I took a few deep breaths and started to silently berate myself for not recognising the signs when she and Catherine, came for their break between Christmas and New Year. She looked so pale and tired that week, her appetite for food, almost non-existent.

"Ruby...no doubt you already realise this, but you're going to have to do something...and soon. Does the father know?"

She cringed and I instantly knew this was not a subject she wanted to discuss. "Yes, I know. That's why I've come to you, Helen. But the father doesn't know, and...he's never going to. He's...in France. It happened when we were there with Mum...at half-term."

"Oh! Some French Romeo! No doubt he told you he loved you before he seduced you?"

I couldn't seem to stop the sarcasm from slipping out of my mouth. "What's his name, Ruby?"

Her face turned a glowing, deep shade of crimson; her eyes glazed over once more and they darted all over the room, anywhere where they didn't have to meet mine.

"He's...he's your neighbour, the one in Paris...André."

My heart sank, I couldn't look at her any longer as I tried to take in her revelation and make sense of it.

"WH...WHAT? RUBY! WHAT.THE.FUCK?" I shouted and she suddenly looked so fragile and scared so I lowered my voice. "Ruby, what were you thinking? You're only sixteen and he's...he's too old for you."

I could feel my anger grow with each passing second, from the pit of my stomach upwards, but it wasn't anger at Ruby.

"He...I...I went to see him...on the Saturday afternoon. I only went to...to thank him...for scooping me...off the pavement, that night...the night I was off my head. That's all, I promise you, Helen. We chatted...and then...he's gorgeous... he kissed me...and... It happened twice, that's all."

I found myself in a mental turmoil that seemed to eat away at me. Anger, hurt, worry for Ruby, and desperation; all emotions bombarded me relentlessly and I felt like I wanted to vomit as my glass of wine rose as acid up into the back of my throat. Because of the love I felt for David, I never told the girls that André and I became an item for a short time. I somehow doubted that André would have made Ruby any the wiser before taking her to his bed. I couldn't decide whether she needed to know but if I did eventually tell her, it would be in the future, when all this crap was a distant memory.

Quite sensibly, Ruby acknowledged the fact that her only option was to have a termination. She told me she wasn't particularly keen on children anyway and she was desperate to continue her education and go to university, but I could plainly see on her face the guilt that consumed her. We talked for hours, but not once did I dare to mention the obvious; that her mother needed to know. In the hope of easing her guilt I told her about Gavin and how he cheated on me, and the abortion I had just weeks after quitting my studies. Her mouth opened wide in horror as I told her how I walked in on the pair, to find them at it.

We exhausted ourselves well before ten o'clock and at my suggestion, Ruby went up to bed to try and get a decent night's sleep. I intended on telling her, the following morning, that she must speak to her mother. Although I suspected she would probably be reluctant to entertain the idea, I had to at least try.

Shortly after Ruby went upstairs, I'd gone up to bed myself. Laying there for hour after sleepless hour, I let my anger build to the point where my heart was racing and although I was laid down, my breathing was ragged, as if I just completed a marathon. I was furiously going over and over the André and Ruby thing; suspicious that he slept with her deliberately to get at me; pay me back for hurting him. Other thoughts surfaced, too; ideas that I struggled to get out of my head, but they were perfectly feasible. André had known how hard it was for me to get over David. He also knew that Ruby was David's daughter. Had this been his idea of a sick joke; sleeping with David's daughter, to get back at David, hurt David because I still grieved for him, therefore unable to love him...André? I sincerely hoped that hadn't been the reason. I prayed that it was just because he was a typical, horny bastard, who in the presence of a beautiful young girl, just couldn't help himself; couldn't keep his cock in his trousers. It hurt too much for me to consider any other sinister reasoning he may have harboured, but I couldn't help but...consider!

Confusion then entered my wreckage of a night's sleep; my nocturnal Hell on Earth. The questions kept shooting at me, one after the other. What would David want me to do? Persuade Ruby to tell her mother? Or help her to seek what David would want for her, an abortion with or without her mother's knowledge? Would David even approve of an abortion? It was his grandchild after all. Or would he want Ruby to complete her education and achieve her ambition to become a psychologist? What would he think of me for seeing her only option as abortion? I didn't have the answers, not one. I tossed and turned in frustration, battering my pillow in desperation, attempting to find a softer base which would serve to ease the tension which knotted each muscle in my neck. The only thought I kept repeatedly visiting was that it was all down to André; he was the one to blame.

Sometime after six am, as my eyes reluctantly closed, I recalled sleepily voicing my anger, to the twittering dawn chorus of the birds. "You are going to pay for what you've done to Ruby. You bastard, André!"

CHAPTER 45

Saturday...the day I was eagerly awaiting arrived at last.

Much later on, the same night I found out where she lived, I came to a decision, after weeks of pissing about getting nowhere. There would be no more sneaking around trying to keep my identity hidden while following Helen home from work. I would no longer need to stand in the shadows of that dark and fucking dismal doorway watching her office once, or sometimes twice, each week. No more freezing my nuts off in sub-zero temperatures, then heading home afterwards, unable to thaw out my frozen bones for hours. I looked forward, probably more than anything, to doing what was now done on waking; shaving off my ridiculous-looking beard, or stubble, as some might call it. What a relief it was. My face felt clean for the first time in months. The next task I set myself, was to deal with the baseball cap I'd been wearing on most of those outings. I started by attempting to cut it up, and when my scissors struggled, due to being anything but sharp, to make much impact, it, and the scissors ended up in the dustbin. I sighed in relief once it was gone. No more wearing the hideous thing. No more looking like a prize prat. I was back to my own identity to complete *the job in hand; all bad disguise features, scrapped. They served their purpose well, though. That, I couldn't deny!*

I left my flat about one o'clock in the afternoon and made straight for the tube. I was feeling quite euphoric. My only teeny, nagging doubt was whether she'd be at home or not. But then again, that was always going to be an issue, being as I didn't have access to her personal diary. Saturday was after all, the day that ladies habitually go out for lunch and shopping with friends. While I sat eyeing up the sexiest of the women in my carriage, I was visited by an attack of the jitters, and wondered for a short time at least, if I should just get off at the next stop, admit defeat and head back home. 'But think of your prize', I cajoled, 'this is how you get to be with her, hopefully for good. Stop being such a wimp and grow a backbone'.

Trying to remain strong and focussed, I carried on with the journey, but on arriving at Maida Vale, I went in search of a pub, somewhere not too far away, where I could indulge in a few tiny glasses of whisky, better known to anybody who might be on the outside looking in, as...Dutch courage. Instead of turning left when I emerged from the station, I took a right down Elgin Avenue. Without having to walk too far out of my way, the Elgin was the first pub I noticed, but it was a decent enough place to take a few tipples and find some inner strength to do what needed to be done.

I felt quite calm when I left the pub, my two shots of Jack Daniels had done the trick, and I even accepted, and smoked, the cigar kindly offered to me by a guy sat on the adjacent bar stool. Together, we ventured out to the smoking area at the back of the building. As I sat relaxing, enjoying the flavour of the cigar on my palate, he proceeded to tell me the whole of his life story in five minutes flat. Whether he was expecting a similar outpouring from me, I didn't know, but I gave him nothing in return. Unlike he had, I hadn't felt comfortable enough to speak about my personal life to a total stranger. It was the wrong time, and the wrong place, even though half an hour passed by a little faster than it might otherwise

*have done. I thanked him for the cigar and chat and, having
downed the last drop in the glass, I made my exit.*

*Having approached the Mews, I stood beneath the arched
opening for a few moments to take some deep breaths. My heart
started racing, and I could feel the perspiration trickling down my
forehead. Not letting my eyes stray from her front door, I slowly
started to saunter down the cobbles. Suddenly, I was distracted by a
hurried clip-clop of high- heels and a deafening rattle of wheels
behind me, then just as quickly, passing by me. A young lady
rushed past me so fast I hadn't even managed to catch a side view
of her face. She was dragging a fairly large suitcase behind her, its
wheels bouncing along the cobbles and threatening to tip over with
the speed she was going. Judging by the way her shoulders were
convulsively shaking, it seemed to me as if she was crying. I slowed
to a virtual stop, waiting for her to get beyond Helen's cottage. Just
as I started moving forwards again she crossed the road...heading
straight for Helen's door. Fuck! Double fuck!*

*By the size of her suitcase, it looked as if the young woman was
intending a fairly long stay. My face burned in anger and my eyes
scanned the cobbles, looking for some small stone or anything I
could kick out at to release some aggression. I turned away,
heading back towards the archway, my plans...fucked up yet again.
When I reached the corner, I kept my head down as I turned back
once more, and just in time to witness Helen embracing her house
guest. She had to be somebody close. I dug into my memories, trying
to recall if Helen ever mentioned a sister. I didn't think so. As I
continued to stare, Helen showed the young woman into the house,
before reaching out to drag the suitcase in over the step.*

*Trance-like, I stood for the next five minutes trying to suss out
what was going on. All these months and thwarted at the last
fucking hurdle. Whatever next? And precisely on cue with my
thought, the door opened again. A tall man, balding from what I
could make out, walked out of the door and closed it behind him.
Neither Helen nor her guest came back to the door to say goodbye*

and see him off. Though I hadn't been near enough for the best of views, he looked old enough to be Helen's father. Surely though, if he was Helen's father and if it was her younger sister who just arrived, he would have stayed a bit longer? Fuck it! I was completely baffled. Whoever the man and young woman were, I wouldn't be able to solve the mystery by standing on the street corner watching her house and letting it eat away at me...with jealousy.

Taking one last glance before I turned to walk back to the station, I whispered, to nobody in particular.

"A month. I'll be back in a month to claim you, Helen. You're mine! But I'll wait for as long as it takes..."

COMING SOON!

THE SCARS
   (A Trilogy – Book 3)

ABOUT THE AUTHOR

ABOUT THE AUTHOR

Eva Bielby was born and raised in North Yorkshire in the North East of England. From the age of seven, she became a member of her local library, and was backwards and forwards perusing the children's section at least twice a week. Eva still lives in her birth town with her son and daughter, and their respective families being in close proximity.

Having worked in accounts offices since leaving school, Eva passed her accountancy qualifications when her children were very young. She has spent over thirty years of her working life as a company accountant.

Eva has always been interested in writing and has written many poems over the years. She started writing seriously in 2014 when she completed the first part of the erotic Goings On series. Book 2 followed in 2015. These two books have now been revamped and given new titles, 'The Hurt' and 'The Healing'. Book 3 is completed and will soon be released as 'The Scars'. Being a reader of many genres of novels, Eva would also love to write a suspense thriller in the future, and possibly a comedy, which she would carry out under an alternative pseudonym,

Eva has many hobbies, which include playing badminton and going on long country walks. She has a keen interest in spiritualism/mediumship, and has attended several work-shops to develop her skills further.

Eva loves nothing better than to have fun with her grandchildren. During quieter moments, she enjoys a cryptic crossword, sudoku and gardening.

Milton Keynes UK
Ingram Content Group UK Ltd.
UKHW020707220923
429186UK00016B/916